The House of Secrets

SARRA MANNING

sphere

SPHERE

First published in Great Britain in 2017 by Sphere
Paperback edition published in 2017 by Sphere

1 3 5 7 9 10 8 6 4 2

A CIP catalogue record for this book
is available from the British Library.

ISBN 978-0-7515-6118-0

Typeset in Baskerville by M Rules
Printed and bound in Great Britain by
Clays Ltd, St Ives plc

Papers used by Sphere are from well-managed forests
and other responsible sources.

Sphere
An imprint of
Little, Brown Book Group
Carmelite House
50 Victoria Embankment
London EC4Y 0DZ

An Hachette UK Company
www.hachette.co.uk

www.littlebrown.co.uk

But one man loved the pilgrim soul in you
And loved the sorrows of your changing face

When You Are Old
W.B. Yeats

2016

PRIVATE SALE

FOUR BEDROOM HOUSE, HIGHGATE £POA

SEMI-DETACHED PROPERTY IN NEED OF COMPLETE RENOVATION AND MODERNISATION.

◆ Two reception rooms ◆ Four bedrooms
◆ Kitchen ◆ Bathroom ◆ WC
◆ Large south-west-facing garden.

Two minutes' walk from Highgate Tube station. Highgate Woods, Queens Woods and the Parkland Walk nature reserve are moments away as are the vibrant cafés and boutiques of Highgate Village.

Applications are invited for purchase of this property, which has been priced considerably below its market value to take into account the work and expense required to turn this house into a delightful family home. Private buyers only, no property developers.

**For further instructions apply in writing to
Messrs Flintlock & Harding, Solicitors,
91 Devonshire Square, Mayfair, London, W1.**

1

1936

Libby

The King is dead.

As Libby travelled across the city, the London she could see from the top deck of the bus was draped in black and when she disembarked at Victoria station, the swirl of travellers and businessmen was sombre and muted and she was glad of it. That, for these few days, until the funeral had passed, London, England, the whole damn Empire, matched the dark mood that she'd carried round with her these past few weeks. Now, no one would dare to tell her to cheer up or to will away her troubles with a smile.

She hurried across the road, breath curling in the air like puffs of dragon smoke, her destination a small hotel down a side street.

Libby paused in the doorway and looked around the lobby. The lighting was dim, the mood hushed. Even the ferns drooping in big brass pots added to the general air of despondency.

There were two men sitting in the darkest, furthest corner

and as Libby squinted in their direction, one of them caught her eye and stood up.

Despite the gravitas of the days since the King had passed, Mickey Flynn hadn't thought to adjust his swagger, his cocky grin or exchange one of his famously lurid silk neckties for a shade more fitting.

'Libby, my darling,' he greeted her, brushing his lips against the cheek she proffered. 'Why the long face? Has someone died?'

'Oh, Mickey,' she admonished him. 'That's in very poor taste even for you.'

Mickey ducked his head. 'Now why would a fellow like me be weeping over the death of an English king?' he asked, exaggerating his brogue so he sounded as if he were fresh off the boat, when Libby knew full well that he'd been born and bred in Kilburn.

'Because someone's dead and that's always sad,' she said as Mickey took her case and guided her to a table near the window, quite some distance away from the corner where he'd been sitting. 'It doesn't feel right not having a king.'

'There's your fellow Edward, isn't there?' Mickey sounded as if he were already bored with the topic and though Libby had plenty to say about how nice it would be to have a young king on the throne, one who seemed simpatico to the plight of the working man (the working woman too), she simply shrugged. Mickey tilted his head. 'You're looking awfully peaky, my darling.'

The last time Libby had seen Mickey had been on a glorious September day. Then, he'd toasted her health and happiness and, along with the rest of their friends, waved her and Freddy off, still in their wedding clothes, as they'd boarded the Golden Arrow, the boat train to Paris. It wasn't even six months ago, but it seemed to Libby that she'd aged a hundred years since then.

In place of the pretty, laughing girl with orange blossom threaded through her red hair who'd leaned out of the train window to shout, 'We'll send you a postcard. Each and every one of you! We promise!' was a pale, thin woman whose hair had faded, the gleam gone from her green eyes. Libby hardly recognised the reflection that stared back at her in the glass each morning.

'That's not a very gentlemanly thing to say, Mickey.' Libby fixed him with what Freddy had always called her basilisk stare but Mickey waved her words away with a brush of his pudgy fingers.

'Never been a gentleman, you know that.' He leaned forward. 'This isn't going to be too much for you, is it?' He glanced back at the corner from where he'd emerged. Still seated there was an indistinct figure hidden by a copy of *The Times*. 'You'll really be helping your good pal Mickey Flynn out of a bind. Got one girl on her way to Hastings with a lord of the realm and another in Margate with the heir to a biscuit dynasty. It's always like this after Christmas. Must be something in the bread sauce . . . January's my busiest month.'

Libby had forgotten how much Mickey liked the sound of his own voice. 'I'm much better,' she said firmly. 'Quite able to manage a weekend in Brighton.' Now it was her turn to nod her head in the direction of the dark corner. 'What's he like?'

'Salt of the earth,' Mickey assured her. 'A diamond among men.'

'Oh, do give it a rest, Mickey, darling. We both know you've never so much as crossed the Irish Sea, never mind kissed the Blarney Stone. I'm going to spend two days with a man I don't know, two nights in a hotel room. So, tell me what he's really like. No fibbing.'

Mickey wiped the oily smile off his face as if he'd taken a damp rag to it. 'Very stiff. Very proper. Ex-army, made his money in the motor trade. Wife's been keeping company with the brother of his business partner. Quite a tricky situation all round, his solicitor said, but Mr Watkins has agreed to do the honourable thing and give Mrs Watkins grounds to divorce him, poor bastard that he is.'

'Isn't it funny that when it comes to divorce, it's the man who always decides to do the honourable thing?' Libby noted with a contemptuous sniff. 'If I were Mr Watkins, I'd bury the bitch.'

'Mind your language!' Mickey said sharply as the principled Mr Watkins unfolded himself from the chair and stood up. 'I told him you were a teacher. Widowed. Respectable. Now, quickly, let's get this squared away. We agreed twenty pounds, didn't we?'

'Thirty,' Libby snapped. They'd agreed twenty-five, but Mickey must be getting fifty and she was the one who'd have to spend two days with a stiff, proper man with an axe to grind. 'Thirty or I'm catching the bus back to Hampstead.'

There wasn't much Mickey could do when Mr Watkins was bearing down on them but nod unhappily and discreetly tuck the money into Libby's coat pocket.

'The Brighton train leaves in twenty minutes,' Mr Watkins said brusquely when he reached them.

Mickey made the introductions. Libby kept her face still and slightly wistful as befitted a respectable, widowed teacher, though she wanted to smile when Mickey called her Marigold. He had flower names for all his girls.

'And this is Hugo Watkins.'

The man nodded tersely at Libby as Mickey went on to explain the particulars. 'From the moment you leave this hotel, you need to play the part of the besotted couple. I wouldn't put it past the King's Proctor to have a detective trail you. Don't forget to sign the hotel register as Mr and Mrs

Watkins and it's not enough to have the maid come in in the morning and catch you happy as larks in bed together, you'll need to be seen having dinner in the hotel restaurant this evening, tip well—'

'You've already covered this in some detail.' Mr Watkins spat out the words as if they were pieces of rotten apple. 'We mustn't miss the train.'

He set off for the door, without waiting to see if Libby was following him. She quickly stood up, though everything in her wanted to stay, to not hurry after this hard-voiced, hard-faced stranger.

Then she wished she hadn't stood up at all, because the dull ache in her side, which was a constant these days, transformed itself into a sharp tugging sensation and she gasped.

'I wouldn't worry about it,' Mickey advised her, mistaking her pain for trepidation, as he walked with her to the door where the odious Mr Watkins was pointedly looking at his watch. 'Two days of sea air will put the roses back in your cheeks, my darling.'

Mr Watkins didn't offer to take Libby's case though he did hold the door for her, even as he held his body rigid so there wasn't the remotest possibility she might brush against him, and when Mickey called after them, 'Don't forget to take off your wedding ring, Marigold!' he snorted derisively.

2

2016

Zoe

'I spy with my little eye something beginning with h.'

'Um, I don't know. House?'

'You're not even trying.'

'I am but there isn't much else in my eyeline right now,' Zoe said.

It was raining so hard she could barely see anything beyond the windscreen. Their little Fiat was packed so full of boxes and bags that she couldn't see out of the back window either. The drive from Swiss Cottage to Highgate had been nerve-wracking enough and it hadn't even been raining then.

They were stationary now; parked behind their removal van, Zoe's mobile sitting on the dashboard. They both tried hard not to stare at it.

'Do you give up?' Win asked.

'I absolutely give up.'

'Hydrangeas.'

Zoe squinted furiously out of the window. 'What hydrangeas?'

'Somewhere out there.' Win gestured at the murky foliage in front of the house. 'You said they were hydrangeas, when we came for the first viewing, didn't you?'

'No!' They'd only been playing I-Spy for two minutes and already Zoe was sick of it. 'Are you talking about the rhododendron bushes, by any chance?'

'Same thing, aren't they?'

'How did I end up married to a man who can't tell the difference between a rhododendron and a hydrangea?' Zoe shook her head sorrowfully.

'You know the nature stuff is your department,' Win said, because Zoe's parents were firm believers in the benefits of fresh air and the Great Outdoors so being able to tell the difference between a rhododendron and a hydrangea wasn't unduly taxing for her. She could even differentiate between a chaffinch and a goldcrest at fifty paces; a talent she rarely had use for. 'While I can add up whole columns of numbers in my head. That's what I bring to our relationship,' Win reminded her. 'Also, I bake. I keep you in cake.'

'For which I'm eternally grateful,' Zoe said and then her phone rang before Win could continue to list what else he brought to their union and they both twitched like they'd never heard a phone ring before.

It was Parminder, their solicitor. All the funds; money from the sale of their flat earlier that day, the savings squirrelled away, the mortgage they'd extended, had reached their final destination, never to return. Now Parminder had been instructed by the vendor's solicitor that the key to the house that they'd just bought and could barely see from where they were sitting, was under a brick in the flowerbed nearest to the front door.

Zoe opened the car door. 'We'd better make a run for it,' she said.

They ran, coats pulled over their heads. There was nothing even near to being a flowerbed by the front door but they both rooted around in the tangle of weeds until Win found the key, then made a dash for the door.

It should have been a special moment. Their first proper house, a brand new start, but rain was dripping down Zoe's neck and the movers were unloading so she took the key from Win and rammed it into the lock.

'Not so fast.' Win wrapped his arms around Zoe's waist before she could jerk away and tried to lift her up. 'I'm going to carry you over the threshold.'

They'd known each other for thirteen years. Lived together for ten of them. Been married for the last three and . . . 'Win! Don't be silly! Please let me down. You didn't even carry me over the threshold on our wedding night.'

'I was too drunk then, I'd have dropped you and anyway, this is our do-over, isn't it?' Win panted as he tried to find purchase on the slippery wet fabric of Zoe's khaki parka. 'Stop wriggling!'

Instead of sweeping Zoe up in his arms, it was more of a precarious fireman's hold.

'Please don't drop me, I really don't want to fracture anything.'

'I'm not going to drop you. You're as light as feather,' Win grunted, which was a lie because Zoe was a good ten stone, most of it dough-based.

He staggered through the open doorway and Zoe had no choice but to cling tightly to him and wish he'd put her down . . .

'Mind your backs!' shouted a voice from behind them and Win did drop Zoe then so they could flatten their spines to the wall, as the first box was brought in. 'Where do you want these then, guv?'

'I've labelled every box,' Win said. 'Half the boxes are

going in the front room, the other half upstairs in the back bedroom, next to the bathroom. All labelled. Clearly. Big black letters.'

'Easy, tiger,' Zoe murmured, but none of this was easy. She'd read somewhere that moving house was meant to be the third most stressful life event after death and divorce. She'd take moving house over death and divorce every time.

Another box was carried in and once again they were asked where they wanted it. From the clenched set of his jaw, Zoe could tell that Win was bearing down on his back teeth and who knew where his mouthguard was – hopefully in one of the boxes marked 'BATHROOM'.

'Stop grinding. You'll end up with lockjaw again.' Zoe plucked at the damp sleeve of Win's anorak. 'Remember, we agreed that we were going to treat this as an adventure. This is a beautiful house and we're lucky we get to live here.'

'It's not beautiful right now.' Win caught Zoe glaring at him and realised he was off-message. 'But it will be by the time we're done.'

They'd never meant to buy a house. They had a plan in place, which involved selling their one-bedroom flat in Swiss Cottage so they could afford a two-bedroom flat at the northernmost tip of one of the Tube lines, the Victoria or Piccadilly, which was as far out as Win was prepared to go, being a born and bred north Londoner.

Then Zoe had seen the ad in the property pages of the *Hampstead and Highgate Express*. A four-bedroom house in Highgate, in need of a complete overhaul and modernisation, and apparently priced to reflect that, though Win said he doubted that very much.

Some people would have read the forbidding words 'in need of complete renovation' and taken fright but Zoe had become quite giddy at the possibility of all those period details

9

left intact. So, the house was a fixer-upper? Well, who didn't need a little fixing-up from time to time?

As requested, she'd written to the address on the advert and subsequently they'd been invited for an interview with a fusty old solicitor at a fusty old firm in Mayfair.

Once it had been established that Win and Zoe weren't soulless property developers who wanted to carve the house up into flats and sell them on at a huge profit, they were told the below-market price of the property. It was a quarter of what a four-bedroom, semi-detached house in Highgate should have cost. It was even less than the price of a two-bedroom flat in Cockfosters, right at the end of the Piccadilly Line.

It was far too good to be true. There had to be a catch. And there was.

The house had been built and purchased in 1936 then never lived in, which was very odd but not odd enough to cool Zoe's ardour. On the contrary, now that Zoe knew for sure that there'd be original period features still intact, nothing Win had to say about dry rot or subsidence was anything that she wanted to hear. She'd made arrangements to view the property on a sunny late-September day.

The house was just across the road from Highgate Tube station on a street off Southwood Lane, which led up to Highgate Village and beyond that the vast green acres of Hampstead Heath.

Although Elysian Place ran parallel to a major arterial road into central London, all Zoe and Win could hear were birds singing as they wandered down the tree-lined street full of solidly built, semi-detached 1930s houses. There were a mix of styles – mock-Tudor, neo-Georgian – but twenty-one and twenty-three had been built in the art deco-ish Moderne style. They were art deco-lite and right now, number twenty-three, their destination, was an art deco fright.

The house stood in an overgrown wilderness that once must have been laid out as a front garden with flowerbeds and a privet hedge. To the left of the plot was a drive, the concrete cracked, weeds valiantly pushing through towards the light. The graceful, minimalist curved lines of the house did give Zoe a little frisson but the white rendering was grey, streaked almost black in places. The original Crittall windows were warped in rotting wooden frames, in a couple of places the glass was cracked. The roof was no better; there were patches of moss clinging desperately to the slates that hadn't gone MIA.

It still wasn't enough to put them off. Hand in hand, they'd unlocked the front door, with its stained-glass sunburst panel, and stepped inside the hall, their path marked out by black and white tiles arranged in a simple geometric pattern. In 1936, it would have been the very latest thing in modern living. The beautiful sleek lines of the staircases and doorjambs, the tiled fire surrounds, the simple, understated architraves and ceiling roses.

Off the hall was a large living room, then a dining room, and at the end, a kitchen complete with walk-in pantry and off it, a small scullery. Up the stairs and behind pitch pine doors were a large master bedroom and a smaller boxroom at the front of the house, then a bathroom, a separate toilet and two good-sized back bedrooms.

Zoe had been worried that neither of them had experienced that special, tingly feeling you were meant to get when you were house hunting – that sense that you'd come home, that this was where you were meant to live. But as Win said, who cared about the feeling? This was a house for the kind of money that might have bought them a beautiful manor house with an orangery and a duck pond in the Scottish Highlands but in London, it wasn't enough for a two-bedroom flat in Cockfosters.

Still, it was Win who went down with a serious case of cold feet first. 'We might as well give up now,' he'd told Zoe when they'd moved on to the next part of the application – writing a letter to the anonymous vendors explaining why they should get the house above any of the other applicants. Zoe thought it made the whole torturous house-buying process a lot more exciting and mysterious than Win filling in mortgage application forms and groaning, but Win had other concerns. 'There's not one good reason why they'd choose us over a family. A proper family. Two kids. Cat. Maybe a couple of hamsters. There'll be other houses for us, although we'll probably have to move miles out of London to afford one. I'm thinking maybe Blackburn.'

Zoe had twitched the solicitor's letter out of Win's hand. 'We are a proper family,' she'd said, folding the piece of paper and tucking it in the pocket of her jeans. 'Two people can still be a family. Leave it to me.'

Leaving things to Zoe didn't always work out so well, because she tended to forget about them, but three days later, she'd presented Win with the handmade book she'd put together. 'Our House' proclaimed the cover in a 1930s' font. It opened on a beaming, #nofilter photo of Win and Zoe on their wedding day in the beer garden of their favourite pub. Win in a vintage Mod-style suit, Zoe in a white lace summer dress with forget-me-nots threaded through her blonde hair, the flowers the same shade of blue as Win's eyes.

This is Win and Zoe, she'd written in a careful cursive script, *who dream of living in a house with enough room for them to live and love and grow old.*

Zoe earned a modest living as a writer and illustrator of children's books so she had the skillset to show the unknown vendors just how she and Win would turn the house that time forgot into their home. She'd included sketches of what the rooms could look like, swatches of original thirties wallpaper, paint samples. Drawn pictures of long lazy summer days with the patio doors they'd install open onto a beautiful garden. Cosy winter nights with the fire in the living room blazing. She'd even drawn the birds and squirrels and hedgehogs that would flock to their garden to feast on the seeds and nuts that they'd leave out for them.

She might not have had 'the feeling' when they'd viewed the house, but when Zoe sent off their finished application, she'd known with absolute certainty that she and Win would be the chosen ones.

And three months later, on a rainy January afternoon, here they were. Walking through *their* house, rediscovering each room. The air that they displaced with their movements was frigid and cold. There was an odd smell too. Something dank and mildewy that seemed to settle on Zoe's skin, but that was nothing that couldn't be solved by a new roof, reconnection to the National Grid, central heating, damp-proofing and a few tins of Fired Earth paint.

'It's darker than I remembered,' Win said as their footsteps echoed on the wooden boards. The house had never been carpeted or wallpapered; it was the barest bones of a house. 'And I'd forgotten about that damp patch.'

They both looked up at the brown tidemarks stretching across the ceiling in the master bedroom at the front. 'We know the roof is leaking,' Zoe said. 'That's why we have scaffolders turning up first thing tomorrow so we can really endear ourselves to our new neighbours.'

Win stood in the centre of the room, which in a few months would be where they'd sleep, hold each other, make love again. For now it was a cold, musty space. Zoe watched her husband as he stared up at damage that decades of neglect had caused. Win was tall and lanky but there was a hunched quality to him these days. He looked tired and rumpled, had done for weeks and weeks.

'This is our new beginning,' Zoe said, because a house that had never been lived in didn't have any memories. Nothing bad had ever happened here. It was a clean slate in a filthy, dilapidated kind of way.

Win turned to look at her. His thin, clever face was cast in shadow for a second and then he stepped forward and smiled. 'You really want to rewind?' he asked.

'God, yes!' Zoe nodded.

Win came forward, his smile as wide as his arms as if he wanted to seal their new resolution with a hug and a kiss. Zoe willed herself not to tense up as he pulled her into an embrace. In fact, she hugged Win back as hard as she could because, for once, it didn't feel as if he were holding every muscle rigid.

How lovely to steal an unexpected moment, a memory of how good they used to be ...

'Jesus Christ! Gonna give myself a bloody hernia!'

The mood was ruined by the prolonged and fluent swearing from one of the movers as they tried to manoeuvre a large cumbersome box around the bend in the stairs.

Win and Zoe broke apart as quickly as they'd come together and stood, hands in pockets, not looking at each other.

'Where do you want this one then, guv?'

Win turned, his expression eager as if he were grateful for the interruption even as he said, 'God give me strength,' under his breath.

3

Libby

Mr Watkins didn't speak to Libby for the entire journey to Brighton.

Indeed, Libby wouldn't have been surprised if he'd deposited her in a third-class carriage and hurried away to avail himself of the rarefied air of first class. He didn't though. There were a lot of other things he failed to do too. Such as ask Libby if she minded sitting with her back to the engine or if she needed help putting her suitcase on to the luggage rack, earning him the disapproval of an elderly gentleman whose splendid handlebar moustache quivered in outrage at Watkins' cavalier attitude. 'Chap's an out-and-out bounder,' he muttered to Libby as he hefted the case for her, but unfortunately he departed at Clapham Junction.

Then it was just the two of them, Mr Watkins seething from behind *The Times*, though Libby was sure he must have read it from cover to cover several times.

Libby had borrowed a couple of Angela Thirkell novels from the library but she couldn't settle to reading. She wrote a list in her diary of things she needed to do on Monday when this hellish weekend would be over, then took out Freddy's letter. She'd already committed it to memory but the same old lines jumped out to taunt her.

It's impossible to love you the way you wish to be loved.

I don't believe that I've ever managed to give you one single moment of the true, pure happiness that you deserve.

If only I were a better man, but I'm not and you always knew that, old girl.

It was a letter from a liar. The confession of a coward. Libby stuffed it back into her handbag and pressed a hand to her belly.

At one point, as they were approaching Hayward's Heath and each jolt of the train along the tracks sharpened the pain in her right side, Libby glanced up to see that Mr Watkins had lowered *The Times*, so his gaze could flicker over her. He caught Libby's eye then and made not the slightest attempt to hide his distaste, as if she were some shabby tart whom Mickey had found hanging around Shepherd's Market.

Then, at last, they were in Brighton. Back in the day when she was still doing rep, occasionally as the female lead, more often much further down the bill, Libby would visit the town at least twice a year to do a run. Sometimes at the Theatre Royal, more usually at the Grand before it became a cinema. The company would take over a ghastly boarding house in Kemptown, sleeping six to a room and three to a bed and staying up to all hours playing gin rummy for ha'pennnies and drinking cherry brandy from enamel mugs.

Now, Libby and Mr Watkins stood outside the station. Libby turned up the fur collar of her astrakhan coat and glanced hopefully towards the one cab that idled on the station forecourt.

'We'll walk,' Mr Watkins decided. 'It's not far.'

He set off, not bothering to check with Libby that she wanted to walk, which she didn't. She was wearing such silly, flimsy shoes because all her others needed mending and when she lifted her suitcase, she winced at the throb of pain in her side.

Libby followed Watkins through the drizzle down Queens Road, which was much longer than she remembered. Halfway down, when all she could see in front of her was a murky greyness so it was impossible to distinguish between sky and sea, the wind picked up. She had to keep tight hold of her hat with one hand, her case with the other, bobbing around people walking towards her, their heads down, their steps brisk, and that terrible wound tightened and pulled so now it felt like the very worst, most agonising kind of stitch.

It was all too soon. She'd only been back in England since mid December, not even six weeks had passed. She was meant to be resting but idling in bed all day didn't pay the bills. To take her mind off the pain, the thin soles of her shoes sliding over damp paving stones, the bitter wind, Libby stared at Mr Watkins's black-coated back and cursed him silently.

'You unutterable bloody sod. Buggering son of a whore. Pox-ridden son of a bitch.'

He suddenly whirled round as if she'd hurled the epithets out loud. 'Don't dawdle,' he barked at her.

'Oh, you *fucking* bastard! You arsehole . . . '

It was that anger that kept Libby going, even once they reached the seafront and the wind all but flattened her against the buildings. Finally Watkins stopped outside a fancy hotel, door held upon by a uniformed flunky. Mr Watkins sailed in before her.

Libby gratefully relinquished her case and with hobbling steps caught up with Watkins, took hold of his sleeve and tucked her arm in his.

17

Though she already thought him impossibly stiff, he stiffened even further at her touch. 'We're meant to be in love,' she reminded him quietly. 'As if a weekend in a hotel together isn't an ordeal by fire.'

'Very well,' he muttered and continued his path to the reception desk, with Libby on his arm as if they'd suddenly become attached and he didn't have the first idea about how to shake her free. No wonder the erstwhile Mrs Watkins had found comfort with another man.

It was as they were taken to their room by a porter, the lift creaking alarmingly between floors, that Libby decided she would simply have to find it within herself to be gay and charming. When she really set her mind to being gay and charming there were very few people who failed to succumb. Mr Watkins might present her biggest challenge to date, but they couldn't spend two whole days together with him either silent or snapping at her.

They were shown to a large, rather nice room on the fifth floor with sea views and its own bathroom. No bundling into one's robe and thundering down the corridor in dread of bumping into another guest. Libby smiled approvingly when Watkins tipped the porter half a crown and as the young boy shut the door quietly behind him, she made her smile bigger and brighter.

It was wasted on Watkins. He turned away from Libby to stare out of the window at the rain-lashed view. He hadn't even taken off his hat and coat. 'It needn't be awful, spending time together like this,' she said to his shoulders, which tightened when she spoke. 'It's only two days. That isn't such a long time. We might as well make the best of it, don't you agree?'

At first, Libby thought that he hadn't heard, though she'd spoken clearly enough. She sighed, put a tentative hand to her side where the pain ebbed and flowed, and was just thinking of the drubbing she'd give Mickey when she got back to town, when Watkins turned round.

Libby wished he hadn't, because those glances he'd given her before, disdainful as they'd been, were nothing compared to the contempt that now contorted his face.

'Just how do you suggest that I make the best of this damned ugly business?' he demanded. 'If you have any ideas then I'd love to hear them.'

'Two days,' Libby repeated with less conviction. 'They'll be over in a flash.'

'Two days for you. Twenty bloody years for me gone down the drain and all I get to show for it is a weekend in a hotel with some floozy ...' He stopped then, for which Libby was grateful, though she'd been called much worse.

'I'm not a floozy,' she said mildly, because there was absolutely no point in antagonising the man any further.

'And I'd bet a pound to a penny that your name isn't Marigold and you're not an impoverished widow either,' he said and sprang towards Libby. She reared back, but Watkins walked past her, to the door, then he was gone.

Libby sank down on the bed – she didn't even want to think about how the bed would feature in her bravura performance tomorrow morning when the maid brought in tea and saw her and Mr Watkins tucked up together as if they'd spent the night hours in the throes of passion. Instead she hung her head until the pain had receded enough that she could get up and, very slowly, take off her coat and hat, then slip off her shoes.

It gave Libby no small amount of satisfaction to stuff her damp shoes with pages torn out of Watkins's copy of *The Times*, then she decided to run a bath.

Soon enough Libby was sinking into the water, head

lolling back, arms on either side of the tub, her eyes closed. She didn't know how long she lay there, occasionally easing up the plug with one foot, so she could let in more hot water, but it was so blissful to simply do nothing. To free her mind from worry.

Then she opened her eyes, glanced down, and the calm was shattered. She always tried not to look at the scar. It made her wonder again and again what they'd done to her in that hospital in Paris, because now she felt so empty.

True, her heart was still intact, beating away, though there had been times that Libby wished that it would simply stop. Her heart had always been a useless thing. Leading her such a dance, making a fool of her, persuading her she was in love time after time . . .

Now Libby had nothing to show for all that love but a jagged, puckered scar across her belly. The raised red skin itched and Libby put her hand between her legs then held it up to see her fingers streaked red. Oh, not again.

There'd been so much blood: thick, viscous, clotted. Libby had had to stumble into the hospital with one of the hotel towels between her legs. Freddy, his face muddy with shock, had clung to her arm, though he'd meant to be the one holding her up.

Libby put her hand between her legs again, and her fingers came away clean and the pain was retreating.

There was a rap on the door. 'What *are* you doing in there?'

It was Watkins. She'd managed to forget about him this last hour. 'I'll be out soon,' Libby tried to say but she needed every ounce of strength to brace her hands on the lip of the bath and heave herself out of the water.

Climbing out of the tub was like trying to scale a mountain but finally Libby was standing on the bathmat, legs shaky, fingers fumbling with her robe.

Another peremptory knock. 'Please come out. You're being very childish.'

Libby pulled a face, but even that made her head swim, as if she were in a dream, pitching forwards. 'I'm not decent.' It was nothing more than a whisper.

'I can't hear you!'

Oh go away, you hateful man.

Libby took a faltering step towards the door and then she really was pitching forward, falling ...

Libby drifted in the hinterland between sleep and wakefulness. Sometimes Freddy's face was all she could see. How she'd missed the soft, tender look in his eyes when it was just the two of them. Other times, she was aware of being jostled and dragged, another man's face, creased with concern, two young women in white caps, black dresses, like nuns, their voices muted as if they were speaking from another room.

Then Libby was awake, in bed, covers pulled up to her chin. 'Ah, she's back with us,' said a voice and Libby looked up see an older man, well fed, with beetling brows and a bulbous red nose. Likes a drink, she thought, as he patted her shoulder. 'You gave your husband quite a fright, Mrs Watkins.'

'I'm not ...' She was Mrs Morton and yet she was in this room, in this ghastly situation, helping another man leave his wife. She turned her head to see Watkins at the other side of the bed.

She'd been too cowed by his contempt to look properly at him before but now she could see dark, glossy hair swept back from a patrician face, dark blue eyes, full mouth. He looked rather like Freddy but his features were broader and there was a weariness to him; a jaded quality Freddy had yet to acquire. 'Did I faint? I never faint.'

'No more hot baths for you,' the doctor said jovially, then

21

he chivvied Watkins from the room so he could take Libby's temperature and pulse. It seemed a pity to waste the services of a doctor when one was at hand, so when he asked her if she was still feeling peculiar, she nodded.

'I lost a baby last November. In Paris. I had to have an operation and ever since then I've had these episodes where I feel quite queer.' Libby described the agonising stitch in her side, the intermittent bleeding, how sometimes she felt so tired, so low, she could hardly drag herself from her bed.

The doctor had a cursory glance at the scar marring her belly then patted Libby's hand. 'These things happen,' he said in the same jovial tone. 'How far along were you?'

'About six months, but I thought . . . I hoped . . . I'd still be able to have a baby.' Libby shut her eyes and sniffed. 'At the hospital, they never really explained and my French isn't very good. There was a letter but it got lost and you see . . . '

'I do, my dear. From the mess they made of stitching you back up and the symptoms you're presenting with, I'm afraid there can be no doubt that they performed a hysterectomy. Removed the whole kit and caboodle. That's the Frogs for you. Knew a French chap once, type of fellow to take a sledge-hammer to crack a walnut. How old are you?'

Usually, Libby told people that she was twenty-seven – she'd always been able to pass as younger. 'Thirty-two,' she admitted.

'Well, you had left it rather late to start a family.' Libby was starting to hate the doctor with his glib pronouncements and air of a man who was long overdue a stiff drink and his dinner. 'Still, best not to dwell on it. I have a sister who never married. She breeds poodles and seems happy enough.'

'I've never liked poodles,' Libby said as there was a soft knock on the door and Watkins came back into the room.

'Maybe gardening then,' the doctor said, as he opened his case. 'I wouldn't be surprised if it turned out that you were anaemic too. We shall have to build you up, my dear. Two spoonfuls of cod liver oil twice a day. A glass of milk stout every evening and if I were you, young man, I'd make sure your good lady has steak once a week.'

'Well ... I ... that is ...' Watkins was wrong-footed and stuttering, so different from how he'd been before. Libby wondered if she shouldn't faint more often.

'Can't afford steak?' The doctor looked around the hotel room in disbelief. 'Liver, then. She'll be as right as rain in no time.' All the while, he was putting stethoscope, thermometer and notebook back in his bag. 'Aspirin for the pain if you really must, but I don't hold with it myself.'

Then he stood there for one awkward moment until realisation dawned on Watkins's face. 'I'll see you out.' He walked the doctor to the door, where they had a brief, hushed conversation before money exchanged hands.

Libby arranged the pillows behind her and when Watkins turned from the door she was sitting up, hands neatly clasped together. Someone, she fervently hoped that it was one of the two maids she'd glimpsed, had dressed her in the mint-green silk nightgown that had been part of her trousseau – the only item in her trousseau, because she'd hardly been a blushing virgin on her wedding night.

She was surprised at how calm she felt. 'I don't know what you must think of me.' Libby wondered exactly what information about her condition the doctor had shared with this man. She decided she didn't much care. After this weekend, she'd never have to see Watkins again. 'I generally don't make a habit of swooning.'

'It wasn't a swoon, it was a dead faint,' Watkins said. His voice was much softer, kinder, now that he wasn't shooting words at her like they were bullets. 'What I said to you, how I behaved, it was unforgivable.'

'Either way, it's forgiven,' Libby said and she meant it. Not just because her forgiveness might prolong this new accord between them but because she also knew exactly how it felt when the person you loved hadn't cared one jot for the 'till death do us part' portion of their marriage vows.

'Shall we start again, you and I?' he asked her, as he came to sit on the bed, in the same spot that the doctor had recently vacated. Not that Libby was alarmed. She liked to think that she could spot a wrong 'un a mile away and only a wrong 'un, the very lowest of the low, would take advantage of a woman who'd been in a dead faint not half an hour ago. 'Is your name really Marigold?'

'It's really not.' There didn't seem much point to the pretence any more. 'It's Elizabeth. Libby, my friends call me.'

'Hugo,' he said, holding out his hand for her to shake. 'Pleased to meet you.'

4

Zoe

They spent the next hour helping to carry in boxes, which Zoe was sure had bred in the van on the journey from Swiss Cottage. They were meant to be travelling light – most of their furniture and possessions in storage as they'd be living in a building site for months. They also had to deal with a man from across the road spitting with fury that the removal van was blocking him from parking his massive Land Rover on their drive, which apparently he'd been doing for years.

It was gone six by the time the removal men left. The house was in darkness, Zoe and Win's only light source a couple of LED lanterns bought from a camping supply shop the day before. It was now that they took stock and came to the awful realisation that they were unable to make tea. 'I refuse to accept this,' Win kept saying as he peered under the sink to see if there was any way they might be able to turn on the water while Zoe dug around in one of the boxes for a saucepan.

'After you've done that, we'll have to figure out how to turn the gas on so we can light the stove,' Zoe said cheerfully as if these were small tasks that were easy to achieve. 'Or we could just go out and find somewhere that serves tea.'

'A nice cup of tea in your own home; it's a basic human right,' Win said mutinously when they heard a knock on the door.

'If it's that man with his bloody Land Rover again . . .' Zoe muttered as she hurried to answer it.

It wasn't the man from across the road. For one thing the three people standing on the doorstep actually looked pleased to see her. 'We come bearing gifts,' said Ed, Win's brother, as he shifted a cardboard box in his hands. 'Torch, batteries, bottled water, biscuits.'

'Everything you might need when you move in to a crumbling old house or when you're facing a zombie apocalypse. Also, hot food and alcohol,' added Amanda, Ed's wife, holding up a bag so Zoe caught a heavenly whiff of fish and chips. 'Are you going to let us in, then?'

'I'm so pleased to see you,' Zoe said as Ed kissed the top of her head. 'You'll have to feel your way, I'm afraid.'

Bringing up the rear was Jackie, Win's mother. 'Everything all right?' she asked as Ed and Amanda fumbled in the box for torch and batteries.

Everything was all right. It was a fresh start, a new beginning, let the good times roll, etc., but Zoe couldn't help the plaintive, 'Not really,' that leaked out of her mouth. 'We're desperate for a cup of tea but we don't know how to light the boiler.' She rested her head on Jackie's shoulder. 'We're not even sure if it is a boiler or a water heater or what the difference is. Win's tried to Google it, but we can hardly get a signal and who knows when we'll get our Wi-Fi set up?'

Win poked his head round the kitchen doorway, at the end of the hall. 'Hello. Did you bring Gavin with you? Why isn't

26

Gavin here?' he asked his mother. Gavin was Win and Ed's stepfather but, more importantly, he'd been in the building trade since he was sixteen.

'Because he's at the football and he doesn't start working for you til Monday morning. Let the poor sod enjoy his last weekend of freedom,' Jackie told Win.

'Anyway, we don't need Gav. Between the two of us, we should be able to figure it out,' Ed said eagerly. 'I've brought my toolkit. I figured you probably wouldn't have one.'

'We do have a toolkit.' Win frowned. 'Except I have no idea where it is.'

All five of them screamed in genuine fright when the contraption in the kitchen lit with a ferocious whooshing sound and a jumping blue flame. Then they drank champagne out of the disposable glasses Jackie had brought. 'From Ken and Nancy,' she told Zoe. 'Your mum asked me to get a bottle so you could toast your new home.'

Tomorrow Zoe would Skype her parents who were spending a post-retirement gap year in South-East Asia, but for now it was comforting to sip champagne, let the bubbles tickle her nostrils, and know that her parents were thinking of her on what they knew would be a stressful day.

After dinner, eaten standing up in the kitchen, Zoe gave them the tour. 'Wow!' Amanda kept saying, as she looked around. 'Wow. I really like what they haven't done with the place.' Jackie, who'd redecorated six times in the twelve years that Zoe had known her, was already talking colour schemes and something she called 'modern deco', while Ed made all sorts of dire warnings about woodworm eating away at the roof joists, silt clogging up their drainage pipes and, worst of all, mice.

'Why would any self-respecting mouse want to set up shop in this house?' Zoe demanded, though she wanted to peer into every corner and crevice to see if there were any droppings. 'They'd choose a house that was nice and warm, where they could gorge on toast crumbs and spilt cereal.'

'Anyway, we're going to get a dog once the house is sorted out,' Win said. 'We'll get a terrier. Chase away all the mice.' He caught sight of Zoe's horrified face. 'The mice that we absolutely don't have.'

'I wouldn't want to sleep here tonight, with no electricity, no heating, maybe with mice, not if you paid me. It's creepy,' Jackie said with a shudder. Zoe loved her mother-in-law. Whereas Amanda was always a little prickly – she and Zoe were sisters-in-law rather than best friends – Jackie had the kindest heart though she'd be the first to admit she didn't believe in sugar-coating things, or even putting a light sugar glaze on them. 'Are you sure you won't sleep in our spare room?'

'No, we're good, and anyway, it's not creepy at all,' Win insisted, as Zoe tried not to look disappointed because actually staying in Jackie's spare room sounded amazing. 'Or it won't be when we've done the place up . . .'

'Painted it cheery colours, knocked down a couple of walls, opened it out a bit . . .'

'Unpacked all our things, laid down carpets, hung pictures. It will look great,' Win said firmly as if he were back on-message. 'It's all going to be great.'

'I still wouldn't want to live here,' Amanda said as they hurried down the stairs. 'But look at the size of your dining room! I wish we had a dining room.'

'Four bedrooms too,' Ed reminded them, though they weren't likely to forget. 'Even if you use one as your studio, Zoe, you've still got two spare bedrooms.'

Two spare bedrooms didn't seem quite as exciting as it had done, not when they could see their breath curling in front of

them as they talked. 'Yeah, it is a lot of bedrooms,' Zoe said –
it was starting to sink in that they really had bought a house.

This house.

Oh God, what had they done?

'And the little room at the front would make a perfect
nursery,' Amanda said, blundering blindly into what Zoe and
Win had already designated as forbidden territory. 'I'm not
pushing or anything, I know you need time, but sooner or
later you've got to get back on the horse . . . '

'I can't. We're not.' She could say the words in her head, but
when it came to saying them out loud, Zoe choked on them. 'I
had surgery. *Major* surgery. It's too soon.'

Win put a stiff arm round Zoe's stiffer shoulders. 'We're not
even thinking about that,' he said. 'Not when we're going to
be paying off this house until we're in our sixties, so we can't
afford to start dropping sprogs. Talking of which, where are
my beloved nephews?'

Amanda and Ed had four sons between the ages of eight
and two and spent most of their time ferrying them between
football games and soft-play centres.

Ed didn't bother to hide his sigh of relief at the change of
subject. 'We decided to let them loose to fend for themselves.
They've probably been adopted by the local foxes by now.'

Amanda jabbed her husband in the ribs with her elbow.
'They're at my mum's.'

'Same difference.'

'And on that cheery note, we should probably get going.'
Jackie pulled Zoe in for a hug. 'I'm glad you and Win got this
house. You deserved some good luck after what happened last
year. And you're looking so much better – you've got a bit of
colour to your face these days.'

Zoe refrained from pointing out that she always had a bit of
colour to her face. Her ruddy complexion, inherited from her

father, was at odds with her wide-set blue eyes, delicate features and fair hair that had never lost its baby fineness. Also, being cursed with permanently rosy cheeks meant that no matter if Zoe was struck down by illness, even when she had literally been hammering at death's door, she always looked in rude health. One of her ex-boyfriends had mockingly called her Heidi because he said she looked like she should be tending a flock of Alpine goats. So Zoe smiled weakly. 'I feel better. Honestly, that's all behind me now.'

Amanda squeezed Zoe's arm. 'I really am sorry. I shouldn't have said anything.'

'I'm absolutely fine,' Zoe said. She ran one freezing cold hand along the curved wood of the staircase. 'Even if I am losing the feeling in my fingers and toes.'

They took the hint, or else the three of them couldn't wait to hurry back to their centrally heated houses. Zoe and Win waved them off from the front door. It was bitterly cold outside, but only marginally less cold inside.

'We should go to bed,' Win said, but he didn't have a lascivious glint in his eye as though he wanted to make a start on christening every room in the house, which Zoe was grateful for because that was the very last thing she wanted to do either. 'We've got no telly, we can't unpack anything other than essentials and I think there's a real danger of hypothermia if we don't warm up soon.'

Getting ready for bed was an adventure too. Or at least that's what Zoe told herself as they hunted down the boxes that contained duvets, pillows and bedclothes, and blew up their air mattress because they'd decided not to risk their proper, comfortable bed getting trashed if the roof suddenly caved in. Then there was a frantic search for the holdall Zoe had packed with all their essential bathroom kit.

Zoe bagsied the bathroom first. The water had a strange

brackish taste when she cleaned her teeth and she had to hop from one foot to the other to try and keep warm, which made putting on her pyjamas tricky. Then she pulled on her thick woollen hiking socks, her baggy sick-day cardigan and scurried into the large back bedroom, which was lit only by the camping lights, desperate for that moment when she could dive into bed, though she'd have sold one of her kidneys for a hot water bottle.

'It's all yours,' she said to Win, who was peering into one of the cupboards built into the recesses on either side of the fire-place. 'I think Ed was right about silt in the pipes. The water tastes foul. What are you looking at? Oh God, is it mouse droppings?'

'No.' Win sounded distracted. 'Pass me a light, will you?'

'Is it a spider's nest?' There wasn't much to choose between spiders and mice. Probably, spiders were the better option, but not by much. Zoe handed Win one of the torches they'd brought upstairs. 'Here you go.'

Win shone the torch on the top shelf of the cupboard then stretched up to grab at something. 'It's been pushed right to the back,' he grunted.

'What has?'

He didn't answer but with torch tucked under one arm, he groped with the other hand then pulled at something that came away from its resting place in a cloud of dust that made them both sneeze.

It was a suitcase. Scuffed brown leather covered in old-fashioned labels from far away places. Paris. New York. Los Angeles. Zoe had seen similar luggage selling for stupid amounts of money in the chicest vintage shops of West London.

'What on earth is it doing here?' she asked, squatting down to peer at the case. There was a tag tied to the handle, the handwriting erased by time.

'Should we open it?' Win asked but he had already snapped open the clasps and lifted up the lid before Zoe could tell him that they should drop it off at the vendor's solicitor. Still, she leaned closer, intrigued, even though she recoiled slightly from the cloying smell as Win took out a parcel wrapped in tissue paper, which disintegrated beneath his fingers. He shook out the folded fabric that was nestled inside.

It was a bottle-green dress cut on the bias. Zoe reached out a hand to gently touch the material. It was made of rayon or crêpe, one of those old fabrics slightly rough to the touch, and there wasn't enough Febreeze in the world to get rid of the dank stench that had permeated it over the years.

'Dead people's clothes,' Win said. 'Amanda was right. Never not creepy.'

'But you can't help wonder who wore the dress, and why it's been left in a suitcase in a deserted house,' Zoe said, her head already full of stories of an unknown woman in a dark green dress. 'It's like the start of a novel.'

'Not one I'd want to read,' Win muttered, and in a way he was right. Zoe wanted to shut the case and stash it at the back of the cupboard again but another part of her, a much larger part, was suddenly consumed by curiosity to see what was inside a large cardboard box, the lettering on it faded, but still distinguishable from the time it had held cakes from Maison Bertaux on Greek Street in Soho, where Zoe had stopped for a coffee countless times herself. Now Zoe could imagine a woman in her pretty green dress, staring at the pastries on display in the window, thinking about what would go best with a pot of tea, then opening the door, greeting the girl behind the counter. She had to know what happened next.

'Let's open the box,' she said. 'Come on, let's do it.'

Win laughed. 'Hang on, Pandora.'

'All the best adventures start with a mystery, a puzzle. And we both agreed that we were going to treat this, the house, as an adventure,' Zoe said as she lifted the lid off the box and scrunched up her nose as she dislodged more dust.

Inside there was a yellowed, folded-over copy of *The Times* dated 17 December 1936, which Zoe quickly discarded in favour of a treasure trove of theatre memorabilia, curling up at the edges, colours faded: programmes, playbills and a handful of identical black-and-white photos. Headshots of a pretty young woman, her hair swept up to one side. She had impossibly doe eyes, an enigmatic smile playing around her lips, her features smoothed and bleached out by the flattering lighting and overzealous retouching. 'Elizabeth Edwards – Contact: Withers & Withers Talent Agency, Greek Street, London W1 Telephone: GERrard 2853.'

'Elizabeth Edwards, who are you?' Zoe murmured as Win pulled out the next item in the suitcase. A diary. Not a large desk diary or a tiny appointment book that would fit into a handbag, but somewhere in between. It bulged temptingly with random pieces of paper and card, lists and letters, stuffed between its pages. 'Now, this does feel a bit like snooping.'

It did but Zoe had already taken the black leather-bound book from Win. She let it fall open at a yellowed page covered in dense spidery writing in smudged and faint pencil, impossible to decipher any of the words in the dim light of the room. The next page simply had a couple of appointments noted down and a to-do list, just like the to-do lists that Zoe typed into the Notes section of her phone every Monday morning then promptly ignored.

Did the diary belong to the enigmatic Elizabeth Edwards? Zoe flicked to the start, hoping for an address, a clue, instructions on how to light the boiler. Instead, a letter fluttered to the floor. The paper was worn thin, soft as feathers, but written in a different hand to the crabbed scrawl of the diary, this script graceful and looped. As Zoe squinted down, words floated up at her.

It's impossible to love you the way you wish to be loved.

I don't believe that I've ever managed to give you one single moment of the true, pure happiness that you deserve.

If only I were a better man, but I'm not and you always knew that, old girl.

Zoe shivered in a way that had nothing to do with the cold. 'You're right,' she said to Win. She scooped up the discarded letter and slotted it back into the diary. 'I'd hate it if someone read my diary.'

'You don't keep a diary,' Win pointed out, as he gathered up the theatre keepsakes and put them back in the box. 'Or if you do, you've managed to hide it from me for the last ten years. Is it full of dark secrets?'

'The very darkest. All those torrid reminders about dentist appointments and birthdays.'

'Anyway, that's all there is, just more clothes at the bottom.' Win was already unfolding the tissue paper to reveal a heart-stopping collection of tiny woollen garments. Booties, a little hat, a cardigan fastened with cherry buttons, now brittle and cracked, everything hand-knitted and yellowed with age.

Zoe put a hand to her mouth to force back the sobs that immediately rose up.

When would it stop hurting?

She kept quiet, even as she saw the pain on Win's face. His expression grave and intent as he stroked the little hat with one impossibly gentle finger.

'It's a sign. An omen. We should never have bought this house.' He pushed the clothes away. 'I should stop putting off the inevitable,' he continued, his voice now loud and hearty. 'Time to brave the Arctic wastes of the bathroom.'

'Do we need to talk about this?' Zoe wanted to touch Win's hand, the same hand that had touched those tiny clothes made with such care and love, but even that small gesture was beyond her.

'I didn't mean it about the house. I just got spooked. It's the lack of lighting in here. It makes everything seem sad when there's nothing to be sad about.' Win still looked as if he was in pain but he stood up, walked away from her. 'I'll meet you in bed in five minutes, all right?'

'All right.' Zoe could feel Win's eyes on her as she kept her head lowered and placed everything carefully in the suitcase.

Win sighed from the doorway. 'So, we're good then, Zo?'

'Better than good.' Zoe forced herself to raise her head and look Win in the eye though now she was glad of the muted lamplight. 'This is our fresh start. Our new beginning. I couldn't be happier.'

5

Libby

As Hannah, Mrs Morton's maid of all work and general dogsbody, moved from bedroom to bedroom lighting meagre fires and taking away chamberpots because the elderly ladies of the house couldn't be expected to use the privy in the middle of the night, she must have informed the residents of 17 Willoughby Square, Hampstead, that Libby was heading into town.

It could be the only reason why, as Libby was taking out the pin curls she'd slept in and surveying the sparse contents of her wardrobe, there were constant taps on the door and plaintive entreaties to be allowed in.

The ancient aunts, Alice and Sophie, wanted a quarter of humbugs, a jar of potted meat, two balls of black wool and if Libby happened to be passing a bakery late in the afternoon, a bag of stale buns. Mrs Carmichael also wanted wool, a pair of size nine needles, a packet of digestive biscuits and a bottle of Milk of Magnesia. Little Miss Bettany sent a note asking for denture cream and a small jar of Bovril, and Potts, though he was perfectly able to toddle to the shops under his own steam, demanded a bottle of gin. Even Hannah, after sneaking the kettle up the stairs so Libby could wash in lukewarm water, presented Libby with a sad collection of farthings and ha'pennies and a request to 'pop into Woolies and get me a half pound bag of weigh-out sweets, Miss Libby, but no Brazil nuts or toffees, please. They play havoc with my back teeth.'

It was quite clear that the old and infirm residents of the house were hungry and cold. Mrs Millicent Morton, landlady and Libby's mother-in-law (though the older woman believed that no woman could ever be good enough for her precious Freddy), ran a tight ship.

Libby had had nowhere else to go. She'd given up her digs in town before she'd got married and when she'd come back from Paris, broke and broken, Millicent had grudgingly offered her lodgings, which Libby had grudgingly accepted. Beggars couldn't be choosers but that didn't mean Libby liked her living arrangements, or Millicent, who ran a teetotal house and refused to even countenance the idea that her darling son had done a runner.

It was little wonder that relations between the two women were strained, not that they'd been particularly chummy before.

It was also hard to feel warmly towards a woman so mean-spirited and penny-pinching that she'd halved the week's coal delivery and had recently decided that the entire household should embrace vegetarianism. 'Meat is so hard to digest,' she'd explained when Libby had defended her right to the occasional rasher of bacon. 'It lies rotting in one's gut and excites passions. I can't have that. This is a respectable house.'

Not that there was anyone in the house who had any passions worth exciting. They were all too cold and miserable to give in to their baser lusts. Libby shivered on the threadbare rug in her bedroom. It had been Freddy's old room, his model aeroplanes still suspended from the ceiling, the bookshelves crammed with tales of derring-do. She tugged on her best dress over her goose-pimpled flesh. The dark green frock she'd been married in. It had been snug then, she'd been four months along at that point though no one was meant to know – she'd couldn't even eat the smoked salmon sandwiches Freddy's editor at the *Daily Herald* had provided for the wedding breakfast for fear she'd rip the seams. Now it hung off her, but Libby added a belt and by the time she'd carefully combed out her hair and applied a little make-up, some rouge, mascara, lipstick, she was quite pleased with the end result. She was still a little faded at the edges, but she looked much better than she had. Felt better too.

Thankfully she'd stopped bleeding, that terrible pain in her side had quietened down – some days it disappeared entirely – and though she'd had to spend a week in bed after she'd returned from Brighton, now Libby fairly skipped down the stairs to the dining room.

It was hard to skip or make any sudden movements when every surface was littered with what Millicent called her 'objets d'art'. Ugly figurines, old-fashioned frames containing old-fashioned photographs of stiff people in old-fashioned clothes, decorative plates on stands. It was all so Victorian; the house dark and dreary, every window hung with heavy drapes, so it was difficult to see where one was going in the gloom of a February day. At least in the morning room the fire was lit and Hannah was just bringing through the teapot and toastrack as Millicent sat at the head of the table, a peevish look on her sallow face, her tone querulous.

'I'm convinced that people have been helping themselves to coal,' she announced, and the little old ladies – the two aunts,

Mrs Carmichael, and Miss Bettany (who hadn't uttered one word the whole time that Libby had been in residence) – quivered where they sat. 'I'm sure that your rooms are quite warm enough without having to take extra so others must go without.'

'Goodness, Millicent, please tell me that you haven't been counting how many pieces of coal there are in the bucket,' Libby said as she took her seat on Millicent's right.

Mrs Morton shot Libby a look of quiet, seething fury as she did every time Libby called her by her Christian name. 'Of course I don't,' she said with wounded dignity. Libby calmly took a piece of toast and waited and she hadn't even counted to ten in her head before one of Millicent's bony hands pressed against her black bombazine bosom. 'Must you always be so strident, Elizabeth? Especially when my heart has been pal-pitating wildly. I barely slept last night and when I did I had such strange, unsettling dreams about my poor late Arthur, then I lay there fretting about poor Freddy. Of what might have happened to him. Something terrible somewhere foreign and how would I ever know? I suppose you haven't heard from him?'

Libby continued to calmly spread butter on her toast, thickly enough that Millicent gave an unhappy whimper at her profligacy. 'No, I haven't,' she said. 'He could by dead in a ditch on the road to Seville for all I know.'

She'd only said it to be spiteful because Millicent was so tiresome but the thought of Freddy dead, or even ill or injured, brought her no pleasure; the traces of her love for him still lingered. Millicent clutched her chest again and her sharp features softened as if she were about to dissolve into tears. 'Dead,' she echoed. 'Dead on a dusty road where those heathens will step over him. Not even give him a Christian burial.'

The argument had gone on long enough. 'I'm sure Freddy is alive and well,' Libby said. 'Probably halfway through writing his novel and he's all but forgotten his own name.' She paused to take a bite of toast. 'Now, back to the coal. If any has gone missing, it's sure to be one of the gentlemen. They come and go at such odd hours. Who can say what they get up to?'

There were three salesmen who rented rooms and disappeared for days on end as they plied their trade (one of them, a Mr North, had once cornered Libby on the stairs and asked if she'd be interested in doing some modelling for his camera club) then would return to change the tenor of the house with their heavy tread and the foul stench they left in the privy.

Peace was restored. Now Millicent and her geriatric paying guests could happily complain about the men and their inconsiderate behaviour. By the time Libby rose from the table, the ladies were preparing for a long morning spent in the drawing room, the only room where the fire was lit during the day, and were chattering about the new King. How handsome he was. 'So nice to have a young man on the throne,' Aunt Sophie said. 'Though really he should be married by now. What good is a king without an heir?'

Libby was pleased to leave the stultifying atmosphere of the house, the smell of cabbage and camphor, to step out into the bracing February day and feel as if she could breathe again.

How she'd missed going into town! Sweeping up the steps at Leicester Square station as part of a busy bustle of people, then ducking through the familiar, narrow Soho streets. Libby had been in every pub, every club, hung around backstage at every theatre, knocked on the door of every casting agent's office. Killed time with a pot of tea and a cake in every café and now, when she popped into Maison Bertaux, she was greeted like the long-lost friend that she was.

Libby took her cup of coffee (Millicent had banned coffee too; claimed that even one whiff of a tin of Camp sent her heart racing) to a corner table. There was just time to gulp it down then powder her nose, reapply her lipstick and set her hat at a more jaunty angle, which she matched with a jaunty wave as she left.

She didn't feel jaunty but if she pretended hard enough, made her smile bright, her voice light, movements quick, then who was to know the difference? Maybe Millicent was right and it was the coffee that made her heart flutter as Libby crossed over Greek Street, slipped through another door and started the long climb up the stairs to the offices of Withers & Withers, Talent Agency.

She'd first climbed up these stairs sixteen years before as a gawky sixteen-year-old, all eyes, elbows and knees. Had goggled at the signed photographs of the stars of stage that lined the walls, all shot by Mr Anthony who had a studio on Bolsover Street and had used the same flattering, diffused light and artfully angled manner when Libby had had her pictures done too. Not that Libby's pictures ever made it on to the wall.

They never would either, not when Deidre Withers glanced up from her cluttered desk and eyed Libby with weary disdain. 'Look what the cat dragged in,' she said, ramming a cigarette into a long ebony holder. 'Married life obviously not agreeing with you then, dearie.'

'And hello to you too, Deidre,' Libby said as she removed a pile of scripts from the chair in front of the desk and sat down. If she waited for Deidre to invite her to sit, she'd have a long bloody wait.

It was impossible to say how old Deidre was. Libby would have sworn she hadn't aged a day in the last sixteen years. Deidre could be forty, fifty, maybe even sixty, for she was

41

tiny, slender and lithe, with close-cropped black hair. Libby had never seen her wear anything but black draped dresses, jet beads strung around her throat and wrists, her lips always painted a vivid blood red.

Libby had hoped that Ronald Withers would be in that morning. Then they'd sit next to each other on the little sofa on the other side of the room and Libby would explain matters, make her voice catch a little, dab at her eyes and let Ronald rest his hand on her knee. A gentle flirtation that neither of them meant because everyone knew Ronald's taste ran to young guardsmen from the Hyde Park Barracks who'd treat him brutally, rough him up, all sorts.

But Ronald had always been kind to Libby. He'd signed her up the very day she'd first come to the offices. 'I doubt you'll ever set the world on fire with your talent, but you're a pretty little thing,' he'd said, after Libby had read one of Titania's speeches from *A Midsummer Night's Dream*. 'I can always find work for a pretty young girl.'

Deidre (who'd waste no time in sliding her hand up one's skirt, squeezing a thigh with cruel fingers, while she stared brazenly, daring her victim to protest) had been furious. 'She has red hair,' she'd announced flatly the first time Libby had met her. 'Everyone knows red hair is unlucky.'

It had set the tone for their relationship, which had limped along feebly ever since. 'Where's that handsome husband of yours, then?' Deidre asked, a malicious gleam in her dark eyes. 'Word is that he left you before the ink was dry on the wedding certificate.'

'He's in Europe. Working,' Libby said, which was true enough. If Freddy were back in London, she'd have heard something.

'And the baby?' Deidre raised her thinly plucked eyebrows as she regarded Libby who tried to affect an air of nonchalance and not grip the sides of the chair. There was always something reptilian and unsettling in the way Deidre narrowed her eyes, the tip of her tongue darting out to moisten her lips as she was doing now. 'Everyone knew you were in the family way, dearie. You chased Freddy for years. Then all of a sudden he decides to do the decent thing and give you his name? Not unless you'd got caught.'

Libby couldn't bear to meet Deidre's obsidian gaze a moment longer. She rummaged in her bag for her cigarettes and matches and it wasn't until she'd exhaled a thin plume of smoke that she could raise her head and say quite steadily, 'I lost the baby. Freddy decided to stay on the Continent and I came back to England and now I'm living with his mother in Hampstead in her dark, cold house with a clutch of elderly spinsters, three boorish salesman and Potts. It's so sad. It's the saddest place on earth. I have to get out of there. I simply have to.'

She'd said far too much and Libby stiffened her spine, braced herself for Deidre to say something cutting and cruel, but it turned out her sympathy, the way she sighed and tilted her head, was far, far worse. 'You need a job, then?'

'Anything.' Libby hadn't planned to sound quite so desperate either but as usual all her plans amounted to precisely nothing.

'Well, you're far too old to play the ingénue or hoof it in a chorus line. As for the character parts, I don't mean to be unkind, dearie, I really don't, but there are heaps of other actresses with better notices and you are looking rather done in. Thin. It doesn't suit you.'

Libby stifled a choked laugh. 'You've always told me that I was too fleshy.'

'You were, but now you're quite haggard in the face. I couldn't even find you a little modelling work at one of the fashion houses.' Deidre sighed again as if her inability to find Libby any suitable jobs was paining her more than it was Libby. 'I could see if anyone might need a secretary. Except . . . Do you type and take dictation? No, of course you don't.'

The weight of it, the sheer despair of her situation, pressed against Libby's chest. 'Maybe some radio work?' she suggested in a voice that quivered with the effort not to break down and sob.

'I don't think so,' Deidre said vaguely as she rifled through a stack of papers on her desk, her bracelets jangling, red-tipped nails a blur. 'You mentioned Hampstead? There was something that came in a couple of days ago. I wasn't sure why it was sent to me, but perhaps it was kismet.' She pulled out a piece of pale blue paper with the air of a magician pulling a rabbit out of a hat. 'Have you ever thought about teaching, dearie?'

6

Libby

It was lunchtime by the time Libby left the office with an interview at a girls' school in Frognal secured for Monday week. It was a hiding to nothing, a sop so Deidre could send her on her way with a clear conscience. Coming into town had been a waste of the Tube fare and now Libby was in dire need of a friendly face. When she opened the door of the café in Wardour Street, she was relieved to see some of her old crowd colonising three tables at the back of the room, much to the tight-lipped fury of Gladys, the owner's wife.

Libby fluffed up her hair, pinned on a smile and strode over. 'Fancy bumping into you reprobates!'

'Libs!'

'Goodness me, hello, stranger!'

'What on earth are you doing here?'

There was Doris and Thea, who had risen up the ranks with Libby. Francis, Tony, Bernard, Janice, May. They'd shared squalid digs, draughty rehearsal rooms, tables at opening-night parties and sat in countless audition lines waiting for their name to be called.

Libby sat down on the chair that Tony pulled out for her, gratefully accepted the offer of a cup of tea and squeezed Thea's hand in greeting.

'It's the oddest thing,' Thea said. 'Your ears must have been burning because we were just talking about you. Saw Freddy's column in the *Daily Mirror* and wondered if you were in Spain with him.'

'Clearly I'm not,' Libby said as the paper was placed in front of her. Her eyes blurred as she saw Freddy's byline on a story about the Popular Front winning the recent Spanish elections. She traced her fingers over his name. So he was still alive, carrying on with his life without a care in the world. Well, wasn't that absolutely lovely for him? 'His editors at the *Mirror* and the *Herald* positively *begged* him to stay on the Continent and file stories for them, but let's not talk about Freddy. I'm dying to know what's the latest gossip, darlings?'

Libby tucked into a plate of liver and bacon, still following the doctor's orders, as she was regaled with a story about a young male lead and his much older, much more venerated leading lady that had Libby spluttering on a mouthful of tea.

But all too soon her friends had to go back to work, to get ready for matinée performances. Libby was lingering over a bowl of apple pie and custard when two hands descended on her shoulders. She didn't jump because she could smell the noxious cologne he always favoured. 'Mickey,' she said with a sigh.

'Fortune must be smiling on me, you've saved me a trip to Hampstead,' he said, turning a chair back to front so he could straddle it and earn himself a seething look from gloomy Gladys.

'I'm not going away for the weekend with any more men,'

Libby said rashly, though lord knows, she could do with another thirty pounds. 'Not again.'

'He didn't try anything, did he?' Mickey asked sharply. 'I told him no funny business.'

Mr Watkins, Hugo, hadn't tried anything. After they'd called their truce, they'd spent the weekend playing gin rummy for toffees and making cordial though rather stilted small talk, mostly about the weather.

'He was a bit shirty at first, but apart from that, he was a perfect gentleman,' Libby said. Watkins had even insisted on sleeping on the sofa in their suite and nothing Libby had said could persuade him otherwise. Not even when she'd offered to 'put my hatpin under the pillow, on the off-chance that you may become consumed with lust in the middle of the night and I'm forced to defend myself.'

Watkins hadn't even cracked a smile. 'I'll be perfectly comfortable on the sofa,' he'd said doggedly and had come out of the bathroom with his pyjamas buttoned up to his neck and his dressing gown tightly belted as if he were rather worried that it would be Libby unable to control her lust.

He'd slid into bed with her in the morning before the maid could bring in the breakfast tray, but he'd been careful not to touch her, kept his face aloof, and when the maid had come in and Libby had snuggled against him, it had been like trying to cuddle a girder. The young girl had averted her gaze and could hardly wait to scuttle for the door, though the maid catching Libby and Watkins in bed was the entire reason they'd come down to Brighton for the weekend. Then there'd still been another day and night to get through before they could go back to London, and the whole time Libby had felt like death warmed over.

Never before had thirty pounds been so hard won. And now Libby wanted the whole business squared away so she never had to think of Watkins again. 'I'm rather glad I've run into you too because I thought you said that you'd be in touch. That you were going to have a couple of witnesses from the hotel come to London and swear before a crowded court, and on a whole stack of Bibles too, that I was the hussy that they'd caught *in flagrante delicto* with Mr Watkins.' Libby peered over Mickey's shoulder but he'd come alone. 'I must say that this divorce nonsense drags on and on, doesn't it?'

'Well, Libby, my darling, that's what I was coming to see you about. There isn't going to be any witness identifying you as the mysterious Marigold because the case isn't going to court,' Mickey said. 'Not unless you agree to testify in person.' He nudged her arm. 'There'll be another thirty quid in it for you, so what's the harm, my darling?'

Libby stared at him in horror. 'What's the harm?' she echoed, her voice rising. 'I'm a married woman.' She wagged a shaking finger at Mickey who licked his lips nervously. 'You promised it would all be hush-hush. That's why I agreed to it. No, Mickey. Appearing in court absolutely wasn't part of the agreement.'

'But dining in the restaurant on Friday night was and you didn't, Libby, my sweet, so Watkins doesn't have enough proof of adultery to satisfy the court.'

'We had dinner in the restaurant on the Saturday night.' Watkins had ordered Libby a steak and a glass of milk stout that they'd had to send out for, which had been very kind of him and had certainly caused a stir and turned heads in such a genteel establishment.

'Had to be Friday night,' Mickey said doggedly. 'There's a certain waiter who works Friday nights that knows the drill.'

'I was poorly on the Friday, Mickey. Won't the doctor give evidence?'

Apparently he wouldn't. Was horrified at the very notion,

and the maid who'd brought in the breakfast tray both mornings and, it transpired, had tended to Libby when she'd been passed out cold, now refused to have any part of it either. She'd somehow got it into her head that Libby was the injured party and said she wouldn't take advantage of a woman 'who nearly died in my arms'.

Libby refused to feel guilty. 'Well, I'm not giving the money back. I've had bills to pay,' she hissed at Mickey, who, as usual, caved at the first sign of resistance and held up his hands to ward off her wrath. 'For goodness sake, Mickey, I couldn't help being ill.'

'Of course you couldn't and you're looking much better than last time I saw you. Got those roses back in your cheeks, the sparkle in your lovely eyes . . .'

'Mickey, don't try and soft soap me,' Libby warned him. 'I'm not one of those silly little girls that you usually inveigle into your tawdry schemes.'

'Of course you're not. You've got class, Libby, my love, but you've left me in a bit of a pickle. My reputation is hanging by a thread and you know how your good friend, your pal Mickey, relies on his reputation.' Mickey placed one of his hands on Libby's, which was resting on the table. His touch was soft, if a little clammy.

'I'm not giving back the money,' Libby said again, but in a slightly more conciliatory tone. 'And I won't appear in court either, but I could write a letter, explaining things. You tell me what to put and I'll happily sign it. Not with my real name though.'

'You're a champ. A real brick.' Mickey smiled ingratiatingly. 'But rather than write a letter, could you have a chat with Mr Watkins? If you're really certain you won't help out poor Mickey in his hour of need and show up for court . . .'

Libby didn't say anything but she was sure her eyes were

promising Mickey a slow and very painful demise if he persisted because he took his hand off her and backed his chair away.

'If you could just meet him,' Mickey said weakly, fishing in the breast pocket of his suit for a business card. 'Call his secretary. Arrange a time and place. He's happy to come to you.'

Libby took the card and glanced at the address, somewhere in Mayfair, then slipped it into her handbag. 'I'll think about it,' she said, then she did think about it. About Hugo Watkins and how kind he'd been, once he'd shaken off his rage and confusion. At least the poor bugger had the possibility of an escape from his wife's betrayal. Some people weren't that lucky. And perhaps some of his good luck might rub off on Libby. 'I will. I promise. I'll call him.'

7

Zoe

Life was grand for Win who toddled off to work each morning, stopping off at his gym on the way so he could have a hot shower. He worked for a small accountancy practice whose offices were on the top two floors of a house on the posh side of Camden Town and they had a kitchen, central heating, a lavatory that flushed first time; all the mod cons.

And Zoe ... Zoe had none of those things.

So as soon as Win left, Zoe would wait for Gavin, their builder and Win's stepfather, and his crew to arrive, parrot back the instructions that Win had asked her to relay while Gavin cast his eyes to the heavens, and then she would leave too.

It was a straight walk downhill through Highgate Woods to Muswell Hill and the childhood home of Zoe's best friend, Cath, who would be waiting for Zoe's arrival, alerted by text message.

'Hot water's on, kettle's on,' she'd call out as Zoe unlatched the gate. 'Do you want tea or shower first?'

Zoe and Cath had met eight years ago at the Hay Festival. They'd ended up in the same cab driven by the most racist taxi driver in the world.

For fifteen minutes he'd taken them on a white-knuckle ride down twisty country lanes as he'd railed against foreigners, immigrants and living in London where nobody spoke English and they 'handed out council houses to anyone fresh off the boat'. Zoe had sat there in an agony of embarrassment, fury and indecision, every muscle tensed in indignation, until she couldn't bear it any more.

'Excuse me! But you're being absolutely offensive,' she'd squeaked at the same time that Cath had said in a furious voice, 'Actually, my boyfriend's black and even if he wasn't, you are bang out of order.'

A minute later Zoe and Cath were standing by the side of the road, somewhere near the Welsh border, because the most racist taxi driver in the world had thrown them out of his cab.

As they tried to get a signal to phone one of the festival volunteers to deliver them to their hotel, they'd bonded over their current dire situation and once they were back in London and discovered that they both had boyfriends who worked in financial services and were obsessed with Arsenal and spending their Saturdays in second-hand record shops, their friendship was a done deal.

Eight years of Zoe and Cath going out and getting drunk together then nursing their hangovers with kill-or-cure fry-ups the next day. Of mini breaks to Paris, Berlin, Prague and New York. Of suffering the slings and arrows of bad book sales.

So, when Zoe needed near daily access to hot water, a Wi-Fi signal and a working kitchen, Cath hadn't thought twice about offering up her facilities and Zoe had accepted with only the most token of protests.

Despite her friend's love of karaoke, gin-based cocktails

and jumpsuits, Zoe had always thought there was something quite Renaissance-like about Cath's beauty; thick brown pre-Raphaelite curls, quite startling green eyes, the elegant sweep of her brow and cheekbones, but lately, she looked haunted and harried as months of worry had taken their toll.

Last summer, Cath's father Clive, funny, clever Clive, had tripped over a wobbly paving slab and broken his hip. The accident had knocked the stuffing out of him; taken away his innate Cliveness. Before the accident, he'd swum three times a week, was a docent at Highgate Cemetery, a keen gardener and organised local history walks. But now after four months in hospital where he'd then caught a superbug that proved resistant to most antibiotics, Clive was diminished: timid and frail and glued to *Homes Under the Hammer*, when Zoe popped her head round the living room door to say hello.

So frail that Cath and her boyfriend Theo had rented out their flat in Finsbury Park and moved in with Clive because Cath's older brother lived in Aberdeen, her older sister had emigrated to Australia and her younger brother spent his days in an anarcho-Marxist squat in Camberwell smoking skunk.

'I think your dad seems a little brighter today,' a freshly showered Zoe ventured, because this morning Clive had managed a smile when he'd greeted her.

'I can't see it myself,' Cath said sourly as Zoe helped herself to toast. 'He wasn't like this when my mum died.'

Cath's mother had died from a vicious form of bone cancer when Cath was still at university, long before she and Zoe had met, so Zoe didn't know how Clive had coped back then. But she knew how he was now and how he'd been before.

'He's lost his confidence,' she told Cath gently. 'He'd been leading a really full, very busy life, just a few aches and pains occasionally, then suddenly he brushes up against his own mortality. That's got to be scary, hasn't it?'

Cath nodded. 'I suppose.' She sighed. 'I just find it, him, the situation, frustrating.'

'Is he doing his physio?'

'Only when I stand over him and nag. I hate nagging but I do it all the time lately. I nag Theo. I nag both my brothers when I speak to them because would it kill either of them to visit? My inner voice has become shrill and hectoring. Ugh! Enough about me.' Cath looked up from her coffee cup. 'What about you, Zo? How are you?'

This was Zoe's cue to rant about how it was impossible to work in a freezing cold house with builders hammering and drilling and singing along enthusiastically to Heart FM. Gavin was constantly knocking on the door of the back bedroom where Zoe lurked to update her on the latest live fuse they'd found sticking out of a wall or to ask her opinion on some topic of house repair that Zoe wasn't qualified to have an opinion on.

But these were minor problems, compared to what Clive and Cath were going through. Compared to a lot of other people who didn't have anywhere to live or anyone to love them. There were people facing terminal illness, life-limiting prognoses. People suffering from mental health issues. There were a lot of people, millions of them, far worse off than Zoe.

'Well, at least Win and I have each other,' she told Cath. 'So, there's that. Someone else to share the pain of splinters. It's amazing how many splinters you get when you have the builders in.'

Cath pursed her lips, exhaled then closed her mouth. Twisted her lips again. 'You know how I have this whole child-hating persona where I bitch about women pushing their Bugaboos three abreast along the pavement and I tut and roll my eyes if I hear children not using their indoor voices? But I hope you also know that if things had turned out differently, I would have been the proudest, most doting honorary aunt the world had ever seen and I'm absolutely here for you if you want to talk about the baby. You get that, right?'

Zoe nodded and she couldn't do any more than that for a moment because there was a throbbing in her throat, a prickle behind her eyes ... She swallowed hard. 'I do get that and thank you, but honestly I ... I ... don't even know how to talk about it or what I'd want to say.' Unlike Cath, Zoe loved children – she made a living from writing children's books so doing author events would have been challenging if she didn't – but she'd been not quite ready yet on the having-a-baby front, while Win had been ambivalent. Zoe had known that at some point in the nearish future they were due a serious conversation about if and when they were going to start a family but now she wasn't undecided so much as terrified, maybe even unable. 'I didn't even know I was pregnant so being sad feels a bit hypocritical.'

'It's OK to be sad though.' Cath gestured at Zoe's sketch pad, which should have been full of drawings for a new picture book proposal about Reggie, a hardened city mouse used to living on his wits and the mean streets, who ended up in the countryside only to be ostracised by the local field mice for his thuggish city ways.

Instead the pages were covered in sketches of a little boy with dark hair like Win's, impossibly big eyes, fat cheeks made for being kissed.

'It's been two and a half months since it happened,' Zoe said, closing her sketch pad. 'I don't know why I can't just move on, stop dwelling over it. So, anyway ... have you heard back from your agent yet?'

'Has Win moved on, then?' Cath persisted, because she was off her game lately and wasn't picking up on the signal

55

that Zoe had just sent out to indicate that the subject was no longer up for discussion.

'Who knows? Mostly Win is obsessed with his day-to-day wall planner, which takes up the entire hall,' Zoe said with great feeling, but not *good* feelings. 'Gavin's meant to place the right colour sticker on each task as he completes it and Win is forever fussing over the bloody thing and moving stickers and drawing pins around like some general planning military manoeuvres. It's the only thing that's occupying his mind at the moment.'

That wasn't fair. Or strictly true. Guilt swept over Zoe like a prickly heat rash. 'I shouldn't be so mean. It's good that Win's on top of all the house stuff, but it's been ages since we talked about anything that wasn't house-related. Last night we talked about flaunching the chimney stacks.'

'Sounds rude,' Cath decided. 'What's flaunching?'

Zoe shrugged. 'I'm still not entirely sure.'

'All Theo and I talk about is my dad,' Cath offered. 'Last night we compared and contrasted various styles of stairlift. When did we become responsible adults?'

'I don't know, but I miss being irresponsible,' Zoe said and then with great responsibility and not much enthusiasm, she reached for her sketch pad again. 'Cath, we really need to stop talking and get working.'

At four, Zoe left Cath's for the walk back up Muswell Hill Road (she was fast realising that there was no way to get any-where in their new neighbourhood that didn't involve a brutal uphill walk) but, as ever, the thought of the wall planner made her delay going home.

Sometimes she would go and work in the library, which was five minutes away from Elysian Place. It was warm and there was free Wi-Fi and a public toilet but the library was also a refuge for mothers and where there were mothers there were children, from impossibly small, tightly swaddled newborns to rambunctious toddlers who ran about shrieking and bashing each other over the head with soft toys.

Each childish yelp made something inside Zoe twist and ache and she'd have to pack up her papers and pens and leave.

She couldn't bear the thought of the library today but walking home and taking the scenic route through Highgate Woods was never a chore. There were babies in Highgate Woods too but they tended to stay in their prams. And much better than babies were the dogs; from large, sleek red Vizslas to silly, curly cockerpoos and everything in between. Zoe had a particular tendresse for the dogs from the local animal shelter who were walked by volunteers, the dogs wearing blue tabards with 'Adopt me!' printed on them. They tended to be mostly Staffies who'd lunge at Zoe, only to bat their big square heads against her hand until she gave in and stroked them.

All the while, as she walked, her left hand kept returning to the pocket of her parka. Even with gloves on, Zoe could feel the round button against her fingertips. A red cherry button once attached to a tiny cardigan for a tiny baby. It must have fallen off the night that she and Win had unearthed the layette set in the suitcase at the back of the wardrobe.

The next morning, Zoe had spotted the button, red and faded, on the dusty floor. It was cracked and brittle, made before plastic was invented. She thought it was probably Bakelite. It was the sort of thing Win would know but she hadn't told Win about the button; she didn't want to talk about anything that would cause his face to grow tight and cold. So she'd put the button away, only to find that she had to keep checking on it; picking it up, turning it this way and that. Wondering who'd bought it and sewn it onto that tiny cardigan.

In the end, Zoe had painted the button with clear nail varnish to stop it cracking further and now it was always there in her pocket. Not a good luck charm, not when even the most abstract thought about babies, of what had been lost, made Zoe curse her own bad luck. She supposed the button was a worry bead, if anything. Something real that she could fuss at instead of the thing that gnawed at the inside of her head whenever she thought about it.

Zoe clasped her fingers around the button now as she arrived back at Elysian Place just as Gavin was packing up so he could give her a detailed progress report, which she'd then impart to Win.

'It would be much easier if you both, oh, I don't know, maybe called each other,' she said to Gavin as he bombarded her with information about the party wall agreement.

'Ah, no. You see, if I start speaking to Win about this, then we'll stop speaking,' Gavin said, which was cryptic but also the truth. Gavin and Win had stopped speaking for two months when Gavin had installed a new kitchen and bathroom in their old flat. They'd both promised that this time Gavin would communicate better and Win wouldn't micromanage everything, but they'd broken those promises within a week. 'Don't worry about it, pet. This is the nature of house renovations. Things get much worse before they can get better.'

'They're not going to get much worse, are they?' Zoe asked with a desperate note to her voice. 'I thought they were already next-level worse. Peak worse.'

'A few months from now, when this place is all shipshape, you'll hardly remember what a shithole it was,' Gavin said sagely and then he was gone.

8

Zoe

This was the hardest time. The two hours or so after the builders had left and before Win got home. The house was dark, full of shadows and strange noises. Things creaking and crackling, not the usual noises that Zoe was used to, like the gurgling of the hot water pipes as they still didn't have any of them. It was also freezing – Zoe had to wear thermals, a onesie, a thick jumper, two pairs of socks, gloves and a Puffa jacket, which was fine as long as she didn't need to move. She sat in her little makeshift office, which was a corner of the back bedroom, the only habitable room in the house, and really tried to sketch out the story of Reggie, the urban mouse, but it was no use. She was *still* drawing the face of the child that might have been hers. Not just hers. It would have been Win's child too.

And like every evening when it got closer to the time that Win would come home, Zoe thought to herself, This will be the night that we talk about it. We have to talk about the baby, no matter how hard and painful it might get.

'Zoe? Are you in?'

Zoe gave a start as she heard Win's voice. Relief seeped through her, because so many evenings when she was expecting him, he'd ring to say he had to work late. She slowly uncurled limbs stiff with cold. Touched the button that now rested on the desk next to her pencil box. 'I'm up here!'

'Well, can you come down?' Win sounded a little terse, which was usual these days.

There had to be enough money in the kitty that they could go out. There was a little Italian restaurant close by with communal seating, and a mid-week bowl-of-pasta-and-a-glass-of-wine special offer. They could go there, Zoe decided, ask for the quietest corner of the communal seating and begin to make sense of something that still felt utterly senseless.

'Good day?' she asked as she carefully picked her way down the stairs, because plastic sheeting on wooden stairs plus Ugg boots was a treacherous combination.

Win, still in his coat, was peering at his vast wall planner, a finger on that day's date.

'Why isn't there a red sticker here?'

'I have no idea,' Zoe admitted cheerfully because she'd done enough moping and brooding today. Time to switch things up. 'What do the red stickers mean again?'

'Zo!' Win squinted at his chart, his nose almost brushing against a little crop of blue stickers. Zoe had forgotten what the blue stickers signified too. 'So, have they started on the plastering? Because it takes weeks to dry out properly.'

This was something that Zoe knew the answer to. 'Gavin wanted to wait until the boiler had been installed. Said the plaster would dry quicker once the central heating was on,' she said knowledgably, like her eyes hadn't glazed over when Gavin had brought her up a mug of tea first thing that morning then stayed for a whole twenty minutes to talk about boilers. 'But we can't have central heating until they've managed to track down some valve-type things that are compatible with the radiators.'

One of the quirks of the house was that although it was unfurnished, undecorated, the original owners had seen fit to install cumbersome but now gloriously retro radiators in every room, which according to Gavin defied all the laws of modern central heating.

'Jesus! How hard is it to find some valves?' Win barked and he wasn't barking at Zoe, he was barking at the situation, but she was the only person around to hear the peremptory pitch to his voice. 'Please tell me that they've narrowed down the choice of boiler.'

'I would if I could . . .'

'Zoe, really! I need you to keep on top of all this.' This time the barking was definitely directed at her. 'I'm not asking you to project manage, as if, but I need you to pay attention when people, Gavin, tell you things.'

It was very hard to remember the Win she'd fallen in love with when the Win that she was currently living with was, well, so hard to live with.

'I do listen,' Zoe said evenly. 'But daily boiler updates get a little wearing, especially when without a boiler it's too bloody cold to think straight.'

Win shuffled a bit nearer to Zoe so they were eyeballing each other in the harsh glare of a naked bulb dangling down from the ceiling on a length of electrical cord. He pulled his hand free from one of his woolly gloves so he could trace her brow bone with the tip of his finger. They'd always used to kiss each other hello and goodbye and sometimes just for the hell of it but this was the first time he'd touched her since he got home. 'You're scrunched up,' he said, because Zoe was frowning. She couldn't help it and frowned even harder when

Win's finger made contact with the deep furrow between her eyes. 'Sorry, I'm being a beast. Should I go out and come in again?'

'There is a lot to feel beastly about,' Zoe conceded. She took hold of Win's sleeve so she could pull him to the stairs. 'Let's sit where we can see the wall planner and I'll fill you in on the latest thrilling developments.'

They sat side by side on the stairs and Zoe very gently told Win that they now needed to install a ventilation unit in the bathroom for reasons unknown. Win groaned and asked how much.

'Does it even matter at this point? I mean, what's another five hundred pounds?'

'Do you remember back when five hundred pounds bought nice things like a week's holiday including flights and hotel transfers?' Win leaned into Zoe, pressed his cold cheek against hers, so she was forced to twist away until she had the rough wall against her back.

'But we've both been in worse places than this.' Zoe pointed at herself because she was talking geographically and not metaphorically. 'I spent my formative years in an army barracks in Northern Ireland, though we did have central heating.'

Zoe could have sworn she saw the faint glimmer of a smile on Win's face. 'Worst place we lived was a flat in Willesden that makes this house look like Buckingham Palace. Crackheads next door, a family of six living in the garden shed in the house on the other side and Ed and I thought we had a poltergeist but our dad said it was just rats. Like that made it any better.'

'Poor Win,' Zoe murmured and she patted his knee in a consoling manner. 'But we wouldn't be the well-rounded individuals we are today if we'd spent our childhoods in one place.'

By his estimation, Win had lived in roughly twenty different locations in and around north London by the time he was twelve. From a house on The Bishop's Avenue, that his dad was minding for a friend of a friend, to the place in Willesden and all points in between. Terry Rowell, Win's dad, was a dreamer, a chancer, a wheeler-dealer. Stories of Win's childhood sounded like episodes of *Only Fools and Horses*, with Terry cast as a Del Boy-type figure who had a good heart, an eye for the ladies and absolutely no business acumen.

Zoe's dad, Ken, was about as far from a chancer as it was possible to get. He'd joined the army when he was sixteen, working his way up to staff sergeant before he'd retired a couple of years ago at fifty-five. He was steady and stalwart – Zoe had always felt safe when Ken was around, even though she'd spent the first six years of her life in Belfast. Then Aberdeen, Germany, Dorset, Larnaca in Cyprus and finally when she was thirteen, Zoe and her mother moved in with Nancy's parents in Cambridge so Zoe could focus on her exams, while Ken was posted overseas again.

Her childhood meant that Zoe could adapt to most things, had always found it easy to make friends, but constantly moving house and school had been hellish for Win, who liked everything ordered, his days carefully planned out and who stumbled over his words when he was in an unfamiliar situation because he was horribly, painfully shy. People often mistook his shyness for an aloof kind of arrogance, as Zoe had when she'd first stumbled into Win's office thirteen years ago.

She'd been a walk-in. A nineteen-year-old art student who needed an accountant as a matter of some urgency. She'd sat in the reception of an accountancy practice in Camden Town for what felt like aeons until she'd been ushered into the office of a young man, not *that* much older than her. 'Mr Rowell,' he'd said. He'd been wearing a grey suit that didn't sit right on him, as if it were a costume, and he was tall and angular as he'd looked down his nose at Zoe.

So haughty, Zoe had thought, and it had wrong-footed her. Her rosy cheeks flushed even redder so it felt as if someone had taken a match to them as she gave him a garbled explanation as to why she was there. 'So, I won a BBC writing competition in my last year of school and I got an agent and a book deal out of it. I didn't think I had to pay tax if I was a student but now my agent says I have to and I've got all this paper and I don't know what to do with it.' She had held up a carrier bag. 'Invoices and receipts and things. I just hoped it would go away and then I got a letter and even the words "Inland Revenue" on the envelope make me want to throw up and so I thought I'd better see an accountant and they're totally going to send me to debtor's prison, aren't they?'

'Sit down,' Win had said gently. He'd taken Zoe's arm and guided her to a chair. 'Of course they won't send you to debtor's prison. They don't have them any more. They'll just send you to a normal prison.'

That had been Win's feeble attempt to break the ice, to put her at ease, but at the time, Zoe wasn't sure if she were going to vomit or cry. She did neither, but shut her eyes. 'Oh God.'

Win had given Zoe's hand a comforting squeeze and said, 'I promise you won't go to any kind of prison.' Which had been uncharacteristically rash of him because Zoe could have been insider trading for all he really knew.

It had taken Win months to sort out her financial affairs. Like trying to squeeze toothpaste back into the tube, he'd said. Zoe would pop in to see him every few days. Living away from home, from her mother, wasn't the wild, liberated ride it should have been because Zoe wasn't wild or liberated. She wasn't cool or edgy either, like the people on her fine art course, and she'd been lost until she'd met Win.

Win. He was the only person Zoe had met in London who was certain of the world and his own place in it. The people she knew at Central St Martins were only certain of things that weren't really important: which bands to like, the hip places to hang out, and how Zoe was the very opposite of cool because she wrote children's books that featured anthropomorphic woodland animals. Whereas Win looked out for her best interests and claimed to be impressed that Zoe had a book deal before she'd left school. And once she got to know Win a little better when he said things in the deadpan, Sahara-dry way of his, Zoe no longer wanted to throw up or cry, but laugh in a way she never did when her college boyfriend Tony cracked jokes.

'Do you remember when we first met, Win?' she whispered now. 'You must have known I had a crush on you a few weeks in because I used to go red every time I walked into your office. Or redder. You did know, didn't you?'

Win made a noise that wasn't yes and wasn't no, but took hold of Zoe's hand and brought it to his lips and even if all else was chaos, they still had each other.

'I thought we'd go out tonight,' he said, but before Zoe could extol the virtues of pasta-and-wine special offers, Win got there first. 'It's the pub quiz at the Maynard. We always used to go and so— Why are you pulling that face before I've even got to the end of my sentence?'

Zoe had already rearranged her features into a grimace. 'It'll be so noisy,' she complained. 'And we can't really afford it.'

'We absolutely can't afford it,' Win agreed. 'But we'll be able to afford it even less a couple of months from now, so, why not?'

'I'm not really in the mood and anyway, the quiz is more your thing,' Zoe said. She wanted to go out just the two of them, so they could find a way to close the distance between them that they'd filled up with packing crates and cardboard boxes.

Win looked at Zoe warily as if he didn't trust her. 'But Zoe, you haven't been out, haven't seen our friends, in ages. Not since you were ill.'

He still couldn't say the words. 'When you were ill' was the closest he could come to describing the events of that November night and its devastating aftermath. Or 'when you had your accident', like it was something that had only happened to Zoe. As if it might even be her fault.

And Zoe *had* seen their friends since she'd come out of hospital. But once had been enough. A Christmas party when she'd still been reeling, trembling and everyone had known why.

'I read somewhere that one in three pregnancies ends in miscarriage,' one of Zoe's friends had said, like that was some kind of consolation, when it wasn't.

'I didn't have a miscarriage, I had an ectopic pregnancy,' Zoe had said baldly and she wasn't a violent person, she really wasn't, but if she'd been feeling stronger there would have been a good chance that she'd have punched Katie in the throat. And she wasn't feeling much stronger than that now. Physically she was better. Her scar had healed and over the coming months Zoe knew it would fade from red to pink and eventually silver. It was the stuff on the inside that took longer to heal.

'I have seen people. I see Cath pretty much every day and anyway, I'm on the verge of a breakthrough with Reggie,' she hurriedly explained.

'The mouse?'

'The one and same. But if you want to go out, that's fine. You deserve a night off and I can stay here and make sure no one breaks in to steal all our copper pipes.' Zoe said this because Flavia from next door had popped round to introduce herself and cheerfully inform Zoe that they'd moved out when they were having work done and their house had been broken into and the thieves had taken every inch of pipe they could dismantle. 'But I am going to crank up the space heater like you wouldn't believe.'

Win no longer seemed thrilled by the prospect of an evening spent in a warm pub with his closest friends, eating pizza from the wood-fired oven, drinking lager and arguing over the sitcom round. 'Are you sure?' he asked again.

'Absolutely sure,' Zoe said firmly, though she wasn't quite as sure once Win had finally been persuaded. She thought about running after him, but then she thought of turning up at the pub and everyone looking at her, heads tilted to one side, and the concern.

'So, how *are* you?'

'No, really how are you?'

'At least you've got the house to take your mind off things. You lucky, home-owning bastards!'

Zoe couldn't do it. She just wasn't ready yet, so she shuffled along to the makeshift kitchen in what had been the scullery, which she wanted to knock through and Win wanted to repurpose as a utility room. More like a futility room, she thought as she made toast and heated up a bowl of soup in the microwave. They had kettle, toaster and microwave but no oven, nowhere to sit either.

Zoe carried her dinner tray upstairs to the back bedroom. She'd get into bed and read something comforting, maybe *Ballet Shoes*, which she always thought of as a literary security blanket, that was the plan, but instead she was marching straight over to the inbuilt cupboard, to the suitcase.

Zoe hadn't forgotten about it. She'd thought about it,

what was inside it, every day. But like the baby, she'd tried not to think about it. Told herself that the brittle button in her pocket was enough. But still she could feel the suitcase's unwelcome presence in her house. Zoe imagined it like Edgar Allen Poe's 'Tell-Tale Heart': beating away in its hiding place, disturbing the rhythms of the house. Perhaps if she got rid of the suitcase, the terrible secrets inside it, then everything else would start to get better.

Standing on tiptoes, she grabbed the handle, gave it an almighty yank and nearly fell over backwards, because she'd expected it to be heavy but it wasn't at all. And as soon as it was in her hands, all her good intentions were gone. She squatted down, opened it, casting aside the dark green dress, burrowing through the papers, to take out the baby clothes again.

They would have once been white. A soft, snowy white but now they were tinged yellow like nicotine stains. Zoe tried to imagine that unknown woman, the mother-to-be, because someone, the woman in the photos, Elizabeth Edwards, maybe, had sat and knitted the booties, the cap with the ribbon ties, the little jacket, her fingers busy, her mind on the baby growing inside her. Would it take after her or her husband? Would it be a fusser? What kind of person would it grow up to be?

Then Zoe remembered the letter that had been wedged in the diary and retraced her steps until she found it again.

I don't believe that I've ever managed to give you one single moment of the true, pure happiness that you deserve.

Zoe couldn't bear to read those lines again. There were so many things she couldn't bear to do these days; she never used to be such a coward.

She forced her eyes down to the page. The letter was addressed 'Dearest Libby'. Wasn't Libby a diminutive of Elizabeth? Elizabeth Edwards, actress, it had said on the back of the photographs. Did that mean this letter, the diary, belonged to her too?

The letter, dated 7 December 1935, had been written on stationery from a hotel in Paris by a man called Freddy. It was a Dear John letter, a Dear Libby letter, explaining why he was leaving her, even though Libby had just lost the baby she was carrying. Their baby.

The words, already faint in their old-fashioned, looped script, blurred in front of Zoe. She brushed her tears away, carefully folded the letter though she wanted to tear it to pieces, and slotted it back into the diary. How she hurt, *ached*, for poor Elizabeth, Libby. Abandoned by the one person who should have been there to hold her, pull her through.

The diary, at least, was a comforting, solid weight in Zoe's hands. She hesitated momentarily, because she couldn't take any more heartache. Not her own. Not other people's. But curiosity got the better of her as curiosity often did.

Zoe started to flick through the book, the pencil marks simply vague indentations on the page in some places, but if she positioned herself directly under the naked lightbulb, she could just about begin to decipher the diary entries.

Elizabeth, though already Zoe thought of her as Libby, was forever totting up her expenses and mostly used the diary to keep track of her appointments, though January had been a quiet month.

January 25th
  Victoria Gardens Hotel, Mickey F, 2 p.m.
  Remember to buy hatpin.

January 30th
  Library books due back. Ask Hannah to renew the
Angela Thirkells.

February 7th
  Library fine – 2d

On today's date, 17 February, Libby had written:

Withers, 11 a.m.

Zoe decided that Withers had to be the theatrical agents, Withers & Withers, whose details were printed on the publicity stills.

There were also several pieces of paper tucked into February's pages. A newspaper report on the Spanish elections, the page carelessly torn out. A business card: Hugo Watkins, Watkins Motors, Park Lane W1, MAYfair 3745. And on a lined piece of paper was a hastily scrawled shopping list.

The aunts: ¼ humbugs, jar of potted meat, two balls black wool, bag of stale buns?????
  Mrs Carmichael: wool – grey (or navy if not too dark), size nine needles, packet of digestive biscuits, bottle of Milk of Magnesia.
  Miss Bettany – denture cream and small jar of Bovril.
  Potts: bottle of gin – hasn't even paid me in advance! CHEEKY BUGGER!!!!!
  Hannah – Woolies pick 'n' mix, no Brazil nuts or toffees!! (Round it up to 2/)

Suddenly, there were so many things Zoe wanted to know about this woman, separated from Zoe by eighty years, a lifetime, but connected to her too through the same sad loss.

Zoe pulled out the photographs again. She was sure she could see a mischievous gleam in Libby's liquid eyes; the curve of her smile seemed more pronounced as if she were about to toss back her head and laugh and laugh. She looked much more like a Libby than she did an Elizabeth.

By the time she packed everything except the diary back in the suitcase, Zoe realised that she'd forgotten to bring the space heater in with her, her soup would be frozen in the bowl by now, and she was so cold that the tips of her fingers were almost numb, but she felt a little better. Even the baby clothes didn't make the sobs start to soar when she placed them at the bottom of the case.

For the first time since it happened, since November, Zoe no longer felt alone.

9

Libby

Spring was just within sight. The promise of sun after such a dreary winter made one long to shake off the doldrums, begin to hope, to think about the future without fear. Libby even dared to imagine that her feelings for Freddy were fading and she was ready for life without him, for starting anew, just as the first crocuses and snowdrops were bravely budding on the heath.

Then the cold snapped. Even though it was mid March, the temperature on the ornate barometer in the hall dropped towards zero, the foolhardy crocuses and snowdrops were snuffed out, smothered by a cruel blanket of snow, and there was a letter waiting for Libby when she came down to breakfast one bitterly cold morning. The aunts and Miss Bettany were swathed in shawls, Mrs Carmichael in an ancient fur coat which reeked of mothballs, and one of the salesmen, Libby couldn't remember his name, was wearing a muffler and fingerless gloves as he tucked into his porridge.

'I saw Freddy's handwriting and I couldn't help myself. I

was sure he was writing to his dear mama,' Millicent said as Libby picked up the envelope and gasped indignantly to find it had already been opened. 'A mother's love cannot be judged too harshly, Elizabeth, dear.'

Libby was so angry she could barely speak. She swallowed down the bitter words forming in her throat, and tucked the letter into her bag.

She didn't have time to read it until the morning break when the girls were playing outside, throwing snowballs and shrieking. Libby could hear them from outside her studio as she sat on the window ledge, feet resting on the radiator, the warmth seeping through the rubber soles of her tennis shoes.

Two weeks ago Libby had been engaged as a teacher of dance, drama and movement at a small girls' school in one of the huge Gothic houses on Fitzjohn's Avenue. The Frognal School for Girls was apparently a Steiner Waldorf educational establishment, though all Libby knew was that it had the same smell that all schools did, of boiled cabbage, chalk dust and Jeyes fluid.

The headmistress, Beryl Marjoribanks, a tiny, blonde thing not much older than Libby, had all but begged her to take the job. 'I never dreamt we might find someone who'd trained in Paris,' she told Libby at the interview.

'Oh, I didn't train in Paris, I've just been to Paris,' Libby had said. 'I'm more of an actress than a dancer. I could muddle through a ballet class but ... '

Beryl had blinked china-blue eyes and flapped her hands feebly. 'I'm afraid the salary is somewhat lacking – you're not certificated – but I can scrape together seven pounds a week during term time. Shall we say a term's trial? Do you think that might suit?'

It suited very well though Libby was given a wide berth and a cold shoulder in the staffroom. She suspected that it was

73

because the other teachers, all women, were university graduates and could sense she was a fraud. Or they disapproved of her outfits because Libby had taken to wearing Freddy's old trousers and jumpers because it was easier to teach dance, drama and movement when one could actually move about.

Besides, the first day that she'd tripped downstairs wearing Freddy's grey flannel trousers and his old school pullover, Millicent had almost choked on her bran flakes, which had been immensely satisfying.

Now, Libby crossed her legs, because her feet were too warm after so long resting on the radiator, and turned her attention to Freddy's letter. Simply the act of sliding the sheets of paper out of the envelope made her heart thump uncomfortably. There had once been a time when a letter from Freddy had been a joy, a treasure, a sign that he was thinking about her.

Freddy's perfect grammar-school script swam in front of Libby's eyes. She blinked, shook her head to clear the fug and began to read.

> *Hotel Splendide*
> *Plaza Santa Ana*
> *Madrid*

Libby, oh Libby, my dearest Libby

So many times I've started to write to you then given up. Put my pen down, paper torn in half because my words are so inadequate.

I imagine that you hate me so very much, but it can't come close to how much I hate myself.

But what I did, why I left, was an act of love, maybe the only loving thing I've ever done for you, because you really are better off without me. I never did deserve your regard, your passion, that fierce, all-consuming love of yours.

74

I was never worthy of it, never knew what I'd done to make you love me so completely, because I never treated you that well, did I, old girl? You wanted all of me and I just wanted you when it suited, then wished I could pack you away, like a toy that I'd grown tired of.

This wasn't what I meant to write. But when I think about you, the thoughts chase around and around in my head, impossible to pluck one at random and search for the truth in it.

What is true is that I did a wicked thing. Deserted you when you needed me most but that love you had for me, it nearly killed you, Libby. No good can come of a love like that.

When I try to think of you, I don't see you any more; your beautiful face, the smile you said was only for me, the curve of your breasts, the sweet promise of your thighs – all gone. Now I see you pale-faced and corpse-like. And the blood. So much blood, pools of it at my feet as I hurried you to hospital, screaming at the cab driver to go faster while you lay on the seat, your head in my lap. I knew the child was no more and I thought I'd lost you too and in that moment I loved you as completely as you'd ever wanted.

And it was also in that moment when love and loss battled for my soul that I saw our differences with a clarity that cut through everything else. You need a man who's more, much more, than me. Steadfast and true, who'll love you and honour you and give you the life you crave. That happy life centred around hearth and home that you had before the war, before your father died, before your mother and your sister were taken by that cruel plague.

I am not an honourable man, Libby, but leaving you is the only honourable thing I've ever done.

Are you happy now, Libby? Or happier, at least? Are you well? I hope you are.

I also hope that living with Ma isn't too much of an ordeal. I'm in Spain (long story, involves a couple of Americans and a bullfighter) and filing pieces quite regularly for the Daily Mirror *and* Daily Herald. *How are you for funds? If you speak to a Mr Gough at the* Mirror *he will send you a money order for however much you need.*

I don't know how long I'll be here, now the elections are over. The political situation is still quite volatile, like a tinderbox, everyone waiting to see who'll light the first match.

If you don't mind, if you can even bear to say my name much less think it, could you ask Ma to send me a few items?

Typewriter ribbons – three (you know the ones I use)

A packet of tea

Two shirts – not white

A good English–Spanish dictionary

Notebooks – the small black ones from Woolworths will do.

There's so much more I want to say, have to say, but it can wait until I get back.

Yours,

Freddy

Libby was crying, tears streaming down her face, because she'd been trying so hard not to think about Freddy. Not even letting herself hate him because that would mean he was still centre-stage when she'd sent him to the wings.

And God knows, she'd tried her very hardest not to think about the baby. In the same way that she always averted her gaze from the still-vivid pink scar across her belly. But it was utter madness to imagine what might have been if the baby hadn't been swept out of her on a sea of blood but brought safely into the world and placed in her arms.

The baby would have been someone to love without rhyme or reason and he would have loved her back in the same way. And now thoughts of the baby rushed at her, reached out to grab her, so that the loss of him was again as raw and as painful as it had been on that day she'd woken up in a bed in a hospital in Paris. Then a couple of weeks later, still in the same hospital, Libby had woken up to find that Freddy was gone too.

Libby crumpled the letter in her fist. How she wanted to howl. Wanted to lie down on the floor and beat at it with her hands, but all she could do was cry quietly for what had been stolen from her.

There were no bells to signal the end of break – apparently the sound of a ringing bell would turn the girls into mindless automatons unable to think for themselves – so suddenly the room was full of shrieking seven-year-olds. They were still rosy-cheeked and boisterous from throwing snowballs.

Libby was glad of their intrusion, the noise and utter joyousness of them. She allowed herself one last shuddering sob and ran her thumbs under her still-streaming eyes. Then she clapped her hands to be heard over the roar of sixteen little girls.

'Goodness me! Is this my class two or have they all been replaced by a pack of savages from darkest Borneo?'

Somehow Libby made it through the rest of her lessons then returned home to be met by her mother-in-law who'd obviously spent the best part of the day preparing to have words.

'I didn't read Freddy's letter,' Millicent burst out before Libby had even removed her hat or scarf. 'I realised my mistake almost immediately but I couldn't help but notice, the words simply leapt out at me, that he'd said that living with me was an ordeal ...'

'That's not exactly what he wrote,' Libby said wearily.

'I'm sure that I've been most welcoming. Treated you like a daughter.' The older woman's chest heaved and Libby wondered, as she often did, what Millicent was made of under all

77

her layers; the stiff black fabrics she favoured, the corseting, the rigging. She was so thin Libby suspected that without all her underpinnings, she might just blow away on a cloud of her own self-righteousness. 'I even took a taxi home when I met you off the boat train, though the driver robbed me blind.'

'You did and I was very grateful, I still am.' Millicent had read Freddy's letter, all of it, several times over. Libby would bet her life on it. So why couldn't she say something about Libby's loss, about the grandchild that she could have had, offer some small word or gesture of comfort? A touch on the arm, a smile soft with sympathy instead of her usual peevish expression as if she'd recently taken a sip of curdled milk and couldn't get the taste out of her mouth. 'If the taxi was that expensive then I could reimburse you.'

Millicent considered it for just long enough to make a mockery of her tight reply. 'Of course not. We're family, but much as I love Freddy, I simply can't be haring around town buying all those things for him. He seems to forget that since his father passed, I'm on a considerably reduced income.' The curdled-milk look crossed her face again. 'I daresay if his editor is in a position to release his earnings, then we should have a discussion about the rent. You *are* paying less than my other tenants.'

'Because I'm family and yet you're still charging me only two shillings less a week than Mrs Lemmon across the road charges her PGs. And she has an indoor lavatory and is plumbed for hot water,' Libby reminded her sweetly. 'If it's any consolation, I'm going out tonight so I won't need dinner. That should save some money.'

Then she swept up the stairs, leaving Millicent Morton speechless.

10

Libby

Libby swept back down the stairs an hour later. From the hall she could hear the muted sounds of dinner coming from the dining room. The clink of cutlery, the twitter of the aunts and Millicent's carping tones: 'Such a disagreeable girl. My Freddy could have done so much better!'

Soon enough, Libby would be able to afford much nicer digs. Maybe even with Mrs Lemmon across the road and all her lovely hot water and indoor lav.

The very notion made Libby grin as she pulled on her coat but the smile was wiped off her face as she heard a heavy step on the stairs behind her. 'Going out, sweetling? Care for some company?'

'Not really, Potts,' Libby said, but she knew any protest would be in vain and as she slipped out the door, Potts was at her side. 'You're missing dinner.'

He sniffed. 'Vegetable slop and brown rice is hardly dinner. A man requires greater sustenance. Talking of which, I don't suppose you could advance me a small cash sum?'

'Absolutely couldn't,' Libby said, pulling her coat closer around her. 'You already owe me eight shillings. Besides, you can't have spent all your earnings from Sunday night. It's only Wednesday!'

'I had various debts to discharge,' Potts said and Libby caught the pungent whiff of stale alcohol, strong enough that she took a step away.

'Well, it's a pity you didn't discharge mine.' She made a shooing motion. 'I'm meeting someone in the Flask on a private matter, you can't come with me.'

'Oh, the Flask. There's sure to be a kind soul *in situ* who'll buy a weary traveller a drink,' Potts said, because he was utterly shameless. 'I'll stay in the public bar, you won't even know I'm there.'

Libby shot him an exasperated look and he rewarded her with a wet, rheumy smile. One always knew when Potts was there. He tended to make his presence felt. What a shock Libby had had when she'd arrived back from Paris to find him in residence.

It had been at least fifteen years since their paths had last crossed. The booze had bloated his slight frame and given his features a reddened, coarse look, but Libby had recognised Potts instantly. He'd always reminded her of a hard-boiled egg with his protruding pale blue eyes and the perfect oval of his head, now devoid of the last few sandy strands of hair, which used to cling forlornly to his scalp.

Potts had recognised her too, though it had taken him a while because Libby was no longer the pretty little redhead bringing up the rear of the chorus line and fighting off the attentions of lascivious directors and ageing matinée idols with a wide-eyed look of indignation and a breathy, 'I'll tell my aunt Dolly if you don't leave me alone.'

'Little Libby O'Malley?' he'd hissed in alarm the first

time he'd got her on her own. 'What on earth are you doing here?'

It was the first time Libby had smiled in weeks. 'Dear old Potts! It's Libby Morton now. I'm the daughter of the house, as it were. And what on earth are *you* doing here?'

When she'd first known him, Potts was already ruined by drink. Aunt Dolly said it was on account of the war, that he'd been different before that, though everyone had been different before the war. Back in those days Potts would stumble onstage whenever he felt like it, weave in and out of the set, step on everyone's lines, unable to remember his own. Then back at their digs, he'd stumble on, down corridors, knocking on doors, begging for a drink, for someone to keep him company and the dark hours at bay.

Then Aunt Dolly had run off with a married man who owned a haulage business in Leeds, Libby had left the company for another that was marginally better, Deidre Withers had made her change her surname and she'd barely thought of Potts again. Until there he was in Willoughby Square, claiming to be in touch with the other side. He spent his Sunday evenings very profitably in fancy houses Up West hoodwinking impressionable woman with 'messages' from beyond the grave.

'Mr Potter has access to a plane of being that we couldn't possibly understand and he's trying to make contact with my dear Arthur,' Millicent had told Libby in sepulchral tones when Libby had asked her why she'd taken Potts in. 'Though my dear Arthur is proving elusive, which is so like him.'

It was all hogwash. The dead stayed dead, however hard one might wish otherwise, and Potts was a charlatan of the worst kind. Giving those impressionable ladies hope where there was none.

Now they walked in silence along frost-dappled pavements. Libby felt nauseous at the thought of whom she was meeting.

Watkins. She hadn't phoned the number on the card, but had sent word to Mickey and asked him to arrange it, but now she wished that she hadn't listened to her conscience and had left well alone.

Watkins couldn't be as angry as he'd been on the way down to Brighton but still, turning up with Potts in tow was sure to make him cross.

'You must promise to stay in the public bar and not bother me at all,' she told Potts sharply as they turned into Flask Walk.

'If you'd just spare me a couple of shillings then we can both go our merry ways,' Potts said.

'You must still have some of your ill-gotten gains!'

'They're not ill-gotten, I do have a gift, sweetling. I see things, people who are among us but not of us any longer, I hear voices . . .'

'If you didn't drink so much you'd have a very quiet, very peaceful life,' Libby protested. 'But that said, couldn't you conjure up a visit from dear Arthur and put Millicent out of her misery?'

'I don't conjure up anything. I'm visited by messengers from the spirit realm.' Potts sounded quite aggrieved that Libby would dare to suggest otherwise. They were at the Flask now and he tried to pull open the door but his hands were shaking so badly that Libby had to do it for him. 'Besides, sweetling, if I may impart some hard-won wisdom – one should never shit where one sleeps.'

He winked as he pushed past Libby. 'You old rogue!' she chided him, but he was gone, shaking his ovoid head in protest at her words.

Libby pressed on through the crowded public bar to the saloon bar. It was cosy with the fire crackling away, lively chatter and laughter, nothing like the stultifying atmosphere of the house in Willoughby Square, and before he even raised his hand in greeting, she saw Watkins sitting by the fireplace with a ubiquitous copy of *The Times*.

He stood as Libby approached and when she reached him, he leaned forward, so for one clumsy moment Libby thought that he meant to kiss her cheek and she leaned forward too, only for him to take a step back and proffer his hand.

She shook it. 'Hello,' she said and she felt inexplicably shy, which was silly when he'd seen the absolute worst of her. Broken on a bathroom floor. It wasn't just the heat of the fire that caused her cheeks to flame and she had to force herself to meet his eyes.

He was older than she remembered. Hair greying at the temples, lines on his forehead, around his eyes. Libby wanted to tug off her gloves so she could place her fingers on the creases on either side of his mouth and smooth them away. He looked so very worn by his cares.

Watkins was looking at her too, eyes sweeping over her from top to bottom. He dipped his head. 'You're looking well. Are you feeling well?'

'I am. Much better,' Libby said and she let him guide her to the chair opposite his. He watched as she took off her hat, fluffed her hair, removed her coat and finally sat down. She had thought, in an act of foolish bravado, to turn up in Freddy's clothes, but now she was relieved that she'd changed into her navy blue as Watkins looked her over once more. His dark eyes seemed to miss nothing, from the scuffed soles of her shoes to the hair that she was still nervously fluffing.

'Good, I'm glad,' he said, after a long pause. 'Would you like a drink? Something to eat?'

'Just a whisky mac, please.'

'Please don't make me eat on my own,' he said. Libby was starving and they'd already had dinner together in the hotel dining room in Brighton, and it would be just as awkward to sit there as he ate than to eat with him. 'Shall I see if they have liver on the menu?'

'Please don't.' Libby pulled a face. 'I know it's meant to be good for me, but it tastes so livery. They do meat pies. I'd much rather have one of them.'

Libby watched as Watkins went to the bar to place their order. In profile, in his dark suit, hair neatly swept back from his face, he reminded her of Freddy again. He had the same colouring, the same slim build, but Watkins was straighter, stiffer than Freddy who always slunk into a room as if he were unsure of his welcome.

Watkins was also a little older than Freddy. Probably only five years or so, just nudging forty, she decided, but those years put a whole world between them. Freddy was the same age as Libby, thirty-two. He'd been too young to be called up. Hadn't come of age on a battlefield, in a trench, surrounded by the bodies of his comrades, his brothers, hands indelibly stained for ever more with their blood.

There was a chasm between those men and everybody else. They were hard in a way that Freddy and his friends could never be.

Watkins was deep in conversation with the barkeep, the man nodding respectfully as he listened to him speak, then Watkins turned away and Libby lowered her head so she wouldn't be caught staring.

'You really do look remarkably well,' Watkins said once more as he placed their drinks on the table and sat down. 'Even your hair is brighter.'

Libby resisted the urge to touch her hair again. 'Thank you and you . . . you're . . . you seem . . . '

'Like a man resigned to his fate,' Watkins supplied drily. 'Was I very awful in Brighton? I was, wasn't I?'

'Of course not,' Libby lied. 'I can only imagine the strain you've been under. How unpleasant it must be. No one could blame you for being a little out of sorts.'

'Very tactfully put, when I was so unkind to you.' When he was younger, Watkins must have been quite handsome. There were still traces of it in the full lips currently curved in a rueful smile, the high planes of his cheekbones, the almost delicate arch to his eyebrows.

'I'm the one who should be apologising. I shouldn't have agreed to go to Brighton when I knew that I was poorly.' He was still smiling at her. Softening her up, Libby knew that, but she may as well forge ahead while he was in such a conciliatory mood. 'Mr Watkins—'

'Hugo, please. I thought we were on first name terms by now.'

Libby pressed her hands together. 'Hugo, then. I hope Mickey made my position clear. I'm sorry that my, er, episode in Brighton scuppered your chances of getting the evidence you need.' She lowered her voice, leaned towards him. 'I live with my mother-in-law, she runs a respectable boarding house. So, going to court, the chance that it might make the papers ... it's simply out of the question, you see. And I've recently started a new teaching job so I really couldn't go away for another weekend either.'

Libby waited for the shadows, the anger to darken Hugo's features, but he simply nodded, then took a sip of whisky. 'Mickey made your position perfectly clear but it now transpires that we do have one witness from the hotel willing to testify. One of the other maids. She helped you when you were indisposed.'

Libby stared resolutely at the amber liquid in her glass and tried not to remember the faces floating above her, white and anxious, as she'd lain on the bathroom floor as weak and naked as the day she'd been born. 'Oh, really?' she managed to squeak.

'The only problem is she won't come up to London to formally identify you – she's never once left Sussex, apparently, and so I wondered, hoped, you might be amenable to meeting me a couple more times . . . No hotels,' he added as Libby stiffened in panic. 'It couldn't be simpler. All we'd do is walk in a public place; a park perhaps, trailed by a private detective.'

It was meant to be one weekend. A chance to make some quick cash, take in the sea air.

'All this trouble,' Libby said, shaking her head. 'Forgive me for speaking out of turn but shouldn't the private detective really be trailing your wife?'

It was like a switch being flipped. A door slamming shut. His beautiful smile dimmed then disappeared altogether. 'I couldn't countenance that,' he said a little forcefully. 'I couldn't do that to the mother of my children.'

There wasn't anything Libby could say to that. The physical pain was gone now but how she ached when she thought that no one would ever describe her as the mother of his children.

It was a blessed relief to see a woman bearing down on them with two heaped plates. The steak and mushroom pie tasted like cardboard, the mashed potato was ashes in her mouth but Libby doggedly chewed and swallowed so she wouldn't have to talk.

Watkins, Hugo, insisted on catching her eye and smiling, once he made an appreciative comment about the food and persevered until they weren't sitting in silence as they ate but conversing about the situation in Europe, what was happening in Germany, then Oswald Mosley and his ridiculous black-shirted buffoons.

'I met him once in a nightclub, years ago,' Libby offered. It seemed as if there wasn't a soul in London that she hadn't met once in a nightclub, years ago. 'We were introduced by the fellow I was with and Mosley looked me over as if I were a horse he were thinking of buying, obviously found me wanting for he couldn't even muster up a "hello". Anyway, I think fascists and their ilk are morally repugnant. So hateful.'

Hugo raised his eyebrows at her. 'But then you live in Hampstead, a hotbed of Bolsheviks and bohemians.'

'The parts of Hampstead I frequent tend to be populated by little old ladies. There isn't a Bolshevik in sight. Besides, no one calls them Bolsheviks any more. Aren't they just Communists these days? I'm sure they're the same thing.'

This was more Freddy's area of expertise than hers. He and his friends would sit in smoky bars arguing happily about how capitalism was finished, a decaying, corrupt system that feudalised the masses and benefited only a few. They could go on for hours, shouting over each other, but whatever Hugo's political allegiances were, he wasn't inclined to share them with Libby. 'So, you're not a Fascist or a Communist? What do you believe in, then?'

'I simply believe that people should be kind to each other, then the world would be a much nicer place.'

He raised his glass to her. 'So, you're an idealist. I always think idealism is the most dangerous of all the isms.'

Libby supposed she should think of something clever to say in return, but the girl had come to clear their plates and Hugo was ordering another whisky mac for her, whisky for himself. 'Everyone has to believe in something,' she said.

'Maybe I don't,' Hugo said. 'Not any more. Does that make me an anarchist?'

'If you are, then you're the most smartly dressed anarchist I've ever met,' Libby said and Watkins laughed and she was laughing too, could feel her cheeks pinking up from the warmth of the room and his approval.

'So, back to the matter in hand,' Hugo said abruptly, as if their camaraderie had been an illusion, a distraction. 'All I'm asking is that you walk with me. Tuck your arm in mine, gaze up at me tenderly so the detective can take a photograph?'

'A photograph?' Libby asked warily.

'So the maid can say you were the woman I was with in Brighton. Mysterious Marigold,' he said. 'No one will ever know your real identity.'

'But are you absolutely certain, hand on your heart certain, that I won't be called as a witness?' There were few things the papers loved more than a divorce case, all the salacious details laid bare for the titillation of their readers. 'You're not famous, are you? Or titled?'

'No. I sell cars, own a garage too. Nothing newsworthy about me,' Hugo said. Perhaps he sensed Libby was wavering for he reached across the table between them to take her hand. Just for a moment. 'I'm happy to come to you. We could walk on Hampstead Heath?'

'No! Not the heath.' It was hard to believe but Millicent had friends, like the vituperative, vile Virena Edmonds who was always sticking her beaky nose where it wasn't wanted. There had been the time when she and Freddy were lying in the long grass, near the Vale of Health, stealing kisses, when Virena had chanced upon them and had made it seem to Millicent that all sorts of indecent acts had occurred. 'My mother-in-law . . . it doesn't bear thinking about it. And I'm a schoolmistress. If some of the parents . . . '

'So, it's not a no then?' Hugo looked around the bar as if he expected to see a map of the area pinned to a wall. 'Regent's Park?'

'Highgate Woods,' Libby said, because it was easier than saying no, however much she wanted to. She suspected Hugo would persist and rather than be worn down, she might just as well agree and get it over with. Like having a tooth pulled. She could easily walk to Highgate from Hampstead and Highgate was positively rural, far enough that she was unlikely to see anyone who could report back. 'It's not on the Tube, I'm afraid, but you could get the bus from—'

'It's not a problem. Highgate Woods it is, and of course, I'd pay you. Five pounds a walk, does that sound fair?'

Libby's first instinct was to refuse, to bristle at the suggestion, but she tamped it down. Five pounds for taking a walk? Some people had more money than sense.

They talked some more, about days and times, until Libby heard the crash of a glass, a muttered apology, and looked up to see Potts weaving unsteadily through the tables towards them.

'Sweetling,' he said as soon as he was in slurring distance. 'I beseech you for one English shilling. Surely you can spare that?'

Libby finished the rest of her whisky mac in one quick, choking gulp. Hugo was staring with a horrified fascination at Potts who, since Libby had last seen him, had managed to spill beer down his shirt and acquire a woman's hat, red with a veil and a feather, perched on top of his bald head at a precarious angle.

She could stay, brazen it out, even introduce them, heaven forfend, but it was easier to gather up her belongings, then Potts who was swaying slowly on the spot where he stood, and make her excuses. 'I'll see you next week,' she said to Hugo who didn't bother to hide either his amusement or his distaste.

11

Zoe

It was as cold inside as it was outside because the builders left the doors open all day so they could mix cement in the front garden and saw wood in the back.

Zoe didn't think she'd ever been so cold as she'd been over the last few days. Ever since Win had gently suggested that perhaps she shouldn't go to Cath's *every* day. 'I know Cath says you're welcome but you don't want to take advantage of her when she's so stressed out about Clive,' he'd said reasonably the week before.

So, Zoe was giving Cath some space. Which was why it was ten on a Wednesday morning and Zoe was unwashed (the builders had turned the water off as they were so often wont to do) and uninspired (her fingers were too frozen to wield pencil or pen) and confined to the back bedroom as Gavin insisted it wasn't safe for her to freely roam the house she jointly owned at vast personal expense.

Instead, she was cross-legged on the floor, Libby's suitcase open in front of her. Maybe it was one of the reasons she'd been going to Cath's every day – when she was home alone, all she could think about was the suitcase. This morning, she'd succumbed to its siren song, after Flavia from next door had very kindly volunteered their Wi-Fi password until Win and Zoe got their electrics properly sorted out.

Zoe had Libby's diary open on her lap while she wrote down names, dates, addresses and Googled them all. She was only interested in the facts, no more reading any entries or letters that would only upset her; Zoe simply wanted to find out who Libby was and what had happened to her. Why a suitcase full of her possessions had ended up in a cupboard of a house in Highgate that had been deserted since the day it was built.

As Zoe jotted down what she knew so far, her eyes drifted over Libby's handwriting, careless and crooked, words crossed out and underlined, as if Libby had very little control over the breathless rush of words that crawled across the pages of her diary.

Libby AKA Elizabeth Edwards AKA Libby Morton/Elizabeth Morton

Actress – Withers & Withers theatrical agency, Greek Street

Married to Freddy – the same Frederick Morton whose byline keeps appearing in the newspaper clippings

Had been in Paris, the year before (1935)

Freddy left her and she came back to London

Business card for Hugo Watkins – garage in Mayfair

Letter of appointment from Frognal School for Girls for position of dance, drama and movement – £7 a week (how much is that in proper money, check?)

There was one fact that Zoe had omitted, for the same reason that she couldn't casually mention it to Win one evening as they sat side by side in deckchairs, Win poring over his renovation spreadsheets, Zoe leafing through a stack of interior design magazines. 'So, I've been poking around in the suitcase we found that first night.'

Win, understandably, would want to know why but Zoe wouldn't ever be able to tell him the truth. That no matter how engrossing Libby's diary might be, Zoe's fascination with the other woman came from the one pertinent detail she'd left off the list in her own notebook.

Libby had lost a baby too. But it was so much easier to think of Libby's loss than her own, which was still too painful to negotiate, still impossible to voice. When Win was staring at his laptop screen at all those columns of figures and muttering under his breath, Zoe wondered if he thought about the baby, their baby, at all. He certainly never talked about it.

Of course neither did Zoe, but the baby was always there, tugging away at the corners of her consciousness. The stone in her shoe. The bank statement she was afraid to open. The keys she couldn't find.

Zoe turned back to her notebook, her list. Took a deep breath and added one more sentence.

Libby lost her baby in Paris.

It didn't make Zoe feel even the littlest bit better or braver as she continued to work through the February pages of the diary, searching for any information that might be useful. There wasn't much, just Libby railing against someone called Millicent, most likely her landlady. A couple of scattered attempts at a lesson plan for a ballet class and then Zoe got to halfway through March, so she and Libby were living the same day eighty years apart and there was a letter tucked between the pages that marked the fifteenth and the sixteenth.

Zoe's eyes drifted down and they came to rest on that word. It used to be such a benign, innocuous word. An endearment. Now it was the saddest word in the English language. Baby.

March 15th

The baby would have been born by now, if he hadn't been lost. I will mark today as his birthday this year and for all the years to come. How easy but so hard it is to love someone who was never truly here.

Zoe hadn't thought there was space for more pain. Except now she was carrying Libby's load too. Mourning Libby's someone as well as her own.

She wasn't here for the pain, Zoe reminded herself, but to find out more about Libby. Lay her ghost to rest, as it were, with facts. Not emotions and feelings and an ache that never went away.

She turned her attention back to the letter, which, serendipitously, was still in its envelope. An envelope addressed to a Mrs Elizabeth Morton, 17 Willoughby Square, Hampstead, London, NW3, England. But when Zoe carefully eased the thin sheets out, as thin as tracing paper, Mrs Elizabeth Morton became *Libby, oh Libby, my dearest Libby.*

Something goose-stepped along Zoe's spine as she bent over the letter, even as she told herself not to read on.

There was another voice in her head. Louder, more insistent, impossible to deny.

Now I see you pale-faced and corpse-like. And the blood. So much blood, pools of it at my feet as I hurried you to hospital, screaming at the cab driver to go faster while you lay on the seat, your head in my lap. I knew the child was no more and I thought I'd lost you too and in that moment I loved you as completely as you'd ever wanted.

Blood. So much blood. Zoe could hardly remember any of that night but now she remembered staring up at the bathroom ceiling. At the one halogen spot that always blew as soon as they put a fresh bulb in. Lying on the bathroom floor, her head in Win's lap. His voice drowned out by the frantic knocking at the door.

Zoe jerked away from the memory. 'What the hell?'

The image was gone. There really was someone knocking at the bedroom door.

'What, Gav? What now?' Zoe called out and the door opened and Zoe steeled herself to appear interested in the latest crisis, but it was Cath bursting into the room, curls bouncing, bringing in a rush of cold, fresh air.

'Gav let me in. So, hello, are you mad at me?' she asked Zoe. Cath was a huge fan of getting right to the point, even though in this instance Zoe had no idea where the point was.

'No! Of course not! Why would I be?'

Cath threw up red-gloved hands. 'Everyone else is. We had an intervention last night via Skype to tell Dad he could either have a stairlift installed, maybe even a walk-in bath, or have carers every morning and every evening.'

Poor Clive. Poor Cath. Zoe pulled a sympathetic face as she put Freddy's letter back in its envelope. 'How did that go down?'

'Like the fucking *Titanic*,' Cath said. She watched Zoe put everything back in the suitcase then heft it into the cupboard. 'You look cold and miserable, Zo. Why haven't you been round mine where you won't be cold and I can work on your misery with hugs and good advice?'

'I think that my misery might be around for a while,' Zoe said because there was no point in deflecting. Cath always called her on it when Zoe insisted that she was fine, absolutely fine. 'And Win said that I shouldn't take advantage of your good nature and—'

'I'm not that good-natured!' Cath protested. 'And anyway, when do you ever listen to what Win says?'

'All the time. Lots of the time. Well, some of the time,' Zoe amended. Cath smiled and Zoe smiled back. 'Now that you are here, I can just about offer you a cup of tea and you can admire our new roof.'

'Such a tempting offer,' Cath said with zero enthusiasm. 'Would you mind if we went for a walk instead? I really need to clear my head.'

Zoe didn't mind. Her own head, her thoughts were so muddied, a bracing walk to Hampstead Heath was exactly what was needed.

'Talk to me,' Cath said, as they set off up Southwood Lane. 'About something that isn't family and elderly parents, or houses or sadness.'

Zoe was silent for quite some time. She had to have some conversational gambits that weren't to do with the bloody house or the sadness that she wore like a favourite cardigan most days.

'I sent off the story about Reggie the mouse to Caroline, my agent, and it's so crap that I'm hoping I don't get a publishing deal because I'm sick of Reggie and his ninety-nine rural problems. Sorry, didn't mean to be such a Debbie Downer.'

Cath shot Zoe an exasperated look but the freshness of the wind, some might even call it gale force, had blown away the worst of their collective worries. For now. 'You're not allowed to talk about work either, because my novel was due at the end of December and it's now almost halfway through March.'

'All right. No shop talk. What else is there? I could bitch about Win and how he's worked late so many nights that he's either going to make partner soon or he's having an affair ... It shouldn't be this hard to think of positive things to talk about ...'

'What were you doing with all the old junk in that suitcase when I came in?' Cath asked. 'I thought most of your things were in storage.'

'They are,' Zoe said. She wasn't sure if she wanted to share Libby with anyone else. Libby felt like a secret. Something, someone, who was hers alone. But perhaps Libby and the suitcase wouldn't have such a hold over Zoe if she shared the secret with Cath, the way she shared most other things. 'Would you like me to tell you about Libby Morton and her mysterious suitcase?'

'OK, now that has me interested.' Cath sketched a courtly bow. 'You may proceed.'

So, Zoe told Cath about her search for Libby, who had proved to be very ungoogleable that morning, even with Zoe's list of facts and Flavia-from-next-door's Wi-Fi.

There were lots of Elizabeth Edwards in the world, but none of them had been employed as dance teacher or actress in the 1930s, or even the 1920s. Libby hadn't managed to land a role in any film listed on the IMDB. There were also a lot of Elizabeth Mortons in the world but none of them was Libby.

'It's a mystery. A sad little mystery,' Zoe summed up as she and Cath left the heath, because they'd 'done' the entire heath in the time it had taken Zoe to bring Cath up to speed. 'I'd hate to think that eighty years from now, some of the things that meant the most to me, like the sketches I made for Win when I first knew him, or my wedding dress, were discarded as if they were worthless, and stuffed away in an empty house.'

'No wonder you looked sad when I came in,' Cath said. She caught Zoe's gaze, held it. 'The baby clothes. Just hearing about them makes me hurt.'

'I know.' Zoe breathed slowly round the pain until it faded into the background, then forced a smile for Cath who had her hand on Zoe's arm, a concerned look on her face. 'So, back to Libby. I made a note of all the dates and addresses that might provide some clues but I don't really know what else to do.'

'Well, we could start by having a look at where she used to live in Hampstead,' Cath suggested with her phone held out in front of her. 'Just for curiosity's sake.' With the aid of Google Maps they navigated along the pretty little streets and alleys between the heath and Hampstead High Street until they came to Willoughby Square.

The square had been through an extensive and expensive period of modernisation, renovation, gentrification. All the houses rendered the same shade of pale cream. The front gardens neatly tended, door knockers and letter boxes gleaming from the loving attention of cleaners 'who work God knows how many hours a week and can barely make their rent while their employers spend millions of pounds digging out three-storey basement extensions for cigar rooms and home spas that they don't even need,' Cath commented scathingly.

Zoe nudged her in the ribs. 'Calm down, Karl Marx.' She gestured at the house nearest. 'Which way do the numbers run?'

Number 17 was obscured behind a big double gate painted an attractive shade of grey that Zoe thought would look quite nice on their own garden gate. There was an intercom but Zoe could hardly press the buzzer and ask if there were any descendants of an Elizabeth Morton née Edwards living there. Instead she stood on the other side of the square, neck craned so she could get a good look at the house.

'I thought this was going to be more exciting,' Cath remarked.

'It is a little bit disappointing, isn't it? I don't know what else I was expecting,' Zoe said, though a tiny, very irrational part of her had expected to be transported back to 1936 and that Libby would emerge from the house, see Zoe standing there and hurry over with a wide, welcoming smile. Her reverie was interrupted by the sound of her stomach letting out an almighty rumble. She checked the time on her phone. 'It's nearly one o'clock. No wonder I'm hungry. I only had a couple of digestives for breakfast because Gav wouldn't let me into the kitchen.'

Cath draped an arm round Zoe's shoulders. 'Let's be really wicked and have a long, boozy lunch in the Flask. Didn't you say that your Libby had met someone in the Flask?'

'The diary just had the time and the place,' Zoe clarified. 'So I don't know who she was meeting.'

'It still counts as research.' Cath was already pulling an entirely willing Zoe along the street. 'Do you think they had Pinot Grigio back in nineteen thirty-six?'

12

Libby

Libby had just reached the top of Muswell Hill Road when Hugo drove up. He pulled over and she waited for him to park and get out of his sleek black car.

Libby had anticipated his shocked look when he caught sight of what she was wearing; Freddy's grey flannel trousers and shabby tweed coat, a pair of sturdy lace-ups and her green felt cloche, which had seen much better days. She had put on lipstick, a vibrant red, but she still didn't look like the sort of woman who stole other women's husbands, which she was rather glad about.

Still, Hugo said nothing apart from a muttered hello and an aside about the weather, which was cold and as wet as one would expect from an afternoon in early April. Libby had worried that the woods would be muddy, but once they slipped through the gate, she was relieved to find that there were proper paths, the trees held at bay but a lovely earthy smell to the air. They started to walk and though Hugo had said that evening in the Flask that Libby would need to tuck her arm in his, she couldn't bring herself to do it. She rather fancied that if she did, Hugo's arm would snap in two. He was so *tense*.

They walked on, turning left to pass a drinking fountain where two little girls in matching navy blue coats were more concerned with splashing each other, much to the dismay of the woman they were with. Too young to be their mother, possibly their nanny or governess, for she took hold of an arm apiece and said crossly, 'I'll tell Cook that you're not to have any pudding if you insist on behaving like street urchins.'

Libby smiled and expected Hugo to smile too but he stared ahead as if he were willing himself somewhere far, far away.

'You said you had children, didn't you?'

'Yes.' The word was dragged out of him.

He really would be so much more attractive if he weren't so pompous, Libby thought, noting again his exquisitely honed profile, the greying hair at his temples and sideburns – though that never mattered much if you were a man. If you were a woman though, it was the end of the world.

'We can walk around this wood in silence if you'd prefer, but we're hardly likely to be having a torrid affair if we can't even have a conversation,' Libby gently scolded. 'You were much more talkative in the Flask.' Inspiration struck. 'Would you like to find a pub? I think there's one by the little railway station.'

Hugo shook his head. 'No pub. Two children. The girl's seventeen. She's in Switzerland being finished at considerable expense and the boy's nineteen. He's up at Oxford, reading History.'

The girl. The boy. If Libby had the baby, he'd be a month old by now, and she would call him by his name, call him precious and sweet. 'Do you love them, your children?'

'Of course I do!' Hugo came to a halt and Libby had

wanted him less stuffy, more animated but she didn't care for the flash of anger that sharpened his features. 'What a ridiculous question.'

Libby stood her ground. 'If you love them, then you should call them by their names.'

He gave her the oddest look, as if she had surprised him. As if he were surprised by his surprise. 'Robin and Susan,' he said eventually. 'Robin is a good sort, fearless, funny, knocks around with quite a fast crowd at Oxford.' Hugo frowned as if fast crowds weren't something he approved of. 'Spends far too much time at Sywell Aerodrome when he should be studying. But he's grown up around cars, always been fascinated by engines. When he was little, he used to beg to come to the garage and would get in everyone's way, pester us with questions until we put him to work. He's never been afraid to get stuck in.'

Hugo relaxed as he talked and Libby decided that it would be all right if she tucked her arm into his. He looked down to where they were joined, frowned again but kept on walking. 'And Susan?'

'Susan. Well, she's a regular chatterbox. Can talk and talk about everything from Clark Gable to the Romantic poets. She thinks Byron is absolutely splendid and wishes he were alive today. Plays the ocarina ... very badly.' He grimaced as if the memory of Susan's ocarina-playing haunted him. 'I didn't want to pack her off to finishing school but Pam – her mother – insisted. I refused to send her to Germany like most of her friends so she's in Switzerland, Lausanne.'

'Because of Hitler? Is that why you don't want her to go to Germany?' Libby asked, because when they'd been in the pub and he'd teased her about Bolsheviks, it had been hard to fathom where his political allegiances might lie.

'People tell me that he's done wonders for Germany, united

101

the nation, made it a model of efficiency, and that rather worries me. We all know what happened last time the Germans got ideas above their station. Besides, I'd rather my daughter wasn't in Berlin or Munich dancing with boys whose fathers may well have killed her uncles.'

'You lost your brothers?'

Hugo nodded and Libby felt a little pang of something tender towards him. Countless people, starting with her aunt Dolly and ending with Freddy, had told Libby that it did her no good to be so soft, that she couldn't suffer for everyone, but she didn't know any other way. 'My father died at Amiens,' she said. It was so long ago now that it didn't hurt.

'So many good men lost. I know that I was one of the lucky few. I was called up in nineteen sixteen, married Pamela before I went. Everyone said we were too young,' Hugo said so quietly that Libby had to strain to catch each word. 'Still, I thought we were happy enough. Evidently not.' He said something else, but it was lost to the wind, the rustling of leaves, the quick brush of a squirrel darting through the undergrowth.

'I'm sorry,' Libby said, expecting him to repeat his words, but Hugo simply nodded as if he were accepting her condolences.

'I'll see you next week, then,' he said and Libby realised that they'd done a complete loop of the woods and were back where they started.

Maybe not exactly where they'd started. They'd forged a truce, perhaps even the start of a fragile, flimsy friendship, despite their footsteps being dogged by a thickset, ruddy-faced man in a gabardine coat who hadn't even attempted to be discreet. And when Libby leaned forward and kissed Hugo's cold cheek, she saw the man raise a small box camera and take their picture.

*

The next week, Libby knew what to expect. From Hugo's mild discomfort, which lasted for the time it took them to reach the second set of gates that led back to Muswell Hill Road, to the private detective lumbering behind them, his heavy breaths and steps puncturing the silence.

'Mickey said that you were well travelled,' Hugo said at last as Libby had been desperately trying to think of something to talk about. 'That you'd been to California and New York and were in Paris last year. I found myself in Paris at the end of the war, I didn't think much of it.'

'Really?' Libby turned to him in surprise. 'I used to love Paris.' She didn't love Paris any more. Vowed that she'd never set foot anywhere near it ever again. 'Every other person you meet is an artist or a poet and the place may be old and decaying but in such a pretty way. London isn't at all pretty, is it?'

Hugo gestured at the trees. 'Oh, parts of it have a certain charm.'

'But it's not charming,' Libby persisted. 'Though Paris would be a lot more charming if the men didn't piss in the streets.'

Libby thought that people only ever spluttered in outrage in novels but Hugo was now beyond words, only capable of huffing.

'Isn't my language *appalling*?' She laughed nervously. 'You'd never think I grew up in a good Catholic home but I went into the theatre at the age of fourteen and I'm afraid it had a detrimental effect on my vocabulary . . . and my soul.'

'How does a good Catholic girl end up in the theatre at such a tender age?' Hugo asked.

So Libby told him about her happy childhood. Loving father, kind mother, adored younger sister. How the days had a steady, safe rhythm that was torn apart by the war and as Libby was still reeling from the black-edged telegram, which meant she'd never see her father again, she'd lost her mother and Charlotte to the flu epidemic.

Her father had been an only child and on her mother's side there'd only been Dolly, her mother's flighty younger sister, who'd eventually been tracked down to a touring theatre company where she was employed as a dresser.

'They'd take a play that was doing very well in London then perform it very badly in the provinces,' Libby told Hugo brightly. He laughed as she'd intended, though at the time none of it had been funny. To leave the house she'd always lived in, only allowed to pack as much as would fit in a suitcase because Aunt Dolly said that she preferred to travel light.

She'd also have preferred to travel without her niece in tow. 'We'll just have to make the best of it,' Dolly had said frequently and unenthusiastically.

Dolly had looked enough like Libby's mother that it was comforting but also a cruel injustice. The same russet-coloured hair and green eyes, but her mother's face had been prettier, sweeter, her smile soft. Dolly always looked faintly exasperated, as if she'd walked to the shops in the pouring rain only to find them shut.

Still, Libby had made the best of it, as instructed. Her old life consisted only of home, school, church and occasional outings to the park or the cinema.

Her new life was full of adults who didn't behave in the way that Libby expected them to. They got drunk and swore a lot. In the dressing room, the women walked about in their unmentionables and talked about their love affairs. She learned that men could love other men, like most men loved their wives, and that it was entirely possible for a girl to get in the family way, even if she weren't married. Then there was the male lead who would pinch Libby's cheek and buy her cream buns but on Friday night when the cast got paid, he would become a mean, snarling drunk who would invariably black the female lead's eyes so the understudy would have to do the Saturday matinée.

Libby didn't even go to school because Dolly said that she'd never sat for her school certificate and it hadn't done her any harm. Instead the company manager, Mr Wilkes, had Libby help him with the accounts and would stick her in the prompt box of an evening, so it was an education of sorts.

It was also Mr Wilkes who'd first put Libby onstage, at Dolly's bidding because she was keen for Libby to start earning her keep.

'I could dance a little, remember my lines and Mr Wilkes said that was a lot more than most of his company could manage,' Libby told Hugo, who seemed gripped by the tale of her early days in the theatre. 'Truthfully, back then I was more decorative than talented.' She put up a hand to her hair, which still hadn't quite returned to the vibrant red it had been before she went to Paris. 'Now, I'm not even that.'

Hugo smiled at her. Libby thought that it might be the first smile of his that reached his eyes. 'Oh, I think you still are. Decorative.'

Libby violently fluttered her eyelashes, which made Hugo smile reluctantly as if he didn't want to encourage her. 'Why thank you, kind sir.'

By now they'd completed their circuit, were back at Gypsy Gate, but Hugo held out his arm. 'Shall we go round again? I'm interested to know how you went from touring the provinces to California.'

Anything was better than going back to Willoughby Square. Though that was rather unfair because walking and talking (mostly about herself) with Hugo was hardly an ordeal. As they set off again, Libby heard their chaperone give an aggrieved sigh.

'Well, if you're sure you won't be bored listening to me prattle on about my misadventures on stage and screen.'

'It's not boring at all,' Hugo said. 'It sounds far more glamorous than my formative years, which were spent at boarding school in Shropshire.'

'Hardly glamorous!' Libby scoffed. 'Not when Aunt Dolly disappeared into the Scarborough sunset with a married haulage contractor without so much as a forwarding address when I was sixteen.' Libby had come back to London, signed with Deidre and Ronald Withers, and progressed to playing bigger roles, though she played them without that spark, that indefinable something that the really good actresses had. Ten years of auditions, rehearsals, opening nights and praying for a long run.

Then she'd been cast in a wildly successful musical revue at the Savoy Theatre, which had transferred to New York. 'New York was absolutely wonderful. So full of life, a little gaudy too, I suppose, but we were put up in this frightfully grand hotel. There were radiators in every room and showers in the bathrooms,' Libby remembered with a wistful sigh. 'I swore that one day I'd live in a house with radiators in every room and a shower in the bathroom too.'

'I can tell you now that if you achieve that lofty goal, your gas bills will be quite prohibitive,' Hugo said in a teasing, but slightly pained manner, which made Libby think Hugo probably did live in a house with radiators in every room and a shower was an everyday occurrence. He didn't have the careless, shabby grace that frightfully rich people did, but he carried himself with a certain assurance that only came when you didn't have to worry about having enough coins to feed the meter. Whatever indignities may have been heaped on him by his adulterous wife he was still sure of his place in the world and Libby rather envied him for that.

It felt perfectly natural now to have her arm tucked into Hugo's and he patted her hand in a gentle prompt to continue with her story and her ill-fated trip from New York to California, after being wooed by a movie producer, who'd seen the revue she was in.

'California was so sunny and there were palm trees lining Sunset Boulevard,' she said. 'I could have stayed there for ever.'

'The palm trees lost their lustre, I take it?' Hugo enquired when Libby sighed at the memory.

'Alas, it was me who lost her lustre.'

'I'm sure that's not true,' Hugo said with another of those strangely assessing looks that he excelled at, his eyes sweeping over Libby from top to bottom and lingering in the places in between in a way that no other man had done for a long while.

Certainly no man in Hollywood had looked at Libby with such keen interest. Instead, the powers that be at the studio had ordered Libby's hairline to be shaved and her nose reshaped with thin strips of rubber hidden under thick panstick, but still, on camera, her face had been doughy and inanimate. There was a squint in her left eye, which she'd never even noticed until the cruel, unforgiving gaze of the camera homed in on it, and then there was her voice. 'I never gave my voice any thought before,' she explained to Hugo as they circled the cricket pitch, swerving to avoid the muddier parts of the path. 'No director I've worked with seemed to find it objectionable, but on tape I had the most terrible lisp and I squeaked. And the more the soundman shouted at me, the higher pitched my voice became, until in the end I couldn't speak at all. It was awful.'

Still dreaming of blue oceans and palm trees, of radiators and hot showers, Libby had sailed back to England, tail very firmly between her legs, sure that nothing good would ever happen to her again.

Deidre Withers had been particularly smug about Libby's fall from grace and had nothing for Libby other than an audition for a part in a ghastly experimental play. 'It's Expressionist,' Deidre had said, though Libby didn't know what that meant.

She had to intone a series of portentous statements while performing calisthenics and wearing a horrid brown leotard and tights, but then she'd been introduced to Freddy who'd been responsible for writing the ghastly experimental play. So as one door had slammed shut in her face, another one had opened, but she wasn't ready to tell Hugo about Freddy.

Freddy! For one whole hour while they'd been tracking through the woods, she'd hadn't thought about him at all. Which meant she hadn't thought about the baby either and as soon as she realised that, Libby felt the hot wash of guilt soak through her.

'You have had some adventures. My life seems very dull by comparison,' Hugo was saying and Libby was no longer in the draughty rehearsal room in Holborn or in that wretched, barren bed in a Parisian hospital, but back at Gypsy Gate.

'I suppose I have,' Libby said, though she couldn't imagine there were any more adventures in store for her. It felt as if she'd done everything, been everywhere, and now her fate was to become like the ladies of Willoughby Square. A decrepit, unloved paying guest in someone else's house.

'So, same time next week?'

Libby raised her eyebrows. 'I thought you said that we need only do this a couple of times?'

'Once more couldn't hurt though, could it?' Hugo glanced behind them, where the private detective was leaning heavily against a tree and looking as if he might cry if they walked around the woods one more time. 'Just to ensure our fat friend has everything he needs. If you can spare the time . . .'

'In that case, of course.' Libby could always do with another five pounds, and also it was so nice to talk to someone who wasn't an elderly PG or a small girl. The other teachers never invited Libby to join in their conversations about the strapping young men who all seemed to be called Nigel or Guy, who would pick them up after school in jaunty little cars. And Libby could hardly bear to be with her old theatre friends who were living a life that wasn't hers any more.

Libby supposed that she was lonely though she'd had this feeling of . . . not belonging for so many years now that she hardly gave it thought.

Even so, she hated being on her own.

13

Zoe

Zoe lay in bed, eyes wide open and fixed on the clock. She must have slept at some point during the night but it seemed that every time she woke up and checked the time, only another fifteen minutes or so had passed. For once, she hadn't been thinking about the thing she didn't want to think about, but of Libby. What she could do next to find her. Perhaps a trip to the newspaper library in Colindale to trawl through archive issues of the *Ham and High*, or the Public Records Office to search for censuses and certificates, though some of that information might be online. And did she really want to find Libby when Zoe couldn't bear to read any more of her diary? Freddy's confession and Libby's heartbreak over the baby was too much, too close to home, so Zoe lay there willing her head to quiet. It was nearly seven now when the alarm would go off and Win would get up, though he'd been twitching for the last half an hour so she knew he was only dozing.

Both of them had their own reasons for finding it hard to

sleep and they had little to do with the very uncomfortable airbed.

Win sighed, long and hard. 'Zo? You're awake.'

'Yeah.' Win rolled over so Zoe felt his breath ghost the tender skin at the back of her neck. 'Win, what's happened? I don't even know who we are at the moment. We're certainly not *us*.'

'It's the house. The building work. It's stressful.'

Zoe couldn't let Win get away with it any longer. 'It's not just the house though, is it? Are we ever going to talk about the baby?'

Win sucked in a sigh, then pulled away from her. 'That was months ago.'

'Not even four months. That's hardly any time at all.'

He flopped on his back. 'What is there to say?'

And when he asked that, Zoe hardly knew where to begin. 'I don't know. Don't you think it's odd that we never talk about it?'

Win sighed again. 'Look, Zo, I have to get up. I planned to have a run this morning.'

Zoe pulled a face and rolled her eyes. 'Don't go for a run. Stop shutting me out and stay and talk to me. Anyway . . .' She angled her neck so she could see the time on her phone, which was on top of a pile of books by the bed. 'You don't have time for a run. We're having a site meeting this morning. There's absolutely no way that you've forgotten about it.'

'That's why I need to go for a run,' Win said. 'I've been lying here thinking about all the issues I want to bring up and I can already feel my blood pressure starting to climb.'

'Maybe a run isn't such a bad idea then.' Zoe tried to offer up something more conciliatory. To show Win that she could be understanding, empathetic to his needs and wouldn't it be wonderful if he could be the same? 'You usually feel better afterwards.'

Win was already flinging back the covers. 'If you want to spend some time together, then you could come with me, if you liked.'

Zoe burrowed deeper into the space that Win had just vacated. It was warm, smelt like him. 'It's raining,' she pointed out, because the faint patter against the windows was all the proof she needed that, although she did want to spend time with Win more than anything, nothing good could come from going for a run. 'Also, I haven't so much as broken into a light jog for ages. Running might actually kill me.'

'It won't kill you.' Win's voice was muffled as he pulled on something black and waterproof. 'It will just feel like you're being killed.'

Maybe it was because Win had cracked a joke, was teasing her, which he hadn't done in weeks, that Zoe decided that there were worse ways to die.

It was still raining when they reached Highgate Woods. Zoe tried to think about the hot shower she'd have after her run, then she remembered that there was still no shower, just a rubber attachment that connected to the bath taps, which invariably fell off, usually when she was trying to rinse out shampoo. Until a new boiler was installed, the water was only ever lukewarm at best too.

There was a small crowd of people waiting for one of the wood-keepers to unlock the gate. Runners jogging on the spot, a frail old man with a West Highland terrier that looked even more frail than him, more dog walkers arriving as one of the keepers finally pulled up on the other side of the gate in his little buggy.

'It still counts as spending time together if we run in the same enclosed space but would you be offended if we headed off in different directions?' Zoe asked Win as they threaded their way through the bend in the now open gate.

Win didn't bother to hide his relief. He preferred to run at the mercy of an app that barked instructions at him to increase his speed and lengthen his gait and beeped to mark every half a kilometre. Win was *that* person cluttering up his friends' Facebook walls and Twitter timelines with smug pronouncements like 'Win ran 8.3 km using the Lets!Run app', though every time he did, Ed and Theo would both post in the comments, 'Dude, nobody cares!'

Now, Win sprinted nimbly away and Zoe tried not to unduly exert herself with a very slow trot. She huffed and puffed as she negotiated a really steep slope, then another one, then a really muddy bit before she came to the big green, the cricket pitch. Past the playground, the toilets and before she knew it, she was back at Gypsy Gate, where they'd entered the woods.

Win had already passed her a couple of times with a cheery wave and now that she was actually *almost* running, taking in huge gulps of clean air, pushing herself that little bit further, relishing the burn in her chest, the ache in her legs, Zoe felt like the person that she'd been before. She could even forgive her body that cruel trick it had played on her because now that she was *almost* running, she felt as if she were back in charge.

Even when Zoe thought she couldn't go on, couldn't make it up yet another slope without her lungs bursting, she had a soundtrack of eighties power ballads, show tunes and Taylor Swift to spur her on. However, it took the big guns, a Beyoncé/Destiny's Child megamix, to get Zoe through the third and final lap.

She was an Independent Woman and feeling no pain as she sprinted down a steep slope then had to suddenly veer off course as something charged at her ankles. Zoe skidded over a muddy patch and into a puddle, arms pinwheeling, barely managing to stay upright.

'What the hell?' She looked down to see what she'd tripped over. Of course, it was a dog. She'd spent her whole run dodging dogs who would appear as if from nowhere.

This was an ugly little thing. Of indeterminate breed, possibly some pug in (Zoe had a cursory look at the undercarriage) her. Rotund and white with brown splodges all over her body and a ferocious underbite, which gave the dog a quizzical expression. She was wearing a bright blue tabard emblazoned with the logo of the local dog shelter and the words 'Adopt me!', and trailing a very muddy lead.

'Hey, doggie.' Zoe crouched down and made kissing noises and the dog bounded over and immediately rested her chin on Zoe's knee. Zoe obligingly stroked behind its ears with one hand and was just about to take her phone out of her sports armband to ring the number on its tag when she heard a faint cry.

'Beyoncé! Beyoncé! Where are you, baby? Beyoncé!'

Zoe blinked to make sure that she wasn't dreaming, though if she was, it was a very sub-par dream unless Beyoncé herself was about to appear at the crest of the hill. Alas, she didn't, just a woman with three other dogs in blue tabards.

'Beyoncé, there you are!' she exclaimed. 'Sorry! I was picking up poo when she saw a squirrel and shot off.'

'It's OK,' Zoe said. She was still squatting, Beyoncé's head resting on her knee as she gazed at Zoe with big brown eyes that looked as if they'd been ringed with kohl. 'We've been getting to know each other. What breed is she, then?'

'A bit of pug and French bulldog, definitely some Staffy, and who knows what else?' The woman picked up Beyoncé's lead and Zoe fell into step with her, trainers squelching, as she explained how Beyoncé had been picked up as a stray a couple of days ago and had had puppies not long before that.

'Probably used as a breeding bitch though there must have been a problem with her last litter and her owners threw her out when they realised they couldn't make any more money out of her,' the woman, Wendy, said as Zoe looked at Beyoncé who was trotting quite contentedly alongside her.

Zoe felt a twinge of solidarity with this odd little dog.

'She seems happy enough, though,' Zoe commented.

'She's happy to be out. She gets very stressed in kennels. We're desperate to place her in a foster home,' the woman said with heavy emphasis as they skirted around the field, but Zoe refused to be drawn. Win wanted a dog but Zoe was the one at home all day who'd get stuck with walking it and picking up poo and handling tins of stinky dog food.

'Oh, I'm more of a cat person,' Zoe said and wondered how to extricate herself before she agreed to foster Beyoncé, who was looking up at her beseechingly. She also wondered where Win was. He should have passed her at least twice by now.

They turned a corner and Zoe saw him. 'Oh God, I have to go.'

She went from nought to sixty, running full pelt, because Win was sitting on a log, face screwed up in pain, one of his legs stretched out before him at an awkward angle and smeared with mud and blood. 'Are you hurt?' she panted before she even reached him. 'Of course you're hurt! What did you do? Are you all right?'

There was an older man in running gear with Win, who turned at Zoe's approach. 'He's a bit winded,' he said, as Win clutched his chest and winced and for one awful, world-tilting moment Zoe thought that he was having a heart attack, then Win took his hand away and shook his head.

'I slipped, caught my foot on a root or a rock.' He winced again. 'I'm fine. More embarrassed than anything.' Win wasn't the type of man who got a mild cold and took to his bed as if he had bronchial pneumonia. He was more of the stoic suffering in silence type.

'You don't look fine,' Zoe said. 'You look the opposite of fine.' His face was pale, grey, and Zoe forced her eyes down to his splayed-out left leg. 'You're bleeding.'

Win's knee still looked like its normal, knobbly self but there was a deep laceration which gushed blood like a small tributary merrily making its way to the sea. So much blood. Zoe turned her head and threw up a mouthful of bile, bitter and acrid.

'Are *you* all right?' It was Win's turn to ask, his voice sharp, as Zoe wiped her hand against her mouth and leaned back against the other man, who was now holding her up, because her legs didn't want to. 'Sorry,' she mumbled. 'So sorry. I don't know what came over me.'

The blood. There was still so much she couldn't remember, didn't want to remember, about that night. Passages of time gone, erased, but she remembered the blood.

Remembered the pain she'd had in her side for a week. A stitch on her right side, which had come and gone then became a constant, slightly worrying thing, which she self-diagnosed after a phone call to her mother and a quick Google search as trapped wind, maybe even indigestion. Nothing that Gaviscon and some yoga stretches couldn't sort out.

And then that night, after dinner, though Zoe could hardly eat a thing and she had a pounding headache, they went through the surveyor's report on the house in Highgate and Gavin's estimates for the work that needed to be done.

Zoe had sat there with her hand tightly pressed against her side as Win did the sums one more time, then looked up from his pad because he preferred to do maths the old-fashioned way with pen and paper. 'Zo, we really can't afford it,' he'd said with genuine regret in his voice. 'If it was just superficial work, then we could muddle through, do it bit by bit, but this is big, expensive, structural . . . God, you look awful.'

'Yeah, really don't feel that great.' Her face twisted with the effort it took to talk. 'I'm starting to think I might have appendicitis.'

Win put a cool hand on her hot, clammy forehead. 'Or you could actually go and see a doctor. Tomorrow, first thing, I'm going to ring up the surgery and get you an emergency appointment.'

'I have to send off some final artwork before lunchtime,' Zoe protested without much vigour. 'I'll go in the afternoon. I promise.'

Then Win had explained about the house. How much they'd have to increase their existing mortgage, make inroads into their savings, that estimates were never a good indication of how much things would cost in the end. Zoe couldn't concentrate. Could hardly bear to sit on the hard kitchen stool.

'Hold that thought,' she'd said and got up, started shuffling to the bathroom because even walking added another level to the pain and she couldn't remember if she'd planned to take a bath, or do some more stretches, but what she remembered next was lying on the bathroom floor, Win kneeling over her, his face as pale as the white bathroom tiles.

'Don't leave me,' he'd said. 'You hear me, Zo? Don't you dare leave me.'

'Where would I go?' She was being carried away on a sea of pain, of blood, could see splashes of it on the floor and Win had put a towel between her legs to try and staunch the flow and covered her with one of the big bathsheets, a shroud stained with a trail of bright red. He'd used their nicest towels; the ones they'd got as wedding presents.

Then Zoe was gone, to a place beyond the pain. The rest was half-glimpsed: the paramedics in green looming over her in the ambulance, the lights dancing over her head as she was wheeled along a hospital corridor.

Waking up, Win on one side of her, leaning over so his head rested on the bed, Jackie on the other side clutching Zoe's hand. To be told her fallopian tube had ruptured as a result of an ectopic pregnancy. A collection of cells, which could have evolved into a brand new person, had taken root in the wrong place. That she'd lost something precious without ever knowing that it was there.

They'd cleaned her up but when Zoe had lifted a heavy hand to her face, there was dried blood caked under her fingernails. It was hardly surprising when there'd been so much of it. So much blood.

Zoe rocked back in her soggy trainers. Forced her attention back to Win and the blood that ran down his leg. 'Can you walk?'

The man, he said his name was Brian, helped them make their slow, torturous way home. Win took tiny mincing steps, his features contorted in pain.

Zoe hadn't ever thought she'd be pleased to see the house, but she was relieved to turn the corner and there it was with its new roof and sacks of rubble in the drive.

Brian stayed with them until they reached their front door. 'You'll be running again in no time,' he said, then looked doubtfully at Win's knee. 'You really should get that X-rayed.'

'You really should,' Zoe said, as she helped Win to manoeuvre through the door. 'We'll cancel the site meeting and I'll drive you to the Whittington.'

Then she shuddered and thought she might throw up again. When Win had called for an ambulance that night, they'd taken Zoe to the Whittington Hospital as the emergency resus unit at the Royal Free, which was nearer, was backed up. 'I am never setting foot in the Whittington again,' Win gritted, echoing Zoe's own thoughts. 'And we are not cancelling the meeting. It's taken weeks to get everyone to agree to be in the same place at the same time.'

14

Zoe

Half an hour later, they were sitting in the lounge, Win's leg resting on an upturned bucket, a bag of frozen peas, borrowed from Flavia next door as their freezer was still in storage, clamped to his knee, as Gavin, Stavros their architect, the plumber and the electrician loomed over them.

The news was not good. Zoe should have been used to that by now. The work was going to take much longer and cost much more than they'd originally thought. Apparently, it wasn't until you started knocking down walls and prising up floorboards that a whole host of other problems showed up; a leaking pipe underneath the bath, dry rot, cracks in the back wall.

Sitting next to him, Zoe could tell that Win had tensed every muscle to try and ward off the pain. You should never ignore pain. Pain was an alarm signal. The body's way of telling you that something was seriously wrong. The last time Zoe had been in pain, she'd ignored it and nearly died.

'Win, you really should go to hospital. Have an X-ray at the very least.'

Win frowned. 'Shhh.'

Zoe didn't appreciate his peremptory tone, not in the slightest, but she shh-ed so they could move on to discussing why the original radiators weren't fit for purpose.

'It's the valves, you see. Not compatible, they'll never pass a safety check . . . ' The plumber was rambling on. Zoe mentally added another five thousand to their running tally though she didn't have an earthly clue how much radiators cost.

Win clenched his fists and made a strange sound like he was about to come to the boil. Zoe knew that sound though she'd only ever heard it the once before when Ed and Win had had an argument over whether to invite their father to the christening of Ed and Juliet's firstborn.

It had been the only time in thirteen years that Zoe had seen Win lose his temper and now she counted to ten but only got as far as six when Win kicked the bucket out from under his leg, then howled in pain before he howled in rage.

'For fuck's sake! We've been here two months and the place looks worse than when we moved in! Why don't we have a boiler yet? We need hot water! We need a shower! We've spent thousands of pounds already and I still can't have a hot shower!' He was shouting. Win never shouted, yet now he was. He swung round to glare at Gavin. 'You should have said that the radiators were absolute lemons!'

'It's not really Gav's fault, Win,' Zoe said, even though Gavin was entirely unruffled, when actually Zoe wanted him to be completely ruffled and appreciating the hideous, expensive enormity of the situation.

'I did try several times, but what do I know? Only been in the building game for forty years.' Gavin sniffed in a martyred fashion. 'But you obviously know better than I do, Win, as you're such an expert in how I should do my job.'

Win hissed in fury or agony, Zoe couldn't tell which, and

Stavros stepped forward. 'I know this is stressful and we haven't moved as fast as we'd have liked but that's the problem with these old houses,' he said calmly. 'Win, please sit down. You look like you're about to drop.'

'I'm fine,' Win insisted, staying rooted onto the spot in the middle of their crummy living room in the crummy house that was going to bankrupt them if it didn't kill them first. 'Actually, I'm not fine. There was a plan. We talked about it! We agreed to the plan and then you just ignored it and did what you wanted without any thought for the consequences. But if you had stuck to my plan, stayed on schedule, then we wouldn't be in this mess. Christ! I don't know why I even bother!'

'Just listen to yourself, Win! Life doesn't work to your plans and schedules. Sometimes stuff, awful stuff, just happens.' Zoe was crying when seconds before she'd been dry-eyed. Win's words had cut into her like the surgeon's blade. He'd had a plan. Zoe hadn't followed the plan and it had made an absolute mess of her, of them. And maybe that was why tears streamed down her face. She choked as she tried to get her words out. 'I know that everything's ruined. I know that!' she sobbed. 'And there's no way to make it better.'

She wasn't talking about the house but Gavin put his arm around Zoe and told her not to worry and that he'd once had a fifty-something investment banker lie on the floor and bawl his eyes out over the wrong kind of porcelain tiles. Only Win didn't react but sat back down in the deckchair (because their lovely comfortable chairs were still in storage), frozen peas on his knee, eyes fixed at some point in the middle distance.

He was stuck in the same pose, hours later, as they sat in A&E at the Whittington, waiting for his name to be called, while Zoe cried. She just couldn't stop crying.

'We can't go on like this,' Zoe managed to say at last, when the sobs had died to a dull roar and she was trying to mop up the stem of tears with a ratty tissue. 'We have to talk about what happened. We have to get through this, otherwise we were never as good, never as strong, as we thought we were. This has to change.'

Win turned to her, his face as bleak as the sky in winter. 'Then make it change, Zo. Think of something, because I am all out of ideas.'

15

Zoe

They were eventually seen by an exhausted junior doctor who diagnosed Win with a significant tear in his meniscal cartilage and put him on a waiting list to see an NHS physiotherapist while Zoe sobbed throughout the entire process. Then the junior doctor, exhausted though he was, sent someone down from the psych team to assess Zoe, who loaded her up with information sheets on miscarriage, ectopic pregnancy, post-natal depression, regular depression, then put her on a waiting list to see a post-partum grief counsellor.

There was roughly a six month wait for either list, but Win couldn't spend the next six months experiencing a hundred agonies as he hobbled about on a knee that made a strange clicking sound. So, twice a week, at forty-five pounds a session, Win went to a physiotherapist.

Zoe went with him the one time to be wifely and support-ive. As she'd watched Henry, the physio, manipulate Win's knee joint and do other things that made Win yelp, she wished it were that easy to fix her. Just as Win started every morning by looping his dressing gown cord round his foot and stretching, then strapped on an ice pack every evening, if only there were a series of exercises Zoe could do to heal the ragged hole in her heart and stem the flow of never-ending tears.

She cried as soon as Win left for work in the morning. She cried when she'd gone to see Cath to be especially encouraging and supportive for Clive's inaugural trip on the newly installed stairlift. She even cried while Skyping her parents and hated herself for it because her mother immediately wanted to fly home. Win was obviously thinking along similar lines because after catching Zoe crying on three separate occasions, he asked her tiredly, 'Does it help? Crying all the time? I could probably try and extend one of our loans if you want to fly out and see your parents.'

Of course, that made Zoe cry harder because there was nothing she wanted more but they couldn't afford it and she couldn't leave Win on his own when he was in such dreadful pain and probably wanted to cry all the time too.

'I'm fine,' she hiccupped. 'It's nothing. Probably just my hormones having one final surge before they settle down.'

It wasn't even as if the crying was cathartic and cleansing. It was draining and in between crying jags, Zoe felt dirty and sweaty, like she'd slept in all her clothes.

But it was as she was walking through Highgate Woods, her fingers closed around the familiar shape of the baby's button in her pocket and the predictable tears about to rally, that Zoe realised that she could just *not*. She could summon up the strength not to cry, if she really wanted to. If she wanted to move on from this awful sadness, then it was up to her to shuffle in a new direction.

After all, it was spring. Everything in the woods was fresh and green. There were buds and blossom and baby squirrels;

the cycle was starting anew and what better time for Zoe to get over herself?

She had read the information sheets the hospital had given her. One in three pregnancies ended in miscarriage, one in eighty pregnancies was ectopic. Which meant that Zoe wasn't alone. She wasn't a special, suffering snowflake. There were all these women walking about, writing shopping lists, wishing their friends happy birthday on Facebook, buying their lunch from Pret, managing to get on with their lives while feeling wretched and incomplete.

And there was Libby, who'd been much further along than Zoe when she'd lost her baby. A real baby. Yet Libby had started a new job. Was going to the pub. Keeping appointments in town. Libby was getting on with the business of life, so Zoe at least had to try. To stop crying. To stop wallowing. Answering her agent's summons so they could talk about Reggie the mouse was a start. One small step in rejoining the world.

When Zoe got off the Tube at Leicester Square, buffeted by the crowds, she was dry-eyed, no threat of tears; she even smiled a little because it felt a bit as if she were coming home. When she'd first moved to London to study at Central St Martins, Soho had been her campus, her neighbourhood, her stomping ground.

She was a little early for her appointment and as she walked along the familiar streets, Libby was on Zoe's mind. Zoe passed Maison Bertaux on Greek Street, then came to a halt outside the building where the Withers & Withers talent agency had been, which was now home to a juice bar and serviced office suites on the upper floors.

Would Libby still recognise the area? The theatres along Shaftesbury Avenue? The tiny Soho cut-throughs like St Anne's Court off Wardour Street? Had the legendary Italian deli on Brewer Street, Lina Stores, been there in Libby's day?

So much had changed even in the fourteen years that Zoe had lived in London. High rents had closed many of her old haunts and huge swathes of Soho nearer to Oxford Street had been demolished to make way for the Crossrail.

'By the time they're finished, there'll be nothing left of London for people to visit,' Zoe said to Caroline West as they sat down to coffee at the Soho Hotel in a small mews off Dean Street.

'When I first started work in a tiny literary agency in the eighties, Soho was still full of clip joints and sex shops,' Caroline said. She was in her fifties and was always stylishly pulled together in interestingly draped dresses and men's brogues and had let her hair go grey though she had a streak of pure white that sprang up from her widow's peak. She'd been Zoe's agent for three years, ever since Zoe's old agent had retired, and had a fearsome reputation for not suffering fools gladly, which always made Zoe feel rather foolish in her presence.

They talked about the children's book market. Who was doing well, what was selling, and all the time, Zoe knew this friendly chat was leading towards a reckoning. After ordering a second pot of coffee, Caroline pulled a clear folder out of her slouchy leather bag. Zoe instantly recognised the drawing of a mouse in a baseball cap and big boxy trainers. She braced herself.

'I can't sell this,' Caroline said, putting the folder down on the table. 'I'm a big fan of your work. It usually has real heart to it but I don't feel convinced by the travails of Reggie and I'm not sure you do either.'

It was Zoe's cue to launch into a passionate defence of Reggie but ... but ... but ... 'I don't love Reggie,' she admitted. 'I wanted to have a solid book proposal for you because I'm out of contract but yeah …' She trailed off, hoped that Caroline would be brutal but brief when she told Zoe to find another agent. 'I've been feeling quite uninspired. It's never happened before,' she added a little defensively.

'I see.' Caroline gave Zoe a look, which seemed to miss nothing. That the only effort she'd made for the meeting was to apply dry shampoo to her lank hair and to hunt through bags and boxes until she'd found her one pair of jeans that didn't have holes in them. 'When I have authors who are blocked, I like to know if there's anything happening in their lives that they're particularly fired up about. I had a writer who was coaching his son's football team and it sparked a wonderful middle-grade series. What's exciting you lately?'

Nothing! Nothing excites me, Zoe thought, but she couldn't say that so she sat in silence trying to rack her brains for the seed of an idea, a tiny nugget of inspiration that didn't involve endless drawings of a little boy. 'We've just moved,' she said at last. 'This house that's been untouched since it was built in 1936. Huge renovation project …' And this was her cue to talk about the suitcase, about Libby, because when Zoe was thinking about Libby it was the only time she wasn't thinking about what had happened, but then sooner or later she thought about those yellowed baby clothes in the suitcase and her hand was in her pocket, fingers curled around the button and she was back to … 'I lost a baby before we moved. It's why we moved. I didn't even know I was pregnant …'

It was the first time she'd had to explain it to someone who wasn't family or a member of the medical profession. And she was crying. Again. Caroline tactfully moved her chair so Zoe was obscured from the other customers. Then she took Zoe's hand and didn't say anything.

It felt like hours before Zoe was able to stop. Caroline nodded as Zoe muttered something about the bathroom.

Zoe splashed her reddened face with cold water and, for once, now that she'd cried, she did feel calm. Resigned, even, as she walked back into the bar and sat down opposite Caroline.

'I'm sorry. I'm not usually a crier,' Zoe lied weakly, but Caroline shook her head.

'Nothing to be sorry for,' she said firmly. 'You've been through a horrible time; I'm still not going to send Reggie out on submission though.'

It shocked a phlegmy giggle from Zoe. Made her brave enough to say, 'Do I need to find another agent?'

'Don't be silly,' Caroline said. Then the waiter, who'd tactfully hung back while Zoe had been in meltdown, arrived with their coffee and Caroline advised Zoe to take some time out. Not to try to force the ideas and in the meantime, she could do some school visits and workshops if she was up to it and Caroline would talk to a colleague at the agency to see about getting Zoe some commercial work.

It had gone better than Zoe had dared hope but as she travelled up the escalator at Highgate station, she dreaded returning to Elysian Place. Back to the house to wander through the empty downstairs rooms, unable to see what Gavin and his team had been doing all day.

They were still without a boiler. The plans for the kitchen were at an impasse as no one could agree on just how scaled back the new plans should be. Zoe could imagine both she and Win having to work long past retirement age, coach parties swinging past to take pictures of the house that hadn't been lived in for eighty years, then had the builders in for another forty.

If she and Win even lasted another forty years. Zoe didn't

know how they could have gone from happy to clinging on to their relationship by their fingernails in the space of six months. Or rather, she knew exactly why.

And before they could talk about it, heal, Win was right, something had to change to free them from the daily grind of house renovations and Win's bad leg and Zoe crying every time someone looked at her funny.

Something good had to happen.

16

Libby

A month after she'd received his letter, Libby finally sent a parcel off to Freddy in Spain. She hadn't planned to at all until a postal order had arrived unexpectedly from Freddy's editor at the *Daily Mirror*. Still, Libby had reasoned that it did Freddy no harm to wait and had taken her sweet time in assembling the items he'd requested. She also included a letter with the parcel – four terse lines, which were entirely inadequate when it came to giving voice to her pain.

> *Freddy*
> *May I suggest that next time you require someone to do your shopping, you write directly to your mother?*
> *I'm so sorry that thoughts of me are disturbing your sojourn in Spain. I hereby give you permission not to think about me at all and I will do likewise. Because you were right – I can't bear to think about you at all.*
> *Libby*

At the time, Libby had thought that the letter was icily dignified but now as she reread it in her head, it seemed childish, especially as she thought about Freddy a lot. But to think of Freddy was to think about the baby and then sadness engulfed everything. Turned her world grey, even though it had been months now since the baby was lost and Libby supposed that it was time to let him go, in the same way that she'd been able to cast Freddy aside. Maybe it was harder because her love for the baby had been pure, unsullied, such a good kind of love, and her love for Freddy had been a bad habit that Libby had had to overcome, like drinking too much or biting one's nails.

'You look out of sorts today,' Hugo said, derailing Libby's train of thought. 'Quite sad.'

'Oh!' She'd forgotten about Hugo, walking silently by her side through the woods, until he took her hand, not to tuck through his arm, but to hold. Neither of them was wearing gloves and the touch of his slightly roughened hand against hers felt like an intrusion. 'Not sad,' Libby assured him with a brightly empty smile. 'Just thinking.'

'These thoughts of yours, they looked like they were worth more than a penny,' Hugo said. Libby hoped he wasn't one of those people who poked and pried and wouldn't be satisfied until you'd laid bare your innermost secrets, but he didn't say any more and instead they talked of whether Edward would make a good king and of Wallis Simpson, his mistress, whom Freddy had told Libby about ages ago, said that it was common knowledge on Fleet Street.

'I've never heard of the woman,' Hugo said. 'Though one can't expect the fellow to live like a monk. And he does seem well-intentioned. A good sort. Cares about the less fortunate.'

It was the third time they'd met to stroll through Highgate Woods. They were halfway through their second lap, walking so briskly that they'd left their huffing shadow long behind them, as Libby told Hugo about Hannah, who was the least fortunate person that Libby currently knew. How Millicent had acquired Hannah from an orphanage, an act of great faith and Christian charity so she insisted, and thought it gave her the right to treat Hannah as slave labour.

'Most of Hannah's wages are paid directly to the orphanage, even though I'm sure they're already funded by wealthy do-gooders. It's a shocking racket, if you ask me. And Millicent is supposed to pay Hannah some small pittance, but she's always docking her wages for breaking things,' Libby said crossly. 'I do what I can. I give her five shillings a month for my laundry and mending, though I don't have any mending left. I have to keep ripping seams and poking holes through my jumpers.'

'Perhaps you could just give her the five shillings?' Hugo suggested.

'She says she has her pride and that her mother didn't raise her to be a beggar. Don't get me wrong, Hannah can be a perfect pest, but she has no one to stand up for her.'

Libby had asked about Hannah's people once and Hannah had said that her mother had died of shock in the kitchen of their basement flat in Penge when she'd lost her grip on a pan of boiling water and spilt it all over herself. Her father was a drunk and a layabout. There were no aunts to take Hannah in, just an aged grandmother who'd seen the eight-year-old girl as simply another mouth to feed and so Hannah had been sent to the orphanage to be trained for service and now she was at Millicent's beck and call morning, noon and night.

'It's such a small, mean life for a young girl,' Libby said to Hugo who hummed in agreement. 'Even when I'd lost both my parents, I still had Dolly who cared for me in her way.'

When Libby was better situated, she'd steal Hannah away, give her a proper wage, bully her into attending evening classes so she could take her school certificate.

How many turns around Highgate Woods before she'd saved up enough? Then there was rent and a hundred other expenses, but she owed Hannah a debt, Lord knows.

When Libby had come back from Paris, so weak that she couldn't get out of bed, Hannah had willingly trudged up the stairs with fresh hot water bottles, had sponged Libby down, brought her cups of tea, despite the many other duties Millicent expected her to perform.

'Hannah has a good heart,' Libby said now. 'Though she never stops talking and she's a terrible gossip. I know things about Mrs Lemmon across the square that I wish I didn't.'

'She sounds quite the character, your Hannah,' Hugo said. 'We have a constant parade of girls, each one of them worse than the last. My wife can't seem to keep a maid for much longer than a month.'

'Oh?' Libby couldn't contain her surprise. 'So you're still living with . . . ?'

'Well, yes, for appearance's sake.' Hugo gave a short bark of a laugh, devoid of all humour. 'It's a big house and easy enough to avoid any awkward encounters when I've been banished to the furthest reaches of the second floor. God knows what the staff have been told. Cook looks at me as if I'm an absolute beast.'

His wife, Pamela, sounded an absolute beast herself. 'A year from now this will all be over,' Libby said. 'These months, the sadness, it will seem like a bad dream.'

'Do you really think so?' Hugo asked. 'I wish I could share your optimism because it seems to me that there's no end in sight to this wretched business. At times it feels as if . . . well, no need to burden you with fanciful notions.'

133

'You're not burdening me and I'm sure your notions aren't at all fanciful,' Libby said and not because it was the polite thing to do, but because she wanted to know what these notions of Hugo's were. She was curious about what lay beneath his perfectly proper, perfectly controlled exterior. Libby fancied that she'd seen glimpses of the man he really was and she wanted to see more.

'It's just ... I have this sense that there's nothing good to come,' Hugo said heavily. 'Nothing to look forward to. When I say it out loud, it sounds so childish.'

'It doesn't sound at all childish,' Libby assured him. 'I know exactly what you mean. I feel the same way myself.'

Hugo didn't say anything else. There was a long pause; silence and sadness shared. They were now doing an unprecedented third circuit, and had passed the detective sitting on a bench and mopping at his forehead with a grubby white handkerchief. Libby decided it was time to talk of brighter things. 'So, Hannah, goodness, I've never met a girl with such a sweet tooth,' she said. 'The old ladies rarely go out and Hannah is hardly ever allowed to leave the house, so I run errands for them. Hannah always wants weigh-out sweets from Woolies. Once I bought her some cream buns as a special treat and you'd have thought I'd presented her with a bag full of diamonds.'

'Oh, you shouldn't have,' Hannah had declared. 'Never even had cream buns on my birthday.' There'd been a look of utter bliss on her usually forlorn face when she'd bitten into one of the buns and the cream had squirted everywhere. It made Libby laugh to remember it.

Hugo laughed too as if Libby's forced jollity was infectious and he was just as desperate to set a cheerier mood. 'Shall we buy her another bag of cream buns?' he asked.

'What? Now?' Libby glanced at her watch. 'The shops will be closed soon.'

Hugo smiled and shook his head. 'Not if we're quick.'

He was still holding her hand, so when he started to pick up his pace, to run, Libby had to run with him, holding on to her hat with her free hand and squealing every time she encountered a puddle and had to jump over it.

When they reached Hugo's car, they were both red-faced and breathless. Libby thought that their silliness might dissipate during the drive to Hampstead, as that was where they appeared to be headed. But then she'd giggle as she thought of the two of them running towards the gate like children rushing to get home before the dinner gong and Hugo would glance over at her, his gaze warm, and he'd chuckle too.

The cake shop on Hampstead High Street was still open, though there wasn't much displayed in the window apart from a few tired-looking Chelsea buns.

'I don't suppose you have any cream buns left?' Libby enquired of the diffident girl behind the counter who shook her head.

'Oh, I think we can do better than buns.' Hugo pointed at an extravagant confection displayed in a glass case; a large cake liberally heaped with fruit, chocolate curls and piped cream. 'We'll take that one.'

They also bought rock cakes for the old ladies, who had more catholic taste in pastries, then Hugo drove Libby the short distance back to Willoughby Square, very slowly and very carefully so as not to jolt their precious cargo.

He handed her out of the car too and even though they were standing right outside number 17 where Mrs Carmichael was known to be an inveterate curtain-twitcher and one of Millicent's dreary friends might walk past, Libby reached up to kiss Hugo on the cheek.

'I've had such a lovely time,' she said. She'd been quite shocked when Hugo had presented her with the agreed upon five pounds in the car because she'd completely forgotten why she was with him in the first place. Certainly it wasn't an ordeal to meet him each week to walk and talk. Hugo was no longer a harsh, judgemental stranger.

Indeed, there were confidences she'd told Hugo about her family, her failed career and fading looks that Libby hadn't confessed to anyone else. Not even Freddy.

It was something to do with Hugo's encouraging tone, the steady weight of his arm tucked into hers and especially the way he would look at Libby; as if she were endlessly fascinating, interesting and not the ridiculous, empty-headed creature that Libby imagined other people found her to be.

'Shall I see you next week?' Hugo asked, smiling as Libby adjusted her grip on the cake-box, the bag of rock cakes and her handbag. 'I could take something for you? See you to the front door?'

'Best not to,' Libby decided, and it was also best not to think too long and hard about this strange friendship of theirs, only that she was glad of it. 'I'd love to see you next week.'

She expected that when Hugo leant forward he was going to straighten her hat or the strap of her bag, which had got tangled but instead he kissed her. It was a chaste kiss, just a glancing blow at the corner of her mouth, but it felt monumental. Important. Maybe even a declaration and not simply an affectionate gesture between new friends.

Libby looked at Hugo, a question in her eyes, but he just smiled, stepped away, touched the brim of his hat in salute. 'Next week, then.'

17

Libby

She hadn't expected Freddy to reply to her letter but he had, even sent it on the mail plane so it would reach her in a timely fashion. How like Freddy to insist on having the last word.

> *Libby, my darling*
> *I'm in no position to do anything other than respect your wishes and leave you free to live and love in peace. Believe me when I tell you that I wish you only good things.*
> *Freddy*
> *PS: Will continue to have my editor forward you funds.*

At least they were finished now and Libby was glad of it. Still the world turned and the sun shone and she was no longer that desperate, half-mad creature she'd been at the start of the year when the days were sharp with cold and so very grey.

Now, it was impossible for Libby not to feel cheery and uplifted when the pink blossom on the trees danced above her head as she walked to school each morning. On warmer days, she took the girls to the heath for their lessons. Instructed them to choose a tree, or a flower, even a blade of grass and become that thing. Libby could hardly believe she was being paid to come up with such nonsense, but the girls had fun, standing in the long grass, waving their arms back and forth and shrieking.

She'd even made friends in the staffroom and often ate her lunch with Beryl, the headmistress, and two sisters who taught art and music respectively and shared a flat in Hendon.

And anyone who saw her with Hugo, walking through Highgate Woods hand in hand, though the detective was long gone now, would have thought Libby didn't have a care. She had colour in her cheeks, her hair was back to a riotous shade of red, and she had a ready smile on her face as they passed other couples making the most of the late-afternoon sun, people walking dogs, children chasing balls along the paths. Libby watched a small girl, no older than three, with a man who could only be her father for they had the same features, both crouched down to inspect a ladybird clinging to a leaf.

'It's only now that you look so happy, that I realise how sad you were before,' Hugo said and Libby turned to him in surprise. She'd thought she'd put on a pretty good show back then.

'Sad? Not really,' Libby assured him in a bright voice and she swung the hand that was holding his, thinking that it would make him smile, but he just carried on looking at her with that steady expression of his.

'Please don't lie to me, Libby. Aren't we past all that by now? Aren't we friends, you and I?'

They were past a lot of things. Like the pretence that they were doing this – meeting not once a week, but twice now, always holding hands, chatting about this and that – to gather evidence to satisfy the King's Proctor and grant Hugo his divorce.

Lately, Libby thought about Hugo when she wasn't with him; how his smile, hard won and rarely given, lit up his features and made him look younger. Less often, she wondered what it might feel like if he kissed her. He'd be quite masterful, she'd decided, though it would take him ages and ages to make up his mind to do so. She'd even started to notice the way other women looked at him with keen and considered interest, sometimes even glancing back as Hugo passed them.

So, they weren't friends but the word that would sum up exactly what they were remained elusive and for all their closeness, there was still one secret that she hadn't told Hugo.

'There was a reason I was sad when we first met. You see, I haven't always been entirely honest with you. I'm not really a widow,' Libby confessed in a breathless rush. 'My husband, Freddy, he's alive and kicking somewhere in Spain.'

'I wasn't sure,' Hugo said carefully. 'You did turn out to be a teacher, after all.'

'Though not entirely respectable,' Libby said and it seemed a lifetime ago that Mickey Flynn had introduced them in that bleak hotel lobby. 'We got married last September, decided on an extended honeymoon in Paris so Freddy could write a novel, though writing a novel really meant sitting round in bars with a lot of other people who said that they were writing novels too.'

Libby and Hugo exchanged a wry smile, though she doubted that he'd spent much time with nascent novelists. 'Sounds quite dull,' he ventured.

'The dullest,' Libby agreed. 'All they ever wanted to talk about were the novels they were supposedly writing.' Then her smile vanished. 'I took ill. Had an operation. It was a horrible business, made more horrible because while I was in hospital he, Freddy, left me.'

Hugo squeezed her hand and didn't say anything but that little gesture made Libby feel rooted instead of hopelessly adrift. 'What kind of man does that to the woman he loves?' he asked quietly, almost as if he were talking to himself.

It was a question that had haunted Libby; the answer too unpalatable to consider so she always shied away from it, like a rat scuttling away from the light, back into the shadows.

'He never did love me,' she said now and hoped the truth would finally set her free. 'Not really. Not at all. He only married me because I was carrying his child.'

Libby expected, and was dreading, Hugo to turn away from her, unhand her, because he was so proper and upstanding and would never countenance any thought of babies conceived out of wedlock, but his hand was still holding her, his gaze concerned, kind even.

'Go on,' he prompted gently. 'Please tell me what happened, Libby.'

There had been a time not that long ago when telling people what had happened was like suffering through it all over again. Libby was stronger than that now. Able to lift her chin and say: 'I *was* carrying Freddy's child and then suddenly I wasn't. Freddy, he took me to hospital, saved my life, I suppose, and sat by my bedside day after day even when he was told to go and then he did go, never to return. Left a note with one of the nurses.' Libby made a helpless, fluttering gesture with her free hand. 'That's about the long and the short of it.'

'The way he's behaved, the way he's treated you, it's abominable,' Hugo said harshly. He stopped walking so Libby had no choice but to stop walking too. There was a bench, which looked out onto a clearing where squirrels madly gambolled, and they sat down. 'I still feel the worst kind of heel for the way I treated you in Brighton when you were so unwell, but to walk out on you when you needed him most . . . he's no kind of man at all. You're better off without him, believe me.'

'But I'm not really without him when we're still married.' Libby looked over at Hugo who was opening his cigarette case. 'The law makes it impossible for us to forget the people who've wronged us. No matter how much you want to be done with them, never see them again, sever all ties, you can't.'

'Never mind that the person that you've married has made a mockery of all the vows they swore in the presence of God and fifty guests.' Hugo lit a cigarette with an angry inhalation of breath then handed it to Libby. It was an oddly intimate gesture. 'If your Freddy's amenable, and it sounds as if he would be, ask him to give you grounds for divorce. Or if your stomach's strong enough for it, you have evidence of your adultery if you name me as the co-respondent.' Hugo shrugged. 'I might as well be hung for a sheep as a lamb.'

Libby blew a series of smoke rings. A stagehand had taught her how when she was fifteen and she'd never lost the knack. She'd been told on numerous occasions that it was common, but she found the action soothing. 'You'd do that for me? Risk your reputation even further? Because if it was just your divorce, then people, your friends, I'm sure they'd know the evidence was cooked.'

'My reputation isn't worth a brass farthing. I'm either a cuckold or an adulterer, the details make no difference,' Hugo said and Libby hated his faithless wife in that moment.

Hugo was a thoroughly decent sort. There weren't very many men like that. Lord knows, apart from her father, Libby had never met one. She took Hugo's hand and she liked that despite the fact that there was a fancy car showroom in Mayfair with his name on the door, his hands were rough and calloused. He'd told her that he still liked to tinker under the bonnet of the cars when he had a chance. They were capable hands and she wondered what they might feel like on her, working her as if she were an engine that wouldn't start.

There was no point in having thoughts like that.

'You're a good person, Hugo,' she said. 'You deserve to be happy.'

'We'd have to make it watertight, the evidence,' Hugo said and Libby thought that he might not have heard her, as he ran his thumb along her knuckles, traced the pale blue veins that threaded their way up the back of her hand. 'I'd rent a flat, make sure a detective saw us coming and going at the kind of hours respectable people don't keep. Embracing at the window. Shocking passers-by with our scandalous behaviour.'

He shot her a look that verged on pantomime villain and Libby laughed. 'My goodness, we'd be the talk of the neighbourhood!'

'If you really wanted to make a clean sweep of it, escape the clutches of the dreaded Millicent, you could live in the flat in the meantime,' he suggested casually as if he weren't offering Libby the one thing she wanted above all others.

Beware of Greeks bearing gifts. It was what her Aunt Dolly used to say to young actresses bowled over by bouquets of flowers and boxes of chocolates left with the stage door keeper. It was sage advice never taken.

'I'll think about it,' Libby decided as she stood up and brushed imaginary crumbs from her dress. 'Shall we start back? It will be getting dark soon.'

Hugo didn't stir immediately but sat there in a contemplative pose, legs crossed, arms folded, lips pursed as he looked up at Libby standing with her hands on her hips. 'I'm not sure you entirely understand my motives,' he said.

'Don't I?' Libby frowned. She suspected that it was more than a friend simply offering to do her a favour, but what kind of favour could it be from someone who was more than a friend? 'Could you explain these motives to me then?'

Hugo shook his head and smiled as if it were obvious. 'Can't you tell when a man is in love with you?'

18

Zoe

At quarter to seven, Zoe was waiting for Win at the garden gate. He used to be home at six thirty but he was walking wounded so everything took him longer now. She watched him limp slowly down the road, his head down, and as much as she hurt for herself, Zoe also hurt for Win. Both of them needed to get back to the people they'd used to be. If Zoe was to take anything from Libby's diary maybe it was a little bit of the other woman's old-fashioned grit and determination. Back in 1936 there was no counselling, no websites offering advice or support, you were just expected to carry on regardless. To somehow still find meaning in your life and Zoe was pretty sure that she'd just found that meaning . . .

'What's wrong?' Win called out as he caught sight of her. 'What's Gavin done now? Or hasn't done?'

'Nothing's wrong,' Zoe said and she tried to smile, which made Win narrow his eyes suspiciously. There hadn't been much smiling lately. 'Close your eyes. I've got a surprise for you.'

Zoe saw hope flare up in Win that she might have found something, a cunning contraption or device, which would make all that was bad and wrong instantly better.

'OK,' Win said warily, closing his eyes. 'Do we have a boiler now? Or did you hand over the house to a TV make-over crew for the day?'

''Fraid not,' Zoe said and she took Win's sleeve to guide him down the garden path, even that inconsequential touch nervous and hesitant. 'Better than that.'

Slowly and carefully she led Win into the house, down the hall, into the kitchen where she'd put the surprise, then let go. 'Can I open my eyes now?' he asked.

'Not yet.' Win must be able to hear the scrabble of something on the floor. 'That's right. No need to be frightened. Come here, sweet girl. That's it. Win, I want you to meet Beyoncé.'

'Meet *who*?' He shook his head, opened his eyes because there was no way, *no bloody way*, that Beyoncé, the lead singer of Destiny's Child, world-famous successful solo artist and bootylicious feminist icon, was in their kitchen.

Of course she wasn't because Beyoncé was a small yet rotund dog, white with brown splodges, including a darling patch over her right eye and a ferocious underbite, which made her bottom incisors poke out of her mouth in a way that Zoe had now decided was completely adorable.

'What have you done?' Win asked, his voice flat as if he didn't even have the energy to snap.

'Well, I've seen the dogs from the local rescue centre in Highgate Woods a few times and that day you fell, I bumped into Beyoncé and we kind of hit it off, didn't we?' Zoe scooped up Beyoncé, who smooshed her face against Zoe's neck. 'She hasn't been coping very well in kennels and everything has been so horrible lately and we both needed cheering up so I

144

said we'd foster her ...' Zoe tailed off as Win looked at the dog and the dog looked at him with an equally discomfited expression.

'How could you think this was a good idea? And who calls a dog Beyoncé? Who in their right mind would do that?' Win demanded of Zoe, who held Beyoncé in front of her like a canine shield to deflect Win's wrath. 'The house is a building site. The garden is a builder's yard. We are broke. Broker than broke and you decide this is a really good time to get a dog.'

'Something needed to change. We both agreed on that,' Zoe insisted. 'And you're the one who always wanted a dog.'

'Sometime in the future and it was meant to be a joint decision ...' They'd hardly spoken to each other these last few weeks but suddenly they were in the middle of an argument, when Zoe could count the number of arguments they'd had in thirteen years on her fingers and still have a hand spare. They weren't shouting at least, but talking in fierce, angry whispers so as not to upset Beyoncé. 'God, that is the ugliest dog I've ever seen.'

Zoe held Beyoncé out for closer inspection. She was very placid, quite happy to nestle in Zoe's arms, comfortingly solid and warm. 'She's not ugly. She's a crossbreed.'

'A cross between what?'

'A pug crossed with a Staffordshire bull terrier with some French bulldog in there too. Come on, Win, look at her little face!'

Zoe thrust the dog at Win and, as if she sensed that her entire future might rest on this moment, Beyoncé cocked her head, stuck out her lower jaw even further and made an odd grunting noise.

'I suppose she is kind of cute.' Win was definitely wavering. She'd heard all about Brandy, the beloved Labrador they'd had when Win and Ed were kids and yes, she and Win might not currently have a back garden but the people from the shelter had said that it wasn't an issue if they had Highgate and Queen's Woods on their doorstep.

Win took the dog from her then Zoe saw his eyes widen in disbelief as he caught sight of her still swollen belly, the enlarged, elongated teats ... 'She's *pregnant*? Oh, Zoe, how could you?'

'She isn't pregnant,' Zoe said hurriedly, snatching Beyoncé back and cradling the dog to her chest. 'She had a litter a few weeks ago but she was picked up as a stray in Chingford. They think she was used as a breeding bitch, but the rescue centre have said that she'll be spayed—'

'No!' Win put up her hands to ward off any more attempts by Zoe to thrust the dog at him. 'She is going back first thing tomorrow. How can you even bear to look at her? What is wrong with you?'

Win walked out without another word. Limped into the living room. Zoe left the dog in the kitchen, to follow him. She'd never seen Win look at her like that. His anger blunted by a dull resignation as if he couldn't see a way to be rid of her.

'You know what, Zo? I can't do this. I can't clear up another one of your messes,' he said, his back to her as he stared out of the windows, his hands resting heavily on the sill.

'Excuse me?'

'I can't always be the grown-up. The one who fixes everything,' Win clarified. 'Fixes you.'

Zoe hated him then. Just a little. For being so dense, so determined not to understand what had happened to her, to them. 'I don't need you to fix me. I'm not broken!' Though in a way she was, Zoe knew that, but she had to believe that she wouldn't stay broken. That the hurt would recede, become something that she'd learn to live with, because if the hurt

146

completely disappeared then it would be an insult, an affront to the memory of what would have been their first child. 'Being sad after what happened is normal. It's not a mess that should be cleared away as quickly as possible. There's no set time to get over it.'

'You'd get over it much faster if you stopped dwelling on it,' Win said. 'And now you get a dog that's a constant reminder of what happened so you'll be even more miserable.'

'I'm sorry. I didn't know you had a schedule for how long I am allowed to dwell on losing our baby ...'

They both winced as Zoe said the three words that they'd somehow silently agreed to never utter out loud.

'I'm not talking about this,' Win said as if that were a surprise. 'Change the subject.'

'No, we are staying on this subject because I'm fed up with you shutting me out, punishing me and I don't even know what for. Losing the baby? Or getting pregnant in the first place, because that was way ahead of the schedule you've mapped out for the next fifty years of our lives?' Zoe had always suspected that Win saw their future as a gigantic to-do list. All the big events: getting married, buying a house, having kids, weren't happy occasions to be celebrated but items to be ticked off.

It was one of Win's more annoying foibles; they'd had their worst ever row in Sainsbury's one Christmas Eve over Win's ridiculously detailed shopping list, which even had sub-sections, but Zoe knew that she had her own foibles too. That her habit of not opening post and how she ate her yogurt off the back of the spoon drove Win to distraction but she'd always thought that was what love was in its purest form; loving someone despite all their infuriating habits.

Maybe that was what this was about; that they'd simply stopped loving each other. It was there in Win's face, the way that he'd shut down, not just since the baby, but how he now responded to Zoe's accusation. Not even trying to deny it, to defend himself.

'We're not doing this,' he said, limping past her. 'And that bloody dog is going back where it came from.'

Zoe rushed after him. 'Don't walk away from me,' she snapped as Win hauled himself slowly up each stair. 'We have to talk about the baby.'

'There was no baby,' he mumbled so Zoe wasn't even sure that she'd heard him properly. 'You were barely even two months gone and you didn't even know you were pregnant so why? Why are you still so down about it? Why, for God's sake, won't you let it go?'

He turned awkwardly on the widest step where the stairs curved around the corner so he could see the stricken, dumbfounded look on Zoe's face. 'It would have been our first child. How can that not matter to you?' she asked. 'I thought that a new house, a new adventure would bring us together again but God, you're not even trying!'

'I never wanted to buy this house,' Win said, turning to continue his flight away from her.

'You know why we had to buy this house.'

Zoe had spent a week in hospital recovering and even though she felt as fragile and as flimsy as a butterfly's wing, she was sent home.

Home.

It didn't feel like home any more, but a collection of rooms that housed her belongings while her heart was somewhere else.

And the bathroom. Someone, probably Jackie, had done a deep clean so the white tiles, the bath surround, were spotless, but even so Zoe was sure she could still see speckles of red clinging to the grouting and when she shut her eyes all she could see was her own body prone and bleeding on the floor.

She came out of the bathroom to find Win waiting for her in the hall,

148

hands hanging by his side, the same helpless look on his face that he'd had ever since she'd woken up in hospital.

'I can't live here any more,' she said without preamble. 'We have to move. Now. Sooner than now.'

'Zo, it's not as easy as that,' Win had said gently.

'It is that easy. There's still the house in Highgate. We can live there. We'll make it work. Do you think we could be in before Christmas?'

Win tried to talk her round. Kept talking money so that Zoe imagined thought-bubbles with a string of numbers in each one floating above his head. She let him talk, use reason and logic, until he ran out of words. 'So, we're agreed, right? We'll wait until the new year and make a decision when you're feeling better.'

She'd never been surer of anything in her life. 'I will never be able to walk into that bathroom without seeing myself nearly bleeding to death on the floor.'

Zoe had expected more arguments, more thought-bubbles with numbers, not Win dropping to his knees in front of her. He put his hands on her hips in that hesitant way that he'd learned in the last week, as if he were scared to touch her. Though Zoe wanted to run her fingers through his hair, hold him to her and make Win promise to never let her go, she couldn't bear to touch him.

Because Win had seen her almost bleed out in front of him and now something between them had shifted, was altered, splintered and would never be made right again.

She'd never be right again, she was damaged and she didn't want to infect Win too so she held herself very still.

Win took his hands off her. 'I know,' he said. 'I know.'

'We're moving, right?' Zoe clarified. 'To Highgate. Something new. Something that hasn't had a chance to be spoiled. OK?

'OK?'

'I can't be happy in this house, when I know we're bankrupting ourselves,' Win said, hobbling into the back bedroom.

'We didn't have to move. We could have found another solution. I told you time and time again that this house was too expensive but it was what you wanted. I did what you wanted, I always do, but enough, Zoe. *Enough!*'

It would never be enough. 'I don't care about the money. I care about you. About us, but I'm not even sure there is an us at the moment.' Zoe raised her head to meet Win's gaze and she wasn't holding anything back, wasn't afraid to let Win see her vulnerability, her pain. He turned away. 'Do you still love me?'

'Of course I do! Do you even have to ask?' Win only had eyes for the holdall he snatched up, the folded piles of laundry that Zoe had placed on the bed earlier. 'But we're not making each other happy right now, are we?'

Zoe was looking forward to a time when she could get through a day without crying, when she simply felt all right. Happiness – something that she used to take for granted – was currently an unattainable goal. 'I know I've been difficult lately but have I been so difficult that you can't even live with me any more? Win! Stop that and talk to me!'

Win didn't stop but continued packing with sharp, jerky movements. 'I love you but I just can't do this. Not any of it. Especially not having to listen to you cry night after night when you think that I'm asleep.'

'I'm not going to do that any more. Look, I want things to be different. I want them to change; but you storming out in a huff isn't the change I want.'

'I'm not storming out,' Win said, which was true. He wouldn't be carefully balling up his socks if he was storming, but he was still packing to leave. 'I'm going to stay at my mum's for a bit.'

'Please don't do that,' Zoe said, when she should have been pleading, imploring, begging Win to stay, but it felt as if he were already gone. Had felt like that ever since they came back from the hospital. 'You know, if you would talk to me about the baby, then we could—'

'We could what? What is talking about it over and over meant to achieve? Not that there's anywhere in this house where we can even sit comfortably and have a conversation.' Win held out his hands to encompass the bare room that like everything else in the house, like her bloody reproductive system, wasn't fit for the job at hand. 'Not that it matters. Nothing is right and no amount of talking is going to change that.'

Win had been picking up speed, voice getting louder, packing more frantic, but his flow was interrupted by the sound of something from downstairs hurling itself repeatedly against the door to the living room and a series of grunts that rose in volume and frequency until they became whimpers.

'The house is fixable,' Zoe insisted but her shoulders were already slumped in defeat. 'And we're fixable too, aren't we? Aren't we?'

'I can't do it any more,' Win said as if it were the only decision he was capable of making. 'I'm sick of being the one in charge all the time. You wanted this house, Zo, and I hope you'll be very happy together.'

Then Win clicked the locks shut on his suitcase, the sound decisive too. Definite. A full-stop.

19

Zoe

The first day that Win was gone, when it came to the time he usually came home, and there was no sound of his key in the lock, the front door opening and closing, then a querulous 'Zoe?' from the foot of the stairs, it felt like a stay of execution.

Besides, even if she didn't have Win, Zoe had Beyoncé. From thinking that she was a cat person, after only one day, Zoe was quite overcome with the rush of affection that swept over her each time she saw that ridiculous, furry face or took a whiff of the warm corn snack smell of the dog when she rolled over onto her back and wiggled her paws imperiously until Zoe rubbed her belly.

Beyoncé also gave Zoe's life a structure she hadn't had in a long time. An hour's walk in the morning, an hour's walk in the afternoon and, unlike Zoe, Beyoncé couldn't subsist on cheese and crackers but needed two proper meals a day. More than that, the dog needed, and gave back full force, unconditional love so that when Zoe inevitably did begin to miss Win after only a couple of days and she'd start to cry, Beyoncé would scramble into her lap as Zoe sat and remembered the Win that she'd first fallen in love with.

She could actually pinpoint the very day when she realised she had more than a crush on the strange, stern young man who managed her accounts.

They'd known each other nearly a year and been friends for a few months by then, but if circumstances were different, if she were braver, Zoe would have preferred to be something more. She settled for frequently visiting Win to present him with silly little sketches of Camden Town life – the stallholders from Inverness Street market, the neighbourhood scenesters taking the air, baby punks hanging around the World's End pub – which made him laugh, before they dealt with the official-looking envelopes Zoe refused to open unless Win was standing over her.

So, that day. THE day. A sunny Friday afternoon in October. First, Zoe had run the gauntlet of the receptionist, Audrey, 'Aud on the board' they all called her. 'He's in his office, just go straight up.' Audrey had given Zoe the usual coy look.

Win had been wearing a very smart navy blue suit, crisp pale blue shirt and a red tie. 'Went to court this morning with a client,' he said to Zoe when he saw her gawp because he looked even more like a proper grown-up than he normally did. Zoe always looked improper in her ubiquitous baggy green jumper and stripy tights, clutching a carrier bag full of sketchbooks and pens. 'Managed to get his impending county court judgement stopped. His former accountant was useless.' He'd rolled his eyes. 'Won't bore you with the details because they really are exceptionally boring. So, what's up?'

Zoe handed him three ominous brown envelopes, which Win had opened, kept two and handed her one back. 'This is from your dentist reminding you you're due a check-up. I'm not getting involved in your medical affairs; that would be crossing a line, though I have to ask why you're standing like that?'

'Like what?' Zoe had immediately straightened up and winced when something pinged in her lower back.

'Like that.' Win had placed his hand on her shoulder. Zoe could smell soap powder and the light zingy scent of his aftershave. 'Like you're in pain.'

'Just backache. My bed sags in the middle.' Zoe had immediately wished she'd invented something more sexy like a salsa dancing injury when Win had sighed and looked at his watch.

'Right,' he said. 'We're going to buy you a bed.'

'But you can't just . . . I mean, how would you . . . Buying a bed is quite a complicated business, isn't it?'

'It really isn't.' Win picked up his briefcase. 'It's fairly straightforward and speaking as your accountant, you can afford a new bed. You could afford several new beds if you wanted.'

They'd taken the bus to Tottenham Court Road, Win folding up his legs to sit next to Zoe rather than in the empty seat behind so he could stretch out, which she tried not to take as A Sign. She'd kept up a steady stream of chatter. What she was doing that weekend; dress shopping with her friend Mercedes, Sunday lunch at a pub in Islington, a karaoke party with a performance art student called Tony Cortes, who Zoe had slept with during Fresher's Week and intermittently ever since, though Win didn't know that, then Zoe had followed Win off the bus and into a bed shop.

'We need a bed,' he'd called out to the nearest salesman.

'A double?'

Win had looked Zoe up and down. 'No, better make it a kingsize.'

Zoe pointed at a bed in the middle of the shop with an

old-fashioned brass bedstead. 'That one,' she said. 'Can I have that one?'

'Certainly, madam.' The salesman managed to peel himself off the wall he was leaning against. 'Do you like a soft or firm mattress?'

'I don't know,' Zoe admitted. 'Um, soft, I suppose.'

'No.' Win came to stand between Zoe and the salesman. 'You need a firm mattress, something with a lot of support.'

'I don't want a hard mattress, Win,' Zoe said and he'd taken her arm, his eyes wide and pleading.

'Zoe! On average we spend a third of our day in bed. Eight hours. On a mattress that should be replaced every ten years at the very least.' He did some rapid mental arithmetic, which made his eyes flicker. 'You're going to spend twenty-nine thousand and two hundred hours sleeping on that mattress.' He'd grinned and Zoe had felt something inside her do a loop the loop. 'I haven't accounted for leap years, because I'm not a total numbers nerd but that's a lot of hours to spend on a substandard mattress. Years from now do you want to be one of those little old women with a dowager's hump all because of this moment in this shop when you chose the wrong mattress?'

Zoe wasn't a person of strong convictions but when she did chance upon one, then even Win wouldn't be able to sway her. But she didn't have any strong convictions about mattresses, just the strongest conviction that if she died now while lying next to Win as they tested a variety of different mattresses, then she'd die happy.

'We'll take this one,' Win decided after they'd spent two minutes stretched out on a very firm mattress but not so firm that it was like lying on breeze block. 'We need it delivered on Monday. How much discount do we get for paying upfront? Fifteen per cent sounds fair.'

It was five minutes after closing time. On a Friday afternoon. Win haggled Zoe a ten per cent discount and when he also persuaded the salesman to throw in two memory foam pillows, Zoe realised that she didn't just have a stupid, debilitating schoolgirl crush on Win. It was so much more than that.

Ever since she'd first met him, Win had looked out for her best interests, be they financial or otherwise. He was a good man. Clever, smart, funny. She liked his face too, couldn't imagine she'd ever grow tired of it. This was someone she'd always want in her life. Someone she wanted to share her life with.

'Because I'm so bossy?' Win had asked, crestfallen, when they'd moved past accountant and client, way past being friends, and he was sharing that kingsize bed with her night after night. 'That's why you fell in love with me?'

'Not bossy – driven, focused,' Zoe had said. 'Anyway, we both know that you're not *that* bossy, like we both know that I'm not as fragile and helpless as people seem to think I am.'

Zoe felt fragile and helpless now as she remembered how good they'd been, she and Win, and she cried as she filled the kettle in their makeshift kitchen in their makeshift house, which was meant to have made everything in their makeshift lives come right.

'Come on, pet, don't cry,' said Gavin from somewhere behind her and Zoe felt a hand descend heavily onto her shoulder. 'I see couples split up over house renovations all the time. It's not the house that needs renovating; it's their relationship,' he added sagely, which wasn't comforting. Neither was the hand rhythmically pummelling her shoulder.

'But the house does need renovating,' Zoe sniffed. 'And we're not split up. We're just taking some space. Well, Win is.'

Her face crumpled again as if it were trying to turn itself inside out and Gavin reached past Zoe for the kitchen roll, tearing off a couple of pieces and handing them to her so she could wipe her eyes, blow her nose.

'The thing about Win, and you know this better than anyone, is that he's sensitive. Always has been, even as a kid. Though it's hardly surprising with Terry being the way he was and all the nonsense that went on.'

Zoe always forgot that Gavin's relationship with Jackie, nine years and counting, was actually pre-dated by a friendship that stretched back decades. He'd been at school with Jackie and Terry, Win and Ed's father, had gone to the same teenage parties and discos, was friends with Jackie's older brother, Keith, so had had a ringside seat for Win's formative years.

She blew her nose again. 'Terry's right up there with Voldemort for people who should not be named, let alone talked about.'

'Volde who?'

Zoe did smile at that. 'I'm just saying that Win hardly ever talks about his dad. Yes, he and Ed have some stories that they always drag out when his name comes up but that's about it.'

Apart from the almighty row Win and Ed had had about Ed inviting Terry to the christening of Extra-Large, as she and Win called Ed's eldest child, most mentions of their father usually involved one of Terry's mad schemes. A business deal gone awry, which resulted in him buying twenty boxes of Pot Noodle sight unseen. The Rolls Royce he'd won in a poker game whose engine had fallen out halfway up Shooters Hill. How he'd broken his leg in a betting shop because he'd fallen over doing a victory jig when his three-way accumulator bet had come good.

Now Zoe remembered that, despite Win's objections, a christening invitation had been sent to Terry who'd promised to come but ended up as a no-show. Terry had finally put in an appearance at Medium's Christening, but he'd been so drunk that Amanda's father had asked him to leave. Zoe had missed all the drama as she'd taken Extra-Large and Large to the park because they were both going through a very loud squealing phase.

When it had come to their own wedding, Zoe had asked Win if he wanted to invite Terry and Win had said no. It had been a very forbidding no and Win's face had tightened the way it always did when Terry's name came up. His voice would become husky too so Zoe never pried. She'd squeeze Win's hand and kiss his cheek so he'd know he didn't have to shoulder any burden alone; which actually hadn't worked out very well as a strategy as now they were shouldering their burdens alone when they should have been a team, working through things together.

'The thing with Terry was that it was all fun and games until it wasn't,' Gavin revealed. 'As soon as things got tough, which they always did and usually because he owed people money, he'd bugger off and leave Jackie to pick up the pieces.'

'Kind of like Win's doing now,' Zoe complained to Gavin, who'd taken over the tea-making. 'I know that I've been difficult to live with and that we took on more than we realised with the house, but he's just closed down. It's what he always does instead of talking things through. He won't talk about the baby at all, like he doesn't even care about what happened.'

'Of course he does. He was in pieces that night when you were rushed to hospital. I've never seen him like that before, Zo. He sat in the waiting room while you were in surgery, face the colour of porridge, and kept saying over and over again, "I can't lose her." Got me quite choked up, but generally, the Rowells are an odd bunch.' Gavin shrugged as if he wasn't concerned that the family they'd both married into were emotionally stunted. 'Don't like talking about their feelings and stuff. Doesn't really bother me. My ex never stopped talking about her feelings and it doesn't mean Win doesn't care. Or Jackie. You know they do. But her way of caring is to put the kettle on.' Gavin held Zoe's own just boiled kettle aloft for emphasis. 'Your boy is drowning in tea at the moment.'

Zoe had to smile at that. Her first week at home after being in hospital, Jackie had all but moved in because Zoe's own mother was far away. There hadn't been anything in the way of a heart to heart, which at the time was something of a relief but there had been cups of tea, every hour, on the hour. 'Win doesn't even like tea that much,' Zoe said, as she took the mug Gavin held out to her. 'Are the two of you butting heads every night when you fill him in on the latest developments in the saga of the boiler?'

'Says he's not interested,' Gavin said, as he picked up the laden tray. 'Be a love and tuck that packet of chocolate biscuits under my arm, will you?'

Later that evening, Zoe called Win. Win was always the one to make the first move when they argued but always wasn't working any more. Her call went straight to voicemail. Her garbled message ('Just calling to see how you are? How's your knee? I miss you. Are you missing me too? I hope you are.') not returned. Her many texts bombarding Win with queries about the house went unanswered too, until he replied with a terse *Your house, you sort it out.*

It did occur to Zoe that Win was behaving like a dick. Cath said as much when she came round with a consolation curry and a couple of bottles of Pinot Noir. 'Which is strange really, because Win is the least dickish man I know. Apart from Theo and even he has his dickish moments.'

It also occurred to Zoe that she could fix her own mess and send Beyoncé back to the shelter and then Win might come back to Elysian Place, but she couldn't bear to be parted from the source of all her current joy and this, their argument, wasn't about Beyoncé. It never had been. She'd just been the catalyst for Win to find his voice, to catalogue all the many ways he was miserable.

Well, Zoe was miserable too. There was nothing left to do but take to her bed to have a good cry and wish that her bed wasn't in a storage unit off the North Circular because taking to an airbed wasn't really the same thing.

It was impossible to cry for any sustained amount of time with Beyoncé around because she immediately curled up next to Zoe and attempted to enthusiastically lick away the tears before they'd had a chance to fall. But despite Beyoncé's best efforts and even knowing that Cath was only a text message away, Zoe had never felt so lonely before and the only other person who she knew would understand was Libby.

Getting the suitcase down and taking the diary out still felt like an illicit act, something secret that she could only do when there was nobody else around, but curiosity always got the better of Zoe and she quickly opened the diary to find solace in its pages.

Zoe had last left Libby at the end of March and as she flicked through there wasn't much solace to be had in her April entries; a series of weekly, then twice-weekly appointments written in some obscure code.

April 23rd 5pm HW/HW
April 30th 5pm HW/HW
May 4th 5pm HW/HW

Then, on a torn scrap of paper:

If loving someone were enough, then the sheer weight of my love for Freddy should have anchored

160

him to my side. Why did I let him go so easily?
Why not become a rebel fighter for love? Go to
Spain and drag him back by his braces? Because
I know deep down that my love isn't enough and
Freddy wants no part of it.

And yet, there is always the possibility of a new
love.

Zoe frowned. New love? She would never be ready for a
new love. It was Win; it always had been for her, but here was
yet more evidence of Libby moving on.

She flicked back a few pages. HW/HW. Zoe leafed back
even further because the initials HW were prodding a dim,
distant memory and there, nestling between the twenty-first
and twenty-second of February, was a business card belonging
to a Hugo Watkins.

A car salesman. Zoe pulled a face at Beyoncé, who gazed
impassively back at her, head tilted to one side. Zoe shouldn't
judge but she'd never had a good experience with a car salesman. At least this Hugo Watkins was a cut above – he owned
a car showroom in Mayfair, but could Libby really have loved
Freddy as much as she claimed if she found it so easy to love
again?

Zoe retraced her steps in the diary to the entry she'd been
reading before she got sidetracked and realised that there was
more. Three drafts of a letter to Freddy. The first was a howl
of pain that echoed in the chambers of Zoe's own heart.

*Oh, Freddy. It's not fair that you can simply walk away. Send me a
few of those pretty words that you write so well and think you've done
your penance when I have to live with the pain, the loss, every minute of
every hour of every day.*

Zoe had to stop there. Not only had they both lost babies –
she and Libby had also been abandoned by the men they

loved. Yes, Win was only ten minutes up the road in his mum's spare room but it felt as if there was a world between them.

'Don't, Beyoncé,' she muttered, as the little dog put her front paws on Zoe's chest, all the better to reach Zoe's face with her tongue. 'Not crying, so stop licking me!'

She settled the dog back in her lap, opened the diary again to read the second draft, which wasn't that much different to the first, then the final version, which Zoe supposed Libby must have sent to Freddy.

Freddy

May I suggest that next time you require someone to do your shopping, that you write directly to your mother?

I'm so sorry that thoughts of me are disturbing your sojourn in Spain. I hereby give you permission not to think about me at all and I will do likewise. Because you were right – I can't bear to think about you at all.

Libby

Then Libby went back to her dates with HW, the mysterious Hugo Watkins, and that was all she wrote until Zoe found Freddy's hurt reply sandwiched between two pages at the start of May.

Libby, my darling

I'm in no position to do anything other than respect your wishes and leave you free to live and love in peace. Believe me when I tell you that I wish you only good things.

Freddy

PS: Will continue to have my editor forward you funds.

Zoe had already cast Freddy as the villain of the piece. Had written him off as callous and cruel and utterly heartless, but there was a wounded quality to his words that resonated with her even if Zoe was on Libby's side. How could she not be? They'd both suffered the same loss.

And yet if Win had left her while she'd been recovering in hospital (and Zoe couldn't think of a single scenario where that might be the case, not even if Win had discovered that she'd taken a whole legion of lovers behind his back), there was no way that Zoe would be thinking of new love, of dating, of meeting up for twice-weekly trysts just a few months later.

Perhaps she and Libby weren't so alike after all, Zoe thought as she turned May's mostly blank pages without really seeing them, until she came to another letter.

It wasn't in Libby's careless scribble or Freddy's elegant, looped hand but in a very old-fashioned, copperplate script.

157–163 Park Lane,
London, W1

17 Willoughby Square
Hampstead NW3

24th May 1936

Dearest Libby

Have made all necessary arrangements and rented a flat in the new mansion block on the corner of Muswell Hill Road and Wood Lane.

If still agreeable, and I hope with all my heart that you haven't taken fright after my declaration, we could meet there this Friday evening at eight in the lobby?

As I've already explained we'll have to spend the night there but I promise to behave like a perfect gentleman. My intentions

towards you are as honourable as they can be – my happiness is
secondary to your own. But that said, I long to spend those hours
with you, to simply relish the pleasure of your company.

This one night may seem like a means to an end, the final nail
in the coffin of our marriages, but I believe it could be the start of
something quite wonderful too.

I do hope to see you on Friday.

Fondest regards

Hugo

Zoe was at a loss. What was the point of spending the night together if Hugo was promising to behave like a perfect gentleman? If they were having an affair, where was the fun in that?

What was clear from his letter was that Hugo was married too, which meant that the bond between Zoe and Libby was weakening still further. Libby knew the agony of being left by her husband so why would she wish that on another woman?

It made no sense. Or perhaps Libby wasn't the tragic heroine that Zoe had wanted her to be.

Zoe tucked Hugo's letter into its envelope and was about to place it back in the diary when she saw that Libby had written in pencil on the back of the envelope. The writing tiny and furious, like ants crawling across the faded paper.

It's not just the loss of the baby, the boy (I know it was a boy) with his eyes, his pilgrim soul, somehow I have to learn to live with the loss of Freddy.

I will be so much happier when I can let him go, not just in a letter, but from my heart too. I tell myself that he was a cold, heartless bastard *but he was so much more than that. If he hadn't been, then I'd never have fallen in love with him in the first place.*

Hugo says that I deserve so much better but I'm not sure that I do. I'm certainly not sure what I've done to deserve Hugo's love or if I can be brave enough to let myself love again.

Zoe thrust the diary away, almost dislodging Beyoncé from her lap. If Libby loved Freddy so much, despite the truly terrible way he'd betrayed her, then instead of moping about it, getting embroiled in some sordid affair with this Hugo, she should have gone to Spain and dragged him back home. If she'd really loved him.

Because when you loved someone, you fought for them. Hard.

Despite recent evidence, Win loved her; it was one of those few things that Zoe had a strong conviction about. She loved him too and love didn't just wither and die. It stuck around. Their love was still there, lurking in the background, and Zoe would do whatever she had to do to drag it, kicking and screaming, into the light.

Win didn't want to come home because they currently didn't have a home but a house in progress, which was weeks behind schedule.

Zoe did dislodge Beyoncé then, much to the dog's grunted disapproval, so she could get to her feet, grab a notebook and walk from room to room. Taking stock, making notes, hatching a plan.

Houses were much easier to mend than hearts so that's where she'd start.

20

Libby

Libby walked along Hampstead Lane then down from High-gate Village as she had done every week since she and Hugo had started their arrangement. But instead of waiting at the entrance to Highgate Woods, she crossed over Muswell Hill Road and entered the manicured grounds of Southwood Hall.

When Hugo had mentioned a flat, Libby had imagined something like one of the places she used to rent. Ramshackle rooms separated by thin partitions with a shared bathroom down the hall. Nothing like this imposing block built in the grounds of a former mansion, with lush green lawns, perfectly manicured hedges and little paths that invited one to take a stroll. Each brick looked as if it had been polished, the windows sparkled in the evening sun, brass fixtures gleaming.

In his letter, Hugo had told her that he'd be waiting in the lobby. It seemed that, like their first meeting, this too would start in a lobby. A place one passed through to get to some-where else though Libby wasn't sure if she were ready for what that somewhere else might be.

All she knew was that Hugo claimed to be in love with her. Probably he meant that he wanted her, but wanting someone, even wanting them quite desperately, wasn't the same as love.

Want was still enough to make Libby giddy with nerves. Earlier, her voice had been quite shrill when she'd told Millicent and the enthralled old ladies that she was going to the opening night of a play; an old friend in the leading role. How else to explain why she was wearing the dark green crêpe that she'd been married in, primped and painted, hair freshly waved and her small suitcase packed and standing in the hall? 'There'll be a party afterwards so I thought it best to kip at my friend's place in Marylebone. I don't want to come home at some godforsaken hour and wake everyone up.'

It still wasn't too late to turn tail and run. Surely Hugo had all the proof he needed for a divorce and though he said he was in love with her, Libby didn't know how he, how anyone, could love a woman who was damaged goods.

But when she glanced towards the grand double doors of the flats, her nerves gave way to a fizzing, tingling anticipation of seeing Hugo again, his smile, the way his eyes lit up at the sight of her.

Then it was quite easy to put one foot in front of the other and walk up to the doors, which were pulled open before Libby had even tripped up the steps, and Hugo was standing there. Smiling, eyes lit up.

'Hello,' he said.

'Hello.' She felt inexplicably shy. 'Have you been waiting long?'

'Not long. I saw you walking up and down as if you were having second thoughts. Are you nervous?' he asked and Libby wondered whether he could hear her heart thundering against her breast. 'I am. Terrified, in actual fact.'

Libby laughed as she let Hugo guide her inside. Her heels clicked across the parquet floor as the porter behind his little desk tipped his cap at her.

Hugo steered her to the lift and they travelled up to the third floor in silence. Then the lift stopped, the doors opened and Hugo took her hand.

'There really is nothing to be nervous about,' he said, as if he were reassuring himself too. They walked down a corridor, softly lit wall lights guiding their way to a door at the end.

Hugo fished for the key in his trouser pocket, then hesitated. It was Libby's turn to squeeze his hand. 'Shouldn't there be a private detective lurking around the corner?' she asked.

'No, he'll be outside,' Hugo said, opening the door. 'Supposedly, the poor soul will be standing guard all night to catch us sneaking out at daybreak.'

'He can't be a very good private detective,' Libby said, as she stepped past Hugo, into the flat. 'If I were him, I'd simply bribe the porter to report on our comings and goings. Oh! This is lovely.'

Though they were standing in a hall, she could see directly into a living room that was open and airy with high ceilings and a herringbone wood floor. Two white sofas were placed at right angles to the fireplace, a low glass table in between them.

Hugo smiled indulgently as he followed Libby who gasped at the kitchen with gas oven and grill, and fitted cupboards. The sparkling bathroom, which had hot and cold running water and a shower, which Libby couldn't resist turning on, though she wished she hadn't when she was pelted by a violent jet of water.

There was a bedroom too, obviously. Glimpsed through the open door was a huge bed, dressed in an oyster satin comforter and heaped with pillows, more pillows than two people could ever need. Libby averted her eyes and let Hugo take her back to the living room.

It was then that she noticed the Fortnum & Mason hamper, the champagne in a silver bucket.

She shook her head. 'I'm not sure what I was expecting, but this is all too much. You rented this flat just for tonight?'

'I took it on a short lease. Landlord's wife kitted it out, has delusions of being the next Sybil Colefax, apparently,' Hugo said, which made sense as Libby couldn't imagine Hugo briefing a decorator on his preference for white sofas or oyster satin bedspreads. Not that Hugo wasn't personable, charming even, and perfectly capable of getting what he wanted, but he seemed to exist in the bubble that they'd created for themselves. It was only ever the two of them, though it felt as if there was always a shadowy figure dogging their every move. Sometimes it was Hugo's wife, occasionally it was Freddy, more often it was the huffing and puffing private detective.

'Is he already outside, the detective, I mean? I didn't see him as I came in.' Libby would have darted to the window to peer out, but Hugo caught her hand. 'What do we need to do?'

'Let's not worry about that for now,' Hugo said. 'Would you like some champagne?'

Libby said that she would, although she could have done with something stronger to take the edge off. The champagne made her feel as if the bubbles were fizzing under her skin and she kept pleating a fold of her dress over and over again.

Eventually, Hugo stilled her motions by covering her hands with his and they sat on the white sofa, side by side, but quite silent. He hadn't even taken off his jacket and Libby wondered if he were one of those men who always wore waistcoat, tie, pocket watch, even on the weekends, even when he was messing about with his car engines.

'We'll have to kiss.' Hugo swallowed hard as Libby turned to look at him. 'At the window. With the light on. The detective, apparently his name is Connolly, has come prepared with binoculars and a camera.'

'Really? Binoculars?' Libby wanted to laugh because it was all so ridiculous.

She took another gulp of champagne and glanced over at Hugo. His eyes were darting wildly about the room, the skin around his tightly pursed mouth was white and a tic at his temple pounded away like a jackhammer.

'Shall we just get it over and done with?'

'I beg your pardon?'

'The kiss,' Hugo said and he closed his eyes as if the thought of kissing Libby was causing him all manner of distress. 'Shall we?'

He was on his feet and halfway to the window that overlooked the street. Libby couldn't help but drag her heels a little. A girl liked a little wooing, after all. With a discontent, inward sigh, she cast a practised eye over the scene; the window where Hugo stood, his hands twisting, the harsh glare of the chandelier on the stark white walls.

'What are you doing?' Hugo asked impatiently as Libby turned off the overhead light so the lamps on the sideboard provided the room with a soft glow.

'I'm creating a mood.' It was as if Libby were back onstage, a director's voice ordering her to play the seductress. There was a lazy swing to her hips as she walked towards Hugo, her voice a purr. 'You should take off your jacket.'

Hugo stared at Libby as if she'd come to steal his soul. 'I should what?'

'You're so buttoned up,' she complained. 'You don't look the least bit like a man conducting a scandalous affair.'

Still he goggled at her. Libby supposed his errant wife was

the only woman he'd ever been with. That she'd found comfort with another man wasn't a great testament to Hugo's skill at lovemaking.

Libby felt sorry for Hugo who'd obviously never known the thrill of making eyes at a stranger, of being held closer than was decent on a crowded dance floor, of kisses snatched in dark corners. All this time, he had been living a half-life. When Libby sidled up to him she could feel his hurried breaths stir her hair.

She put her hand on his chest, felt his heart racing against her palm. 'It's just a kiss,' she said. 'There's nothing frightening about a kiss.'

Then she smoothed her hands up to his shoulder, slipped them under his jacket and tugged him free while he stood there mute, at her mercy. She began to unbutton his waistcoat and the detective, Connolly or whatever his name was, had to be getting one hell of a show, Libby thought as she freed the last button.

She took a half step back. 'That's better,' she said with some satisfaction. 'So, aren't you going to kiss me then?'

Libby had meant to sound teasing, playful, not challenging, but Hugo twitched, his eyes flashed and then he seized hold of her, one arm clamped around her waist, the other hand tangling in her hair.

He kissed her.

It was a clumsy, artless kiss. As Libby had feared, Hugo didn't have a clue what to do with a woman. Libby's hands were trapped between their bodies, neck caught at an awkward angle as Hugo's mouth ground against hers.

She said a silent prayer, then pushed Hugo away. He stood there, panting, a flush staining his cheeks.

'Do you think that was enough?' he asked in a ragged voice then jerked his head in the direction of the window. 'Shall we have another bash at it?'

'Have another bash at it?' Libby echoed sorrowfully. 'We're talking about kissing, not hand to hand combat.'

Hugo stiffened instantly. 'Forgive me,' he said, not sounding the least bit contrite, but as if she'd wounded him, which was rich when Libby was sure she'd cricked something in her neck that would never right itself.

'I'm quite happy to kiss you again,' she said, which wasn't strictly true. 'But not like that. Like this ...'

She took his hands in hers then reached up to press the mere hint of a kiss to the corner of his mouth. Hugo stiffened even further so it was like trying to seduce a plank of wood. 'You could pretend I'm someone else, if it would help,' she murmured. 'Someone you'd much rather kiss.'

'I did ... I do want to kiss you,' Hugo mumbled back, his face stained red. Libby had to turn her head to hide her smile. 'I'm just ... I've never ... well, it all feels so horribly contrived, doesn't it? Kissing with an audience.'

Libby had kissed in front of packed houses before. There was nothing to it. You simply stared into the eyes of whoever was playing your besotted swain and shut out the rest of the world, the mutterers, the coughers and that one person at every performance who loudly crunched their way through a bag of mint imperials.

Libby gazed deep into Hugo's eyes, he had lovely eyes, blue as anything, framed by long lashes. He stared back at her and when she finally felt him relax, his hands stopped clutching convulsively at hers, she kissed him. Softly, sweetly, her lips parted. She tugged her hands free so she could caress the back of his neck, curl her fingers in his glossy black hair.

Eventually Hugo kissed her too, cradling Libby's face in his hands as if she were a thing to be treasured. Gentle, reverent kisses this time. Perhaps a little too gentle, a little too reverent, so Libby opened her mouth and kissed him back in what Hugo would probably call the French manner.

Libby was sure Hugo had stopped worrying about the grubby man outside watching them through binoculars, then Libby stopped worrying too and simply delighted in the feel of being in a man's arms again. Of kisses that made her quiver and how she wanted to coil herself about Hugo, because he wanted her terribly, she could feel it, and it had been so long since any man had wanted her.

She didn't even protest when Hugo pulled her away from the window and backed her up against the wall so he could touch her, palm her breasts, her ribs, with a light, ticklish touch that startled a laugh from her.

It was a dance and Libby still remembered all the steps. They moved through the flat, unbuttoning, tugging, peeling away their layers as they went, until they were in the bedroom, on the bed, and Libby hadn't planned this at all.

Neither had Hugo. Hadn't been spinning a yarn as an excuse to lure Libby to an empty flat because he parted her legs with hands that shook slightly and stared down at her with an awestruck expression on his face.

'Are you . . . ? I never expected this. Never dreamt that you might . . . you would want to . . . ' Hugo stammered, his words falling over themselves in a way that Libby found terribly endearing. 'You do want to, don't you?'

'I do. I absolutely do,' Libby said and he settled himself between her thighs and then he was in her, but what she loved most was that he was *on* her, that heavenly weight of a man in her arms, hard where she was soft, desperate where she was a little removed and so incredibly grateful that Libby was allowing him this.

Afterwards, Hugo held her in his arms and petted her nervously as if she were a skittish kitten.

Much later still, she slipped on the negligee that had been part of her trousseau that she'd taken with her to Brighton and they drank the rest of the champagne, nibbled on cold chicken sandwiches and strawberries from the hamper and much later than that, Hugo took Libby back to bed and made love to her again.

Libby didn't go back to Hampstead on Saturday morning, because Hugo begged her not to and they kissed again at the window still dressed in their nightclothes for the benefit of the detective and this time it was perfect.

Libby eventually left on Sunday evening, clinging to Hugo as they waited outside for a taxi, stealing one more kiss from him and she couldn't have cared if every private detective in London was peering at them through binoculars.

As she was driven through the dusky London streets, Libby thought only of Hugo. How he'd become more assured, more adept, a little more arrogant, though she never minded that, as they learned each other's bodies. The little things, the intimate clues of what it took to make each other gasp, plead for mercy. Libby thought of how she'd climbed on top of Hugo as he sat sprawled on the pristine white sofa and she'd ridden him like that while he mouthed her breasts, muttered invocations into her skin.

Then she thought of the very last time they'd made love, barely an hour before, when Hugo had taken her back to bed and done things that on Friday night he'd never have dreamed he was capable of doing. How she'd trembled and gasped and begged him to stop and to never stop and she'd come quite undone.

In that moment Libby had felt not transported, but frightened, vulnerable, as if she'd shown her hand far too soon. But then Hugo had stroked her skin, the long line of her spine, the curve of her behind, with sure, steady movements and said,

'I'm not falling in love with you, Libby. I am in love with you. I should be worrying about what a damn mess this all is, but I can't, because I'm so very glad about this. About being with you.'

All Libby was sure of was that even though she was sore from his lovemaking, her skin reddened and bruised, her lips stinging from his kisses, she still ached for Hugo's touch. Still wanted more. She could have stayed in his arms for another night, for a week, a month and it still wouldn't have been long enough.

Was that love? As the taxi sped her closer to Hampstead, the green trees and hedges of the heath a twilight blur outside the window, Libby decided that if it weren't love then it was close enough.

21

Zoe

It took nearly three weeks before Zoe was ready to bring Win home.

Then she was standing, at last, on Jackie's doorstep listening out for her mother-in-law's approach, which was preceded by the words, 'Are we expecting anyone, Gav? It better not be someone trying to sell me something.'

The door was wrenched open. Suspicion on Jackie's face, which transformed to a smile of pure pleasure when she saw it was Zoe, tempered with relief that she wouldn't have to put up with Win for much longer (Gavin had volunteered the information that mother and son were waged in psychological warfare over the correct way to load a dishwasher). Finally Jackie's gaze drifted to Beyoncé snuggled in Zoe's arms.

'Jesus Christ, Zo,' she spluttered. 'I've never seen a dog with such a swollen vulva.'

'Nice to see you too,' Zoe said, stepping inside the garden flat, which Jackie had bought for a song at the tail end of the recession before last. Every time Zoe visited there was a new interior design development. Something upcycled or distressed or painted one of Farrow & Ball's latest colours. It was how Jackie and Gavin had turned their friendship into something more; Jackie had his number on speed dial for the bigger jobs she couldn't manage herself and according to Win, Gav had been pining after Jackie for years.

Now, Gavin called out from the kitchen, 'Is that Zo? Is she staying for dinner?'

Zoe shook her head. 'I'm just here to take Win home.'

'Just go through,' Jackie said, squeezing Zoe's arm affectionately. 'He's not back from work yet. I haven't wanted to take sides, but oh my God, that boy is driving me to drink. He wants to clean everything *before* he puts it in the dishwasher and then he has the cheek to tell me that *my* way is the wrong way.'

'Win and dishwashers are never a good combination.' Zoe shifted a wriggling Beyoncé in her arms. 'So, I know you and Gav have been put in an awkward situation and I'm sorry about that but . . .'

Jackie was already shying away. 'I'll put the kettle on, shall I?'

Zoe looked round the living room as Jackie busied herself in the kitchen. Jackie's interiors aesthetic was best described as country cottage chic. Everything from TV stand to coffee table and radiator covers was distressed and Zoe counted at least five different floral prints, though it was the huge red roses on the curtains that really drew the eye. Pride of place on the mantelpiece was Zoe and Win's official wedding photo, though Zoe could have sworn that it used to live on the shelf above the TV.

Jackie might not be great at dispensing advice and talking about feelings, but she had other ways of getting her point across, Zoe thought as she heard the front door open. She

177

didn't even have time to arrange her face into a welcoming smile before Win appeared in the doorway.

Zoe's body, heart, her everything, gave a joyful tug in his direction because it had been three weeks and six days since they'd last seen each other.

From the day of their very first meeting all those years ago, when she'd walked into Win's office with two carrier bags full of invoices and receipts, they'd never gone so long without seeing each other.

It would have been the easiest thing in the world to rush over to Win and hug him, say she was glad to see him but Zoe was frozen, held back, by the uncertain look on his face. And when he saw Beyoncé sprawled on his mother's favourite armchair (Zoe hadn't thought to ask Jackie what her position was vis-à-vis dogs on furniture) he tensed up. Zoe found that she couldn't bear to meet Win's gaze. She stuffed her hands into the pockets of her coat, felt for the baby's button, as she tried to build herself up to launch into the speech she'd been rehearsing for days and days as she carried out her grand scheme to make Win happy. Or happier, at least.

The way her heart was twitching unpleasantly, teeth chewing at the inside of her right cheek, the words just out of reach, reminded Zoe of the night of Win's twenty-fifth birthday party.

By then, Win occupied an odd, undefined place in her life. Technically he was her accountant, but mostly he was her friend, though he had no idea how much Zoe yearned for him to be something more. Because they were friends, Win had invited Zoe to his party in a little Spanish bar in Camden and she'd gone with Tony Cortes in the hope that it would make Win furious to see her with another man. Zoe had been nineteen and everything she knew about relationships had been gleaned from *Cosmopolitan* and watching rom-coms.

So Zoe had walked into the bar, Tony Cortes following

close behind because he was already a bit drunk and he always got quite possessive when he was a bit drunk. Zoe had introduced the two of them.

'Tony, Win. Win, Tony.'

Tony had sized Win up; his tall lanky frame, his short back and sides haircut, jeans and neatly pressed T-shirt. Zoe could tell that he didn't think much of her new friend.

'Yeah, whatever. Nice to meet you, mate,' Tony had said, which was pretty civilised of him considering he'd done nothing but moan about having to go to 'some accountant's birthday party'.

Win had worked his jaw, much as Zoe was doing now, his face getting tighter and tighter, until he was all cheekbones and taut skin. Then he'd drawn himself up as if he were about to address the United Nations and said, 'Well, yeah, I'd say it was nice to meet you too, but it's not because I'm in love with your girlfriend. I'm in love with Zoe.'

It was still the singularly most romantic thing that Win, or anyone for that matter, had ever said to Zoe. Then Tony had tried to smack Win and Zoe had thrown herself between the two of them. Ed had intervened as it all spilled out onto the street, Tony shouting about 'his fucking bird' and insisting that he was going to fight Win to protect Zoe's honour.

She and Win had left the party, to wander along the Regent's Canal towpath and he'd barely said a word as if his declaration had used up all his powers of speech. The silence hadn't even mattered.

But now Win's silence mattered terribly and their positions were reversed. Zoe needed to say something singularly romantic, to speak the truth that was in her heart, the right combination of words that would bring Win back to her.

'What?' he finally asked in a hoarse voice. 'What are you doing here, Zo?'

It felt like a make or break, do or die moment in their marriage. That what happened or didn't happen in the next five minutes would change their lives, their relationship for ever.

Zoe shook her head, eyes imploring because she was trapped in a prison of her own inarticulacy. 'I ... You ...' She shook her head again. 'Get your coat, love, you've pulled.'

'*What?*'

Sometimes, all the fancy rehearsed speeches came to nothing and you blurted out the first thought that popped into your head.

'Come home with me,' Zoe said. 'Please, Win.'

'That house isn't a home,' Win said, his eyes down, his expression mutinous. 'I hate that house.'

Zoe wanted to scream or scoop up their official wedding photograph from the mantelpiece and hit Win over his incredibly thick head with it.

She didn't. She didn't cry either but tried to pick her words with care, speak them with meaning, imbue them with all the love she had for Win. 'The house might not be a home yet but your home is with me, Win. We're meant to be together.'

'You could move in here,' Win offered, stepped closer to Zoe, bridging the gap between them a little. 'Mum wouldn't mind.'

It would only be a temporary reprieve; a sticking plaster over the open fracture in their relationship. 'No. We both know that wouldn't work,' Zoe said with strong conviction. 'I want to fix this. Fix us, but I can't do it alone so you need to come home with me.'

There was a pause that lasted a lifetime. Whole civilisations rose and fell in the length of that pause. Then Win nodded. 'All right,' he said and within ten minutes he was packed and in the car, Beyoncé settled on his lap. The first time they'd met Win had been less than complimentary but Beyoncé wasn't the type to bear a grudge. She rested her head on his chest and gazed up at him with trusting brown eyes.

'I'd almost repressed the memory of how ridiculous her name is.' Win pulled a face. 'Sorry, I'm really not trying to pick a fight.'

'I said I'd foster her until she was spayed. She can't be put up for adoption until then,' Zoe said a little stiffly. 'And she can't be spayed until everything's calmed down a bit.' She gestured at Beyoncé and Win glanced down, lifted the small dog to see her undercarriage.

'Yeah, she is still looking a little er, pendulous,' he said and Zoe hummed in agreement and then neither of them said anything for the ten minutes it took to drive back to Highgate.

The house looked just as it had done when Win had last seen it. The skip on the drive full of rubble, heavy plastic sacks full of sand lined up on the garden path, broken crazy paving, the weeds. Zoe's spirits sank as she tried to take in the scene through Win's eyes.

Win cradled Beyoncé in his arms as Zoe unlocked the front door and then the smell and taste of plaster and dust assailed them both as they trod over the ubiquitous plastic sheeting laid down to protect the tiled hallway.

The house was in shadow but Win would be able to see that it was still broken. He took a step towards the living room, but Zoe held him back.

'Upstairs,' she said, struggling slightly with his hold-all because Win was still limping heavily. 'Can you carry Beyoncé? Otherwise she slips on the sheeting. I should have asked, how's the leg?'

'Better than it was,' Win said. 'My knee's still clicking and I'm not going to be running a marathon anytime soon, but it's improving. Slowly. So, are we still camped out in the back bedroom?'

'Not exactly.'

Four weeks ago the back bedroom was still the only vaguely habitable room in the house but after they'd made their laborious way up the stairs, Zoe paused at the door of the big front bedroom. 'I can't click my fingers so the last six months never happened,' she said. 'I can't give you the dream home that you want either, all I can give you right now is three rooms.'

She pushed open the door. The last time Win had been in here it had been a barren space with bare plaster walls, unvarnished floorboards, the ceiling bearing the marks of water damage from the leaking roof, a light bulb dangling down from looped electrical cord.

Win took one step over the threshold, then stilled. 'Oh my God,' he breathed, because now ... The walls had been painted the soft smudgy grey blue that they'd talked about, the floorboards sanded and painted white, the ceiling was pristine.

Zoe had retrieved some of their furniture from storage; the chest of drawers and nightstands. The lovely vintage dressing table set that Win had bought her for her twenty-fifth birthday had been placed in the alcove in front of the bay window, where their curtains hung. And of course, the bed Zoe had bought with Win's guidance all those years ago. Now the pillows seemed a little plumper than they used to, the duvet billowed like a cloud and the Orla Kiely bedlinen Zoe had bought in a flash internet sale was as smooth and wrinkle-free as any millpond.

Zoe had worked hard to get every detail just right. Perfect. The alarm clock set for seven thirty, the book that Win had been reading before he left and the fancy docking station for his fitbit and iPhone all arranged on Win's bedside table.

'Oh, Zo,' he said. 'How did you do this?'

'With a lot of help from Cath and Theo. Gav stayed behind for an extra hour or so some evenings. Even Ed came over last weekend to sand the floorboards.'

'No one said anything.'

'They were sworn to secrecy and there's more,' Zoe said. She rapped the wall nearest to her. 'In an ideal world, there'd be a door here so we could have an en-suite bathroom but the budget wouldn't stretch to it.'

'I think we'll manage somehow,' Win said as they left the bedroom to enter the bathroom next door.

It wasn't such a huge transformation. There were still the same 1930s' fittings but, along with the original mint-green and black wall tiles, they'd been buffed to a glossy shine. There were matching black tiles on the floor now, a proper shower installed because a showerhead above the bath wasn't good enough. Zoe's favourite thing of all was the vintage display unit, an eBay find, that looked as if it had come from an old-fashioned apothecary's shop, where their towels and bathroom products were neatly stacked.

Win was still in a daze as she showed him into one of the back bedrooms on the other side of the bathroom. 'For now, this is our lounge while they're working downstairs.'

There were the same white floorboards as in their bedroom, the walls a soft chalky white and, instead of the deckchairs they'd been sitting on, their velvet grey sofa and armchairs had been rescued from the storage unit.

Apart from the fridge and the microwave, which had now migrated upstairs, as a temporary living room the space was also perfect, right down to Win's collection of *Mojo* magazines on the coffee table and two wineglasses to go with the bottle of Sauvignon Blanc Zoe was taking out of the fridge.

'I don't know what to say.' Win gazed around him and blinked. 'Should I go away more often?'

'No, you really shouldn't. Please, sit down,' Zoe said, as if she were interviewing him for a job. 'I need to talk to you about the house.'

It was easier to talk about the house, a tangible thing made of bricks and mortar, plasterboard and pipework, than the other things that were less solid but had still driven a wedge between them.

Win settled himself on the sofa, Beyoncé still in his arms. He put the dog down beside him. 'Will you sit down too?' he asked Zoe, who'd poured out the wine and was standing over him. 'What you've done with these rooms, they're amazing. You're amazing.'

Zoe's smile was an echo of what it could be. 'Look, we're stuck with this house. We've sunk every penny we have into it, signed a covenant that said we'd live here for five years before we even think about selling it but they don't have to be awful years. We could be happy here. I want us to be happy again, Win.'

Win looked round the room again at all their dear familiar things. Sofa, armchairs, cushions, curtains, it was just *stuff* but all of it carefully chosen, deliberated over, as they'd made a home. Together. 'I want us to be happy again too,' he said slowly and even now there was half a metre and a gulf between them. 'It's just . . . the thing is . . . I don't even know . . . '

When Win was stumbling over his words, trying to force out his thoughts and give them voice, Zoe knew not to prompt him, talk over him, but it seemed as if he were done.

Beyoncé shuffled over to her and curled up so her head was nestled in Zoe's cleavage again, her preferred resting place. 'I shouldn't have agreed to foster a dog without discussing it with you,' Zoe said. 'But even before that, we'd hardly talked in weeks. Not properly.'

'You, of all people, you should know that my quietness . . . ' Win groaned in pure frustration. 'My quietness doesn't mean

I don't care. You know that, Zo. And these last few months . . . ever since it happened, you won't let me touch you, won't let me see you. These are worse things than not speaking.'

'That's not true,' Zoe began then stopped. She replayed all those times when she shied away from Win's hand, tensed at his touch, crept as far as she could to the other side of the bed every night. Got undressed in the bathroom or like she was struggling to get out of a swimming costume under cover of a towel on a windy, public beach. 'I'm sorry. It's just that ever since I left hospital, I haven't felt right in my own skin.' She shook her head, cuddled Beyoncé a little bit tighter. It was still so hard to try and make sense of the mess and muddle inside her head. 'I've been so let down by my own body. All those weeks with a time bomb lodged in me, like a virus, and sometimes I think it's still there, ticking away, ready to infect anyone that gets too close. That's why I didn't want you near me.'

'Zoe . . . ' Win breathed out and he didn't say anything but didn't try to touch her either, which Zoe was grateful for. Not because she still felt tainted but because one brush of Win's fingers against her arm, her cheek, and she would break down and cry and this was not the time for tears. Her tears hadn't solved anything.

'I'm sorry too. For being so silent when I knew you were hurting but God, it's always impossible for me to find the right words. I'm sorry about what I said about the pregnancy.' Win flinched as he said the word. 'When I told you to stop dwelling on it, it's because I can't bear to dwell on it at all. I know we need to talk about it but I can't. Not yet. But I can talk about the house, I can do that . . . '

It was something. Something was better than nothing. Zoe nodded. 'What do you want to say about the house then?' she asked a little dully because she was sure it was going to be the usual litany of complaints.

Win tipped his head back and sighed. 'We moved round so much when I was a kid. I know that Ed and I talk a good game, make it sound like it was all larks, but it wasn't. A lot of times it was unpredictable, scary.' He reached out to gently scratch Beyoncé behind her ears. 'The dog we used to have, Brandy. One time we had to move in a hurry and Terry just left her behind. Said someone was coming to pick her up, but the next time he got drunk, he confessed. Always cracked under the pressure, did Terry.'

He took a huge gulp of wine and seemed comforted that Zoe was letting him speak. Didn't pepper him with questions.

'We moved all the time. Not just every few months, but sometimes every few weeks, even days. It got to the point where we didn't bother to unpack. So, I'm not being a princess, I'm really not, when I'm bitching about the lack of a kitchen or hot water. That there are wires and holes everywhere. I can't handle the chaos and the upheaval because in my experience it only leads to bad things; bailiffs banging at the front door or scary-looking men who want a word with my dad knocking at the windows then us having to clear out in a hurry and start all over again. Every time I come back to this house, it's a sense memory of some of my worst times.' Win let out a shaky breath and Zoe moved closer so he could list to the right and she was there to lean on.

'I knew things were tough when you were a kid but I had no idea they were that grim.' Zoe tried to keep the heat, the hurt, out of her voice because she really didn't want this to turn into a row. 'You hardly ever talk about Terry.'

'Because there's nothing good to say about him. Nothing worth burdening you with, anyway.'

'But I don't mind being burdened,' Zoe persisted. 'Honestly, I'm stronger than I look; you know that better than anyone. I've even gone quite a few days without crying.'

It was a weak joke to let Win off the hook and he smiled dutifully.

'It's all ancient history: Terry, all the crappy places we lived. It's in the past,' Win said, as if what belonged in the past never ever impinged on the present and the future. 'At least I hope it does, the bailiffs and all that.'

'I promise you there will be no bailiffs,' Zoe said because she never made promises she couldn't keep. 'I can also promise you that the house renovations aren't going to come even close to bankrupting us.' Now that she was on a steadier ground, she couldn't help the smugness creeping into her voice.

'Really?' Win sounded hopeful. 'Have you had any film rights optioned? Or did you get five numbers and the bonus ball on the Lotto?'

They always said that winning the Lotto was too greedy but five numbers and the bonus ball would be just enough money.

'I wish. Actually, I've been revising our budget.' Zoe sniffed, as Win looked at her like she was talking in tongues. 'It was horrible. I have a new appreciation for how hard your job is. Do you want me to hit the highlights?'

'Knock yourself out,' Win drawled with a little of that old archness that Zoe had missed so much.

The good news was that a combi-boiler compatible with their rare 1930s' radiators had been sourced at last. 'I had to go on a central heating engineers' forum board and throw myself on their mercy,' Zoe explained. 'I now know more about radiator valves than I ever wanted to.'

'So, you're saying that we don't have to fork out for new radiators?' Win clarified hopefully.

'Exactly that and I've massively scaled back our plans for the kitchen. We're going for the cheapest kitchen I can find. It will probably be made entirely out of plastic. And for the rest of it, well ... I'm going to do a lot of the decorating myself. You're going to help, by the way.'

'OK,' Win said, with apprehension because he was fond of saying, as if it were something to be proud of, that he didn't possess a single artistic bone in his body. But even he could slap paint on a wall. With supervision. 'It's not like we can afford to go on holiday this year so I can take some time off work.'

'And weekends. Gavin says that they'll prep everything and your mum says she'll help too. She's promised not to ragroll anything.' Zoe and Win both grimaced at the thought. 'Also, when my parents fly back from Vietnam, they're staying with us for a fortnight and have offered to sort out the garden.'

'Thank God for Ken and Nancy.' Win's hand shot out to clutch Zoe's knee. 'All of this ... it would have been better if they'd been here, don't you think?'

'A hundred thousand times better.' It was hardly a ringing endorsement of their joint coping skills.

Zoe covered Win's hand, which was still on her leg. 'I'm not the nervous nineteen-year-old that walked into your office all those years ago,' she said quietly. Now, instead of refusing to look each other in the eye, Zoe couldn't tear her gaze away from Win. Nearly a month apart and she had to relearn every inch of him. 'You were right when you said I expect you to fix everything. That's how we started our relationship, with you fixing my problems, and the habit stuck. But I'm perfectly capable of fixing them too. And there are some things that can't be fixed anyway, we just have to deal with them in the best way that we can.'

Win raised Zoe's hand to his lips so he could press a kiss against her knuckles. It was the most intimate gesture they'd shared in months. 'I need to be in control. And when we moved in here, I thought that at least the house, the renovations, would be something I could control.' Win shot Zoe a knowing look. 'Dare I ask if my handy wall planner is still in operation?'

'Best not to.' Taking it down had been her very first act as project manager. Gavin had got down on his knees and kissed her feet. But that was the only secret Zoe wanted to keep from him. Though the other secrets, the things still to be said, could wait. For now.

They sat and drank the wine, with Beyoncé burrowed between them, as they looked at kitchens online. They'd had wilder evenings than this, but when Win brushed his hand against the back of her neck, Zoe's skin warmed to his touch, and instead of shrinking back from it, she couldn't think of anywhere else she'd rather be.

22

Libby

'I've decided to stay with my friend in town on the weekends,' Libby explained to the assembled company at Willoughby Square. 'Now that it's summer, there's so many invites; picnics and parties and dances, and it's such fun to get ready then go home with one's chums isn't it?'

'I would never have dreamt of going out without my dear Arthur.' Millicent quivered magnificently at the head of the breakfast table. 'Certainly I wouldn't have been gallivanting to all hours as if I were still unwed.'

Libby couldn't imagine that Millicent had ever once gallivanted. She wasn't the gallivanting sort. 'Freddy's in Spain,' she said evenly. 'Besides, it's the nineteen thirties. Times have changed.'

If possible, Potts, hardly a paragon of virtue himself, was even more disapproving than Millicent. 'This will not end well, sweetling,' he'd warned later that same Friday afternoon when Libby dashed back to Willoughby Square for long enough to snatch up her small weekend case.

'Oh, Potts, I don't know what you mean,' Libby said, as she primped her hair in front of the mottled hall mirror. 'Or are you simply passing on a message from your spirit guides?'

'I see things,' Potts said, coming up behind her. He wasn't drunk, for once, but so pale and trembling that he did rather look like a ghostly apparition in the glass and Libby couldn't help but tremble too. 'I see angels on your shoulder, Elizabeth.'

'Angels? That's a good thing, surely?' Libby insisted. 'Angels are on the side of right.'

Potts shook his head, assumed a pained expression, even when Libby stuffed a half crown in his shirt pocket because she wanted to be gone. Didn't want doubt and uncertainty dogging her when she was so happy, already hoarding the forty-eight hours she'd spend with Hugo.

And when she walked through the door of the flat, Hugo was waiting for her. How she lived for the smile that slowly crept over his face as he got up from the chair where he sat and walked over to her. As he came closer, the early evening sun backlit him so he rather looked like an angel himself.

'You're so beautiful,' he said, taking her case so he could place it on the floor and pull her into his arms. 'I always forget how beautiful you are. Then each week you take my breath away all over again.'

'I'm many things, beautiful isn't one of them,' Libby scoffed because certainly no casting agent or director had ever thought so. At best, she'd got 'pretty' in an offhand voice.

Hugo cupped her face in his hands, though Libby had learned by now to ward him off until she'd checked he hadn't been up to his elbows in a car's innards and had missed a streak of grease or oil when he'd washed afterwards. 'Quite beautiful,' he declared. 'All of you. Every single inch of you.'

Hugo was already unhooking her dress, kissing the hollows and dips of her collarbones, the curve of her breasts.

Dropping to his knees to pull the material free of her hips as if Libby were some sort of goddess.

Then he slipped down her knickers so he could worship her there and it was only when he tumbled her down on to the floor, right by the front door, that Libby remembered that she wasn't some divine being but made of flesh and heated blood and she could kiss Hugo back. Arched back from his insistent body so she could unbutton his trousers, take him in her hands because much as she loved him, she loved to see him truly come apart even more.

He was magnificent when he was inside her, rearing back, the muscles in his arms taut, a slick of dark hair falling into his face. His eyes clouded, jaw clenched, his lips curled back and still he managed to say it even as his thrusts became more brutal, more desperate. 'I love you. I love you. I love you.'

It should have come as no surprise that a man as stiff and as starched as Hugo would become so fierce, so passionate, so out of control once he'd loosened his collar, taken off his tie, unbuttoned. Libby had wanted to know what was beneath the prim and proper face that he showed to the rest of the world and it was this man, his eyes dark with wicked promise, the mouth, that did such wonderful things to her, curved in a smile. This man who touched her skin, her breasts, the secret place between her thighs with a knowing, tormenting ease. This man proud and naked as he lay in bed next to her, the curtains still pulled back so they could see the sun set in a glorious sky streaked pink and orange. This man who, once again, said, 'I do love you, Libby.'

Libby smiled. 'There's nowhere else I'd rather be than right here,' she murmured as she settled back in his arms.

'You don't love me too?' Hugo asked casually, though Libby could feel the tension thrum through him.

'When I tell a man I love him, then it's guaranteed that I

won't see him for dust.' There was little point in prevaricating. Hugo already knew that Libby's past was as chequered as a draughtboard.

Hugo stroked a finger down her profile; her chin, neck, between her breasts. 'I'm not like the other men,' he said as if he were making Libby a solemn promise.

'And that's why I love being with you,' was the best she could offer him, until she was absolutely certain of his heart, his intentions.

'We should be together. Always,' he told her.

'Always lasts for ever,' Libby said carefully because those other men had talked of always too and it turned out that always never lasted that long. 'You might grow tired of me halfway through for ever.'

'That's not possible. I could never have enough time with you.' Hugo pressed his mouth to the line of freckles that adorned the underside of her left breast and though Libby could have sworn she was spent, her nipples hardened, her insides turned liquid and molten. 'These weekends hidden away as if we should be ashamed; I want to spend every day with you. Wake up with you, come home to you.'

'You do?' Libby couldn't think of what she'd done to inspire such feelings but she hoped, how she hoped, that Hugo would feel this way for a little longer. Oh, she wasn't ready for this to end. 'It would be nice to have someone who wanted to come home to me.'

'I was hoping for better than nice.'

'Wonderful, then,' Libby amended. 'To have you thinking about me all day as you were tinkering about with your cars, then coming home to me every evening. What a lovely life that would be.'

Considering all those years on the stage, all those parties, nightclubs, romantic intrigues, it should have sounded a

193

boring way to end up; the little woman waiting for her man to come home, but it didn't. It sounded heavenly.

Hugo rolled over, presenting Libby with the long line of his back as he reached for his jacket, which had been tossed on the floor. Libby marvelled at how at ease he was now in his own skin, a throaty rumble coming from him as she pressed a finger to the dimple at the base of his spine, because she was more than ready to go again.

Hugo returned with his cigarette case and lighter and Libby hoped that they were finished with talking about a future so rosy, so golden that it was impossible.

'It's easy enough if you're the King of England, I suppose,' Hugo said as Libby took the cigarette he was offering.

'What is?' Libby asked.

'Obtaining a divorce for that woman of his. Wallis Simpson.'

There hadn't been anything in the papers about Wallis Simpson for weeks and so if she'd stopped to think about it then Libby supposed that her affair with the King had died a death. It would have to. 'He could never marry her,' she said.

Hugo blew out a thin plume of smoke ruminatively. 'Why? Because she's been divorced?'

'That, and she's an American!' It was clear that Hugo had no interest in ravishing her for the time being so Libby sat up and tucked a pillow behind her, drew the sheet up to cover her breasts, the scar that Hugo always avoided, no matter how thorough his attentions to the rest of her body. 'You say that it's easy for him, but he's the King and yet he can't get married to the woman he loves.'

'Tell that to Henry the eighth,' Hugo said with a snort.

'Isn't it precisely because of Henry the eighth that they don't let today's kings run about willy-nilly doing whatever they please?'

'Then I'm glad I'm not the King and that I can get married to the woman I love.' Hugo took Libby's hand, his finger worrying at the ring that Freddy had placed there. 'Not right away, you understand. After my divorce is granted. Do you think your Freddy would put up a fight when you ask him for a divorce?'

'Oh, please, let's not talk about this, about divorces, about Freddy and your Pamela,' Libby begged. 'It gives me such a horrible, gloomy feeling.'

'If we don't talk about it now, then when? I love you. Do you love me too?'

Libby couldn't stall any longer. 'Don't be silly. Of course I love you!' She must have said 'I love you' hundreds of times but now she tried to convey the true depth, the heft of the words, in the tone of her voice. 'All I want is to be loved, to have someone who loves me, who makes me happy.'

'You do realise that it's not quite as simple as that,' Hugo said, and he tried to settle Libby back into his arms but she wouldn't go.

Love was never simple for Libby – but for everyone else love was an absolute breeze.

'I didn't mean to upset you, darling. Don't look so sad.' Hugo kissed one of the downturned corners of her mouth. 'It's just that once the judge in his infinite wisdom allows us to walk away from the two people who wished they'd never married us in the first place, we can't see each other for six months.'

'Six months?' Libby repeated incredulously. 'What business is it of theirs?'

'Six months when we can't have any contact until our divorces have been finalised. The King's Proctor's office employs detectives to ensure we're obeying their ridiculous rules, though I'm damned if I can see what difference it makes.' Hugo viciously stubbed out his cigarette in the ashtray on the nightstand. It was one of the reasons why Libby hated it when they talked about his divorce – it made him so angry. Seething with the injustice of it all. 'But it needn't be so bad. We can write to each other. Talk on the telephone.'

'I'm not on the telephone,' Libby reminded him and she thought about how it would be not to see Hugo for six months when she'd seen him once a week since February. More than once a week. Being with him had given her life, which always felt so transient, new purpose. Given her something to look forward to, to get her through the week. And now there was this Friday night to Sunday afternoon when he made her heart stop hurting and taught her body how to sing again.

It this wasn't love, then Libby didn't know what was.

'We'll have to put you on the telephone then,' Hugo said. He was so determined now his affections had been declared that Libby let herself be cheered up.

'You really are the sweetest man.' She curled herself around him and Hugo smiled as if just her touch was enough to make him happy. 'But we're not on the electric at Willoughby Square and surely you can't have a telephone without electricity. Besides, Millicent might just explode if she found out that my fancy man was going to connect us to the local exchange.'

'More than just your fancy man, Libby. At least, I hope I'm more than that,' he said quietly, leaning down to kiss the top of her head.

'Much more than that,' Libby said. 'But I could just be your fancy woman. Afterwards, we don't have to get married. We could be together and what we are, husband and wife, or simply lovers, well, it's nobody's affair but ours.'

It was when she expected something from her men, made what they called 'demands' on them, wanted an indication that she was more than just an amusing diversion, that their so-called love inevitably turned sour.

Libby realised her mistake immediately for Hugo took his hands off her. 'I'm not the sort of man to take advantage of a woman,' he said in the same acid-drop voice that she remembered all too clearly from that first weekend in Brighton. 'Certainly not the woman I'm in love with. I'd marry you tomorrow if the law would have it.'

'It's just a piece of paper. It doesn't mean anything. We both know that. I want to be with you, that's enough, surely?'

Her marriage had barely lasted two months. It hadn't made Freddy love her more. In truth, it had made him restless and desperate to be free once he was tied to her by dry words recited in a town hall, their names scratched on official documents.

So, Libby really didn't need to be married again. It was tempting fate.

'You're not still in love with your Freddy?' Hugo asked.

'He was never my Freddy.' Libby struggled upright, accidentally digging Hugo in the ribs with her elbow so he hissed in pain. 'Darling, please, what we have is so precious, more than I ever dared hope I'd have again, let's be content with that. For the time being, at least.'

Then she leaned over and peppered his face with kisses until she'd wiped away his mulish expression and he was laughing at her onslaught.

'This is no way to win an argument,' he protested, trying to hold Libby back as she climbed astride him.

'I'm sick of talking about it,' she said firmly as she ground her hips against his, once, twice, three times and was rewarded by his eyes darkening and the tiny groan he gave, before he rose up with a dramatic roar to rival any villain's, which made Libby shriek in turn, and rolled them so she was underneath and he was on top, plucking the sheet away from her, to drive her quite mad with his mouth and fingers.

23

Libby

Libby had known that the conversation wasn't over, merely deferred.

The following Wednesday, when she left lessons early because she had a queer sort of headache and her limbs felt heavy like they were made from sandbags, there was a letter waiting for her.

It had a London postmark, her name and address written in a hand that Libby recognised but that most definitely wasn't Freddy's, so it had escaped Millicent's curious scrutiny, though Libby wouldn't have put it past her to steam it open.

Libby headed straight for the garden in the hope that the fresh air would clear her head. There was a patch of grass between the apple trees at the bottom where she could sit in shade while she read.

Darling girl
I have to write this so that you have unassailable proof of my feelings, my regard.

I love you. I want to marry you. I must make plans for our future.

Not just the future that we'll spend together but for those six months, after our divorces, when I must not even drive over to Hampstead to gaze up at your windows like a lovesick schoolboy.

It would make me happy, set my mind at ease, if you'll agree that it's for the best if you move out of your mother-in-law's house.

If it suits, I could start arrangements to purchase the flat in Highgate.

All I ask is that if you do return even a fraction of my love, and if you could bear to spend the rest of your life with me, will you write to Freddy? Make him understand that he needs to return to London to start divorce proceedings.

Such a sordid business, isn't it? But if we can get through these few ugly months then our days ever after will be golden.

All my love

Hugo

Libby folded the piece of paper with a sigh. Her head was swimming, clouded with thoughts, stomach churning. The air was so heavy and close that she wondered if it might storm.

She would have to write to Freddy, there was nothing else for it. As it was, their marriage was long dead. But that didn't mean Libby had to rush into marriage with Hugo. Perhaps it was just as well they'd have to wait six months after their respective divorces before they could reunite. All sorts of things could happen in six months. Hugo's ardour could cool. He might meet someone else, fall in love with them ... it wouldn't be unprecedented.

Just the thought of it was enough that there was a very real possibility Libby might be sick in the nearest overgrown flowerbed. But fighting her way through the weeds was Hannah, eyes squinting against the glare of the sun, as she carried a loaded tray towards Libby.

Libby didn't have the heart to tell Hannah that the sight of the cheese sandwich and slice of fruit cake that had been placed on Millicent's finest bone china made her feel bilious. Instead she smiled wanly. 'Tea? What a sweetie you are.'

Despite the heat of the day, Hannah looked pale and pouty. Even though fires no longer needed to be lit, the sun brought its own tasks, showed up the dust and grime that collected in every corner of the house. Libby couldn't remember the last time that Hannah had been given an afternoon off.

'Why don't you stay?' she suggested. 'Here, have a sandwich.'

With an anxious glance at the house as if she expected to see Millicent suddenly burst through the kitchen door in a righteous fury, Hannah arranged her sturdy limbs on the grass. She took a sandwich from the plate Libby was proffering and anxiously nibbled the edges.

'She said that when she was my age, she'd never have dared to be as ungrateful as I am,' Hannah said through a mouthful of bread and very thinly sliced cheese. 'Says that she'll have to dock my wages because I broke the milk jug. It was chipped anyway. Chipped before I even got here!' she finished on an aggrieved note.

'Oh dear.' Libby tucked a lock of Hannah's unruly brown hair behind her ear. 'Let's talk of something happier. If you showed me a picture of a style you liked in one of your magazines, I could cut your hair for you.'

She was tempted, Libby could tell, but then Hannah stuck out her chin.

'There won't be time to cut my hair before I run away,' she declared. 'First chance I get, I'm off!'

'Well I wouldn't do that.' Libby had to bite her bottom lip to hide her smile. 'You might get abducted by white-slave traders and you wouldn't want that to happen, would you?'

'I'm sure they couldn't treat me any worse than Mrs Morton.'

'Oh, I'm sure they could. I knew a girl, was in rep with her, who was abducted by white-slave traders when she wasn't much older than you,' Libby said, lowering her voice for dramatic effect. She did love to spin a yarn and Hannah did love to listen to yarns being spun. 'They packed her off on a steamer boat to Morocco and there they beat her savagely until she learned to do the dance of the seven veils, then they changed her name to Salome and she was forced to perform that salacious dance every night, sometimes twice a night, for all sorts of louche, debauched men who'd stare at her nubile body with their opera glasses until all seven veils had been removed.'

Libby had known a girl who'd performed the dance of the seven veils twice a night in a less than salubrious club in Soho but white-slave traders had nothing to do with it. Monica had been left high and dry by her husband who'd buggered off with a chorus girl half her age and poor old Monica had two kids to feed and rent to pay.

Hannah didn't know that. 'Being abducted by white-slave traders sounds marvellous,' she breathed.

'My friend was beaten savagely,' Libby reminded her with a grin and Hannah, gloomy no more, grinned back. She was only sixteen and if Charlotte had lived she'd have just celebrated her twenty-sixth birthday, but still Hannah was a small reminder of what it had been like to have a little sister.

Hannah scrambled to her feet. 'Mrs Morton wants me to take the kippers back to the fishmonger. Says they're not fresh and he's trying to ruin her.'

Though true vegetarians eschewed fish, Millicent wasn't one of them. Alas. The mere thought of kippers, fresh or otherwise, brought up a mouthful of bile and Libby had to wash it away with a hasty gulp of tea, which made her feel sicker. 'Could you take the tray? I'm really not at all hungry.' She clumsily got to her feet though suddenly being upright made her head swim and sparkling spots dance in front of her eyes. 'I have things to do. Can't be lazing the rest of the day away.'

As Libby hauled herself up the stairs, the higher she climbed, the sicker she felt, she resolved to write to Freddy to ask for a divorce right away.

When one had a decent man pledging his undying love to you, it was best to hang onto him as hard as one could.

24

Zoe

The long summer days had finally arrived and on weekday evenings, Zoe would meet Win at the entrance to Highgate Woods with Beyoncé and a packed supper.

As soon as the little dog caught sight of Win limping across the road at the traffic lights, she'd go rigid in her harness. Her pump-handle tail would wag with a manic metronomic rhythm, she'd start to shake, ears pricked up, and as Win got nearer, she'd strain at the lead, her whole body a quivering arrow pointing in his direction.

When Win was finally close enough that Zoe could kiss him, Beyoncé would force them apart so she could twist and turn in an effort to make sure that every part of her body made contact with Win's legs. For her final act, she'd roll onto her back and present her belly to be rubbed. Panting, huffing and wheezing as Win stroked her tummy, legs frantically pedalling in the air, until the ecstasy was just too much and she had to push Win away.

It was one hell of a welcome.

'How come you're never that pleased to see me?' Win asked Zoe, because they were trying hard to get back to that place where they could tease each other.

'It's not just you,' Zoe said, as they wound their way through the twisty gates into the woods. 'When I get back from the shops, she greets me like I've just come home from a twelve-month deployment in Afghanistan.'

Once Beyoncé was done worshipping at the altar of Win, Zoe would slip her long lead on and they'd head for the playing field to eat their supper. Supper was usually sandwiches made from whatever was on special offer in Lidl, then they'd walk the shaded paths, the canopy of trees providing them with some relief from the heat of the sun still high in the sky.

Zoe had thought that by getting out of the house, they could talk about the house, without arguing about it as they had done in the past. But now that Win's wall planner had been decommissioned and Win had agreed to be consulted only on a need-to-know basis, it turned out there wasn't really that much he needed to know about, and he seemed quite relieved not to be getting daily updates.

They didn't talk about the baby either though Zoe had hoped that they might be able to test the edges of the wound to see if it had begun to heal – but it was still too sore.

So mostly they talked about Beyoncé because as Win noted, 'She's got quite a lot of personality, hasn't she?' She was the most human of dogs; bustling up and down paths looking for all the world as if she were carrying out a health and safety inspection. She also delighted in policing the other dogs they met, wading in to stop fights or break up behaviour she deemed too boisterous, which had inspired Zoe to invent a silly crime-fighting caper with Beyoncé as its heroine.

It was a relief to know that she could still make Win laugh

as she described a 1930s' Beyoncé ('though obviously she wouldn't be called Beyoncé') and her owner, an officious little girl called Beatrice and how they'd patrol the woods and sniff out wrongdoings: a brooch stolen by a gang of magpie thugs. Bullies in the playground vanquished. A lost baby squirrel reunited with its siblings. Beyoncé and Beatrice were free to right these wrongs because Beatrice's French governess was more interested in being wooed by a dashing woodsman – that was Win's contribution.

'Though it was the nineteen thirties,' he'd mused. 'I think they had a very lax attitude to childrearing. Not like Amanda and Ed. The nephews aren't allowed out on their scooters without so much protective padding that it's a wonder they can still scoot.'

The woods didn't close until nine fifteen on these midsummer evenings and it wasn't until they heard the bell ring the fifteen-minute warning that they'd gather up their stuff and go back to the house.

Zoe knew it couldn't last: these few precious weeks, their walks in the woods, putting the past on hold. Caroline, her agent, had been as good as her word and wangled Zoe a week's worth of children's workshops in Edinburgh under the auspices of the Scottish Book Trust. 'I think someone who's sold way more books than me cancelled at the last minute,' Zoe had explained to Win wryly. 'But it's three hundred quid a day.'

So, even though Beyoncé was due to be spayed on the Monday, Zoe was booked on a train from King's Cross first thing Saturday morning.

'I feel horrible deserting Beyoncé when she needs me the most,' Zoe said, as she stuffed socks down the side of her case on the Friday night. 'Are you absolutely sure you can work from home Monday and Tuesday?'

'Absolutely sure,' Win said, stroking behind the ears of the dog in question who was slumbering on top of his pillow, although he'd been quite adamant that she was never to be allowed on the bed. 'And she won't be on her own the rest of the week, Gavin will be here. She'll be fine.'

Zoe ran a hand through her hair, which was too long but in their latest economy drive, trips to the hairdresser were out. Amanda had offered to cut it when they'd met for lunch. 'I do the boys' hair,' she'd said, but the nephews' hair always looked as if someone had chewed the ends so Zoe had politely declined. 'What if she has complications?'

'There's no need to whisper, I don't think she's listening,' Win said. He considered the problem for a minute as he wrestled with his knee support, which had stickily cleaved itself to his skin. 'If she's not doing well, needs someone to keep an eye on her, then I could take her into work.'

'See, this is why we can't have a dog. You can't be spontaneous with a dog. No suddenly taking off for the weekend.'

'I don't do spontaneity,' Win reminded her with a slightly sheepish smile. 'I need at least six weeks' notice before I can agree to a minibreak. But it's true, we're not in the right place in our lives to have a dog.'

They really weren't, but it was still with the heaviest heart that Zoe walked with Win and Beyoncé to Highgate Tube station on Saturday morning, where Cath, Theo and Clive were waiting.

Cath had decided to spend the weekend in Edinburgh with Zoe, then travel on a to a writer's retreat in Stirling, with no Wi-Fi, no TV and lots of stirring and inspiring views so she could finally finish her novel.

'But first we lay Edinburgh to waste,' she announced with relish.

Win looked sceptical. 'Oh, really?'

'I've already emailed all the mothers in the Midlothian area warning them to lock up their sons,' Zoe deadpanned. 'What will you be doing while we're gone?'

'Manly pursuits,' Clive said. He was leaning heavily on his walking frame, a new acquisition, which he'd railed against almost as much as the stairlift, but the fact he'd left the house and the lure of the television spoke volumes for how much better he was doing. 'There's a cricket match on the field at Highgate Woods tomorrow, for one thing.'

Zoe had hoped that these manly pursuits might also involve sanding down the stairs but that wasn't important right now. 'Please keep Beyoncé out of the path of any stray cricket balls.' She'd also written a detailed list of the dog's daily requirements; it rivalled any list that Win had ever written, and ended with the particular way that Beyoncé liked to be tucked up of an evening. Then there was the spaying ... 'She'll wonder why I wasn't there to save her from a trip to the vet,' Zoe said as Win held Beyoncé up and waggled her front paws like she was waving goodbye. 'She hates going to the vet.'

'You'll miss your train,' Win warned her. 'Beyoncé will be fine. They'll give her the good drugs. She won't know a thing. Now, text me when you arrive and don't forget to bring home some shortbread. Hope the ankle-biters don't actually bite.'

Zoe was pretty sure that Win would rather attend a week-long conference on corporation tax or changes to the law surrounding bankruptcy procedures, a week-long conference on anything, than five days doing back-to-back workshops with a bunch of under-sevens.

He adored his nephews who adored him right back even though he called them Extra Large, Large, Medium and Small because he said he couldn't be expected to remember their names. Then there were Milo and Maisie, Flavia-from-next-door's twins, who were always coming round to ask if

Beyoncé was allowed out to play and who Win regarded as a source of much amusement.

But when confronted with large groups of children at family parties or friends' barbecues, Win became awkward and ungainly. Even worse, he assumed a cringing voice of forced jollity like a children's TV presenter on steroids, which didn't fool anyone, least of all your average child.

'Aren't you terrified?' Win had asked Zoe that morning. 'You hate public speaking.'

Zoe would rather have root canal treatment without an anaesthetic than have to speak in front of a grown-up audience but thirty six-year-olds didn't faze her.

'It's all good,' she'd said lightly. 'What I lack as an authority figure, I make up for by being able to draw dinosaurs.'

The thought came to Zoe as the train chugged into Newcastle station. Cath had disappeared to the buffet car for more crisps and Zoe's attention was a caught by a man across the aisle reading *Room on the Broom* aloud to his two small daughters.

She and Win would make great parents.

Whatever qualities Zoe lacked, Win would more than compensate. He'd be firm, consistent, all about establishing boundaries, but silly and indulgent too. And kind, so kind. All the reasons why Zoe loved him were all the reasons Win would make a wonderful father. Suddenly she had an image of him bent over a child, their child, a tiny downy head cradled in his large hand, and she had to catch her breath.

The image kept coming back to her the entire week she was away. The picture made sharper by the time spent with so many small children and her evenings in a hotel room on the phone to Win for Beyoncé updates, house updates and then just chatting about nothing and everything in a way they hadn't done for ages.

This time, Zoe dared to hope that being apart would bring them together.

Then, on the Thursday night, Win made her cry.

'Beyoncé was adopted today,' he said without even a gentle warm-up.

'Say that again.'

'A really lovely couple – they're going to spoil her rotten.'

'But you don't know that ... It's too soon. Have the rescue centre even done a home visit with them? Has she gone already?'

'We talked about this, Zo. You knew it was a possibility,' Win reminded her. They had and she did and now she could hardly speak, but rang off with a choked grunt instead of a goodbye.

The loss of Beyoncé, when she still wasn't over losing the baby, was too soon.

It was too soon for a lot of things. Because if they still couldn't talk about the baby they'd lost then they were nowhere near ready to talk about the baby they might have in the future. 'Might' and 'in the future' were vague, neb-ulous terms but over the course of the week Zoe was aware that her grief was changing shape and texture; transforming into a sharpening want for a child of her own. When she got back home, she and Win had some long, hard conversations ahead of them.

It was a relief that on the final night of her stay in Edinburgh, she had a party to attend, rather than chasing her own tortured thoughts around a hotel room. Four months ago she couldn't face going to a pub quiz with Win but now Zoe was quite happy to attend the book launch of someone she knew through Cath and had only met a couple of times. When Zoe arrived at the crowded bar on Canongate, Helen greeted her with a fervent hug like she was a long-lost friend, and it was never an ordeal to drink wine and guzzle sausage rolls and talk about books, though it was quite a surprise to bump into Caroline at the end of the evening.

'I was hoping to run into you,' her agent said, even though they were both four hundred miles away from home. 'Had a meeting about the Edinburgh Book Festival and couldn't face rushing to catch the last London train. Shall we travel back together tomorrow?'

Zoe would have preferred not to spend a four-hour journey in the company of a woman who didn't suffer fools gladly and had been witness to Zoe making a total fool of herself the last time they'd met, but Caroline turned out to be an exemplary fellow traveller. Mostly because she was a fervent fan of a train picnic. After a bacon sandwich and a medicinal gin and tonic for their respective hangovers, they settled into a long gossipy conversation about editors they'd both known and disliked intently.

'So, how have you been since I last saw you?' Caroline asked once they'd finished putting the world of publishing to rights.

'Much better now,' Zoe said and somehow she was, though she didn't know how she'd achieved this state of betterdom. 'I've discovered a talent for grouting and we've been fostering a dog. Beyoncé. Except now she's been adopted by some people who will never love her like I love her.'

Zoe showed Caroline several favourite photos of Beyoncé because she had more pictures of Beyoncé on her phone than her grandparents had had taken during their entire lives. She even found herself sharing what she and Win were now calling *The Amazing Crime-fighting Adventures of Beyoncé and Beatrice*, because two gin and tonics before lunchtime had left Zoe light-headed and loose-lipped.

'Does Beatrice have parents?' Caroline enquired. 'Where are they while she's upholding the forces of law and order?'

'Win, my husband, decided that Beatrice had a French governess who was more interested in a burly woodsman called Jim than fulfilling her job remit,' Zoe explained. Caroline held her gaze and Zoe wondered if this was a hint to go to the buffet car and get another round of gin and tonics in, when Caroline smiled.

'Well, that's your next book right there, isn't it?' she said.

'I suppose it could be a middle-grade series,' Zoe said slowly. 'I'm not in the mood to do a picture book, but I'd love to do some illustrations and maybe the crime should be a bit more serious. No murder, but pet thefts or a house broken into and a stash of jewellery hidden in the woods.'

Her mind was suddenly racing with possibilities for several different plots. She could also visualise quite clearly the clean lines of the simple pen and ink illustrations and . . .

This! This is how I used to be! Zoe remembered. It had been gone too long, that part of her that never felt quite right unless she spent time writing or drawing every day, and now she realised how much she missed it. Wanted nothing more than to pick up her pens and pencils and sketch pad and make stories again.

'And a dog called something other than Beyoncé,' Caroline was saying firmly. 'It's the end of June now, I'd like a workable draft, something ready to be pitched, beginning of September. Then we have a month to send it out to editors before the Frankfurt Book Fair. Agreed? Let's toast in lukewarm gin and tonic.'

'Agreed.' Zoe knocked her plastic glass against Caroline's. 'I can't wait to get started.'

25

Zoe

When Zoe walked through the front door, Win raced down the stairs as if he'd been watching out for her. She felt quite bedraggled after spending a sticky four hours on a train then wrangling her suitcase and the several carrier bags she'd acquired home from King's Cross. She'd also had another little weep in the smelly train toilet when she'd thought about coming back to a Beyoncéless house but that didn't compare to the reality. There was no frantic whimpering, no scrabble of claws on the floor, no small, compact body set on a collision course for Zoe's shins.

'Good journey?' Win asked brightly as if he hadn't noticed Zoe's dejected stance.

'The air conditioning broke down before we'd even got to Berwick-on-Tweed,' she said as she gratefully relinquished her carrier bags, which had dug welts into her wrists, to Win's care.

'Sounds grim. Do you want a shower? Cold drink? I made us something to eat.' Win employed a strange jazz hands-style gesture, which was most unlike him. It was as if he were nervous, though Zoe couldn't imagine what he had to be nervous about. Unless he hadn't performed a single act of DIY while she'd been away, in which case he had every reason to be nervous. Shouting could wait though.

'Cold drink first,' Zoe decided and Win hadn't even kissed her hello, although she was sure she smelt a little ripe and she definitely had gin breath so maybe it was for the best. 'I travelled back with my agent. I told her about *The Amazing Adventures of Beatrice and Beyoncé* and she wants me to have a draft ready to be submitted by September. Also, there's a new guy started at the agency who'll hopefully get me some illustration work. I'm feeling properly fired up for the first time in ages.'

Win blocked Zoe's path down the hall. 'That's good. Fired-up Zoe is one of my most favourite Zoes.'

'She's a lot more fun than mopey Zoe.' She tried to move him aside. 'Win! All I've been able to think about for the last five hours is the ice-cold can of Diet Coke I'm about to drink.'

Win didn't budge. 'You have to close your eyes. I have a surprise for you.'

'Have you been baking?' Zoe's nostrils twitched. Her sense of smell overcoming her own sweatiness and the stale gin fumes to pick up the mouthwatering scent of cake; all buttery and lemony and warm. 'How have you been baking when we don't have an oven?'

'No more backchat, just shut your eyes,' Win said and Zoe sighed but did as he asked and let him guide her down the hall towards the kitchen and then he stopped, which meant Zoe had to stop too. 'OK, you can open them now.'

Zoe opened her eyes then she shut them again, sure she was hallucinating. It couldn't be true. Considering how long it took to do anything in the house – fitting a ventilation unit in the bathroom had taken *weeks* – Zoe had only been gone seven days and yet in that time, they suddenly had a kitchen.

A bare shell of a room was now transformed into an actual working kitchen with fitted cupboards, a French plate rack and a Belfast sink that Zoe immediately rushed over to so she could stroke it again and again as if it were a lover returned from a long trip to faraway lands.

'Do you and the sink need some alone time?' Win asked from where he was standing by the pantry, which had a new door in the same very hideous, very dark wood veneer as the rest of the kitchen, which actually was not what Zoe would have chosen.

'It's not *quite* what we discussed, is it?'

'It was *literally* being given away,' Win said very quickly. 'Someone up the road was ripping out their old kitchen. Me and Gavin had a chat with their builders and they let us have it, all in, for four hundred and a crate of lager.'

'Four hundred quid?' Zoe squeaked. She looked round the room with new, far more appreciative eyes. 'Even the range?'

'Even the range and no veneers either: it's all solid wood,' Win added a little defensively as Zoe opened the nearest cupboard door and rapped on it with her knuckles.

'OK. OK. Yeah, it's quite eighties rustic at the moment but we can work with that. I'm thinking that we repaint in a light cream, or even a pale sage green with a very matte finish and cup handles in that gunmetal silver we both liked. Wow! I can't quite take this in.' Zoe turned a slow circle. 'We have a kitchen table! Chairs! This is amazing. A new kitchen just slotted straight into place.'

'It didn't just slot into place,' Win recalled with a shudder. 'It took much measuring. Also a huge amount of cutting to fit and unbelievable amounts of effing and blinding.'

Zoe looked around again. There was a lot still to be done.

Painting, sealing, and at some point apparently Gavin was going to show her how to tile and grout the splashback but they now had a kitchen. 'Oh my God, what *is* that smell?' She sniffed the air again. 'Oh! Don't tell me. It's your boozy lemon drizzle cake, isn't it?'

'It is,' Win confirmed and things hadn't been this good between them, this happy, this playful since . . . last November. Zoe dropped to her knees in front of the range so she could peer through the glass like a contestant on *The Great British Bake Off* checking on the progress of their signature bake. 'Zo, are you kissing the oven door?'

'Maybe. Just a little bit,' she admitted.

'It's just I have one more surprise for you,' Win said and when Zoe turned round, he had such a smug smile on his face that she was immediately suspicious.

'What have you done?' She'd seen that smile before when Win had signed them both up for a charity fun run, even though there was nothing fun about running ten kilometres, or the time he'd decided to reorganise the fridge and found the very expensive, budget-busting chocolate truffles she'd been hiding behind the mustard. 'Is it a nice surprise?'

'Well, I think so,' Win said and he waited for Zoe to take a can of diet cola out of the fridge, because their fridge was now in its rightful place in the kitchen, and finish it in five greedy gulps. He winced as she burped.

'Sorry.' Zoe wondered if the surprise could wait until after she'd had a shower but Win was already hustling her out of the kitchen and up the stairs.

'So, I have to tell—'

'It's weird not to have Beyoncé rush to greet me . . .' Zoe pulled a face. 'You were saying.'

'I know that you're going to miss her so I got you a little something to make up for it.' Win's voice was pitching up and down now like a kite on a windy day. 'It's in the bedroom. You coming?'

'Just what kind of present is it?' It probably was time for them to resume their sex life but Zoe wished that she wasn't so sweaty, that she was more in the mood but then, there were times when Win could be very persuasive.

Zoe opened the bedroom door and there, asleep on the bed, a pink bow tied round her neck was ... 'The dog formerly known as Beyoncé,' Win said and the sound of his voice woke Beyoncé up from the kind of slumber that only came from two hours chasing squirrels in Highgate Woods. She yawned, stretched, then saw Zoe standing behind Win and began running in circles on the spot.

'Oh, Win, you didn't ... '

He had and he stood aside so the dog could launch herself off the bed with a joyful yelp straight into Zoe's arms so she could paint Zoe's face with her tongue.

'Are you crying?' Win asked Zoe, which was a completely redundant question when tears were streaming down her cheeks. 'Oh God, I know you agreed that we couldn't have a dog right now, but I've got so used to having her around, I suppose I sort of love her, and I was pretty sure that you did too ... '

He waited for Zoe to say something but she just shook her head, her arms full of squirming Staffy/pug/French bulldog cross.

'I should have asked first but I wanted it to be a surprise and you are OK with this, aren't you? I mean, you did seem really upset when I said she'd been adopted by a really nice couple, not a lie by the way because we are a really nice couple, but you did point out how expensive owning a dog was but we can get a good deal on the pet insurance if we go with the same company we get the—'

Zoe looped one arm round his shoulders and pulled Win in for a slightly sour-smelling hug so he could get his fair share of the face licking. 'Best present ever, Win,' she said, her words thick with emotion. 'And you? Are you really OK with her bankrupting us?'

'We'll be fine. We might have to make some more economies and stop splurging on the fancy quilted loo roll, but I think she's worth it, don't you?'

Because it was a special occasion, they pulled up a third chair to their new kitchen table and gave the official addition to their little family a small bowl of watermelon as they had dinner. Win kept one hand on Zoe's knee and entertained her with a long funny story about a band whose finances he'd been managing since they signed their first deal, who'd always had delusions about their own greatness. 'Now, apparently, they're number five in some obscure iTunes chart and they want me to set up an offshore account for them,' Win said. 'I had to give them a very stern talking-to.'

Zoe grinned and stroked the hair back from Win's face then turned to look at Beyoncé who was gazing at their platter of watermelon, feta cheese and budget-brand ham with her tongue lolling and two delicate trails of drool starting to descend. 'What did you mean when you said the dog formerly known as Beyoncé?'

'I'm not shouting Beyoncé across the playing field any more, Zo, I have my limits,' Win said sternly. 'I've been calling her Florence-ay for the last two days, and in a week or so we can start calling her Florence. It will make her feel more at home. All the other dogs in Highgate have names like Ruby and Daisy and Archie, like they work below stairs at *Downton Abbey*.'

'How do you feel about your new name, Florence?' Zoe asked, and the former Beyoncé instantly turned her head to gaze at both of them with a look of utter adoration as if she understood that she'd never have to worry where her next organic dog treat was coming from. Zoe shrugged. 'Florence it is then.'

It wasn't until they were clearing up after dinner, Zoe washing as Win dried because they both agreed it would be profligate to run their old dishwasher, which had been reinstalled, that he cleared his throat. 'The dog's not a child substitute, is it?' he asked as if he were genuinely curious to hear Zoe's answer.

Zoe knew that they were nowhere near ready to have this conversation yet here they were, having it. 'I don't want a child substitute. I want a child, Win.' It was hard to keep the longing in her voice corralled. 'Not right now. But soon.'

Win's hands stilled around the plate he was meant to be drying. 'Back up for a second, will you? You don't even know if ... after what happened. The accident.' He turned away from her, ostensibly to put the plate he'd been drying in the plate rack. 'We don't have to have children, you know.'

The pain was sudden and overwhelming. As if he'd just slammed her hand in the cutlery drawer or picked up one of the knives, still smeared with feta cheese and plunged it into her heart. It was hard to speak. 'You don't want children?'

'I'm not saying that.' Win shook his head as if he weren't sure exactly what he was saying. 'I don't think you're in a position to think about this rationally yet.'

'There's nothing rational about it. It's a need. A biological imperative, which guarantees the survival of the species,' Zoe said, which sounded very pompous even if it were true.

'Channelling David Attenborough there,' Win muttered. 'Look, where is this even coming from? Because, well, we agreed we'd wait at least another two years.'

'But that was before.' How to even explain the new feelings

that were sweeping her grief and sadness to one side? 'I don't know where this has come from. But I've spent a week surrounded by kids and I've seen how you are with Bey—Florence. You're lovely with her, Win. You'd be such a great dad.'

He pulled a face like he could smell something foul. 'I don't know about that,' he muttered. 'Not sure Terry passed down any great fathering talent in his DNA.'

'What rubbish!' Zoe couldn't help but roll her eyes. 'Ed had Terry as a father too and he's managed to raise four gorgeous boys and the nephews adore you. Maybe you do have good dad DNA and it skipped a generation with Terry.'

'Maybe.' Win didn't sound convinced. He held his tea towel in front of him like a matador's cape to deflect any more of Zoe's thrusts and parries. 'Let's just park this for now, shall we?'

'I don't want to park it.' She was fed up with having to put her feelings away until a time when Win wanted to deal with them. 'This is like a primal thing. Another couple of weeks more of this ache to have a child and I'm probably going to pin you down, rip off your clothes and beg you to impregnate me.'

Win looked alarmed rather than aroused. He put down the tea towel, folded it into quarters, and then stared at the neat square rather than at Zoe. 'I'm still undecided on the whole kids thing.'

'And how long is it going to take for you to reach a decision?' Zoe demanded.

'I'm sorry, Zo, but I can't pretend to feel something that I don't,' Win said and it was probably best that he was being honest. Setting his stall out, as it were. Determined not to give Zoe false hope, but then again he hadn't given her an outright 'no'.

'I want to go and see someone, a consultant,' Zoe insisted. 'I was meant to have my six-month check-up a couple of months ago but I couldn't face it then. I need to know what our options are. If I even can conceive. But there's always IVF and—'

'Don't get carried away.' Win's lips twisted when Zoe glared at him. 'Well, OK, I can agree to seeing a consultant,' he said as if Zoe was asking his permission.

She knew to let the subject drop and there was so much else to talk about; Beyoncé (Zoe didn't know if she'd ever be able to remember to call her Florence-ay), the fraught installation of the new kitchen, how to work the range ... and if things were a little scratchy between them, they both tried hard to ignore it.

But now that she knew that Win had absolutely zero interest in making love, though it had been *months* since they'd last had sex, Zoe got undressed in front of him for the first time in all those months. Though Win lingered in the doorway of the bathroom as Zoe brushed her teeth, he was hardly overcome with lust at the sight of Zoe in her underwear. 'I remember what I wanted to ask you now,' he said, as Zoe rinsed out her mouth. 'That suitcase ...'

'What suitcase?'

'The one we found that first night with the clothes in it ... Did you know that it was still in the cupboard in the back bedroom?' Win asked. 'I thought you were going to drop it off at the solicitors or throw it out.'

Zoe clutched onto the side of the sink for support. 'You didn't, did you?'

'No. I wondered if there was some reason you were keeping it.'

'Aren't you even a little bit curious about what we found inside it?'

Win pulled a face. 'It's ghoulish. Creepy.'

220

'It's not. I've been reading Libby's diary,' Zoe admitted. It felt like she was confessing to a crime though Win seemed more confused than anything else.

'Who's Libby?'

It had been weeks since Zoe had checked in with Libby. The last thing she'd read was the letter from Hugo arranging a tryst in the mansion block not five minutes' walk from their house. The letter had made Zoe see Libby in a new, not altogether flattering light and so she'd packed her away, concentrated on getting her own house in order. Her only daily link with Libby was the button that she'd transferred from coat pocket to jacket pocket and now that the weather was too warm for even a cardigan, the button lived in a side pocket of her handbag.

'Come with me.'

Win followed Zoe into the bedroom and watched as she took out the diary. Then he sat down on the bed next to her and took the book, turned it over, but didn't open it. Instead Zoe told Win about Libby. That she'd been keeping up with Libby's year as her own year unfolded, but that it was a slow process because Libby's handwriting was almost indecipherable. Told him about the house in Hampstead and its occupants. The job in a school that was long gone. About Hugo ('he's her lover') and Freddy ('he's in Spain, reporting on what's going to become the Spanish Civil War. There's lot of his clippings in the diary').

'I suppose it's all quite romantic.' Zoe took out Hugo's last letter and handed it to Win, who took it as gingerly as if Zoe had handed him a full poo bag to be deposited in the nearest bin. 'No one ever pledges their undying love by letter these days, but I don't understand why they're going to spend the night together without any funny business. You'd think funny business was all they had in mind.'

Win made a noncommittal noise but he started to read the letter as Zoe opened the diary and angled the bedside lamp the better to pick up the faint trace of Libby's pencilled entries. In some ways Zoe felt as if she knew more about Libby than some of her own friends and in other ways it was impossible to know someone when you were following paper trails in an eighty-year-old diary.

It was June in 1936. Libby complained about the heat, headaches, a run-in with Millicent over her laundry then another letter from Hugo to Libby, which made it clear that Hugo was in love with Libby. Was writing not to just talk about their divorces but so that Libby had '*proof of my feelings, my regard, my love for you.*'

'It was actually really hard to get a divorce back then,' Win piped up, causing Zoe to nearly slide off the bed in alarm because she was so intent on Libby and Hugo she'd forgotten all about him. 'We did study divorce law as part of one of my accountancy modules. Problem is I've slept since then.'

'But Win, you never forget anything,' Zoe said, because his memory was elephantine and he could always be relied upon to drag up the most obscure facts when she was stuck on the general knowledge crossword.

'I'm thinking … thinking … That's it! Nineteen thirty-eight Marriage Act!' Win clicked his fingers in triumph. 'Before that, the only grounds for divorce was adultery. So, even if there wasn't adultery, or if your lover didn't want their reputation tarnished in court, you'd go to a hotel with a paid witness, a co-respondent, jump into bed with them, make sure the maid caught you at it or a private detective was prowling the place with a camera and you had your proof for the court. There was a bit more to it than that, but you get the gist?'

Zoe did and it made some of the mysteries of Libby's diary clearer and in other ways, she was still fumbling in the dark.

There was one thing in particular that struck her. 'It's odd, that it was so hard to get a divorce back then,' she said, closing the diary. 'Now divorce is so easy, it's the staying together that's hard work.'

Win froze on the bed next to her. 'Oh. So you've thought about divorce then?'

'What? *What?* No! Never!'

'Are you sure about that?'

Win was hurt. Zoe could tell he wanted reassurance, which was reassuring in itself but if anyone should have been worried about divorce, it was her.

'You were the one who walked out,' she reminded Win, because she still hadn't made her peace with that. Didn't think she ever would.

Win rested his hand on her knee. 'But I came back.'

'Only because I made you,' Zoe reminded him. She rested her hand on top of Win's. 'And why do we still keep arguing? We never used to argue this much.'

'I know.' Win leaned over so they weren't just sitting next to each other but pressed side by side. 'We *are* going through a rough patch.'

Zoe rested her head on his shoulder. 'I was hoping we were past that.'

Win's sigh ruffled her hair. 'I'd say it's still ongoing. But, let's get this into perspective; we've managed nearly thirteen years and this is our first rough patch, so I'm hopeful, actually I'm certain, that we'll come out the other side.' He tapped the diary that was on Zoe's lap. 'So, anyway, what happened to the baby?'

'What baby?'

'The baby clothes in the suitcase? What happened to the baby? Any clues about that? I guess, yeah, maybe I am a little curious,' Win said with a smile.

Zoe's smile faded. 'She lost the baby.' She began to gather up the detritus from the diary, slot it back into the right places. 'But Libby's working towards being happy again.'

Even to her own ears it sounded weak and Win looked spectacularly unconvinced. 'You really need to get rid of this stuff.' He gestured at the diary again. 'I'm sorry, Zo, but I don't see how this can lead to anything good.'

26

Libby

School had broken up, the little girls all gone to the coast so they could spend the long days sticky and sunburned.

Hugo was going away too. To spend four weeks with his wife taking in the sea air at Aldeburgh, strolling along the promenade, sitting out in the lush green garden of the house that they rented every summer.

He'd waited until after they'd made love and Libby was stretching languorously, waiting for Hugo to light and pass her a cigarette as he always did. Instead he cleared his throat and told her the news in a flat voice.

Libby felt as if every one of her nerve endings had been zapped with an electrical charge. She'd known it! Known it all along! That Hugo, for all his fine words and talk of love, was just like the rest of them. 'You're taking a holiday with your wife? The same wife that you're so desperate to be free of?'

'Darling, don't be like that. Susan is back from Switzerland and Robin's down from Oxford. This is the last chance for all four of us to be together. As a family.' Hugo had met Libby's wounded expression with an even stare as if she were the one being unreasonable. 'Please be understanding about this.'

'How can you expect me to be understanding when you tell me that you love me, you want to marry me and then, without a by your leave, you go off with *her*?' Libby was already sliding out of bed, tugging the sheet with her because she felt vulnerable and naked enough without actually being naked. 'Besides, what do I know about being part of a family? Not a bloody thing!'

'Is there any need for that kind of language? There's certainly no need to be such a dog in the manger about this when you know you have my heart, that I want to make a home and a life with you and yet you haven't even said you'll marry me.' If Libby had expected Hugo to be more conciliatory she'd been sorely mistaken. 'Be honest with me, have you even written to Freddy to ask for a divorce?'

'I said I would and I have, though now I wish I hadn't when you're waltzing off with your precious Pamela!'

Libby had written to Freddy after the first weekend she'd spent with Hugo. *I'm in love with someone else,* she'd said, quite plainly. *There's enough evidence to divorce me on the grounds of adultery so please contact your lawyer soonest to start necessary arrangements. It's best this way, don't you think?*

It had been hard to draw this final line through their brief, unhappy union but Libby wasn't the type of woman who would string two men along. Not when one man said he loved her and the other man couldn't give a brass farthing for her affection. No wonder she was teetering on the precipice of a quite majestic flounce out of the room, but still she had to pause to wonder why she was behaving like this. Being so shrewish, so petulant, when she'd refused to make any claim on Hugo's affections, only admitting that she loved him under duress. But who could blame her when her heart had been broken so many times? It was a miracle that it still worked at all.

Swathed as she was in the sheet, Libby could only stagger as far as the window seat, then collapse upon it. 'You're being so silly,' Hugo told her in a gentler voice, once it was clear that the storm had passed. 'I can't wait to see Robin and Susan, to remember happier times when they were little, but Pamela and I are agreed that at the end of the holiday we'll tell them about the divorce.'

Another poisoned dart lodged itself in Libby's heart at the thought of Hugo and Pamela's cosy tête-à-têtes as they discussed how best to break up their once happy home. 'Will you tell them the truth? That she was the one who ... ?'

'No!' The word was torn out of him. 'She's their mother. It's the whole reason ... ' He smiled, though Libby couldn't imagine why, then got to his feet to walk over to where she was sitting and drop to his knees. 'How can I be angry with her any more? If it weren't for Pamela, I'd never have met you, would I?'

Libby caressed his cheek with the back of her hand and he leaned in to her touch, his eyes closed as if he were exactly where he wanted to be and damn a month in Aldeburgh. 'You're still pleased that you met me, even though I can be absolutely horrible sometimes?'

'Not so horrible,' Hugo decided, with a tiny playful smile. 'Most times, you're adorable.'

She wasn't but it was so sweet of him to say she was. 'Will you tell them about me? It will come out sooner or later, with the court case; there's sure to be reports in the paper.'

'There might not be,' Hugo said, but they both knew there would be. There was nothing people liked more than reading all the titillating details of a divorce as they ate their

227

toast of a morning and lingered over the last cup of tea from the pot. Before all this unpleasantness, Libby had been one of them. 'Let's worry about it then, for now I'm only going to worry about how much I'll miss you. Might you miss me too?'

Libby pretended to give the matter some thought. 'Perhaps,' she decided at last. She held up her thumb and forefinger, maybe an inch apart. 'I'll miss you that much.' She fluttered her eyelashes. 'If you take me back to bed and make love to me again, I promise I'll miss you even more.'

With Hugo gone, no lessons to teach, nothing much to do but brood, Libby wished that she wasn't spending summer in town on her own. There had been a time, when she was performing, that she'd visited what felt like every coastal resort in England, and quite a few in Scotland and Wales too.

Libby had loved doing summer season. They barely bothered with rehearsals and would spend each day on the beach. She remembered what fun it had been, splashing through the water then retreating to the safety of a big parasol as she did burn so easily. Sand between her toes, the illicit feeling of the sun caressing her bare legs, usually hidden under stockings, sending the most juvenile of the male leads off to buy ices.

This summer was a world away from those carefree summers of the past. It was probably the strain of Hugo gone and waiting for Freddy to reply to her letter requesting a divorce, but all through the hot sticky nights Libby hardly slept but would lie very, very still because even kicking the covers off made her head pound and her stomach heave. The only thing that helped was when Hannah thudded up the stairs each morning with a glass of ginger ale and a couple of arrowroot biscuits and wondered aloud if Libby was dying of consumption ''cause you are awfully pale and in a book I read where the heroine died of consumption she was awfully pale too'. After sipping the ginger ale and nibbling on the biscuits, Libby would be restored, until late in the evening when it would start all over again. So, during the day when she felt quite well, Libby was glad to leave her bed and take in some fresh air.

At the end of term, Libby had asked Beryl Marjoribanks if anything might be done for Hannah – if there were some benevolent organisation that might deliver the poor girl out of Millicent's clutches and offer her a scholarship so she could go back to school. Beryl had promised to look into it and when they'd discovered that they were both staying in town for summer, it seemed silly not to meet for a walk.

Libby hadn't expected that a stroll on the heath one afternoon would mean that she'd end up seeing Beryl every day. She suspected that the other woman was lonely. Her family, two aged parents, an older brother and his domineering wife, lived in Devon in a small village and never came to London to see Beryl.

'They visited Cambridge once when I was at university, but they didn't like it much. Said it was far too noisy, too many people,' Beryl had recalled sadly, that first day on the heath, before embarking on a long treatise about how dismayed they'd been that Beryl had turned out bookish because being bookish could only lead to a lonely life of spinsterdom.

Spinster she might be, but Beryl had travelled to Germany to study under Rudolf Steiner himself. She'd also visited Austria, Hungary, Norway, Holland, Belgium and along the way embarked on many intense friendships with other bookish women, only to have her hopes cruelly dashed when her affections weren't returned.

Libby suspected that Beryl's tastes ran in the same direction as Deidre Withers, but Beryl, for all her travelling and good works among the needy, was a *naïf*. Libby was sure Beryl didn't even know that two women could be together in that way. 'I could never see myself married,' she'd said to Libby as they meandered across the Vale of Health one day. 'I've met some perfectly nice chaps in my time, but you can never truly be yourself with a man.'

Still, it was no hardship to meet up with Beryl to go swimming in the Ladies' Pond, even though Libby was terrified that there might be pike or carp or some other sharp-toothed fish lurking in the weeds to strike at her legs. The two women would float on their backs then lounge in the grass meadows and wait for their cossies to dry off.

Libby had missed the camaraderie of the dressing room; the confessions and confidences shared after the curtain came down. And if Beryl weren't also Libby's employer, then Libby may well have confided in her too. Instead, she stuck to just one side of her sad story – that her husband was in Spain, reporting for the *Herald* and the *Mirror*, and when she mentioned Freddy by name one hot July afternoon, Beryl gasped, her eyes especially wide.

'Frederick Morton? I've read all his pieces. He writes awfully well, doesn't he? Makes one feel you're there in Spain, seeing it for yourself,' she said. 'You must be terribly worried about him.'

'Why should I worry about Freddy? Gosh, I'm sure he's having the time of his life,' Libby snorted rather inelegantly. 'Yakking it up with all the other reporters and also-rans in the hotel bar. Drinking too much. Arguing about politics. Pontificating. He'll be in his element.'

'Sounds rather fun,' Beryl said a little wistfully then assumed a more serious expression. 'But the situation's a bit sticky out there. Riots, strikes, talk of a military coup.'

Libby sank back down on the grass. 'Freddy will be fine. He's not one to get his hands dirty. Honestly, he's the sort to run away at the first sign of trouble.'

Libby refused to worry about Freddy but not two days had passed since Beryl's dire warnings when it was in all the papers, the big black letters striking dread in her.

STATE OF WAR DECLARED IN SPAIN
Franco's Nationalist forces seize control of Morocco,
Canary Islands, Seville.

'I never knew Morocco was in Spain,' Libby said, as she squinted at the words.

'That's because it isn't! Just as well you don't teach geography, Libby.'

In the end, Beryl drew a map in pencil on the paper bag from the cherries that Libby had bought on her way to the heath. The cherries were then deployed to portray the different factions: the Republicans – who Beryl said were the good guys, even though they seemed to be a motley collection of anarchists, Trots and concerned citizens – had taken up arms against the Nationalists, who were Fascists trying to seize control of the country. Libby knew enough about politics to know that she wouldn't trust a Fascist as far as she could throw one.

'But Freddy's in the press corps,' Libby said as Beryl made her head spin with all the Spanish names: Franco, Quirago, Giral; and places: Majorca, Minorca, Sierra de Guadarrama, Pais Vasco. 'He won't be fighting. He'll simply be reporting on the fighting from a safe distance away, won't he?'

'I'm sure he will,' Beryl said. 'He's in Barcelona, isn't he? I think the Republicans have managed to hold Barcelona. Let me just see.'

231

Libby scrabbled for the *Daily Mirror* and they both bent over it to read about the police, soldiers and ordinary men fighting with any kind of weapon they could muster against Franco's rebel army. How roads full of shops and houses and offices had become battlegrounds.

'Could you imagine if there were hundreds of men fighting along Hampstead High Street?' Libby wondered.

'Did we learn nothing the last time? Men! It's always men, isn't it? Wanting what isn't theirs and sacrificing the lives of thousands to take it.'

There couldn't be another war. It was too horrific to contemplate but Libby did contemplate it, and from her silence she supposed Beryl was too, then their reverie was abruptly broken as a shadow cast over the two of them.

'Disgusting! Mrs Morton, have you no shame?'

Libby blinked because Mrs Morton was cloistered in Willoughby Square, then she looked up into the furious, jowly face of one of Millicent's friends. An awful woman called Virena Edmonds. Unlike Millicent, who fancied herself an invalid, Virena was often to be seen yomping about Hampstead poking her large red-veined nose into matters that were absolutely nothing to do with her.

She'd once reported Hannah for loitering in the library and 'reading filthy books', though Hannah had been on an errand for the aunts and was flicking through the new Florence Crawford, which they'd specially requested. Virena had also tattled on Potts when she'd spied him eating a meat pie 'in the street like a common vagrant', and now she was glaring at Libby and Beryl as if they were personally responsible for the many wrongs in the world.

'Will you cover yourself?' Virena hissed. 'You're a married woman, even if you fail to act like one.'

Libby glanced down at her pale legs, made paler by the lush

green grass. Her swimming costume was hardly indecent. It covered just as much of herself as the leotards she'd used to wear at dance rehearsals.

'We're at the ladies' bathing ponds,' Libby pointed out, though she wondered why she was bothering. Arguing one's case with Virena was as much use as howling at the moon. 'We've been bathing, hence our swimming costumes.'

'Besides, there's nothing shameful about the female form,' Beryl piped up. Beryl wasn't the sort to back down when injustice was afoot. 'It's one of God's works, after all. When you stop to think about it, it's like saying trees or lambs or flowers are shameful too.'

Virena must have been bathing too but now, despite the heat of the July sun, she was back in tweed skirt and twinset, her fleshy face sweaty, iron-grey hair frizzing at the temples.

'God made woman from one of Adam's ribs,' she intoned wrathfully, which was neither here nor there. 'I've held my tongue until now, out of respect for dear Millicent but . . . this brazen display, your impertinence, it really is the last straw. She deserves to know that she's been harbouring a viper in her bosom.'

27

Libby

Beryl offered to come back to the house with her, but Libby demurred. Best to face the music alone, especially as Virena had hinted at other crimes. The only crime that Libby was guilty of was adultery and she'd rather that Beryl didn't know about that. Their friendship was so new, even precious in its way, and for all her knowledge of the wider world, Beryl knew nothing of the smaller world, that tiny sphere only big enough for a man and a woman.

By the time Libby had queued for a changing room and changed into one of her tired summer frocks, Virena had a good twenty minutes on her.

She traced her steps back across the heath, the long grass bleached by the sun and scratching at her legs. Libby could feel one of her heads coming on again and as she turned into Willoughby Square, dread making her feet like lead, the churning in her stomach had returned with a vengeance so just climbing the three steps to the front door made her feel as if she were in a rowing boat perched on precarious seas.

She'd barely got her key in the lock when the door was wrenched open and Libby was almost mown down by Virena Edmonds. 'Well, I've said what I had to say,' she announced, as she descended the steps. 'Not that it gave me any pleasure, I quite assure you. When I was a girl, we believed in the sanctity of marriage. You young people carry on as if it were the last days of Sodom and Gomorrah.'

'Hardly Sodom and Gomorrah,' Libby muttered, though as a very impressionable nineteen-year-old she'd been taken to a party in an old Turkish baths and had seen such shocking sights that the next day she'd gone to confession for the first time in years. Whatever gossip Virena had taken great delight in sharing with Millicent couldn't come even halfway close.

As it was, Millicent was standing with her mouth agape, hand in its favourite position atop her chest, not moving, so it was easy enough to brush past her.

'I'm going to bed,' Libby said. 'I don't feel at all well.'

'Are you expecting?' Millicent hissed, reaching out to seize Libby's wrist. 'You weren't well last time you were expecting a child out of wedlock!'

It was the cruellest of opening parries, cutting to the quick and thrusting deep. 'No, I am not,' Libby hissed back because it was impossible, though at times it did feel like the same kind of wretchedness she'd experienced a year before when anything and everything had made her nauseous. There were even moments during the night when she couldn't sleep that Libby wondered if those damn doctors in Paris hadn't left part of the baby inside her. A ghostly limb, a puny organ, skin and bone festering deep in the heart of her. 'What a nasty insinuation,' she added, aware of a rustling, the drawing room door ajar and no doubt the old ladies lurking behind it, desperate to catch every word. 'I insist that you apologise.'

235

Libby was on safer ground now. Unless Virena had happened to be wandering along Muswell Hill Road one Friday evening a couple of months back and had glanced up at the windows of a mansion block, she had nothing incriminating to report to Millicent.

'I will not apologise. You were seen with a man in the bakery on the High Street buying cakes!'

Libby nearly laughed in her face. 'That wasn't a crime last time I checked. Shall we go down to the police station just to make certain?'

Millicent took a deep breath, nostrils flaring, and drew herself up as if she were a decrepit, ancient dragon desperate to breathe fire one last time. 'And one of Virena's bridge friends saw you walking in Highgate Woods with a man too!'

Libby could have cobbled together some tale of a colleague, a friend of Freddy's, someone who'd stopped to ask her for directions, but she simply couldn't be bothered. She wasn't a married woman. Hadn't been ever since Freddy abandoned her. She could do what she liked. Was free to fall in love again without being spied on by a gaggle of spiteful old ladies. 'How ridiculous you sound! Just listen to yourself,' she demanded, hands on her hips. She closed her eyes just for a second so she wouldn't have to look at Millicent's furious, sallow face but that made the world swim about her.

'I will not have a trollop under my roof. Yes! A trollop! How do you explain this?' Millicent thrust something at Libby, a piece of paper.

It was a postcard. A beach scene. Sea, shingle and some distance away, a row of higgledy-piggledy houses. 'Greetings from Aldeburgh.'

Libby turned the card over, Millicent sucking the air in between her teeth as she did so.

Dearest L

Weather good. Bathed or boated with the children most days.
Having a lovely time – would be even lovelier if you were here too.
Nothing else to report as yet.
Yours, H

A few lines on a card that meant everything to Libby and would mean nothing to anyone else, unless that person was determined to twist the innocent words into something ugly.

The indignation rose in Libby like bile, even though she *was* guilty. She *was* carrying on – a married woman having an affair with a man who wasn't married to her. Those were the facts, but the circumstances of their affair absolved both her and Hugo of their sins. Even if they didn't, Libby was so used to playing a part, to becoming a different character, that now she'd assumed the role of the innocent party, the wronged wife, as if she were born to it.

'It's unspeakably rude to read someone else's mail, especially when it's a postcard from an old friend, nothing more,' Libby said in hurt, injured tones. 'Goodness, I doubt there's anything that Harriet, yes the H stands for Harriet, has written that even the Archbishop of Canterbury could object to.'

'But you've been seen with a man on several occasions and who knows what you're about when you disappear on the weekends,' Millicent said, determined to win back the upper hand.

She stepped closer to Libby, who took a step away until she felt several hard protuberances against her spine and realised she was backed up against the umbrella stand and quite unable to escape Millicent bearing down on her, reeking of menthol and musk.

'I'm not even going to dignify that with a response,' Libby said. 'Besides, I have far more pressing concerns.' She pulled out the now-damp copy of the *Daily Mirror*, which had been folded up next to her swimming costume in her string bag. 'There's a war going on in Spain and Freddy is caught up in the middle of it. Shouldn't you be worrying about him?'

'My darling boy!'

Millicent was shrieking now and though her voice had reached a piercing pitch, Libby could barely hear a word. She watched the other woman's lips move, spittle collecting at the corners of her mouth, could smell the damp wool of her swimming costume mix with the other smells of the house. Camphor and Brasso, boiled cabbage and the cloying scent of violets; all the old ladies loved the scent of violets. Libby felt sweat break out along her brow, her head grow thick and heavy so it was an effort to hold it up and then she couldn't even do that, but sank to her knees.

'Elizabeth! Elizabeth? What on earth is the matter?'

Libby bent so far forward that her forehead brushed against the horsehair rug that covered the tiles in the hall.

There was more rustling. Black skirts flapping about her like moths as the old ladies gathered around her.

'Is she going to faint?'

'I have my smelling salts!'

'Such a to-do!'

The pounding in her head felt as if her brain was trying to break through her skull and she had such sharp pains in her side that it seemed to Libby as if she were back in Paris, with Freddy. That she was dying all over again.

'*Betwixt the stirrup to the ground, mercy I asked and mercy I found.*'

She muttered the words out loud so if she did die, she really would be absolved.

Then she fainted.

Libby debated whether she could go to the doctors at all, but Beryl called around later that afternoon to see if all was well and

238

she knew of a women's health clinic in town. That sounded more simpatico than the glib doctor Libby had seen in Brighton, so Beryl rang up to make an appointment for the following week.

Of course, over the course of the week, Libby began to feel much better in that annoying way that always happened when you were about to throw away good money on seeing a doctor.

Still, she decided to keep the appointment, mostly because Beryl was adamant that she should and that she should accompany Libby, as if now that they were friends they had to do everything together.

The clinic was on Great Titchfield Street, around the corner from the flat Libby had shared before she got married. After a short wait Libby was called in to see a Dr Parkinson who looked as if she were no older than sixteen. She poked, prodded and palpated Libby. Asked all sorts of questions about her menses and the first pregnancy. Even about how frequently she enjoyed intimate relations with Mr Morton but flushed bright red when Libby said, without thinking, that Mr Morton had skipped out rather than enjoy intimate relations with her. 'But then he came back,' she lied. 'And we resumed, er, marital intimacies . . . gosh, it would have been May. Early May.'

'It's the first week of August now so by my reckoning, you're about twelve weeks along,' the doctor said.

Libby couldn't believe what she thought she'd just heard. 'I beg your pardon. Do you mean . . . that I . . . ?' She gestured in the vicinity of her belly.

'Yes. I'd say you were three months pregnant, give or take a week or so.' Libby shook her head, set her mouth in a stubborn line, and the doctor smiled. 'There is a test we could do to be certain but if I were you I'd keep the money and put it towards a pram. I suspect that you're probably a little iron deficient too.' She went on to talk about Libby's diet, recommended the ubiquitous liver and a glass of milk stout every day, assured Libby that she could attend a clinic each month so they could keep an eye on her, even deliver the baby in the Hospital for Women in Soho Square, and all the while, Libby sat there in a daze.

She was absolutely befuddled. That against all odds, despite feeling that she was empty, a useless husk, there was a seed growing in her. A baby.

' . . . I'm sure your husband will be delighted when you tell him the news, so I won't keep you any longer.'

The doctor had come out from behind her desk to chivvy Libby along, to see her to the door, and she thought of Freddy. How cavalier he'd been when she'd told him he was going to be a father. Panicked. Evasive.

Then she thought about how Hugo might take the news. She hoped that his serious expression would lighten; that he'd look softly happy in the way he did when they were lying in each other's arms.

It didn't really matter what Hugo, or anyone else, thought about it. There was going to be a baby. Her child. Libby could feel a strange sensation in her chest as if her heart were already swelling, expanding, to make extra space for all the love welling up inside her. She was suddenly crying, laughing, an odd, strange, choked combination of the two so Beryl, who was sitting in the waiting room, jumped up from her chair.

'Are you all right?' she asked in a concerned voice. 'Are you happy or sad? It's impossible to tell.'

'I'm happy. Happier than I've ever been.' Libby shook her head. 'I don't even know what to do with so much happiness.'

28

Zoe

Zoe had lost the baby on 27 November.

The embryo had been between eight and nine weeks old. About the size of a jelly bean, one of the doctors had said.

Lately, Zoe had been rewinding those eight or nine weeks to a Sunday morning at the beginning of October. Summer about to give way to autumn so the days were sun-dappled and warm, but the nights had a chill. They were staying with her parents in Yorkshire for a week in their lovely stone cottage on the edge of the Dales before Ken and Nancy went off on their big adventure to South-East Asia.

Zoe and Win had waited for her parents to go to church before they made love in the guest bedroom with the headboard that banged against the wall, her father's history books, arranged by military campaign, on the shelves next to her mother's WI files.

'I really hope that they don't come back early. Sometimes the vicar keeps his sermon very short,' Zoe had said before she'd peeled off her T-shirt.

Then she'd straddled Win, who'd grinned and said that actually he'd much rather have a lie-in so if Zoe was determined to have her wicked way with him he was just going to lie back and think of England.

Zoe could still remember the blissed-out look on Win's face as she'd ridden him slowly and then, when he was already halfway to heaven, she'd paused.

'Did you just hear a car on the drive?' She'd frowned. 'Seriously though, did you hear a car pull up?'

'Zoe! Really?' Win had shaken his head as if he couldn't think about anything but Zoe, all around him, on him, but he'd frozen under her and . . .

'Oh well, too late to stop now,' Zoe had said and she'd taken him inside her again, hands pinning his to the bed and laughed. 'Unless you really would prefer to catch up on your beauty sleep.'

'Serves you right if they duck out before the sermon,' Win had managed to groan and Zoe remembered the enraptured but goofy look on his face and how she'd been overwhelmed with love for him. The sunlight streaming in through the window had turned their skin golden and she was sure that was the moment they'd overridden all the progesterone released into Zoe's body by the tiny contraceptive implant that had created a little ridge under the skin on her left arm. That was the moment they'd made a baby.

The baby should have been with them by now. A little boy, fair of face and hair, blue eyes, which would later focus into a solemn and wise gaze, skin as soft as rose petals and Zoe, even Win too, would have loved him fiercely and quietly and deeply.

She thought about that little boy now as she and Win walked through Highgate Woods late on a Sunday afternoon, past what they thought of as 'their' bench. They stopped so

Florence could take a drink at the little trough at the back of the water fountain then headed towards the playing fields.

'We'd have a baby,' Zoe said because she couldn't wait any longer. It was time to talk about this or she'd burst. Not even burst, but slowly collapse and deflate. 'If things hadn't ended like they did, we'd have a baby now.'

'I know,' Win said quietly. 'I know we would.'

He didn't say anything else but shot Zoe an anxious glance as if they weren't navigating the uneven path but stepping over landmines, walking unarmed into enemy territory.

Soon, they came to the field. Cricket was over for the day. The men in their grass-stained whites packing away wickets and bats. Florence circling Zoe and Win hopefully, waiting for her plastic ring to be thrown. Win sent it skimming as far as the benches that bisected the field, then sat down next to Zoe on a log.

'I never used to believe those stories about women who didn't realise they were pregnant until they went into labour, but I was pregnant and I didn't know.' Zoe braced her palms on the log, so she could stretch out her legs. 'I was still having my periods, still had the contraceptive implant. And that pain. I insisted it was just indigestion and you told me to go to the doctor but I always know best, don't I? If I hadn't left it so long, if I'd gone to the doctor sooner, then maybe ... things would have turned out differently.'

'We still would have lost the baby.' It was the first time that Win had spoken of the baby, instead of referring to what had happened as 'it' or 'the accident' or even occasionally 'the pregnancy'.

'Maybe I wouldn't have lost one perfectly good fallopian tube though.' This was the first time she'd been able to say that particular truth out loud. Even thinking about it could make her tremble so she'd always pushed the thought back into the dusty corner where she'd hidden it. Enough! It was time to face the facts, no matter how cold and hard they might be. 'I've made an appointment with my GP to get a referral to see a consultant at University College Hospital. It won't be for a couple of months, but you'll come with me, won't you?'

'If you want me to,' Win said in a voice that was as neutral as Switzerland but that might have been because his attention was elsewhere, hand shielding his eyes so he could scan the field for Florence who'd gatecrashed a picnicking gang of teenagers. 'What happens at the hospital?'

Zoe blew a strand of hair away from her face. 'It's at the Reproductive Medicine Unit. I have what sounds like an MOT for my lady bits,' she said with a grimace. 'That's before I even get in to see a consultant.'

Win nodded but didn't say anything else. There were times he seemed a different person from that golden boy of last year. Now he could be so hard, impossible, to read. Zoe sighed. 'You know, Win, I always thought being an adult would be more fun than this.'

'I hear you. I thought I'd eat ice cream for every meal and in between meals too,' Win said. 'I never expected that there'd be times I'd crave vegetables.'

'Or that I'd look forward to an early night. Being an adult can be very dull.'

'Oh, I think there are still some things about being an adult that can be very exciting.' Win turned to her with a smile that made Zoe's heart falter. Something in the curl of his lip, the way his eyes darted down to Zoe's breasts, which was … unexpected. It had been nine months since that sunny Sunday morning when they'd last made love and since then, it had been the last thing on Zoe's mind. On Win's mind too, she'd thought.

They both glanced towards the end of the field where Florence had outstayed her welcome and without having to discuss it, they got up to retrieve their errant hound. 'Being a kid was horrible,' Win said. 'I had no control over what happened to me. I always thought that when I was a grown-up, nothing bad would ever happen because I wouldn't allow it.'

Zoe took his hand. 'Win, you can't plan against bad luck. It's luck. It's random.'

'I wish you could though,' he said wistfully, waving at Florence as they got nearer, though she pretended that she couldn't see them. 'A comprehensive flowchart to cover all eventualities so that random bad luck simply couldn't occur. It could take up the big long wall in the kitchen.'

'Because that would look much more aesthetically pleasing than the framed David Bowie album covers you were going to put up there instead,' Zoe said drily and Win smiled. 'Anyway, you can't plan for random good luck either. I'm pretty sure that they balance each other out. Right?'

'I'd have to work out the probability to be certain,' Win insisted in his stuffiest voice, the one he used to pull out to make Zoe laugh, and she laughed now, but she thought it might be from sheer relief that they hadn't completely lost who they used to be.

They hardly talked at all on the way home. Ever since that charged look he'd given her, his veiled reference to their once healthy sex life, there'd been a tension between them that was so different from the tension of a relationship in turmoil, the awkward gaps, the silences, the things left unsaid.

It was the kind of tension that made Zoe feel as taut as the telephone wires overhead, as they turned into Elysian Place. Zoe unlocked the front door and Win came up behind her, too close, so he could lower his head, nuzzle away the fall of her hair and breathe in the scent of her. It felt primal, maybe even a little intrusive, but Zoe stood there and let him.

It had been a long day. They'd sanded down the skirting

boards and doorframes in the upstairs hall to prep them for painting and Zoe hadn't showered yet, so Win would smell the faint, tired tang of her perfume, the sour note of sweat and another fragrance lurking beneath it all, that she didn't have words or descriptors for but knew it was unique to her – in the same way that Win had his own scent that would sometimes make Zoe bury her face in one of his shirts or jumpers when she was sorting out a wash. And now Zoe thought about just how many times Win had buried his face between her breasts, inhaled and then sighed in satisfaction as if he were home.

Too many times to count. A life of times. But lately, not at all. Before, Zoe wouldn't have thought twice about turning around, looping her arms around Win's waist, tucking her head into the crook of his neck, but now it felt like such a brave thing to do.

'Florence,' Win muttered and with a sigh, Zoe let Win go so she could unclip Florence from her lead and harness, then take her into the kitchen for fresh water and food.

Win had followed her into the kitchen and was standing in the doorway. They hadn't turned the lights on and the night was slowly, imperceptibly drawing in, so again, it was hard to tell what he was thinking.

The gap between them got smaller and smaller until Win was standing in front of Zoe. She'd never wanted to kiss him as much as she did right then. Not even in the days when all she did was imagine what it might be like to kiss him.

'Hello,' Win said, as if they were meeting again after a long time apart.

Zoe smiled. 'Hello.' She pressed her hand to his face. 'It's been a while, hasn't it?'

Win kissed her then. Not the lazy, heatless kisses of a couple who'd known each other for thirteen years, but as if they'd never kissed before. His touch, his taste, all shockingly new all over again.

But even after all this time, they still fitted together. Win's mouth on hers, Zoe's hand in his as she led him up the stairs.

It was a lot like the first time all over again. And it *was* a first time in this new house as well as slipping back into the old and familiar routine as Win undressed her. Zoe raising her arms so he could slip off her T-shirt, presenting him with her back to kiss as he unclipped her bra.

Then it was Zoe's turn to unbutton his shirt, palm her hands over the ridge of each of his ribs, her touch firm enough not to tickle because she still remembered what Win liked.

'Hello,' Win said again, when they were lying on the bed that they'd bought together all those years ago, and he was about to slide inside her. 'Hello, old friend.'

'Hello, hello, hello,' Zoe whispered in his ear, as she wriggled, then tightened her arms and legs around him. 'Hello, I've missed you.'

She'd never take this for granted again. She vowed, as Win's hands gripped her upper arms, to savour every second. She wanted to memorise all the little details that she thought had been forgotten but were now flooding back. The hitch in Win's throat, the flush on his face, the way he stared down at her, his gaze as blue and as deep as oceans.

She waited for his first thrust, was so ready for him, but he stilled, fingers on the slight pucker of skin on her left arm.

'Your implant?' he muttered. 'Did you have it removed?'

She had as soon as she'd registered with her new doctor. She'd wanted it gone. Now really wasn't the time to be remembering all this.

'It's fine. It doesn't matter,' she said, trying to pull him down on her, in her.

'So, are you on something else?' Win asked, holding his body very still. 'Because I don't have any protection.'

Protection. He wanted to protect her, but Zoe didn't need protecting any more.

'Let's do it anyway,' she said rashly, trying to wriggle against him. 'Let's just see where fate takes us.'

Win didn't even have to think about it. 'Let's not.' He rolled away from Zoe to lie on his back.

'Win!' Zoe didn't even have the will to be angry with him. She was too disappointed. Too frustrated because Win had wound her up, then left her with nowhere to go. 'Is this going to be yet another thing that we don't talk about? I thought we were getting back to being happy and God knows, sex used to make us both happy.'

'I'm all on board with having sex,' Win said through what sounded like gritted teeth. 'I am not on board with you getting pregnant through sheer carelessness, not after what happened last time.'

It was a fair point. Reasonable, responsible, though three minutes ago reason and responsibility had been the last things on Zoe's mind.

Win lifted a hand. 'I could still get you off ... if you wanted.'

'Not really in the mood now,' she said, flopping onto her back too.

Win was saved from having to reply by a whining and thumping of a paw at the door. With a sigh he slid off the bed to mollify a furious Florence. 'I'm going to grab a shower, OK?'

They hadn't put the lights on and the room was in shadow. Zoe snapped on her bedside lamp. She lay there for a while, felt her body begin to quieten, her heart return to its usual steady pace. She listened to the sound of the shower running, then rolled over and pulled Libby's diary out of the drawer of her nightstand.

It had been a while, out of respect for Win's thoughts on the subject of Libby and her diary. At this precise moment, Zoe didn't feel that inclined to respect Win's wishes on the matter. She was heartily fed up with respecting Win's wishes, his boundaries, the half a dozen things he wasn't ready to talk about.

But now, seeing the familiar scrawl, Zoe was surprised to find that she'd missed the other woman. At least Libby was trying to live her best life, Zoe thought, as she turned to July, only to find that Libby had forsaken her; the diary for that month was little more than a record of appointments.

Heath with Beryl.
Heath with Beryl.
Heath with Beryl.

A postcard from Aldeburgh signed only H but Zoe recognised Hugo's handwriting.

Weather good. Bathed or boated with the children most days.
Having a lovely time – would be even lovelier if you were here too.
Nothing else to report as yet.

So, Hugo had children. Once again, Zoe was baffled by Libby's bad life choices. If the decades hadn't separated them, if she had been friends with Libby, then Zoe would have taken her out, plied her with booze and told her in no uncertain times that while Freddy was bad news, Hugo was even worse news. He was married, had kids, was going through a messy divorce and the best thing Libby could do was forget both of them.

'Plenty more fish in the sea,' Zoe would say, even though it was the singularly most annoying thing to say to anyone who was having relationship problems. 'Anyway, there's nothing wrong with being single.'

It was a conversation she'd had countless times with countless friends – though those friends liked to point out Zoe had gone straight from Tony Cortes to Win, with no waiting, no cooling off period and so she had no idea what being single was really like.

And she never wanted to find out, Zoe thought. She heard Win step out of the shower and she turned back to the diary, squinting to make out the words of Libby's first proper entry in weeks.

July 29th
Awful scene with Millicent. Just awful. Accused me of terrible things, a lot of them true, but they didn't feel true. Then I came over all queer. Thought I was going to DIE.
    M scared enough to want to send for the doctor but I felt better after a cup of tea.
    I know what's wrong with me. Those Parisian doctors have ruined me, butchered me.

Zoe put a hand to her own stomach. To the scar. Even in the dark, Win had avoided touching the jagged line down the right side of her belly. Not some neat little keyhole incision. No time for that.

Libby's fears set off her own fears again. Zoe imagined them as a set of dominos arranged on the floor in an endless, intricate pattern and if she wasn't careful, didn't watch her step, then they'd all come tumbling down. She put Libby's diary away. Shoved it right to the back of the drawer just as Win came back from his shower. Skin pink from the hot water, hair slicked back, in just a pair of shorts.

'What are you doing?'

'Oh, nothing.' Zoe sat with her back to the nightstand, one hand behind her at an awkward angle to shut the drawer. 'Looking for something. Didn't find it. Not to worry.'

She was tripping over her words, as if she were guilty of something. But she was also nervous because she hadn't seen Win like this, practically naked, for a long, long time. Despite his accident, Win still had a long, lean runner's body, deceptively strong, which had always come in handy for carrying suitcases and hefting bags of charcoal back from the shops during barbecue season.

It had always turned Zoe on, added a dark thrill to their lovemaking, that Win could pin her down, hold her captive.

Despite the fact that she absolutely wasn't in the mood now, Zoe couldn't help the little shiver as Win came towards her, his gaze intent. 'Shower's free,' he said, while his eyes said something completely different.

'Is it? I should head for the bathroom then.' Zoe made no effort to move from the bed as Win shook his head.

'No point. Not when I'm about to get you all messy,' he said. 'It's been a while . . .'

'It's been nearly a year!'

'But I do dimly recall that there are a multitude of things I can do to you, with just my hands and mouth, that will still have you screaming my name. In a good way,' he added, when Zoe raised her eyebrows sceptically.

Zoe wanted them to be all right and she wasn't averse to screaming Win's name in a good way but she was still cross enough that Win was going to have to do better than that. Work much harder.

She folded her arms and tilted her chin in a mutinous way. 'These things you're going to do, what exactly are they?'

Win rested one knee on the bed, a tiny, teasing smile on his face. 'They're not the kind of things I can explain. It's probably best if I just show you.'

'Fighting talk, Mr Rowell,' Zoe said, resisting the smile that wanted to lift the corners of her mouth. She leant back against the pillows, arms still folded. 'Go on then, do your worst.'

29

Zoe

Zoe had been banished to the kitchen by the builders, who had finally reached the back bedroom she'd repurposed as a temporary lounge, the very last room that needed their attention, which would become her studio.

She had raced through a draft and rough illustrations of the first instalment of *The Highgate Woods Mysteries* starring the irrepressible (according to Mademoiselle Marsaud, her governess) Miss Elizabeth Edwards and her dog Florence as they foiled a petnapping ring. Zoe was scheduled to do two readings at the nephews' primary school, because it was the best way to get both constructive and utterly crushing criticism, then she'd start on a second draft.

In the meantime, in response to a nagging email from Hardeep, her new illustration agent, using all shouty caps, she was updating her online portfolio.

Being busy again, in work mode, was yet another indication that Zoe was fast becoming the woman she used to be. Although, truthfully, Zoe knew one of the reasons she was happy to throw herself back into the loving embrace of her work ethic was because she certainly wasn't able to throw herself back into the loving embrace of her husband.

What Zoe had thought was the happy resumption of their sex life had turned out to be a one-off. A mercy hump. Win throwing her a bone. The next evening when Zoe had cosied up to Win in bed, freshly showered, with loving on her mind, he'd held her back with one arm and a copy of *Record Collector*.

'I wasn't sure if you'd want to and I haven't had a chance to get any condoms,' he'd said in an offhand manner, as if he'd much rather be reading about how much a test pressing of David Bowie's *Life On Mars* was worth than having Zoe kiss his neck.

Zoe wasn't to be swayed. 'We can do other things,' she'd said, her hand delving downwards. 'You did some pretty amazing other things last night.'

Win had intercepted her hand before it reached its target. 'Let's not until after we've seen the consultant. Otherwise, it's only going to muddy the waters.'

'Muddy the waters? Is that really how you want to describe us having sex?' Zoe had demanded, her voice rising along with the flush that swept over every inch of her skin, so different from how pink she'd been the night before when Win hadn't stopped with his hands and his mouth until she was limp and giddy.

'You know I didn't mean it like that,' Win had said, his own voice getting tight, his lips thinning. 'You're being ridiculous.'

'*I'm* being ridiculous? *I'm* being ridiculous?'

The argument that followed culminated in Win taking himself off to the spare room to sleep on the air mattress, Florence opting to go with him, which was another dagger in Zoe's side.

So, she was relieved to immerse herself in work, to use parts of her brain that had lain dormant for months. Even the fiddly job of updating her online portfolio, which involved a lot of scanning illustrations then tarting them up on the computer, was a welcome respite from replaying the fight with Win and thinking of all the snappy retorts that had eluded her at the time. But when Zoe realised that she'd spent the last twenty minutes filling out increasingly inane personality quizzes on Facebook, she remembered now that the woman she used to be was also a champion procrastinator and it was time to step away from her screen.

Florence was always ready for a walk and the woods beckoned, the trees providing shade from the August heat as Zoe slowly ambled downhill.

She was almost at the gate that led on to Muswell Hill when Florence's ears pricked up and she bounded over to a man sitting on a bench.

'Florence! Come back!' Florence seemed to think that people sitting on benches were simply waiting for her to arrive so they could lavish attention on her. 'We've talked about this before!'

Florence had already sat down in front of the man, front right paw held aloft in greeting because she really was the most appalling flirt, but as Zoe got nearer she realised that Florence was among friends.

'Hello, Clive!' she said in surprise, because last time she'd seen Clive out and about he had a walking frame and wouldn't have dared try to navigate the uneven paths of Highgate Woods.

'Hello, lovely girl,' Clive replied as Zoe sat down next to him. 'Before you nag me, this is about as far as I go under my own steam. Just taking the air.'

'Glad to hear it. You look much more like your old self,' Zoe said. Clive was wearing socks and sandals, baggy knee-length khaki shorts, a white T-shirt that proclaimed YOLO, which Cath had brought him as a gag gift for his eightieth birthday, and a New York Yankees baseball cap. It was quite the look but Zoe was of the firm belief that by the time you got to eighty-odd, you should be able to wear what the hell you wanted. 'I like your cane.'

Clive's walking frame had been replaced by a sturdy stick with a flame motif on it.

'I was about to say the same thing about you,' Clive said, peering at Zoe's face. 'Lost that peakiness you had a few months back.'

'I feel so much better.' It was good to be able to say that and have it be the truth, rather than a means to stop people asking questions.

They talked about Clive's recovery. How he was swimming again and how he loved his new stairlift and the independence it had given him so much that he was now having a walk-in bath installed.

'I don't want carers in and I certainly don't want to be a nuisance to Cath and Theo,' he said. 'They're making noises about moving back to their flat. Apparently they have to give their tenants notice quite soon.' He sighed. 'Getting better seems a bit like a double-edged sword.'

Zoe patted Clive's hand. 'If you don't want Cath and Theo to move out, then perhaps you should tell them that,' she suggested gently because she'd had a similar conversation with Cath a couple of days before about how living with Clive gave her peace of mind and a garden but that she didn't want to make him feel that he'd become a burden.

'They could have the run of the top floor, turn one of the bedrooms into a sitting room,' Clive said, and he and Zoe talked a little more about home improvements, because there was very little Zoe didn't know about improving a home, then Clive fixed her with a stern look. 'Actually, I have a bone to pick with you, young lady.'

'A bone?' Zoe immediately felt guilty though she couldn't have imagined what she might have done to offend Clive. 'Me?'

'Yes, you!' Clive clarified. 'Cath told me ages ago you'd found a mysterious suitcase in your house and that you wanted to pick my brains about local history. I sorted out some maps and things for you, but have you called? You have not!'

Zoe was suitably chastened, though she did point out that she had been rather busy. Clive wasn't to be appeased until Zoe agreed to come to tea the next day with Libby's diary and any other information that might be relevant.

The following afternoon, with Libby's diary swathed in bubble wrap, Zoe took tea with Clive.

He'd been as good as his word and while he tried to read Libby's diary with the aid of his varifocals and a magnifying glass, Zoe sifted through the items that Clive had set aside for her.

There was a 1935 Ordnance Survey map for Muswell Hill, which included Highgate Woods but stopped just shy of the Archway Road, which meant that any land further south, including what was to become Elysian Place, wasn't on it either. There was also a Ward Lock *Red Guide* to London from 1937, which was full of all sorts of interesting facts. How much it cost to travel on the bus (thruppence) and where to find a vet or an after-hours chemist.

It was all very interesting. Clive even had some background on Southwood Hall where Libby and Hugo had met for their trysts. It had once been a grand mansion. The smart mansion blocks that had replaced it were built in 1932 and it was possible to sneak into the grounds and find statues in the gardens from the building's illustrious past, but none of it got Zoe any closer to discovering what had happened to Libby after 1936. Or why her diary for that year and a suitcase full of her possessions had been left to moulder in Zoe's house.

'I can barely make out a word she's written,' Clive complained after an hour of squinting at Libby's faint scribbles. 'If we had a time machine, I'd quite like to travel back and present this Libby with either a pencil sharpener or a fountain pen and a bottle of black ink. I'm afraid I haven't managed to glean any more information than what you already have.' He gestured at the sheet of paper where Zoe had typed out all her salient Libby facts.

'Oh.' Zoe puffed out a frustrated breath. 'That's disappointing.'

'Except, I've deciphered all that HW nonsense. One of the HWs is obviously Hugo Watkins as you suggested, the other HW must be Highgate Woods, which is why Hugo picked Southwood Hall as the venue for their affair.' Clive took off his glasses to rub his eyes and smiled at Zoe's dumbfounded expression.

'Of course! Highgate Woods.' She slapped her forehead with the palm of her hand. 'Why didn't I think of that?'

'I'm guessing that you don't do many cryptic crosswords,' Clive noted.

'More Win's department,' Zoe admitted. 'My brain doesn't work that way.' She didn't want to think about Win, for obvious reasons. Also, he wouldn't be impressed that she'd got a third party involved in her search for Libby. 'He thinks that all this is morbid,' she added, as she took in the various papers and books arranged on the dining table in front of them. 'That it will end in tears.'

'It might.' Clive shrugged. 'At my age one tends to dwell on the past too much, whereas you have your whole future ahead of you to become too preoccupied chasing ghosts.'

'Hardly my whole future,' Zoe said, though at the mention of ghosts, a shiver trickled along her spine. 'I'm thirty-two!'

'You're a child.' Clive picked up the well-worn bulging diary in a hand that trembled slightly with the effort. 'Have you read all of this?'

Zoe shook her head. 'Not all of it. You've seen the problem I have with the handwriting, it's not the kind of thing you can just flick through. But I've data-mined it,' she added, picking up her Libby factsheet. 'I've collated all the addresses and important dates I could find. Even had a look on the internet for census information and public records. Not that it was hugely successful. You can't access very much unless you sign up for one of those find your ancestor sites.'

'It's very curious,' Clive said. 'You have all those addresses, except the one address you should have.'

It was all sounding terribly cryptic again. Zoe studied her list. 'No, these are all the addresses that were in the diary, or on letters and cards. I'm sure I haven't missed one out.'

'You haven't got your address on there though,' Clive pointed out. 'You have nothing that puts Libby in your house. You don't even know what her connection to the house was. That's what's really baffling and I'm afraid I haven't been much help.'

'You've been lots of help,' Zoe assured him. 'Especially with the local history.' But she hadn't got much further in her search and it felt as if she might never have the answers she was looking for.

The thought niggled at her as she walked home. In her head was an image of Libby, on her own, no Hugo, no Freddy, taking the same path through Highgate Woods that Zoe was currently taking some eighty years later. But as they both slipped out of the gate to walk up to the Archway Road, Libby stopped. Froze on the spot, as if there was a sign blocking her way that said, Thou Shalt Not Pass, so she was unable to cross the road and head for Elysian Place.

To come home.

30

Libby

Three more days dragged by, then Hugo was back from Suffolk.

They met in the woods. Hugo was waiting for her at the water fountain. Burnished by the sun, his teeth gleaming white in his tanned face as he smiled at the sight of Libby hurrying towards him. In deference to the heat, maybe because he was still in a holiday mood, Hugo was wearing a light-coloured blazer and no tie. Half a world away from the man she'd met in January.

'You look very exotic, as if you should be strolling along a riviera on the Continent,' Libby told him as she reached his side.

'And you look positively beautiful,' he said. 'But then you always do.'

She tucked her arm in his and they began to walk, taking their preferred path opposite the fountain. The trees were denser, the ground more roughly hewn so one could believe that you really were in a forest, miles away from town. Even the squirrels were more plentiful along this secluded stretch.

There was a bench halfway along the path and Libby pulled Hugo down next to her. 'Aren't you going to kiss me then?' she asked, because it had been over a month since they'd last seen each other.

'Let me look at you first.' He took her chin so he could tip her face towards the sunlight that slanted in through a gap in the leaves. 'Yes, everything seems quite present and correct, though you are looking a little thinner. I shall have to fatten you up, my darling.'

She'd be fat enough soon. Was even looking forward to feeling her waistbands pinch and waddling about like an elephant. Libby smiled and Hugo smiled too, though he couldn't know the joke, then he kissed her.

It was a gentle, unhurried kiss. Not quite as passionate as other kisses of his, especially when he'd been away so long. Libby made a small sound of protest, leaned further into him, opened her mouth under his and for one, quicksilver moment she felt the dart of his tongue against hers, but then Hugo pulled his mouth away, hands on her shoulders, as if to ward her off.

'Not here,' he said. 'Back at the flat ... you still haven't said if you want me to buy it.' He was looking so grave again. 'Because I did say I would take care of you ... '

She couldn't contain the words any longer. 'Us. There's an us to take care of now. I'm having your child.' Libby hadn't meant to announce it in such a clumsy way but she wanted to shout the words at the top of her voice. But then her throat seemed to close up and she could hardly look at Hugo.

He took her chin again, raised her face so she had to look him in the eyes, which had never seemed so blue before, as if Libby might drown if she gazed into them for too long. 'Really? Are you sure?' he asked hoarsely.

Libby nodded and that queer feeling of wanting to laugh and cry all at once was upon her again. 'I'm absolutely sure. I can't believe it myself. Please say you're happy about the news, darling.'

He curved the palm of his hand to fit her cheek as if Libby were something to be revered. 'After what you told me had happened in Paris, well, I assumed . . . '

'So did I. Thought it was hopeless and now I'm so full of hope that I'm quite mad with it.' Libby took hold of his hand and placed it on her belly, which she was sure had a more pronounced curve to it. 'It will be perfect. We'll be together and there'll be a baby too. You are pleased, aren't you?'

'I don't even have the words for how I feel. Pleased, happy, they hardly come close,' Hugo said and finally he smiled. His smile reeled her in, wrapped itself around her as surely as his tightest embrace, made her feel so loved, so wanted, so needed. 'I'm ecstatic, Libby. Delirious. Quite, quite transported and if you weren't *enceinte*, I'd pick you up and twirl you in my arms.' He grew concerned. 'You are well though? You look well.'

'Positively blooming,' she assured him, as his fingers stayed warm and splayed on her belly. 'I felt rotten while you were away, but I'm fine now. A little dizzy if I stand up too quickly but the doctor says that's because I have a touch of anaemia. Back on the milk stout and liver, I'm afraid.'

'I'll buy you steak every day,' Hugo promised and it was so different to how Freddy had behaved when Libby had told him she was carrying his child.

They'd been in a dark, dingy pub in Soho with his dark, dingy friends. The fug of beer and tobacco had made Libby bilious and she'd dragged an unwilling Freddy outside. He'd lit a cigarette as she'd told him the news.

'Well, that's that,' he'd said flatly and taken a long drag on his cigarette. 'It is mine, then?'

'Of course, it's yours,' Libby had said, stung, and as an afterthought she'd slapped him round the face in a half-hearted

262

fashion – it seemed the right thing to do – then she'd flounced away and Freddy had sighed and come after her.

Perhaps the baby had known it wasn't truly wanted, not by its father, and Libby's love, her devotion, hadn't been enough to keep it safe.

'Darling Libby, you've given me more than I ever dared to dream,' Hugo was saying. She tore herself away from the unhappy memories to where he was sitting next to her, his body angled towards her, her hands in his. 'Let's go back to the flat now. And I'll call the agent first thing in the morning.'

Libby didn't want to be ungrateful when Hugo was offering her all of himself, but now it was her turn to pull away. 'Not the flat,' she said haltingly. 'I don't want to start our new life, be a family, where something so illicit happened. That our first kiss, our first moments of being truly together, were witnessed by a detective. Please say you understand.'

Hugo kissed her again, but it felt as if her words had punctured the joy that had surrounded them. He said that he'd see her as far as the heath and neither of them even looked across the street at the mansion block as they left the woods.

They crossed over Archway Road, then the road that curved behind it, full of houses being built. Over the last few months as she'd walked to meet Hugo, Libby had always checked on their progress. She could see now that the houses were mostly complete, their scaffolding and canvas draperies all but gone.

'What about these?' Hugo asked, as he saw Libby glance down the street.

'What about them? They look nice, I suppose,' Libby replied. 'Awfully smart.'

'Let's have a proper look,' Hugo suggested and he steered her down the street where the houses had all been built to look like miniature Tudor or Georgian mansions.

'How odd,' she said to Hugo. 'Why would you want to live in a new house that looks like an old house?'

'Not this one.' They were standing outside a house still obscured by scaffolding but even so Libby could tell from the sleek lines, the gleaming white of the frontage, that it had been designed to look as if it were built in the last ten years, not during the reign of Elizabeth I. 'This one looks more modern, don't you think?'

'Coincidentally, the style is called The Moderne,' said a youngish man, in trousers and shirtsleeves, his face ruddy from recent exertions, who'd just emerged from the house and was walking down the path towards them. 'With an e on the end, in the French style. For the potential homeowner with a more discerning eye.'

Libby turned to hide her smile at his salesman patter. 'It's for sale then?' Hugo asked.

'Last one. All the others have been snapped up. I'm Gordon Shaw, master builder.' He and Hugo shook hands. 'Welcome to Elysian Place. Don't know if you're cognizant of your Greek mythology but Elysian pertains to all matters heavenly.' The man spread his arms wide. 'And who wouldn't want a small piece of Paradise in leafy Highgate to call their own?'

'We would.' Hugo turned to Libby. 'Wouldn't we?'

'A whole house? Have you gone quite mad?'

Hugo grinned. 'Well, what use would half a house be?'

Gordon Shaw, master builder, was very agreeable to letting them have a look around the house. It was finished enough that Libby could see the stained-glass panels in the front door and the window in the stairwell adorned with sunbeams, so one might always feel lifted and cheery when one glanced at them. The rooms were bright and cheery too and it would have electricity, and hot water simply by lighting the geyser in

264

the kitchen. There was a scullery with a sink in it and a pantry and if Libby had been asked to design her dream home, it would look a lot like this one.

'You could have radiators in every room.' Hugo came up behind Libby so he could close his arms around her waist again as she stood in the kitchen gazing out of the window at the garden that was just topsoil though Mr Shaw had promised it would be laid to grass and fruit trees planted. 'Shaw says they can put a shower in the bathroom too. I'll give you every modern convenience you could possibly want.'

'Don't be ridiculous, Hugo! A house! You can't buy a house as casually as if you were buying a pair of socks or a new tie. I don't need to be spoiled like this. It would make no difference to me if you were poor.' Libby laughed nervously because even though she loved Hugo, she wasn't sure what she'd done to deserve all this love. Certainly no one else that she'd loved so doggedly, so desperately, had loved her back even half as much. Only her own flesh and blood – father, mother, sister – and all that love had died with them. It seemed to Libby that she'd been searching for its replacement ever since.

'Not spoiled. Cherished,' Hugo said, guiding her down the hall and into the front room. The lounge, he called it. 'Shall we get rid of the nasty old-fashioned fireplace?'

The fireplace was simple and elegant, the outer tiles and the ashpan a lovely duck-egg blue, the inner tiles and the edging a darker French navy.

'Even with radiators, there's something so lovely and cosy about a fire on a winter's night,' Libby decided. She looked around the room. It was all clean lines, no nooks and crannies and queer little angles where shadows could lurk. The house would hardly need any cleaning at all. Just a char to come in twice a week. 'Everything here is perfect. I'd hardly change a thing.'

They walked through hand in hand, peering around doors, exclaiming at each new discovery. Libby didn't want Hugo to think that she was a horrid little gold-digger but she couldn't help but get caught up in the madness of it all.

'This could be the nursery,' she said when they came to the last unexplored room upstairs, with its view of the garden where the baby would lie in its pram on sunny days, fat fists curled, as it watched the leaves dance on the trees, the clouds roll by.

'I never even asked how far along you are,' Hugo said and she noticed that already he looked at her differently; almost as if he were slightly scared of her. Before he'd gone away, he'd always looked at Libby hungrily, as if he couldn't wait to make her naked.

'Three months, the doctor said.' Libby found that she was blushing. 'I think it must have been the first time that we ... we were together.'

She'd often wondered, before she'd become pregnant the first time, if there were something wrong with her. She hadn't lived chastely, but she was one of the few women she knew who hadn't got caught even though there had been times that she'd been careless; had been too poor to bother with Volpar gels and too drunk to douche with vinegar after. So many girls she'd known had had to marry in haste or disappear to stay with distant relatives only to return a little diminished, a little less than they once had been. Or there was always Mickey Flynn who, for a small fee, would affect an introduction to a doctor with rooms in Harley Street. Or for a smaller fee, would put a girl in touch with a doctor who worked out of a cheap hotel in Marble Arch.

It had never been anything that Libby had to worry about until she was thirty-one and positively ancient. And now, at thirty-two, when she'd been told that her dancing days were over, here she was about to take to the floor again.

'Well, it was a memorable night,' Hugo said with a wolf-ish smile that was so out of character that it made Libby laugh. 'So, February, then. Six months from now.' His expression grew serious once more. 'Even if we've gone to court, the divorce won't be final by then. The child will be born a b—'

'Don't say it!' Libby covered his lips with her hand. 'I'm so happy, don't ruin it, because the dates, this legal nonsense, they're simply not important.'

'I'm not even sure I'll be able to put my name on the birth certificate.' Hugo moved away from Libby to lean against the window sill. 'If the divorce isn't final, if I'm meant to have no contact with you for six months.'

'I don't see how it counts. It's the contact you had with me which led to the divorce in the first place.' Libby was bored with talking about it. It was the dullest subject on earth. 'I've already told you I don't care. You don't have to buy a house, you really don't, because wherever we live, even if it's a mud hut, we'll be happy, we'll be a family. I'll call myself Mrs Watkins and no one need be any the wiser.'

Hugo ran a hand through his hair, though it took more than that for it to fall into disarray. 'It's not how things should be. I don't suppose you've heard from your erstwhile husband?'

The situation in Spain had escalated at a quite frightening pace. The Nationalists were on their way to Madrid. Libby was sure that Freddy, allied as he was to the Republican cause, was having far too much fun to think about writing to her, much less coming back to London so he could denounce her as an adulteress in front of a packed court. 'Not so much as a postcard,' she said and Hugo cursed under his breath, his eyes no longer dark and full of promise, but squinty and cold. 'I swear to God, if you say one more word about any of this,

I will scream. If you don't want me, don't want the baby, you only have to say. We'll manage, just the two of us,' Libby said hotly, then she couldn't say any more because Hugo had stood up and he was kissing her quite desperately.

As if he loved her more than anything.

31

Libby

Hugo told Mr Shaw he would buy the house and there was nothing Libby could say that would persuade him otherwise. He also set up an account at Heal's and Libby was to order anything she needed from bedroom sets to sideboards, sofas, a dining table.

'Don't worry about the cost,' Hugo had said and because he'd made his own fortune, it meant a lot that he wanted to share it with Libby.

She travelled up to town to spend the day in Heal's, taking notes and making lists. It was a rather daunting task for someone who hadn't had a home to truly call her own for nearly twenty years and it was late afternoon by the time she got off the Tube at Hampstead. Libby was hungry – she was hungry all the time now – and although she was hot and sticky too, she was of a mind to go to the Flask for something hearty to eat instead of making do with the usual unpalatable vegetarian fare at Willoughby Square.

'Miss Libby!' There was an urgent voice in her ear, a hand

tugging at her arm and Libby turned to see Hannah standing there. 'I've been waiting for ages! You're to come home immediately.'

All thoughts of pie and mash were banished. Libby had taken to carrying her diary with her, all her correspondence stuffed in its pages, as she didn't trust Millicent not to have a good snoop through her things. So she was sure there was no incriminating evidence lying around but even so she felt her stomach clench in anticipation.

'I said I'd be back by five,' she said lightly. 'I'm sure I don't need an escort from the station. What ever is Millicent fussing about now? Are you all right, Hannah? You look very out of sorts.'

Hannah's big round face was bright red. 'You're to come home right away,' she said again, her words forbidding yet her voice was bubbling with glee as if she couldn't quite believe that she'd been appointed the bearer of bad news. 'There's been a telegram from Mr Freddy's editor. He's been mortally wounded and Mrs Morton's in hysterics.'

Libby ran all the way back to the house with Hannah at her heels. Hannah had left the front door wide open. Her mother had left the front door open too the day the telegram arrived from the War Office. Had run out into the middle of the street, where Libby and her sister had been playing, and dropped to her knees. Wailed. A keening. Such an awful sound. And all the other doors on the street had opened, women spilling out, wiping hands on aprons grubby from a day spent keeping house for men who might not come home.

There was no wailing when Libby stepped inside number 17. She paused with her hand to her heart, which was racing, then slid her hand down because the doctor had told her not to exert herself. But her stomach felt as solid as ever, though it roiled alarmingly as she pushed open the door of the parlour.

It was like a scene from a painting, something Dutch and gloomy. Millicent in her long black dress was arranged on the chaise longue, hands clasped together, the aunts and Mrs Carmichael sitting like three wise monkeys on the sofa opposite and little Miss Bettany perched on a chair, currant eyes filmy and swimming with tears.

For one awful moment Libby thought that Millicent might have died. She was lying there so still, her face an awful jaundiced yellow, then she whimpered. 'Elizabeth, is that you, my dear?'

It had to be the very worst news if Millicent was calling her dear. Libby dropped to her knees by Millicent's side. 'I'm so sorry about Freddy,' she said.

'My poor Freddy, my darling boy.' Millicent moaned and waved something at Libby. The telegram.

Libby smoothed it out and began to read, her brow knotted first in dread, then fury.

```
FREDDY SHOT MADRID STOP STABLE STOP
ARRANGING PASSAGE TO LONDON STOP CANST
MEET HIM IN PARIS QUERY ADVISE EARLIEST
CONVENIENCE STOP FLEET SIX THREE FIVE
NINE STOP
```

Libby rounded on Hannah who shrank back. 'I've a good mind to box your ears,' she snapped. 'Mortally wounded means dead, you little ninny!'

'Been shot though.' Hannah was determined to stand her ground or at least stay in the parlour and watch the theatrics for as long as possible. 'Don't see how anyone could survive being shot. They never do in the pictures.'

Millicent gave another guttural whimper, the ladies twittered, Hannah leaned in closer and Libby felt sweat break out on her brow. 'Stop talking nonsense and go and make some tea. Strong, sweet tea,' she said firmly to Hannah, because tea would have to do when there wasn't a drop of alcohol in the house.

'My Freddy. Just like my dear Arthur,' Millicent moaned and when Libby took her hand she clutched it tightly. 'Both of them gone!'

'Freddy's not gone,' Libby said gently. 'He's stable. If it were serious, if he were badly wounded, they wouldn't be packing him off to Paris, would they?'

Of course they wouldn't. Unless the situation in Spain was so dangerous that it wasn't safe for Freddy. And hadn't Libby read in the paper only a week or so ago that France had closed its border with Spain? Libby could feel one of her heads coming on; a deep throbbing between her eyes.

'Elizabeth, you'll go to Paris and fetch my darling boy back for me, won't you?' Millicent tried to sit up and for all her usual histrionics, her face was still that awful yellow colour and in the gap between words she was making a ghastly rasping sound. 'Will you go and phone Freddy's editor? Will you do it now?'

'You really can't be comfortable like that.' Libby rose to her feet and rearranged the stiff embroidered cushions so that Millicent was propped up. 'Now, if Freddy is well enough to get to Paris, then he can get back to London under his own steam,' she added doubtfully. 'It's quite simple. A train to Calais, then the boat and another train from Dover to Victoria.'

Libby had done the journey, still weak and trembling from her weeks in a Paris hospital, so Freddy could do it too. It was a fitting sort of retribution.

'But he's been shot! The bullet may still be lodged inside him. He might be bleeding or infection might set in. He might die on the train. In a third-class carriage!' Millicent's voice was rising to a piercing pitch, her movements agitated. 'Do you want him to die on his own on a filthy French train?'

'I can't go to Paris,' Libby said and she cast her eyes about the room for a more suitable candidate. Someone who wasn't expecting again and as the doctor had said, 'lacking a certain youth', so a jaunt to Paris was out of the question. 'Maybe Potts could go. Or even Hannah?'

'Hannah! Hannah? I hardly dare send Hannah to post a letter!'

'Is she hysterical?' Hannah was back with the tea and didn't seem the least bit offended by her employer's damning assessment of her capabilities. Her eyes gleamed. 'Perhaps you should slap her, Miss Libby?'

'Nobody's slapping anybody. Perhaps someone from the newspaper could travel to Paris to fetch Freddy. Or Virena Edmonds,' Libby added sourly, as Virena would enjoy nothing more than bossing and bullying Freddy and spoon-feeding him broth while being unspeakably rude to anyone foreign or from the lower orders. 'Yes! Virena would be perfect.'

'It has to be you, Elizabeth.' Millicent seized Libby's hand in a bruising grip. 'Freddy is all I have. My only child; without him I have no one. Yes, you've had this silly argument but I know you love him and that he loves you. You're the only one I trust to bring him safely back to me.'

'But I haven't been well, Millicent, you know I haven't.' Libby was starting to waver. The babies, the one she'd lost and the one she already loved, she'd do anything for either one of them. Would have laid down her life if the choice had been given to her, so she knew a little something about the maternal bonds. Still, Libby had trodden the boards long enough to smell ham at a hundred yards. Now that she'd taken some tea, Millicent was back to being sallow rather than yellow and liverish, and when she saw the assessing look that Libby was giving her, the older woman coughed delicately and placed her hand over her heart.

'Perhaps Virena could go,' Millicent agreed in a faint voice. 'But she's so busy with her committees that it might take her some time.' The fingers resting on the bodice of her black bombazine twitched. 'Oh! My heart is trembling so; it makes me feel quite giddy. I could be dead by the time Virena brings poor Freddy home.'

Libby knew when she was beaten. 'Millicent, I'm quite sure that you'll outlive us all. Certainly you'll still be alive when I fetch Freddy home from Paris. I'm counting on it, otherwise it would be rather a wasted trip.'

32

Zoe

Zoe was furious with Win. Absolutely bloody furious.

But this time it was the fury that any reasonable woman would have when her husband took two weeks off work to help decorate then turned out to be so spectacularly bad at decorating that she was close to *begging* him to go back to work.

'If you show me how do it, then I'll do it,' he'd say and Zoe would show him how to tape over the skirting boards so he didn't get paint on them and yet Win still managed to get paint on them. Hanging wallpaper for the first time together was not a watershed moment in their relationship but something that would haunt Zoe until her dying day.

'Yes! For God's sake, they match up! How many more times?' Win had had the audacity to snap at Zoe when she'd asked if the two strips of very expensive wallpaper she'd just pasted and hung were perfectly aligned. Of course they weren't. They were a good centimetre out as any fool, except Win, could have told Zoe. As it was, Win would never know how close Zoe had come to upending the bucket of wallpaper paste over his head.

It was two weeks of decorating or rowing about the decorating, with only the occasional trip to B&Q providing a brief respite. And when they weren't embroiled in their interminable home improvements, they still weren't having sex. For all Win's hurt that Zoe had shied away from his touch when she'd been grieving, now it was Win giving Zoe the widest of berths. Even in bed, *especially* in bed, he acted as if he'd much rather be in the spare room on the airbed. It was as if he didn't trust Zoe not to force herself on him or pierce holes in the condoms, which she'd bought and presented to Win with great ceremony. Not that Zoe felt much like having sex herself; your husband acting like a skittish virgin was hardly an aphrodisiac.

They were brewing for another fight and they ended up having it in the middle of IKEA in the soft furnishing department, Win shouting, 'This is not about the curtains for the guest bedroom and my supposed lack of design aesthetic, this is about you wanting to have a baby and I have already told you that I am not having a conversation about that until after we've seen the consultant.'

All eyes were upon them as he'd stalked off, leaving Zoe to manoeuvre that unwieldiest of beasts, the IKEA trolley, all by herself. Win did catch up with her at the till but only so they could have another row in the food shop over a packet of frozen cinnamon buns.

None of this was what Zoe wanted. Not when they'd been through so much already. And not when they should have been celebrating that the builders were finished, bar the snagging. It had taken eight months, tens of thousands of pounds and Win threatening to charge Gavin rent.

The day after an obviously relieved Win went back to work, Gavin finally left the premises. 'From now on, I'm only coming through your front door as an invited guest and not a paid contractor,' he told Zoe as they did a grand tour of the house to retrieve all his stray tools, including the tiny Philips screwdriver which had been sitting in their toothbrush holder for weeks.

'Unless we start getting electric shocks every time we turn on a light or the ceiling suddenly collapses,' Zoe said. 'Then once you've fixed those problems, you'll never be allowed to darken our doorstep ever again.'

Gavin pretended to cry and as Zoe hugged him, she thought how much she'd miss his little nuggets of well-meaning advice, perfectly brewed cups of tea and strong, steady presence in the face of disaster. What she wouldn't miss was Gavin eating marrowfat peas with his lunch, then telling Zoe 'best to give it fifteen minutes' when he came out of the new downstairs loo with a copy of the *Daily Mirror* tucked under his arm.

Once Gavin had driven off in his van, giving a triumphant toot on the horn as he rounded the corner, Zoe took the Tube to Warren Street. She'd dutifully peed in a bottle clearly not designed for the task, now double-Ziplocked in her handbag, which she handed to the nurse when she arrived for her blood tests and scans at University College Hospital.

'Not squeamish about the sight of blood, are you?' the nurse asked her as she skilfully inserted a needle into the vein in the crook of Zoe's right elbow.

Zoe remembered throwing up at the sight of the blood pouring out of the gash in Win's leg, but now she watched intently as the crimson drops became a steady stream that flowed into a test tube. She imagined each drop as a harbinger of hope. That it would be tested and the results would be perfect. One hundred per cent. A-starred.

A week later, when she and Win were shown into the consultant's office, Zoe felt as if she were about to sit an exam. They were still doing DIY on the evenings and weekends, which involved a lot of eye rolling and passive-aggressive sniping at each other, so the atmosphere between them was strained. But this morning, Zoe clutched tight hold of Win's hand until he had to adjust her grip so her wedding and engagement rings didn't gouge holes into his skin. Her other hand was in her pocket, fingers worrying at the cherry button, which she'd plucked from the side pocket of her handbag that morning, though for the life of her, Zoe still couldn't decide if it were a good luck charm or a curse.

'There's nothing to be scared about,' Win whispered as the consultant came in. Dr Shetty was a middle-aged Asian woman, with a calm, serene manner that didn't even begin to dispel Zoe's fears.

She glanced through Zoe's notes and asked about the doomed pregnancy. Had Zoe had periods after getting her contraceptive implant? Had she still had periods when she'd been pregnant? Had she had any other symptoms of pregnancy? Nausea? Just the pain? Could she describe the pain?

'I didn't even know I was pregnant. That's the thing,' Zoe said in an exasperated voice. 'I've already explained this a million times.'

'Steady on,' Win murmured and he stroked his thumb across the back of her white-knuckled fist. Zoe realised that she hadn't explained this a million times. She'd been rushed to hospital in an ambulance, siren blaring, lights flashing, but she'd been oblivious to it all. Unconscious, pumped full of drugs, and she'd only woken up when it was all over.

She might have relived it in her head over and over again. To wonder if something might have been done if only she'd realised what was happening. If the baby could have been saved, because she'd read in the paper only a few weeks ago about a woman who'd brought her ectopic pregnancy to term. But these had been conversations that had never gone anywhere, but doubled back on themselves because they'd been one-sided and Zoe didn't have any of the answers.

'Usually there are reasons for an ectopic pregnancy,' Dr Shetty said and Zoe knew this too. Knew that in her case it was none of the above. She hadn't had endometriosis or PID. Hadn't had previous abdominal surgery or a coil fitted. Had never smoked, had never taken the morning-after pill, it was just ... 'In this instance, there are no factors to indicate why the foetus didn't develop *in utero*.'

It wasn't at all comforting. That there was nothing Zoe could have done, or do in the future, to ensure that ...

'There has to be a reason,' Win said tightly. 'I've run the numbers. There's a one in a hundred chance of getting pregnant with a contraceptive implant fitted. One in ninety pregnancies develop into an ectopic pregnancy. Only one in four of those results in the fallopian tube rupturing. And you say there were no indicators? There has to be, because do you know what the odds are of those different calamities happening together? Because I worked that out too and—'

'I understand why you want facts and figures, but I'm afraid that sometimes it's a series of unhappy coincidences.' Dr Shetty stared impassively but kindly back at them, as if she'd sat in front of countless other couples and they'd all merged into one anxious-faced, shrill-voiced whole. 'You're obviously a man who sets store by numbers, so let me give you a good number. Sixty-five per cent of women are healthily pregnant eighteen months after an ectopic pregnancy. There is research that suggests that figure could be as much as eighty-five per cent after two years. Those are good odds, aren't they?'

'What about the thirty-five per cent of women who aren't healthily pregnant?' Win asked.

Zoe nudged him. 'But two out of three women are. I'd bet

on those odds.' Hope, sharp and bright, flared to life then dimmed. 'Except how many of those sixty-five per cent only have one fallopian tube?'

'I've treated women who've lost both fallopian tubes but have still conceived with IVF,' the doctor said and hope gave another rallying cry. 'Not that we need to discuss options like IVF right away,' she added quickly. 'You've had one fallopian tube removed but there is a fifteen to twenty per cent chance that an egg produced on that side can still travel down what's left of your tube. So, it's not as if your fertility has been halved. I'd say, at a conservative estimate, that you have a seventy per cent chance of conception. That is, if you did want to start thinking about another baby . . .'

'I do,' Zoe said because she had already thought about another baby. And she hadn't let herself want any more than that. To think about its sex, whether it would take after her or Win, what colour eyes it might have. 'Please say we do, Win.'

Win made a noise that was neither yes nor no, but kept hold of her hand as Dr Shetty asked lots of questions about Zoe's menstrual cycle, talked briefly about ovulation, then handed her an array of leaflets.

'Let's give it a year,' she said, which made Zoe's heart sink, because she couldn't wait another year. 'Let nature take its course and if it needs a helping hand, we can talk about next steps then. Until then, the most effective method of getting pregnant is by having lots of sex.' Dr Shetty smiled as she rose from behind her desk to show them to the door. 'Sometimes we get so caught up in percentages that we forget that making babies should be a lot of fun too. Go home and have some fun.'

33

Zoe

'We'll talk about it later,' Win said before they'd even made their way outside, as if Zoe was intent on dragging him into the first empty room they found so she could get on with the babymaking there and then. She must have had a mutinous glint in her eye as she muttered, 'fine' because Win held up his hands in protest. 'Really, Zo, I promise we'll talk about it but not right now.'

They'd already agreed that after their appointment they'd treat themselves to a tapas lunch at a fancy gastropub near Regent's Park. They couldn't afford it but Zoe had said, and Win had readily agreed for once, that they'd need a bit of cheering up. Now, however, as they walked along in silence, there really wasn't any need for a glass of wine and some marinated chicken skewers as a consolation prize.

The news was good, better than Zoe had dared hope. Yet Win was pinch-faced, taking long strides so she had to scurry to keep up with him. The buses and lorries thundering past as they shot out of the underpass on Euston Road meant that Zoe had to shout to make herself heard.

'Do you want children, Win? Yes or no?'

For a moment Zoe thought that her words had got caught up in the traffic's slipstream. Then Win glanced across at her and she'd never seen him look that way, as if he wanted to hurl himself headfirst in front of a juggernaut to not have this conversation.

'I said not now.' Win strode on. Zoe let him go on ahead and by the time she got to the pub he'd found a table; even better there was a bottle of wine and two glasses. He didn't look up as Zoe slid into the chair opposite, but poured her a glass of Malbec. 'You hate me a little bit right now.'

He didn't even pose it as a question, but a statement of fact, though it didn't come close to being true, even if Zoe had spent the last few weeks raging at him. In the early days when she was just getting to know him, Zoe had thought Win's taciturn ways were enigmatic and mysterious, but she was older, though not that much wiser, and no longer found his quietness intimidating, or sexy.

Now, his quietness was infuriating and frustrating. Win wielded it like a weapon. He always shut down when Zoe wanted to have things out. And there were things that absolutely had to be said so he could just sit there, silent as a bloody grave, while Zoe said them.

'This isn't an argument for one of us to win,' she began. 'We're not going to be able to reach a compromise like when I want a Chinese and you want curry. If I want children and you don't, then we're at a complete impasse. Aren't we?'

Win took a sip of his wine, eyes down. Zoe knew he was playing for time. 'You didn't even know, an hour ago, if we could have children and now you're trying to railroad me into making a decision that has serious repercussions.'

'We're talking about a baby, not investing in some high-risk bonds!' Zoe's voice was so perilously high that something pinged in the back of her throat and when she glanced down, though it hardly needed confirming, her chest above the neckline of her T-shirt was mottled red. 'I know that you were ambivalent about having kids but you're going to have to be more specific than that.'

'We were happy before. Are you saying that you wouldn't be happy if we can't have children ... or decide we don't want to?'

Sometimes Zoe thought that they hadn't been truly happy since that weekend in Yorkshire when they'd last made love, maybe made a baby, and their lives had been sun-dappled and golden. At least then they'd been bumbling along in the same direction. Tragedy hadn't come between them.

'I want children,' Zoe said as simply and plainly as she could when everything in her wanted to scream the words in Win's face. 'Something would always be missing without them. I wouldn't feel complete. I'd never be really happy.'

'You wouldn't be happy with me?' The question tore a hole in Zoe, made something inside her wither a little, but Win saved her from having to answer by shaking his head. 'A sixty-five per cent chance of a healthy pregnancy ... '

'She said seventy per cent ... '

'Basically a one in three chance that something would go wrong,' Win said. 'One in three.'

'Not that something would go wrong,' Zoe argued. 'A one in three chance that I wouldn't get pregnant.'

'I won't go through that again.' Win was speaking so quietly that Zoe had to lean across the table to catch his words. 'To walk into the bathroom and find you like that and have to pull you back ... '

'Win, darling,' Zoe said softly, because he still was her darling. She wanted to take his hands, to touch him, but suddenly she was scared to. There was something lost in his eyes, his

283

face tightening, as if he were about to tip his head back and howl.

'You very nearly died. You almost didn't make it. I know I said that you wouldn't let me touch you, but actually I was scared to touch you too. For a long time afterwards when I looked at you, all I could see was you on the bathroom floor. All that blood, Zo. And I can't let that happen to you again. Not if it means losing you. You can't expect me to. Nobody could.' Zoe could see the damp trickle of tears rolling down his cheeks until he scrubbed at them furiously.

Every day Zoe gave a silent prayer of thanks that Win had found her when he did. Had kicked the bathroom door off its hinges. If it weren't for Win, she *would* have died. It wasn't a dramatic retelling of the events. It was right there in her medical notes.

'You know something? I don't think I've ever thanked you for saving my life.' Zoe got up, scraped her chair back so she could come round the table and kneel in front of Win who refused to look at her, but stared up at the ceiling. 'I'm so sorry for putting you through all that but it turned out all right. Or, you know, seventy per cent all right. See, I can even joke about it.'

Win shook his head. 'I can't. It will never be funny.'

Zoe took Win's hands. They were cold to the touch and she clasped them tightly as if she could breathe life back into them. 'I did nearly die but I didn't. And it isn't a good enough reason to never try again.'

It was odd how Win's hands went limp in Zoe's grasp as if they'd suddenly become boneless. She felt him tense up before he snatched himself away from her touch, folded his arms. 'What if you lost another baby?' he asked hoarsely. 'What then? What if I come home to find you collapsed and bleeding and this time I'm too late? I won't risk it.'

Because he loved her, even after all they'd been through. The coldness, the distance, the arguments, the rough patch that had lasted months now. Win still loved her but he'd always been risk-averse whereas now Zoe was ready to risk their relationship. Or at least test its new boundaries. Push Win into the same direction that her heart wanted to go in.

Zoe took his hand and raised it to her lips, kissed it. 'I love you,' she said, because it was the only thing she could say. It was the truth and she hoped that it was the talisman which would keep them safe along these rocky paths they were continually navigating. Here be dragons. 'I want us to have a baby and I cannot give you any more time. I do not have time. Do you know the perfect age for a woman to have a baby, biologically speaking?'

'I don't,' Win said rather unwillingly, because it was very obviously a rhetorical question and Zoe's blood was up. All of her was red, not just her neck, and Win knew her well enough to know that she was seconds away from ranting, even though she'd wanted to present a calm and measured argument.

But how could Zoe be calm and measured when every time she looked at a paper or turned on the radio, she was being screamed at on all sides?

'Twenty-five!' she exclaimed. 'At twenty-five, everything – ovaries, fallopian tubes, uterus – all in splendid, tip-top condition. At twenty-five, you're young and healthy and strong enough to sail through a pregnancy and labour and deal with all those sleepless nights and—'

'I think you have a rather rosy view of what being twenty-five was like.' Win put his hands out in front of him pleadingly. 'When you were twenty-five, your career was just taking off, mine too. We were still renting because instead of saving for a deposit we liked to go out, a lot, and you were even worse getting up in the morning than you are now.'

'It's still meant to be the best age to have a baby,' Zoe insisted doggedly, because she knew, without having Win to point it out for her, that in her mid twenties she'd barely been able to look after herself, without having a tiny human relying on her to keep them alive too. 'I'm thirty-two now. Seven years older. In three years' time I'll be thirty-five and do you know what doctors call expectant mothers who are thirty-five and older?'

Win shook his head again. 'I don't,' he said flatly.

'"Elderly primigravida" or "Geriatric mother". Take your pick.' The unfairness of it struck Zoe anew. She'd been waiting to have a baby so that it would grow up in a stable, financially secure household. And yes, she wasn't quite ready to give up big nights out and lovely holidays abroad, even though the longer she left it, the more chance there was of birth defects and all manner of other developmental problems. Anyway, this wasn't just all on her. 'You *are* thirty-five and that means your fertility has taken a huge nosedive too,' she informed Win, who was still listening intently but with a very beleaguered air.

'I'm not entirely sure that that's true,' he said.

'Well, it is. Don't be fooled by all those ageing rockers having babies well into their seventies. At thirty-five, you're half as fertile as men under twenty-five. There was a study done recently. It was in the papers. The *Guardian*!' Zoe added defensively when Win raised his eyebrows and opened his mouth as if he were about to challenge that claim.

'Zo, I don't really think this is helpful—'

'It might not be helpful but it's the truth,' she said. It seemed to Zoe as if there was just a five-minute window in a woman's life when it was the best time to have a baby. Just five minutes. Zoe was sure that she'd passed it long ago and along with her one fallopian tube, with every day that went by her oestrogen levels were dwindling and her ovaries were packing up shop.

'We do not have the luxury of time. The longer I wait for you to make up your mind, the more our chances of having a baby decrease and don't think that IVF is going to be the answer because—'

'That's enough, Zoe!' Win said. 'I hear you.'

It wasn't enough. Not any more. 'I want a baby,' Zoe said, because that was what all these facts and figures and fear came down to. 'A fat, gurgling baby.'

She was still on her knees in front of Win. He pulled her up and onto his lap so he could kiss her; the simplest press of his lips at the corner of her mouth. All the love Zoe had for him, the overwhelming, complicated feelings that often felt too large to be contained, welled up in her, even though she knew what was coming.

'I need more time,' Win said. 'I'm still not over what happened last year when you lost the baby, when I nearly lost you. And it just feels that right now, we've lost us too. How we were. Who we used to be.'

It was what she'd felt herself now, so how could Zoe deny it? 'But how much time do you need?' she asked.

'Not that long,' Win said, brushing his thumb across Zoe's cheekbone to catch the first tear. 'Before we make this decision, jointly, we need to get back to being a couple. We live in the same house, sleep in the same bed, most of the time anyway, eat at the same table, but we're not together.'

'I know,' Zoe admitted and she wished that she could do this, have one serious conversation without crying. She'd never used to cry this much. She sniffed and tried to pull herself back from the brink. 'How do we get back to being together?'

Win smoothed the hair back from Zoe's face. 'I don't know. Maybe a joint project, something we can do as a couple.'

'But something fun that absolutely doesn't involve DIY

or IKEA trips,' Zoe said slowly. Maybe this was the answer. Exactly what they needed. A few weeks to get back to the Win and Zoe they used to be. 'Did you have anything in mind?'

'Now, don't dismiss this out of hand,' Win said, which immediately had Zoe on edge. Her fears turned out to be well founded. 'How would you feel about training to do another ten k race or maybe, and I'm just putting this out there, a half marathon? I'm still out of condition after my injury and if I promised to match your pace, we could make it fun and chart our progress—'

'Have you completely lost your mind? You call that fun? I'd rather assemble flatpack furniture every day for the rest of my life,' Zoe said aghast, not even caring if she was hurting Win's feelings, which was a relief in itself. 'Pick something else. Something that actually could be described as fun.'

They sat there in silence for an uncomfortable few moments though it really shouldn't have taken any time at all to come up with at least five fun activities to get them back to their happy place.

Zoe looked around the pub for inspiration. In the corner, gathered around a large table, were a group of people having lunch, discarded tissue paper and cards next to a middle-aged woman who was unwrapping her last present.

This year they'd let their birthdays pass almost unnoticed and had hardly seen any of their friends so it was actually pretty obvious what their joint fun project should be.

'Party?' Zoe suggested at the same time that Win said, 'Housewarming?' He smiled. 'See? We're not that far out of sync, are we?'

'We're not. Thank God.' Zoe held up her glass. 'So, we're in agreement, then? Housewarming party?'

'Or as I like to call it, Project Fun,' Win said, as he clinked his glass against Zoe's.

34

Libby

Someone at Freddy's paper made the necessary travel arrangements and Beryl told Libby not to worry about missing the start of term. 'You must go to Freddy in his hour of need,' she'd said, like a character in the aunts' romantic novels.

Hugo was less understanding. They met in the woods, walked to what Libby thought of as their bench, and she told him that she had to go to Paris to collect her injured husband.

There was something perfect and beautiful about Hugo's fury. The way his jaw clenched and a vein at his temple suddenly bulged. He lit a cigarette with abrupt, jerky movements – not offering her one as he usually did.

'I forbid you to go,' he said in a clipped voice. His Mr Watkins voice. 'I absolutely forbid it, Elizabeth.'

Secretly, his words thrilled Libby. He might have bought them a house so they could have a life together, she was having his child, but it seemed to her that he'd been slightly distant ever since he'd come back from Aldeburgh. Now, however, his ire was up at the thought of Libby with another man, even though the other man was Freddy.

Libby had often wished for someone to look out for her, to have her best interests at heart, but ever since her parents had died, she'd had no choice but to rely on only herself. Truth be told, there were times she rather enjoyed being independent so no one, not even Hugo, was going to clip her wings.

'I'm a grown woman,' she said sharply. 'You can forbid me all you want and flare your nostrils and beetle your brow, but I will do as I please.'

'You can't go haring off halfway across the world—' Hugo stopped as Libby scoffed at the ridiculous suggestion that Paris was halfway across the world. 'What about the baby? A woman in your condition should be resting.'

Libby didn't think that her condition meant that she needed to be confined until the baby arrived, but Hugo did have a point. She was only just starting to feel better and spending a day on trains and boats was always tiring for some reason. 'I promised Millicent. He's been shot, Hugo. And in the eyes of the law, we, Freddy and I, are married.'

'Then the eyes of the law need spectacles,' Hugo muttered. 'He left you, Libby. Left you high and dry when you needed him the most.'

'I'm not likely to forget that. Let's not argue.' Libby tucked her arm through his and rested her head on Hugo's shoulder, glancing up at his face to see if he still looked angry. 'Besides, with Freddy back in London, weakened by injury and utterly shamed that I didn't leave *him* high and dry, he's really in no position to argue about the divorce.'

Libby had expected Hugo to be pleased, but he hmmmed in a sceptical manner, then took out another cigarette. 'Perhaps,' he acquiesced, which was just as well because Libby was going to Paris and there was little he could do to stop her. 'Let's see how things settle when you're back from your jaunt.'

When Libby arrived at Victoria station it was heaving with young men and not so young men all bound for Spain to take up arms against the Nationalists.

Libby couldn't help but feel, as she hurried after the porter who she'd charged with carrying her case because Hugo had been quite insistent about that, they were doing the Nationalists a favour. Most of them looked like the pale, doughy men that Freddy had kicked around with, who'd only been adept at skipping out when it was their turn to buy a round of drinks, and would be useless in armed combat.

But that was men for you. Always spoiling for a fight.

The porter handed Libby and her case into the right carriage. Libby couldn't imagine that any of the Fascist-fighting hordes would be travelling first class, but she'd only just settled herself into a window seat when the door opened and two men entered in a flurry of luggage, booming voices and pipe smoke.

Neither of them appeared to notice Libby as they went about putting their bags on the rack above the seats and discussing some fellow called Simmons who apparently needed to be hung out to dry, but then they sat down and one of them, a tall, stout man not that much older than Libby, dipped his head.

'This must be Morton's wife,' he announced to the other man as if there was absolutely no reason to address his enquiry to Libby herself. 'Damn fool, getting himself shot like that. Still, worked out rather well for me.'

Freddy *was* a damn fool but Libby wasn't going to have a complete stranger, and such a rude one at that, cast aspersions on him.

'I'm Elizabeth Morton,' she said icily. 'And I'll thank you to keep any remarks about my husband to yourself, thank you very much.'

291

The man had a florid, round, beaver-like face – his front teeth looked as if they could be put to better use gnawing logs. It was the kind of smug, self-satisfied face that Libby quite longed to punch.

'Chivers,' he said, not the least bit chastened. 'Off to Spain to replace Morton. This is Maxwell. Takes pictures.'

The other man couldn't have been any older than twenty-five but he managed to give the impression that his top lip was curling in derision even when his face was in repose. He nodded briefly in Libby's direction then the two men resumed their conversation as a whistle blew and the train moved off with a clumsy lurch.

Chivers and Maxwell yapped like two old women all the way to Dover. Even worse, Chivers puffed away on his pipe while Maxwell chain-smoked Turkish cigarettes, their scent acrid at the back of Libby's throat.

' . . . of course what's happening in Spain is merely a dress rehearsal for what will come.'

'Goes without saying. Herr Hitler has his fat sausage fingers in several of Franco's pies.'

Libby had planned to spend the journey knitting a layette for the baby but she felt sicker and sicker, her head aching from the smoke and their incessant chatter. As the train finally pulled into Dover station, they were still busy extolling the virtues of Communism from the comfort of their first class seats and the air in the carriage was a fug.

It was a relief to leave the train and board the boat. Not surprisingly, Chivers regarded himself as an expert in Channel tides as well as world events. 'A smooth crossing,' he decided, even though any fool could look at the sea, only the faintest ripples disturbing the surface, and would have arrived at the same conclusion.

Libby found a seat on the deck. The fresh air, the tang

of sea salt, would do her the world of good. Anything to get away from all those men smoking foul-smelling things who never stopped talking, as if their opinions counted for nothing unless they were being aired frequently and at great volume.

The sound of a horn almost frightened the wits out of her and then they were on their way, England at the rear, France too far in front of them to be anything more than a suggestion when she squinted her eyes and looked at the far horizon.

'Fancy some company, love?' Libby swivelled her head to see a shabby fellow, who looked as if he'd slept in his clothes, about to sit down next to her. 'Can't have you being lonely.'

'Oh, do go away,' she snapped, brandishing her handbag in front of her. 'I'd like to be quiet. Is that too bloody much to ask?'

He called her a bitch as he shuffled off and Libby didn't care. Only cared that she felt even more awful in the fresh air than she had in the stuffy train carriage. Could feel her stomach lurching in rhythm with the listing of the ship.

Oh, Lord, no! Libby struggled to her feet and just made it to the railings before she was unspeakably ill. One hand clinging to her hat, her handbag dangling in the crook of her other arm as she all but hurled herself over the side of the ship again and again and again and—

'Mrs Morton! Whatever's the matter? Sea's as smooth as a millpond. I have to say, Maxwell, I've never met a woman who was a good traveller.'

'Do shut up, Chivers. Go and get the poor woman a nip of brandy, will you?'

Then someone was removing her hatpin, taking off her hat, relieving Libby of her handbag, then finally and soothingly rubbing circles on her back. 'Oh God, I'm not sure if I want to die of shame or nausea,' Libby managed to moan.

Maxwell chuckled. 'I'm sure you'll die of neither and there's nothing to be embarrassed about. My mother can't go more than half a mile in a car before she's indisposed.'

It took at least another ten minutes until Libby could be guided to a seat. Maxwell was waiting with a glass of soda water, which Libby gratefully took. When she'd drunk half of it, she poured the brandy Maxwell had managed to procure into the glass.

'Thank you,' she said a little stiffly. 'You're very kind.'

Maxwell waved her words away. 'No trouble at all. You're very pale, Mrs Morton. Here, I begged a blanket off a steward. Let's tuck you up. You'll feel right as rain in no time.'

Now that she no longer felt so terrible, Libby was seized with worry for the baby. Hugo had been right – a woman in her condition had no business haring off to France like this.

But she wasn't in any pain. She no longer felt queasy, even her headache abated after she'd drunk most of the brandy and soda and had a cigarette.

'You really don't have to stay with me, I'm perfectly fine now,' she told Chivers and Maxwell, but they insisted on keeping her company. Maxwell went off to get more brandy and some crackers and they talked about Freddy. How much everyone liked him, what a tremendous writer he was and how it was a damned shame that he was pulling out of Spain, but it would be wonderful for Libby to have him back home with her.

Libby refused to be drawn, but once they'd disembarked and were settled in another first class compartment, Chivers and Maxwell kept her entertained with absolutely scurrilous stories about the King and Mrs Simpson. It turned out that Wallis Simpson would no sooner be Queen of England than Libby would. Not when she had a high-ranking Nazi lover on the side. And especially not when she'd enslaved the King, who Libby had always said had a weak face, with a trick called the Chinese Grip that she'd picked up in a Shanghai brothel.

The three of them shared a taxi to a hotel in the fourteenth *arrondissement* where the newspaper had booked rooms for them all, including Freddy, though neither Maxwell nor Chivers knew if his train from Perpignan had arrived at Gare Austerlitz yet or what state he might be in.

'Hopefully he's lucid,' Maxwell said cheerfully as their taxi pulled up outside a small, elegant hotel with a doorman who looked at them and their cases with a studied disdain. 'Meant to give me the lie of the land before we set off for Spain.'

Libby had an image of a sweaty, feverish Freddy, his wound leaking and infected, thrashing around on sweat-damp sheets, but when she introduced herself as Madame Morton to the disapproving-looking woman behind the reception desk, she was greeted with a torrent of unhappy invective.

'*Monsieur Morton est déjà ici. Il dérangé tous mes clients avec son bruit infernal. Si égoïste!*'

Libby could barely follow what the woman was saying but as she was shown to the elevator – evidently she didn't warrant the attentions of the porter – she imagined Freddy's feverish shouts and moans going unanswered just because he'd had the audacity to disturb the other residents. So she was quite surprised to hear the frantic clackety-clack of a typewriter being hammered by impatient hands when she reached the door of his room.

She knocked on the door, but her rapping was no match for the drumming of the keys and if Freddy was typing he was hardly on his deathbed, Libby thought exasperatedly, because he was absolutely exasperating. She opened the door and there he was; hunched over his typewriter, which was sitting on a small *escritoire*. He had a cigarette clamped between his teeth, a tumbler of whisky stood next to the pile of small black notebooks that he favoured and he'd discarded his shirt in favour of sitting in his vest like a navvy.

35

Libby

Libby was going to say something, though she hardly knew where to start, when Freddy glanced up and saw her in the doorway. His eyes widened, bulged really, and his mouth fell open so that the cigarette dangled from his bottom lip, then fell into his lap and he came to life with a curse.

'Goodness, Freddy, you look like you've seen a ghost,' Libby said, as she came into the room and shut the door behind her.

It would have been quite a nice room if Freddy didn't have the curtains drawn and a large collection of dirty plates, glasses and cutlery littering every surface. Libby knew only too well how cross he got if someone tried to distract him when he was writing. No wonder the lady downstairs had looked so furious at the mention of his name.

'Libby. What the hell are you doing here?' Freddy turned in his chair to watch as Libby strode over to the windows, drew back the curtains, then wrestled with the handle to get some air into the room. It was dark now, but she could hear the hum of conversation, the chink of glasses, from the bar across the street. 'You're the very last person I expected to see.'

'I'll bet.' Now that she'd arrived at her destination, Libby was dog-tired and the bed, even with crumpled sheets and blankets, looked inviting. 'Your Mr Gough at the *Mirror* was going to send a cable.'

'Madame la Receptioniste hates me. I'm not surprised she's withholding my messages,' Freddy said. He held up a packet of cigarettes. 'Do you want one? And are you ever going to tell me what you're doing here?'

'Yes, please.' Libby perched on the window sill. Freddy had his back to her and she could see a dressing taped to his shoulder, which looked as if it hadn't been changed in days. 'We got a telegram saying you'd been shot and that someone needed to fetch you home from Paris. I drew the short straw.' She was determined to be aloof, a little haughty. 'Are you in terrible pain?'

'Hardly. Here, catch!' He threw Libby a cigarette, then a box of matches. 'It only hurts if I forget and do something silly like try to stretch my arms when I get stiff. Anyway, Libs, you've had a wasted trip; I'm going back to Spain, you see. First, though, I've been commissioned to write a book about what's been happening in *el hermosa pais*. Publishers want fifty thousand words by Friday week. Quite a decent advance too. What day is it?'

Libby had forgotten this; Freddy's quicksilver mind, his thoughts everywhere all at once. It was impossible to keep up, one just had to sift through and pull out the most pressing pieces of information. 'You are coming home, Freddy. Both your editors at the *Mirror* and the *Herald* were quite adamant. Said that you'd taken the most appalling risks while you were in Spain and that neither of them wanted your death on their consciences.'

Freddy snorted in derision. 'What rot!' He was pale, though Libby couldn't tell if it were because of his wound or because he'd been shut up for days, the only light coming from his desk lamp. 'I was accidentally shot by a pal, a Spanish poet called Jorges, who didn't know one end of a rifle from another. We laughed about it.'

'Oh, Freddy, you don't change! You're absolutely infuriating!' Libby took an angry drag of her cigarette, as a poor substitute for slapping some sense into him. 'Your mother is beside herself – claiming that she's having palpitations and goodness knows what else – and you are coming back to London because I've just travelled over with your replacement and—'

'Oh really, who? Hollis, I shouldn't wonder, though he can't write for toffee. Always thought his political allegiances weren't as—'

'Freddy! Shut up!' It was a pained scream. 'They've sent a man called Chivers and a photographer called Maxwell, who have both been very kind.'

'Chivers? That pompous old windbag. Or pompous young windbag, rather. And Maxwell? I expect he was only kind because he wanted to make love to you.' Freddy leaned back in his chair then winced as if the movement had jarred his shoulder. 'You've come all this way, Libby? That's very noble of you.'

'It's not at all noble of me.' She'd also forgotten this truth – that when she wasn't with Freddy she loved him more than when she was with him. He was just too much. Too bloody much. 'Did you not get my last letter? I sent it to your hotel in Madrid.'

'The letter when you told me you were done with me? That if I cared anything for you, that I'd let you be, not write to you again.' Freddy pushed his hair back from his face. 'I do care for you, Libs, so I honoured your wishes. Besides, I haven't been in Madrid for months.'

It would have been so much easier if Freddy hadn't claimed to still care for her. If he didn't look so thin and tired, like he hadn't shaved or washed or eaten a proper meal in weeks. She couldn't tell him now. Couldn't kick a man while he was down. 'Chivers said to meet in the bar across the street at eight. You need to wash and shave first. Do you have clean clothes?'

'I won't go.' Freddy shook his head. 'I have work to do and there's no point in meeting my replacement when I'm heading back to Spain myself. Don't look at me like that, Libs. My mind's made up – there's nothing anyone can do to change it.'

They were half an hour late to meet Chivers and Maxwell, by which time Libby had bullied Freddy into having a tepid bath, while two maids restored order to the room. Then Libby took great pleasure in tipping iodine on Freddy's wound as he shuddered and swore at her. The bullet had been removed, the hole crudely sewn up with black thread. It looked sore, the skin still knitting together, but not infected.

'I'm not at death's door,' Freddy grumbled when Chivers and Maxwell greeted him like a conquering hero. 'It's barely a scratch.' Though he didn't need much persuasion, or whisky, to describe what life was like on the Republican lines. Men and women coming from all over Europe to join the International Brigades, though too many of them had a romantic notion of what it was like to fight for a worthy cause. 'The romance soon ends when you're outnumbered, surrounded and being shot at.'

The two men peppered Freddy with questions, Chivers quite deferential now he was face to face with 'a comrade who's taken a bullet for the cause'.

'Not at all,' Freddy laughed. 'Was just in the wrong place when someone was playing silly buggers with their rifle.'

Then he sketched out the key positions with the help of the hardboiled eggs that were a feature of most Parisian bars, though a hard-boiled egg was the very last thing Libby ever wanted to eat when she was drinking.

As it was, after a small cognac, she was done. Maxwell stood up when she did, though Chivers and Freddy stayed seated, oblivious as they blethered on about Franco. 'I'm going to leave you boys to it,' Libby said, swaying on the spot. 'I'm absolutely fagged.'

Maxwell insisted on accompanying Libby and lingered on the hotel steps making pointless conversation about his sister who longed to go on the stage so that Libby thought there might be some truth to what Freddy had said about him wanting to make love to her. In which case, he was doomed to disappointment, especially when Libby yawned in his face.

'Sorry! How rude!' she trilled. 'You'd better go back to the bar. I can see Freddy glaring at us through the window.'

Freddy was doing nothing of the kind and Libby was sure if she and Chivers made love in the middle of the road Freddy wouldn't give two hoots.

Libby hadn't planned to share a room with Freddy, but by now it was too late to make other arrangements in her rudimentary French. She pulled off the creased clothes she'd travelled in, gave herself a whore's bath with cold water and a flannel then dropped onto the bed like a stone. She'd left the window open, could still hear the chatter from the bar opposite, but she was soon dragged under by sleep.

'I didn't think I'd ever see you again, Libs. And yet, here you are. Are you sure you're not a dream?'

In the foggy, groggy hinterland of awake and asleep, Libby

thought that she was the one who was dreaming, but then Freddy closed his arms around her, nosed that spot on the back of her neck as he'd used to.

'Of course you'd have seen me again,' she mumbled, her words thick. 'I'm living in your mother's house, for one thing.'

'Ah, but I'd planned to exile myself for the wrongs I'd done you. Do you hate me or have you forgiven me?'

Now, Libby was remembering when she'd loved Freddy the best and it had been these still, quiet hours in the dead of night, the world slumbering, when he'd put his arms around her and whispered things that she could hardly believe he was saying.

'I don't hate you,' Libby said, because she never had, no matter how hard she'd tried. 'But I can't forgive you, Freddy. You left me when I was … You left me in the very depths of despair and I had to claw my way back out.'

She felt Freddy flinch but he didn't retreat, instead he tightened his arms around her. 'I'm sorry things didn't work out, Libs.'

'You can't even say it, can you?' she asked a little sadly. 'Can't say that you're sorry about the baby. I know that it's silly to still be so blue about a baby that was never even born but I loved him already and I think I always will.'

'Darling Libs.' Freddy kissed her nape, his fingers threading through her hair. 'It's not that I didn't care; it's just so impossible to find the right words.'

He let go of her and Libby was unanchored, alone, as he moved off the bed then stumbled about in the dark as if he knew that hot tears were coursing down her cheeks and that she didn't want him to put the light on. Libby heard him rummage in a corner and then he was back, kneeling at the side of her bed, to take her hand. 'I carried these with me,' he said. 'They were all I had of you, of the baby.'

Libby felt something soft and warm and it was she who reached out to snap on the bedside lamp to see that he was holding the white layette; jacket, trousers, little hat and booties, that she'd knitted for the baby as she'd sat on the sidelines in Parisian cafés and bars while Freddy had taken centre stage.

Perhaps the bitter memory of it gave her that little edge of spite to say what she had to say. 'The letter you never received . . . I wrote asking for a divorce.' Libby marvelled at the clear, steady beat to her voice. 'I've fallen in love with a man, he loves me very much too, and I'm having his child.'

Freddy's gaze was dark and serious. 'Does he treat you better than I did?'

'That wouldn't be difficult, would it?' Libby smiled to take the sting out of her words and Freddy smiled back.

'Then I'm happy for you, truly I am.'

Libby sighed. 'You could at least pretend to be angry, Freddy. Even a little piqued. Makes a girl feel wanted, you know.'

Freddy turned off the light. 'I've certainly never met a girl who falls in love as often as you do. This chap, me, that fellow you ran off to New York with . . .'

'Jack and I didn't run off, he cast me in his revue, which he took to New York . . .'

'And before that, the man who seduced you when you were . . .'

There had been five or six men and Libby had been in love with each of them: that wonderful giddy, heart-skipping feeling as if champagne ran through your veins. When she'd greedily count the hours that they'd spend together; the afternoons taking tea, walking in parks and the nights, those wonderful nights that seemed to last for ever but ended too soon. But always, *always*, their love gradually withered away to nothing and all the tears and the gin in the world couldn't wash away Libby's pain.

But this time, Hugo loved her back. Had never treated love like a silly game but declared his intentions from the start. So, this time, the love was different. Safer. Solid, so that Libby sometimes imagined that she could reach out her hand and be able to touch it.

Or maybe it was Hugo who was safe. Solid. A man of honour, who kept his word. Still . . .

'I'd much rather love and have my heart broken, than never know love at all,' Libby said as Freddy got back into bed, put his arms around her again, his hands coming to settle on the swell of her stomach where another's man's child grew.

'Your need to be loved – it will be the death of you, Libby,' Freddy murmured in her ear and Libby thought that he was probably right, but she couldn't find it in her heart to care.

It would be such a lovely way to go.

36

Zoe

Win was always cheerier when he had a project on the go and very soon he had a spreadsheet devoted to the housewarming party, which he lovingly tended of an evening. Zoe was in charge of the guest list and food, while Win totted up columns of figures and drove himself into a frenzy cross-checking the price of Prosecco across half a dozen supermarket websites.

It also helped that Henry, Win's physio, had decided that Win could finally begin running again. Nothing too strenuous – just one lap of Highgate Woods, keeping an eye out for exposed roots, rocks or small dogs, and if anything started hurting Win was to stop immediately. Within days, his face had lost its haunted quality, which he'd worn for so long that Zoe thought it had become a permanent feature, and in the mornings, Zoe could hear him whistling in the bathroom.

It was odd, what with the September days getting shorter, that Zoe was imbued with purpose too as if it were spring, rather than late summer. She was . . . optimistic. Her book was out on submission, which was always scary but hopeful too.

Cath and Theo had decided that they would stay on at Clive's so that meant Cath was only down the road, and best of all, Zoe's parents were due back from Vietnam and were staying for a couple of weeks before they travelled on to Yorkshire.

Zoe had imagined that after spending four months travelling through South-East Asia and six months building an orphanage just outside Saigon, her parents would want to put their feet up. Maybe take a couple of gentle strolls up to Hampstead Heath . . .

'Put my feet up? Why on earth would I want to do that?' Nancy Richardson had demanded when Zoe suggested it on their first day in London. She and Zoe's father, Ken, were determined to stay up, jaws clenched to stifle their yawns, and not give in to jet lag.

'We can put our feet up when we're dead,' Ken had added. They were sitting at the kitchen table, new sliding doors open. He nodded his head in the direction of the barren expanse of land outside. 'Anyway, we said we'd sort that out for you.'

The garden was a plot of churned mud bordered by collapsed and rotting fence posts, its only redeeming feature two apple trees that needed serious pruning. Within the space of a week there was proper fencing and foundations dug for a patio. They even had a lawn (which had started life as what Zoe called a 'massive grass carpet' and her mother called 'rolled turf') with flowerbeds dug out on either side. It was almost ready for the housewarming, which had become a barbecue as it looked like the good weather would hold and because they were homeowners now and didn't fancy people spilling wine on their new rugs.

Despite Win's best efforts, the invite list soon spiralled out of control. Originally, they'd planned to invite all the friends they'd barely seen in months but Zoe pointed out that if they were going to invite Gavin, because he was family *and* a friend, then they had to invite his crew to thank them for all their hard work and it would be rude not to invite their wives, girlfriends and kids too. They also owed favours to all their immediate neighbours for putting up with the noise, rubbish and lorries coming and going at all hours. But Elysian Place was such a friendly street (or as Win put it 'everyone is all up in everyone else's business') that somehow Zoe ended up inviting all the neighbours, apart from Pernicious Peter across the road, who'd tried to do a land grab on their drive when they'd first moved in. It all added up to a hell of a lot of people.

Fortunately, the Saturday of the barbecue was a glorious, late September day. Mellow and warm, with not one hint of autumn crispness to the afternoon. Zoe had given her parents strict instructions that they weren't to do anything but sit on the new garden furniture and be waited on hand and foot but Ken quickly commandeered the grill and at the other end of the patio, Nancy had created a salad station and was supervising Cath and Theo who were setting up a makeshift bar, even though Cath insisted she was an expert at drinking alcohol so serving it couldn't be that hard.

Win was ferrying food from kitchen to garden and Zoe was meant to be on front door duty but when she greeted each new arrival standing on the doorstep clutching a bottle of something cold, the first words out of their mouths were: 'So, are you going to give us the guided tour, then?'

It never got old though. Explaining how the house had just been a shell. 'No carpets, buckled window frames, don't let's even talk about the roof,' then throwing open doors and hearing the gasps of admiration and the barrage of questions: 'Is that French linen grey or Parisian grey?'

There was a real sense of pride in intimately knowing every centimetre, every corner of the house because Zoe had sanded, primed and painted most of it herself. Had agonised over the muted blue tones that ran through the downstairs because she'd decided to make a feature of the two-tone blue of the fireplaces. Had fought long and hard for her Edison bulb/timber beam light fixture in the kitchen. Had hung thirty-seven framed prints along the stair wall; the little sketches of Camden Town life she'd drawn for Win long, long ago. Had hunted down all the jumble sale, car boot sale and eBay finds to furnish each room.

Talking about the house made it easier to face her friends. At least Win had met people for lunch, sometimes gone to the Monday night pub quiz. He'd been present and Zoe had been . . . absent.

She simply hadn't been strong enough before. But now when Chloe, one of Zoe's old Central St Martins friends, or Olivia, one of her writing buddies, or even Mercedes who was the first person Zoe had become friends with when she'd moved to London, tilted their heads and asked, 'Really, Zo, how have you been?' or variations on that theme, Zoe could truthfully say, 'Busy. We bought a derelict house and we got a dog.'

'And you're better?'

'Yeah, I'm still sad about losing the baby, these things break your heart, but they happen, don't they?'

Every time she said it, Zoe would get something back in return: a hug, a brush of lips against her cheek, a hand squeezing hers. A few months ago these gestures would have reduced her to tears. Now they made Zoe wonder how many of her friends and acquaintances had suffered a miscarriage or cried when a missed period arrived weeks late. Experienced a hurried trip to A&E then a phone call to work claiming a tummy upset or food poisoning. They lived in an age of TMI, where every waking moment, each thought, was posted on social media, and yet there were still things that people never talked about.

During the week as they'd dug out flowerbeds together (Nancy was always more comfortable having a heart-to-heart while doing something else, whether it was peeling vegetables or pulling up weeds), Zoe had talked to her mother about the baby, about desperately wanting to try again despite Win's reluctance. Then Nancy had set down her spade and said that when Zoe was a month shy of her second birthday and they'd been living in Northern Ireland, miles away from home and Nancy's own mother, she'd had to deliver an almost full-term baby boy who'd inexplicably died in the womb.

'Most of the women back at the army base could hardly bear to look at me when I left hospital,' her mother had said. 'I think it was a case of there but for the grace of God, but I felt so alone.'

'Why did you never tell me?' Zoe had asked, putting down her own spade so she could take her mother's hand.

'Because it was the very worst time of my life and it hurts even now to remember it. It's a very hard thing to grieve, much less talk about, a person who was never there,' Nancy had said with a surety because she'd had years to come to terms with these painful feelings. 'You have no real memories of them, just the memory of all the hopes and dreams you had for them.'

It was comforting, rather than dispiriting, to Zoe to know she'd always carry the grief around with her. That the baby, though he'd never grown beyond the size of a jellybean, would never be forgotten, would stay in her heart.

The party was in full swing. It was standing room only in the kitchen as people clutched drinks and talked, mostly about property prices.

Zoe stepped out onto the decking where Amanda and her mum, Linda, had taken over the salad station. Ed was arguing with Gavin and his brother, Steve, over how long to cook a medium rare burger. Florence was in her element as she glee-fully herded a small pack of children made up of the nephews, Maisie and Milo from next door and a few stragglers up and down the garden, when she wasn't darting off to scavenge for stray bits of sausage and burgers. Zoe was going to be clearing up dog vomit in the very near future.

'Thought you might need a refill,' Zoe called out when she was a few feet away from Jackie and Nancy who were sitting on the little bench outside the shed Ken had built and painted a jolly sky blue.

Jackie obligingly shuffled up so Zoe could sit down and held out her glass to be topped up. 'I was just saying how nice the garden looks and trying to persuade your mother to overhaul mine.'

Nancy beamed. 'I'm sure Ken could manage without me for a week or so in the spring if Zoe wouldn't mind putting me up.'

'I warn you, she has very strong opinions about the ratio of lawn to decking,' Zoe told Jackie, then turned to her mother. 'Actually, Clive was looking for you. Wanted to know if you and Dad still fancied going out for lunch tomorrow?'

'Oh, yes! We did make vague plans earlier in the week.' Nancy immediately got to her feet. Zoe watched her mother hurry up the garden, her steps brisk, so much life and vitality in her small, trim figure.

'I love my mum but she makes me feel like such a slacker,' she remarked. 'When I told her that occasionally Win and I spend a weekend having a boxed set binge, she was horrified.'

Jackie made a noncommittal noise and took a sip of her wine. Zoe liked to think that she and Jackie were close. Over the last decade, she'd spent more time with Jackie than her own mother. When she'd woken up in hospital, it had been Jackie holding her hand. Nobody could be further from the stereotypical, tyrannical mother-in-law, but now they sat there in silence, which felt like the safer option.

But safe wasn't always an option.

'I realise that I never thanked you for looking after me when I lost the baby,' Zoe said, stumbling only slightly over the words. Jackie immediately stiffened.

'You never, ever have to thank me for that, Zo,' she said firmly. 'It was the least, the very least . . . I wish I could have done more.'

'You did so much,' Zoe insisted but Jackie put a hand on her arm, a warning, and when Zoe glanced over at her tanned face, it was set and tight and she was blinking rapidly to stave off the tears. It was exactly how Win looked when he was overcome with emotions that he wanted nothing to do with. 'I just wanted you to know how grateful I am, how much I love you.'

Jackie patted Zoe's arm, which was an 'I love you' back, then she wiped away an imaginary crumb from her mouth. 'So . . .' she began heavily, 'Gav said you and Win have been rowing a lot. That he dreaded turning up in the morning in case you'd murdered each other. Now, you know I don't like to interfere . . .' Jackie pulled an agonised face at the very thought of being even a little bit like Reenie, Gavin's mother, a ninety-year-old cockney matriarch who had made interfering into an art form.

'You don't ever interfere,' Zoe rushed to assure her. 'And I thank you for that as well.'

'But you and Win; you're all right now, aren't you?' Jackie asked hopefully.

Zoe nodded. 'Yeah, we're getting there.' It wasn't fair to get Jackie involved but desperate times and all that. 'I really want us to start trying for a baby but Win's on the fence about it. I think he'd be an amazing dad, but he's not convinced.'

Jackie caught Zoe's eye and they both shook their heads, looked up to the heavens. 'He would be an amazing dad,' Jackie agreed. She wiped away another phantom crumb. 'Terry, when he could be bothered, was a good dad. Or he was a better dad than he was a husband. Not that that was hard.'

'Win never talks much about Terry . . . he goes all twitchy if I even mention his name. It makes me sad for Win.' Zoe took a sip of her wine. 'Makes me sad for Terry too because he's lost out on so much by not having Win, or Ed, in his life any more.'

'I know the boys took it hard that Terry cut all ties . . .' Jackie took a huge gulp of her wine too. 'Between you and me, and you have to promise not to tell Win . . . do you promise?'

She and Win didn't have secrets, or rather they didn't use to and Zoe wanted to get back to them being the most open of books. But she also wanted to know more about Terry, why things had broken down so irrevocably and why Jackie had the most anguished look on her face as if she couldn't keep the truth in any longer. 'I promise,' she said rashly.

Jackie touched glasses with Zoe by way of a solemn and binding agreement. 'Terry didn't walk out, I threw him out,' she said quickly, as if she wanted to be done with it. 'The way we lived, it was so unfair on the boys, but you end up getting used to even the most awful situations. When I brought Ed home from the hospital we were living in a static caravan in Borehamwood. Terry always said it would get better . . . but it never did. Not for long, anyway.' Zoe wanted to take her mother-in-law's hand, but she didn't know if Jackie would let her so instead she scooched over to be closer. 'So many times I thought about leaving him, when he was away on one of his trips, which actually meant that he was in prison . . .'

'You pretty much raised Win and Ed single-handed,' Zoe told her. 'And you did a bloody good job of it.'

'I need a tissue.' Jackie sniffed, then looked around for her handbag. She bent her head as she retrieved one then blew her nose. 'I put up with so much for so long, thought the boys were better off with us together. The last time he got sent down, it was only for a month for handling stolen goods, but I told him I was done. He swore on his mother's life that things would be different. We moved into a nice house in Winchmore Hill and I really thought he'd turned over a new leaf. We'd only been there a few weeks – I came home from work and I thought some of his associates had done over the place.' She blew her nose again. 'That shouldn't be your first thought when you come in and find your house ransacked. I went into Win's room and his moneybox was lying on the bed completely empty. So was Ed's. It turned out that Terry owed someone something he couldn't pay back so he'd stolen from his own sons but I didn't know that then. I just stood there in Ed's room and he hadn't even unpacked because he knew that we'd be moving on in a few weeks because we always did. Enough was enough. The boys deserved so much more. I got my dad and my uncle to track Terry down and I told him that he couldn't live with us any more. You never met my uncle Ron, he had a boxing gym under the old railway arches in King's Cross, and you really did not want to get on the wrong side of him. Anyway, so Terry went and I'm sorry . . .'

'You don't have to be sorry.' Zoe decided that it was time to put her arm round Jackie. 'You deserved more than that too. And I love how the three of you look out for each other. That's something special. You should be proud about that.' She let out a shaky breath. 'Do you miss him?'

There was a pause and Zoe wondered if she'd pushed too

hard. Jackie ducked her head as if she didn't have enough courage to look Zoe in the eye. 'I'm sorry that the boys missed out on their dad being around.' She swallowed hard, like she was choking down a sob. 'But we were happier, much happier, without him. And it was down to Terry that he never wanted to see the boys after that. Never got in touch on their birth-days or Christmas. That's what I really can't forgive.'

Zoe had to let go of the older woman because she was in danger of crying too. It was her turn to sniff and Jackie smiled tremulously then lifted her hand to smooth it through Zoe's hair. 'I would hate it if telling you this makes you think less of me.'

'Of course it doesn't.' Zoe felt as close to Jackie as if the bond between them weren't simply a by-product of marriage, but made of flesh and blood. 'But you should probably tell Win. You know what he's like. On some level, he probably blames himself for Terry disappearing so if he knew what had really happened, it would give him some peace of mind.'

Jackie nodded like she'd give it some thought. 'You've been so good for him, Zo. Even as a kid, he was so quiet, sensitive, that sometimes I don't think he was truly happy until he met you.'

The love she had for Win at that moment felt as if it couldn't be contained by the frame of her body and was seeping out of Zoe's pores. 'Well, I'm not saying he's perfect and God knows, I'm certainly not, but I think we're good for each other.'

'But if the worst did happen ...' Jackie persisted.

'It's not going to,' Zoe said, because even the thought of it made her guts churn and she really didn't know what she'd do if Win decided that he didn't want children. It would shatter her heart into a million pieces.

'But if it did, Gav and I have already discussed it, and we're getting custody of you. Win will have to fend for himself,'

Jackie said, as if Zoe without Win was so unthinkable that it was all right to make jokes about it. Zoe really hoped that was the case.

'Look, if our relationship can survive the Sunday that you dragged me to every architectural salvage yard in the Home Counties before you found the right size Belfast sink, then it can survive anything.'

Jackie smiled, just as Zoe had intended. 'I don't know about you, Zo, but I really could do with some more wine. Wish I hadn't brought the car now. I told Gavin that he was all right to get a bit pissed because I'd drive us home.'

'Have some more wine,' Zoe said firmly. 'Get the bus. It's a ten-minute ride. You can pick up the car tomorrow.'

'Well, if you're going to twist my arm.' Jackie was already holding her glass up. 'But can you break it to Gav that we're taking the bus home?'

37

Zoe

By seven, the sky was dusky, streaked with thin, wispy clouds of dark blue and people were starting to leave.

Zoe wandered through the house to gather up stray wine-glasses and plates. She followed the sound of voices coming from upstairs, cursing when she saw that someone had spilled rosé wine on the runner, to find Win in the spare bedroom talking with a man from across the road who she was on nodding terms with.

The man was in his sixties, grey hair a mass of wild curls, and wearing a Ramones T-shirt, jeans and Birkenstocks. He had the benign, unfazed look of someone who'd lived well and partied hard. Zoe didn't like to interrupt when he and Win were deep in conversation.

'We bought our place in the eighties and all the period details, ceiling roses and whatnot, had been ripped out,' the man was saying. 'We even had these nasty fitted wardrobes with mirrored doors that took up half the bedroom. Oh, hello!' he added as he caught sight of Zoe hovering in the doorway.

Win was leaning against the window sill, backlit by the sinking sun, his face pink from slaving over a hot barbecue all afternoon. 'This is Geno from across the road. He lives next door to Peter the Drive Stealer.'

'I think you know my wife, Trish,' Geno said as he shook Zoe's hand. 'I was just saying to Win how lovely it's been to have a good snoop round your house. Such a shame that it stood empty for all those years.'

'Actually, Zo, Geno told me something about the house that gave me tingles all the way down my spine.' Win shivered as if he felt them all over again.

'Really? Good tingles?' Zoe asked. 'Or bad tingles?'

She sat down on the bed, Geno sat next to her and told her that before Pernicious Peter had bought his house ten years ago, it had been in the same family since it was built in 1936.

'A woman called Anne lived there. She was in her fifties when we moved here, which was in nineteen eighty-four, and she'd inherited the house from her parents who'd bought it off-plan when she'd been five or six. Lovely woman, got Alzheimer's, terrible way to go. So, one day, we asked her about your house and she said it had always been empty for all the time she'd lived there. When she first mentioned it, it was all quite vague but as the Alzheimer's took hold, she became quite fixated on your house and the details became much clearer.'

Zoe waited patiently because it seemed, she hoped, that Geno was building up to something and Win, who'd already heard the story, looked as if he were about to burst with the effort not to chime in. 'The details ... ' Zoe prompted, because she couldn't be patient any longer.

'She said her family moved into their house in the July of nineteen thirty-six, just after Anne's birthday. Your house wasn't quite finished but they'd occasionally see a pretty red-headed woman coming and going and Anne's mother would stop to say hello. Her name was Lizzy, Livvy ... It's twenty-odd years since I last heard this story so forgive me if I'm getting things muddled up.'

'Libby,' Zoe said. 'The woman's name was Libby.'

She glanced over at Win who raised his eyebrows as if he was intrigued too, despite all his dire warnings about getting involved with a ghost, a phantom.

Geno nodded. 'Yes, that might be the name. So this woman was expecting a baby and getting the house ready for her and her husband to move in to but before that could happen, there was an incident in the December. Anne was very specific about the exact date, though I can't remember it now. Apparently there was a terrible commotion in the street and most of the neighbours rushed out to see two men in the front garden of your house, door wide open, shouting and almost coming to blows with this Libby woman standing by the gate crying. Then she and one of the men disappeared up the road and the other man got into his car and drove away and that was the last anyone ever saw of her.'

Geno leaned back and looked with some satisfaction at Zoe who sat with her mouth hanging open. 'Curious, isn't it? You don't know anything about who you bought the house from?'

'It was a private sale,' Zoe said. 'We only dealt with the vendor's solicitor.'

Win stirred. 'They must have details of the original owner. They'd be on the deeds, I think.'

'We could ask Parmy.' Parminder, their friend and solicitor, worked from the ground floor of the house in Camden where Win's accountancy practice occupied the first and second. Zoe got up. 'I wonder if she's still here. I could go and check.'

'Or it can wait until Monday.' Win smiled at Geno. 'We found a suitcase when we moved in. It belonged to that woman, Libby—'

'Short for Elizabeth.' Zoe took over. 'The suitcase had some of her things in it, but we're not sure how it ended up in a cupboard in one of our bedrooms.'

'How fascinating,' Geno said, his eyes dancing. 'A house not only with all its original features but a mystery to solve too.'

'I'm very confused. Are we sure this happened in nineteen thirty-six? Because, according to her diary, Libby was pregnant in nineteen thirty-five, but she lost the baby.' Zoe couldn't reconcile the facts but to finally have Libby at their house, corroborated by an independent witness, was another piece of the puzzle slotting into place. A very important piece. Although now there were even more pieces missing. One of the men had to be Hugo, so who was the other man? And why had they all been so angry?

As the foundations of her own marriage seemed to crumble, it had been too painful to read about Libby coming between Hugo and his wife. But now Libby was back again. Almost close enough to touch and this time Zoe was determined not to let her dart out of reach.

Later that night, she left Win to finish unloading the dishwasher, and hurried upstairs to open the drawer of her nightstand and pull out the diary.

Zoe was a couple of months behind and her heart was pounding, hands clammy, as she skimmed to where she'd last left Libby at the end of July and an impending doctor's appointment.

August 7th

I'm with child. Up the duff. Expecting. Enceinte. One in the oven. Pregnant.

I'm going to have Hugo's baby and it seems fantastical, impossible, but the doctor says it's so. It shouldn't be possible to be this happy. I could die from this much happiness.

When Win came up to bed, he found Zoe sitting cross-legged on the floor, head hanging down, shoulders shaking from the force of her sobs.

He was at her side instantly, pulling her out of her slumped position, smoothing his fingers over her damp face. 'What is it, Zo? What's wrong?'

Zoe didn't answer at first. She took several shuddering breaths then picked up the diary and thrust it at Win. 'Libby did get pregnant again.' She saw him take a few seconds to process this, remember who Libby was and why her pregnancy had such significance. 'I have to find out what happened to Libby and the baby, because if everything worked out for her, then it will work for us too. It will. I know it will.'

Win looked at the diary as if it were an unexploded bomb. 'You do know that there's no way that what happened to someone eighty years ago will have any effect, any bearing on you, on us, on our lives. That doesn't make any sense.' He looked at Zoe's tear-streaked face, wiped away a streak of mascara with his thumb. 'Is this really so important to you?'

'Yes!'

'OK. We'll find out what happened to your Libby.'

38

Libby

As soon as Libby was back from Paris, Hugo had to go away. To Manchester, he said, where he was going into business, opening a car showroom, with an old army pal.

They met in Highgate Woods on a Sunday morning, at their bench, their secret little place. Summer had lingered a little but now it was dead and gone and Hugo was back in his drab dark clothes but still smiled when he saw Libby. Then his smile died too and his face lost all its warmth.

'You were gone over a fortnight, Libby,' he said harshly as soon as she was in earshot. 'I didn't know what had happened to you.'

Libby took a deep breath. 'I'm so sorry.'

'I feared the worst,' Hugo said and stood like a statue when Libby brushed her lips against his cold cheek.

'I wrote to you at your Mayfair address, did you not get it? I would have sent a cable but the French pretend they don't understand English though I'm sure they do.' Libby took Hugo's hand, wound her fingers through his and willed herself to stop her nervous chatter. 'There was no need to worry. Freddy behaved like a perfect gentleman but he had just been shot. The doctor said that he shouldn't even think about travelling for at least a week.'

It was a little lie. There was no point in explaining about Freddy's bloody book and how he'd refused to leave the hotel until it was written. That he was 'in the rhythm' and couldn't possibly be disrupted.

Hugo frowned again. 'So the doctor was one of the few Frogs who did speak English, then? How convenient.'

'Please don't be like this. I've been longing to see you,' Libby said because it was the truth. The time she'd spent with Freddy had been a salutary reminder that he was maddening, infuriating, always determined to have his own way. Whereas Hugo, when he wasn't radiating this cold anger that chilled Libby right through, was kind and loving. 'Besides, now that he's back in London, he says he'll go to see a lawyer about the divorce.'

Freddy had said no such thing. They hadn't even talked about it since the first night in Paris, but Freddy had agreed in spirit and Libby would frogmarch him to the Inns of Court if she had to.

'It's still too late for the baby to have my name,' Hugo said and Libby thought she might scream, because it was very disheartening to love someone who spent so much time pointing out all the ways in which that love was an encumbrance to him. 'But the little one's well, isn't he?'

'It might be a she,' Libby said, somewhat mollified. 'In fact, I call it the pickle. I'm five months gone now and I imagine it's about the size of a gherkin.'

Hugo looked quite startled that Libby would compare his child to the pickled cucumbers that were all she craved but couldn't eat because they gave her terrible heartburn. Then he grinned. 'The pickle, then. I hope the pickle's well. And you look well too. Positively blooming. Quite, quite ripe.'

A moment ago, Libby had been exasperated with Hugo but now she'd all but forgotten how to breathe as his eyes rested on the burgeoning swell of her breasts that strained against her blouse. It was odd because as her body grew heavier, ungainly, clumsy, more unattractive, Libby constantly felt the pull of desire throbbing in her. How she'd hungered for him during their time apart. She was soft and pliant whereas Hugo was hard, so male. 'There have been some nights I haven't been able to sleep because all I can think about is you,' her voice a sultry whisper as she leaned close to him. 'Of how much I want you. I'm quite mad from it.'

'Oh, Libby . . . ' he half groaned and pulled her closer so he could kiss her. Not a chaste Sunday morning kiss but desperate open-mouthed kisses, his hands clutching hold of her arms to keep her still. 'What you do to me.'

Libby strained to get closer, kissed Hugo with just as much fervour, pressed her aching breasts to his chest and it still wasn't enough to assuage her.

'More. I need more,' she hissed, seizing hold of his hand to guide him to where she wanted him most.

'Someone might see,' Hugo said against her mouth but his hand was already at her knee, smoothing up her thigh under her skirt to trace the edge of her stocking top. 'I should stop, don't you think?'

At any other time Libby would have revelled in his playfulness. 'No one will see. There's no one about. They're all at church or still in bed. Please, Hugo. Please don't stop. I'll scream if you stop.'

She'd barely finished begging when his fingers were there, where she was slick with need, knuckle deep. Libby half rose up on the seat then sank back down, so his grip on her tightened, their foreheads touching, Libby letting out every breath that Hugo took in.

It took no time at all for Libby to reach her crisis, to cry out so that birds pecking the ground in the little clearing cried out too, then flew for the safety of the treetops. It was barely enough; she could have gone again and again. 'Let's go back to the house,' she said and his fingers, still inside her, trembled at the notion. 'We could spend the whole day in bed. Wouldn't that be lovely?'

But then he was pulling free of her. 'It would be wonderful but I'm afraid I can't.' Hugo prised her hand off his prick, which was hard and eager, unlike the rest of him. 'It's not that I don't want to,' he added as Libby's face fell and a shameful blush crept over her. 'I do. More than anything, but I have to be in Manchester before dark and there isn't a stick of furniture in the house.'

'There isn't, is there? I was meant to be organising that before I had to go to Paris.' Libby smoothed down her skirt. 'Once all that's sorted, we can move in, can't we? Be together properly, no more sneaking about.'

Hugo fished in his coat pocket. 'In a perfect world this would be a ring,' he said, handing her a door key. 'But my world is far from perfect. Go back to Heal's, tell them to deliver as soon as they can. Can't have you living in Hampstead now that your Freddy's back. It's hardly appropriate.'

Living in the same house as her husband was the most respectable thing Libby had done in months but she doubted Hugo would appreciate the joke. Not when Hugo's smile was already slipping, his eyes half closing as if he were anticipating a heavy blow. 'You needn't worry about Freddy. He won't cause any trouble. He knows you're the one I love, the one I want to be with. I wish I could be with you right now for ever and ever,' Libby said a little desperately, because it felt as if Hugo were slipping away. 'You'll be back soon?'

'I'll be back before you know it.' Hugo put his arm around Libby, pulled her in for a kiss so sweet, so solemn, it made Libby want to cry.

It was as if all those months spent in Spain, in heat and light and sun, had left an indelible impression on Freddy.

Not only did he insist that Hannah opened the curtains each morning so the rooms of 17 Willoughby Square were no longer dark and gloomy, but he had the house crawling with workmen installing electricity. There were wires, mysterious little boxes and other strange apparatus in every corner of the house though Libby simply couldn't fathom how the electricity would happen once they were done with their hammering and drilling and doing things with teeny, tiny screwdrivers.

Libby had expected Millicent to have a serious attack of the vapours at all this shocking modernity, but Freddy had a way of bringing light into the house that was nothing to do with the boxes of bulbs waiting to be fitted.

'Come on, Ma! It's like the Dark Ages in this place,' he'd laughed when Millicent expressed her unease at his plans for electrification, even though he was paying for it all with his book money. 'Time you started living in the twentieth century.'

With her darling boy back, Millicent swept about the house with a vigour which Libby wouldn't have believed possible. She also had the men from the electricity company to harangue for making a mess, which meant that Hannah was free from her constant scolding, so she was cheerier and the old ladies were quite giddy that Freddy also had plans for a boiler that would issue forth hot water.

'When a kindly American publisher buys my book,' he promised, joining them for dinner one evening, though usually he sequestered himself in the morning room during the day; pounding at his typewriter, drinking endless cups of coffee and chain-smoking.

The salesmen came and went, mostly went, so their opinions weren't canvassed but Potts was the only resident of Willoughby Square not taken with the new improvements. 'I don't trust electricity,' he told Libby as he walked out with her one Monday morning. It wasn't even halfway through October but felt later in the year, the night creeping in far earlier than it should so that Libby welcomed the arrival of electric light. Couldn't come quick enough, though she doubted she'd still be around by the time the work was finished. 'I don't trust things I can't see.'

'You don't trust things you can't see, but you say that you can see ghosts. Can you understand my scepticism?' she asked drily.

'I do see things.' Potts shot Libby a sideways glance. 'I can see that you're in the family way, sweetling, for one thing.'

'Hardly. I just spent two weeks in Paris waiting for Freddy to finish his damn book with nothing to do but go to cafés and eat cake. Ever such a lot of cake,' Libby said with all the wide-eyed candour of her ingénue days.

'Cake? Bun in the oven, more like,' Potts muttered darkly and Libby sniffed as if she were offended and was glad that it was now time for them to part ways at the top of Hampstead High Street.

She *was* showing in a way that she hadn't been before she went to Paris. Then, she'd had a slight thickening of her middle. Now, her skirts would only fasten with the help of a safety pin and her belly had become rounded and plump.

Soon people would notice and intrude and interfere. Pass judgement, which was why she was hurrying to school early to catch Beryl before assembly.

Libby had bought presents from Paris; a pretty tin of biscuits, a jar of cherries steeped in brandy, and she waited nervously as Beryl exclaimed over her gifts. She'd never have imagined that she'd be nervous of Beryl but her loose navy wool dress was suddenly constricting and making her skin itch.

'I'm going to have a child,' Libby heard herself say while her mind was still plotting the right way, the right moment, to say it. And there was more. 'It's not Freddy's. I've been seeing someone else. We're in love, Beryl.' Love was the ultimate excuse. It was unimpeachable, irrefutable.

'What on earth do you mean?' It came out as an indignant squeak. 'You never mentioned being in love before.'

'Hugo, he's the father, he's married,' Libby explained. 'He's getting a divorce. Though that's nothing to do with me. Although it is how we met. It's quite an amusing story really.'

'You never told me anything about a Hugo either. I thought we were friends,' Beryl added, and she wrapped her arms around her bird-like frame, a hurt, reproachful look on her face as if Libby had just pinched her. 'Friends don't keep secrets from each other.'

'We are friends. I'm very fond of you, which is why I didn't want you to think the worst of me.' They were standing in Beryl's minuscule office. There was barely enough room in it for a desk, a bureau and a couple of chairs. Libby only had to take two steps to reach Beryl's side. 'I appreciate I've put you in a terrible bind. That if word got out, it would cause a scandal, parents pulling their little darlings out of school and such.'

'Not that it's any of their business and it's not as if they're to know that your husband has been abroad.' Beryl gasped indignantly again. 'Freddy was in Spain risking life and limb to report on the creeping Fascist menace and you . . .'

This was the bother with telling the truth. It led to revealing yet more unpalatable truths. 'Don't go painting Freddy as some tragic hero,' Libby said sharply. 'He left me in Paris last year in the most hurtful, callous circumstances and I won't be condemned for finding the courage to love again.'

She drew herself up. It was easy enough to tower over Beryl even when one wasn't standing on the moral high ground. 'Shall I resign? Save you the trouble of firing me?'

Beryl rubbed her upper arms as if she were cold, her bulging gaze resting on Libby's bulging belly though she still had her coat on so there wasn't much to see. 'Very well, stay until the end of term,' she said rather ungraciously. 'Once it, the baby, is born, you'll give up work anyway.'

'I suppose.' Libby hadn't given the matter much thought, though she wasn't sure that she'd want to be solely reliant on Hugo providing for her. Enough that he had her heart to do with what he wanted. She remembered her father coming home from work of a Friday evening. He'd sit down at the kitchen table and hand his pay packet over to her mother. 'I've put some by and taken what I need for the week, the rest is your housekeeping, Ida.' He had the softest brown eyes, her father, and a droopy moustache that tickled when he kissed Libby goodnight. 'Don't spend it all at once.'

'I'll try not to,' her mother would say. She'd send Libby and Charlotte to fetch their Friday fish and chips and when they got home, her mother would be perched on her father's lap and the mood in their little house would be so light and gay.

Libby blinked back tears at the memory dredged up from where she'd long buried it. The best, brightest memories were also the most painful ones.

'Libby? We're agreed then? You'll stay until the end of term?' Beryl said querulously in a way that was at odds with

327

her anxious expression as if she hated having it out with people more than anything else in the world.

'December it is.'

'I won't be here come January anyway,' Beryl added a little defiantly, sitting down at her little desk and shuffling a pile of papers, so she looked as if she were pretending to be grown up; a respectable headmistress. 'I've been offered the chance to open a Steiner Waldorf School in New York. I had half thought you might come with me. You did say how much you wanted to go back to America. I don't suppose you will now.'

'Babies are rather portable,' Libby said heatedly. 'In China, the peasants give birth in the paddy fields and carry on picking rice with the babies strapped to their back. Not that I plan on doing that but there are women who work, travel, all sorts, and manage to be mothers too.'

The clock chimed the hour and all at once there was the sound of many pairs of little feet running down the corridor outside. 'You'll be late to take the register,' Beryl said coldly, which didn't suit her.

Libby wondered if she'd be added to the list of other women who had failed to hold Beryl in the same regard as she held them. She was at the door when she heard Beryl get to her feet.

'I don't understand, Libby,' she said plaintively. 'How other people seem to fall in and out of love so easily. Shouldn't love mean more than that?'

Libby turned to see Beryl standing there, looking utterly woebegone. 'Falling in love is the easy part,' she said. 'It's falling out of love that's difficult.'

39

Libby

It wasn't until Saturday that Libby had time to go to the house in Highgate. It was getting dark by the time she left school at four and though she was in the rudest health, not queasy at all, she was so tired that most nights she was tucked up in bed by eight o'clock, with a hot water bottle and a novel, eyelids already drooping.

Freddy had cleared out the little junk room next to his bedroom and was sleeping in there. He told Millicent and the ladies, though no one seemed to care, that he often got up at odd hours as inspiration struck and he didn't want to disturb Libby. No one seemed to care either that Libby was wearing a motley assortment of smocks and loose blouses or that she appeared for every meal with a book strategically held over her stomach.

There would be murders eventually, when she packed up her belongings and left, but Libby rather hoped that she'd be long gone and wouldn't be able to hear Millicent's histrionics as far away as Highgate.

Not that the house was ready to move into, Libby thought, when she unlocked the door that chilly Saturday morning. The radiators had arrived – huge cumbersome appliances – but various complicated things had to be done to them before they started emitting heat. Still, she found it thrilling to walk through the house again. It was so clean, so modern. She'd never get used to the novelty of flicking a switch and lo! There was light! To turn on the tap in the kitchen and the boiler roared into life and hot water gushed out.

Libby drifted upstairs. She and Hugo would sleep in the large back bedroom, its windows looking out on to the gardens and the woods beyond. The bedroom next door would be the nursery though she'd have the pickle in with them at first. They'd need a cot, a little chest of drawers, a set of shelves for toys and books.

Libby took out her diary and wrote out a list then moved to the front bedroom. Four bedrooms, two more than they needed, but perhaps if she were lucky, there might be another child. An only child was a lonely child and she'd loved having a little sister; had adored bossing Charlotte about and having a playmate on hand. Libby peered out of the window. The house opposite was already occupied. Mrs Lister had introduced herself the first time Libby had been by and now they always exchanged smiles and said hello. She had a little girl of about five or so and a baby in a pram so the pickle would have friends here.

She stepped back from the window as a car pulled up outside. Didn't want to get a reputation as a curtain twitcher, even if there were no curtains to twitch. Now, what were they to do with this room? Maybe Hugo would want it for a study or Libby could take up a hobby. Scrapbooking or sewing or something.

What did one do with oneself all day if one didn't work?

There was a sudden ring on the bell. Libby's heart thudded as she hurried downstairs. This house, the life she and Hugo would have, even the pickle, was a secret and yet there was someone at the door. Perhaps it was Mrs Lister being neighbourly.

Libby patted down her hair, licked her lips nervously then opened the door, a bright, welcoming smile on her face.

'Hello!' she trilled at the woman standing there, who certainly wasn't Mrs Lister. This woman was older, blonde, swathed in a fur coat. The woman fingered the diamond necklace round her neck as if it were a rosary and at last Libby focused on her face. There was something petulant in the downward cast of her mouth, the cold look in her pale blue eyes, which made her prettiness seem brittle.

'You're Libby?' the woman asked. 'I'm Pamela, Hugo's wife. I thought it was about time we had a chat.'

It was all very cordial. Libby agreed that they should have a chat, though what they needed to talk about she dreaded to imagine. They decided that the house wasn't an appropriate venue so Libby had slipped on her coat and got into Pamela's racy little car and they'd driven to Crouch End, chattering politely but stiltedly about the weather.

Now they sat in the tearoom of Wilson's department store with the battle lines, consisting of a cake stand and teapot, drawn between them.

'I thought you'd be younger,' Pamela said coolly, though up close she had a good ten years on Libby.

'Really?' Libby countered with just as much *froideur*. 'I hardly thought about you at all.'

That much was true. Pamela had been packed away in a box and tucked out of sight where she couldn't do any harm. Yet here she was.

Pamela worried at her diamonds again. 'I didn't mean to sound so rude,' she said. 'It's just if you were younger, I could pretend you were just a silly little girl who'd caught Hugo's eye, that it was a meaningless fling; but you're not and it's not.'

'It's not,' Libby confirmed. Every word she spoke felt charged as if she weren't speaking so much as walking a tightrope and each placement of her foot was the difference between life and death. 'I love Hugo and he loves me.'

'But I loved him first,' Pamela protested as if her prior claim trumped everything. 'Please, Libby, I've made a terrible mistake and I'm asking you, begging you, woman to woman, to send Hugo home, to me.'

It was a pretty speech and Pamela's performance was note perfect. Her rather thin lips trembled, pale eyes glassine, one tear clinging to her bottom lashes.

'You humiliated him,' Libby reminded her. 'Carrying on with the younger brother of his business partner and yet Hugo was still determined to do the decent thing and let you divorce him.' She was indignant on Hugo's behalf when she remembered how ashamed, how furious, he'd been that weekend in Brighton. 'You've behaved abominably.'

They were forced to hiss. Loud enough that they could hear each other over the melodies of the string quartet in the corner yet quiet enough not be overheard by the woman and her two young daughters at the next table.

'You're the last person to lecture *me* about behaving abominably. You knew Hugo was married . . .' Pamela pressed the tips of her fingers together and blinked her eyes at Libby. 'If you only knew what it was like. All those years married to a man who was so cold, so angry with me.'

Libby could feel herself being drawn in. 'Why would he be angry with you?' she asked, lifting the teapot to refill her cup because she couldn't think of anything else to do with her hands. 'It sounded to me as if you had the perfect life. The children, summers in Suffolk, the house in Maida Vale, isn't it?'

'St John's Wood.' Pamela held her cup aloft so Libby could fill her up too. 'It does sound perfect, doesn't it? It's a lie, an illusion.' The tears were flowing unchecked now and Libby had heart enough to shuffle her chair round to block Pamela from view. 'I couldn't give Hugo children, carry on the Watkins name, which was the one thing he wanted. It's the reason why, as the years passed, he grew more distant. No longer wanted to be intimate with me,' she finished on a choked whisper.

It was all Libby could do not to roll her eyes. 'That's simply not true. What about Robin and Susan?' she asked. 'Hugo has said, repeatedly, that you were the mother of his children.'

'They're my sister's children.' Pamela dabbed ineffectually at her eyes with a lace-edged hankie that she'd produced from her handbag. 'She and my brother died in a car crash in nineteen twenty-four. Hugo and I had been married for eight years by then and I just . . . ' She buried her face in her hands, shoulders shaking. Surely her grief had to be genuine, absolute?

'I'm sorry,' Libby said and she meant it. 'That sounds awful.'

'Eight years,' Pamela repeated as if Libby hadn't said anything. She seized hold of Libby's arm to pull her closer. 'Eight years of desperately wanting a child and when we adopted Robin and Susan, it was the answer to all our prayers but they were eight and six when they came to us, old enough that they still remember their own mother and father and we could only ever be second best. So Hugo and I kept hoping for children of our own but every time I lost another baby, I could feel him pulling away, becoming more aloof. I've been so lonely, so very unhappy for such a long time. Made an utter fool of myself over a man just because he showed me a little affection. Everything would have been different if Hugo and I had had a child of our own.'

Libby was close to tears herself. It had been far easier when Pamela had been bundled away in that box, instead of a living, breathing, crying woman sitting across from her, who knew, even more than Libby, the unceasing agony of losing a child. Libby couldn't, wouldn't, be able to go through that again, without losing her mind too.

'I'm so sorry,' she whispered and she was crying as well, fishing in her own bag for her hankie. 'I think ... Men, they couldn't possibly understand what it feels like to carry a baby, to fall in love with someone who hasn't even drawn breath. It would be so much easier if one's love died with it.'

Somehow, she and Pamela were clutching each other's hands, united in sorrow. 'Libby, oh, Libby.' Pamela sounded quite unhinged now. 'This could all come good if you let Hugo and I have the baby. I promise you I'll love it as if it were my own. Hugo will love it too and it won't want for any—'

Libby reared back in her chair and yanked her hand free so she could wrap her arms around her middle. Feel the bulge of the baby as solid and comforting as ever. '*What?* What on earth ... ? How could you possibly ask me something like that? You must be quite mad.'

'I feel as if I'm thinking clearly for the first time in years,' Pamela said. 'Before I left for Suffolk, John threw me over. Said he'd met someone else.' She'd stopped crying now and straightened up, her voice not thick with grief any more. 'I don't see why I should be punished for one silly mistake. Besides, the whole business with John, well, it made me realise, you see, that what Hugo and I had wasn't so bad.'

'Have you even bothered to apologise to Hugo for the hell you put him through?'

'Of course I have.' Pamela narrowed her eyes as if she simply couldn't comprehend the impertinence of Libby's question. 'Then I told him that we'd simply have to make the best of it. That he couldn't obtain a divorce without my consent and I refused to give it. But when he came back to town and discovered you were expecting, I realised there was a way that Hugo and I could really be together again, be happy as we used to be.'

'I'm sorry about the disappointments you've had, I really am, but if you think you and Hugo could ever be happy, you're a fool. I love him and he loves me . . . '

'No, I don't think it's love,' Pamela said as if she'd given the matter much thought. 'I'd say it was infatuation on Hugo's part. But that's not important. Now, Libby, I need you to be honest with me: is Hugo really the father?'

Libby had her hands braced on the edge of the table, all ready to hoist herself up and run away. Escape from Pamela's lies, her casual disregard for the truth, twisting it this way and that so it was ruined, spoilt. She wanted to rush to the station, board a train to Manchester and find Hugo. Beg him to put his arms around her, hold her, repeat the promises he'd made to her so she'd know that all this was the last spiteful act of a spurned woman. But Libby stayed where she was. She wasn't even sure that her legs would hold her up and she couldn't tear herself away from Pamela's knowing gaze. 'I'm not some cheap little tart who jumps into bed with any man who bats his eyes at her,' Libby said in such strident tones that the woman at the next table shot her a fearful look and urged her two young daughters to make haste with their iced buns. 'Of course Hugo is the father.'

'Then he has certain rights, rights that will take precedence because what kind of life could you give the baby, Libby?' Pamela's expression and tone grew softer, more cajoling. 'Really? You're an actress—'

'I'm a teacher,' Libby interrupted. 'Not that it matters because I would happily die rather than give up the baby.'

Libby half expected Pamela to say that Libby's death could be arranged. The other woman was staring, transfixed, at Libby's belly as if she planned to rip her open with the cake slice and snatch the baby there and then. 'If you love the child, then you'll want to do the right thing,' Pamela insisted. 'We could give it more than you ever could. You have a rickety sort of life, living on the edge, going away to hotels with men; yes, Hugo has told me everything. What does someone like you truly know of love?'

'I would never have gone away to that hotel if . . .'

'Freddy hadn't left you. You couldn't even keep your husband,' Pamela said, though she was a fine one to talk. If Pamela hadn't been *fucking* another man, Hugo would have had no need to go away to a hotel with a paid colluder. 'Deep down, you know this is the right thing, the kindest thing, to do for the baby.'

For one brutal moment, Libby considered it. Imagined Hugo gone, the baby asleep in the corner of a dressing room as she tried to earn a living, begging for parts she'd have turned her nose up at a year ago. Then the vision cleared and she imagined the baby at her breast, the fierce pull of love. She'd never known a love like it.

'No,' Libby said. 'No.'

'It's not the end of the world for you, Libby. You and Freddy could make a go of it. You could even have another baby.' Pamela tried to reach for Libby's hand again but she scraped her chair back, flinched away from her.

It was quite clear that things had ended with her lover, Hugo was intent on leaving her, and Pamela was desperate to cling on by any means necessary.

'Hugo,' Libby said, as she struggled to her feet because

never had she felt so weighed down. 'Hugo,' she said his name again as if it were a lifebelt being thrown out as she flailed in choppy waters. 'He loves me. I love him. That's what you seem to forget. I'm having his child and we're going to be very happy together and there's absolutely nothing you can do about it.'

'You stupid girl, he doesn't love you,' Pamela said, rising to her feet as well so they stood facing each other and glaring over the sandwiches with their crusts cut off, the delicate array of cakes arranged on bone china. 'He told me himself that he could never love a woman who let him do the things that you've let him do.'

40

Zoe

The Friday after the barbecue, when Zoe got home from a day of meetings in town she found Win sitting at the kitchen table, engrossed in the book he was reading.

'I forgot you were out,' he said, briefly looking up as Zoe stumbled into the room, Florence dogging her heels and intent on tripping her up. 'I came home early.'

'Did you?' Zoe said. 'You should have texted.'

'I was going to but then I started reading Libby's diary.' Win held up the object in question. 'She can't add up to save her life. I'm not altogether sure she even knows how many shillings there are to a pound. Sorry, had to get that off my chest.' He smiled sheepishly in a way that made Zoe want to perch on his lap and brush the hair out of his eyes, so she did. Winding her arms round his neck once she was finished with the brushing then bussing the end of his nose with her lips. 'I've read through to the end and now I'm going back over a few things.'

'I haven't read through to the end. Not properly. I'm only up to the beginning of August . . .'

Win's eyebrows shot up. 'So, you haven't seen the telegram saying Freddy was sh—'

Zoe slapped a hand over Win's mouth. 'That doesn't mean you can spoil it for me.' She narrowed her eyes. 'You know how I feel about spoilers.'

Win did know how Zoe felt about spoilers because she'd once unfriended him on Facebook when he'd ruined the series finale of *Mad Men* for her.

He took Zoe's hand away from his mouth. 'Spoilers show a callous disregard for authorial intent,' he parroted, looking up at Zoe from under his lashes with a sly smile. 'You're really red. You've been slurring your words and you appear to be sitting on my lap. Have you been drinking?'

'Yes. Yes I have.' Zoe had had the best part of a bottle of champagne inadequately mopped up with several portions of triple-cooked truffle fries. 'That reminds me. Do you want the good news or the bad news?'

'The good news, always.'

'The good news is that I've got a three-book publishing deal for *The Highgate Wood Mysteries* but the bad news is that it's a very small publishing deal.' Zoe held up thumb and forefinger so Win could get an idea of just how small it was. 'But there's always foreign sales, right?'

'Foreign sales have been good to us over the years.' Win pulled her closer so he could kiss Zoe's pink cheek. 'But still, it *is* really good news, Zo.'

'I was starting to worry that no one would pay me to write or illustrate another book ever again. I also hate it when I'm not pulling my financial weight.'

'Rubbish,' Win said. 'Yeah, you have your quiet periods and then all your advances come in at once and you end up bringing in more in a month than I do in a year. It's all good, Zo.'

Zoe kissed him for that because not once, not even at their very worst when they were screaming at each other daily, had Win ever brought up Zoe's current lack of earning power though she'd strong-armed him into buying a money pit.

The kissing became quite heated, quite quickly. Hands starting to wander, which was unexpected and exciting, but then Zoe remembered what else she'd been about to say and pushed Win away.

'I also have really, really good news and quite bad news. Shall I lead with the good news again?'

Win nodded, his expression hopeful, his eyes dark, face flushed.

'It's just as well you're already sitting down because I'm about to blow your mind.' Zoe shot finger guns at her own head for emphasis. God, she really was quite drunk. 'So, like, do you remember that picture book I did about the robin who was down on Christmas and how he'd pull the berries off holly bushes and perch on the window sill of houses with their decorations up and tap on the glass in an annoying fashion until the Christmas Eve when he was flying along and he came across Santa Claus and—'

'Are you going to give me a page-by-page rundown of a book that I've already read?' Win jiggled Zoe on his lap. 'Could we skip the plot?'

'I suppose,' Zoe agreed. 'Anyway, I've been drinking champagne with Hardeep, my illustration agent, to celebrate being commissioned to design all the Christmas packaging for a leading high street store for next year.' Zoe shook her head and blinked. It still hadn't sunk in. 'Confectionary, cakes, novelty food items too. Gift tags. Wrapping paper. Christmas cards. All adorned with a family of fat red robins getting up to all manner of festive high jinks.'

Win jiggled her on his lap again. Zoe didn't have the heart to tell him that the jiggling was making her feel sick. 'Which store?'

'I can't tell you. I signed a non-disclosure agreement but *it's not just any store*,' she revealed with heavy emphasis.

'Oh my God, you clever, clever woman.' Win clasped his hands in the prayer position. 'Will we get free food? Vouchers? Christmas hampers?'

Zoe glared at him. 'Please don't rain on my parade. Not when my fee will pay the mortgage for the next year and keep Florence in organic dog food.'

'She has got very expensive tastes,' Win agreed and his smile was equal parts pride and relief that they no longer had to live on just his salary and Zoe's paltry royalty payments, which dribbled in twice a year. 'Dare I ask what the quite bad news is?'

'I need to have over a hundred preliminary sketches done and signed off by December twentieth,' Zoe said and she pulled a horrified face for dramatic emphasis, though Win didn't seem that bothered by the daunting task that lay ahead.

'Oh, you'll be fine.' He pulled Zoe closer so he could kiss the top of her head. 'Honestly, Zo, this is amazing news and just as I was about to instigate another round of quite brutal budget cuts and insist we *finally* gave up the quilted loo roll.'

'Not the quilted loo roll!' Zoe shrieked in genuine alarm. 'I told you I'd give up alcohol before I give up cushioned toilet paper.'

'Talking of alcohol, you really are hammered, aren't you?' Win peered intently up at Zoe's face. One sniff of the barmaid's apron and her complexion upgraded to lobster red. 'We should have dinner. Sober you up a bit.'

'Or you could get drunk too?' Zoe suggested.

They compromised with a quickly pulled together carby

dinner of pasta and pesto and a bottle of Cava left over from the barbecue and when Zoe put the bowls down on the table, Win opened his laptop.

'We haven't even talked about your Libby properly. I was wondering if you'd looked her up on the census for nineteen forty-one?' he asked.

'No, because the censuses are sealed for one hundred years,' Zoe said around a mouthful of pasta. 'But I couldn't find her on the nineteen eleven census either. The problem is that I have no idea what her maiden name was – I'm pretty certain it wasn't Edwards, I think that was a stage name, even though it's the name she registered when she got married.'

Without log-in details for one of the commercial ancestry sites (and Zoe could tell that Win was sorely tempted to sign up) their only option was to use a free site that only logged the barest details of births, marriages and deaths.

Zoe had already confirmed that Libby and Freddy had been married in the Parish of St Pancras in September of 1935, but after that the trail went cold.

There was no marriage to a Hugo Watkins. No birth certificate for a baby either, even though they tried looking under Edwards, Morton and Watkins. In fact, there were no births for the first half of 1937 registered in London that fitted the scant information they had. Thankfully, there were no death certificates either.

Zoe was pleased that Libby was no longer a secret or the cause of more disagreement, but something she could share with Win. Win was always a great sounding board when she was drafting a new story, and he was a great sounding board now; happy to listen to Zoe's theories or suggest new avenues they should search. Besides, it was lovely to do something together that didn't involve spreadsheets or random acts of DIY.

'We're going round in circles now,' Win said at last when they'd bounced around the internet for an hour but hadn't come up with any new leads. He closed the laptop lid to prove his point. 'The thing is, Zo, we're butting up against the Second World War so if Libby did stay in London, what with the Blitz and everything, then chances are ...'

Zoe didn't want to hear it. 'The important thing is that Libby got pregnant again. When she was sure that she couldn't, when she'd lost a baby already. They didn't have fertility-enhancing drugs or IVF then but she still managed it.'

'I know what you're doing, Zo, and I get it but stop looking for signs where there aren't any.'

There *were* signs everywhere. Cycles. Circles. Strange coincidences, which couldn't be explained by reason and logic. In January when she'd been raw with grief, Zoe had moved into this house and found a suitcase and diary belonging to a woman who, eighty years before, had been grief-stricken too.

Maybe the house had stood still all this time because it had been waiting for Zoe to finish Libby's story. Zoe remembered back to that first evening, Win recoiling as they uncovered the house's secret. 'You said it was a sign when we found the suitcase,' she reminded him. 'A sign we should never have moved, but I think we were meant to turn this house into a home.'

Win was halfway to the sink with their dishes, but he paused. 'Does it feel like home to you? When did that happen? Somewhere between the new kitchen being installed and the Tuesday when we had that row in the middle of IKEA? I'm not there yet.'

Neither was Zoe really. There were some things missing before 23 Elysian Place became their home. The house needed a pram in the hall. The bedroom next to theirs transformed from spare room to nursery with a sunny mural painted on the wall, and in the cot, solid and real, their child. Zoe could see it, feel it, so completely that it had to come true.

If Libby could do it, against all the odds, then so could she.

When Win committed to a project, he really *committed* to a project.

When he'd decided to take up running after his nan had warned him there was a history of high cholesterol in the family, he'd completed his first marathon within six months.

Then there'd been the Great KonMari Purge of early 2015 when they'd started sprucing up their old flat ready to put it on the market. Win had become so obsessed with decluttering that Zoe became dry-mouthed each time he appeared with another black bin liner full of things that absolutely didn't need to be thrown out.

And now he was about to embark on Project Libby and Zoe recognised the signs that indicated that he was all in. Their kitchen whiteboard had been repurposed so it looked like Win was conducting a Missing Person investigation, he'd taken a huge pile of books on English theatre and the car industry between the wars out on inter-library loan and was fielding phone calls from the Highgate Historical Society.

Whereas Zoe was about to sequester herself to draw more robins than any other person had ever drawn in the history of illustration. But first, before he left for work one morning, Win sat her down with a serious expression on his face and Libby's diary in his hands.

'You should finish reading the diary before we go any further,' he said gravely. 'In case you decide that it's best to leave Libby to rest in peace, as it were.'

The way that Win put it was ominous so that Zoe had a

metallic tang of fear at the back of her throat, like she'd been licking batteries. But it wasn't just the diary.

'And you're meeting Jackie for lunch,' she reminded him.

'Yeah, I know I am,' Win said as he gathered up his brief-case. 'Said she wanted to have a chat about something. I hope it's not her VAT return.'

Win squatted down to pet Florence goodbye so he missed the anguished look on Zoe's face because she knew the mother/son lunch-date was nothing to do with Jackie's VAT return.

The look was still on Zoe's face after she'd made a pot of tea then reached for the diary with some hesitation. Taking a leaf from Clive's book, she was armed with a magnifying glass, which made reading much easier as finally Libby talked about the house and though she didn't give its address, Zoe knew that she meant *their* house when she wrote about her hopes and plans for it.

I want it to be light and bright, no dark wood, no cumbersome Victoriana. A place where we can live and love and be happy, she'd written in mid October. Just as Zoe had, Libby was planning to go white with accents of blue in the downstairs room and had even drawn a rudimentary sketch of their living room; sofa and armchairs in roughly the same place but a radio-gram instead of a television.

And then.

28th October 1936

Hugo's still not back from Manchester. I phone the garage in Mayfair every day. Twice a day! I'm sure the man who answers the phones suspects something when I say that it's Mrs Morton calling about the car Mr Watkins sold her. But what else could I possibly say?

345

He hasn't even sent a letter, or a postcard. It has only been three weeks, I suppose that's not such a terribly long time and I might be overreacting but who could blame me? He must have known that Pamela was coming to see me. From what she claimed, they have no secrets. How else could she know about the baby? I was so determined not to believe her, but the longer Hugo stays away, crushes me with his silence, then the more I doubt.

Oh, I don't know what to think! People would have it that love is wonderful but in truth, it can be such a horrid business.

It was in all the papers that Wallis Simpson was granted a divorce from her husband yesterday. Everything is so much easier when you're rich and have influence.

Freddy says that there's nothing to stop Wallis and Edward getting married six months from now when her divorce becomes final, but he doubts she'll ever be queen. Says it's even odds on whether Edward will actually be crowned king, but Freddy says the most ridiculous things. Of course he will. He's the king. He can't just stop being king. There's an order to these things or else it all descends into chaos.

Oh God, I'm so sick of chaos, of feeling so unhappy. Since last Saturday when I was ambushed by Pamela, I've had dreadful pains in my side. Like the stitch I had in Paris before I lost ... No! Can't even think it. The pickle is not for turning.

And one final entry.

11th November 1936
  4pm Doctor Richardson 57 Great Titchfield Street,
WC1

That was how Libby's diary ended. Not with a bang, but a pained whimper and a doctor's appointment.

Zoe had wondered if Win might come home straight after his lunch with Jackie. If he'd be angry with Zoe for asking Jackie about Terry when he was *persona non grata* in their lives, but Win was home at half past six as usual and even called out a cheery 'hello!' as soon as he came through the front door, kissing the top of her head when he walked into the kitchen a moment later. She tugged hold of his sleeve. 'How did lunch go?'

'Fine. As it happened, Mum didn't want to talk about her VAT return after all,' Win said mildly. He kissed the top of her head again then busied himself with putting the kettle on and making tea, though Zoe didn't know if he was genuinely desperate for a cuppa or if was punishing her a little by withholding. 'Do you want tea or coffee?'

'Tea, please. So, what did you talk about?' she asked a little desperately with an eye roll at Florence who cocked her head like she couldn't believe Win either.

'I know that you know what we talked about already,' Win said, placing a mug down in front of Zoe. 'Mum said I had you to thank for giving her the courage to come clean about Terry.'

'Right. OK.' Zoe blew on the tea before she took a tentative sip. 'I wasn't prying but we had a heart-to-heart at the barbecue and the subject of Terry came up.'

'I'm not mad at you, Zo,' Win said, as he sat down opposite her. 'Mum and I needed to talk it out and I'd always suspected that something he'd done had finally made her snap. Ed did too. They always fought a lot but why else would Terry disappear for good instead of popping up like he usually did, when we'd just got used to him not being around?' He looked thoughtful as if his mind were still on the conversation he'd had with his mother over lunch. 'You know, I did sometimes worry that Terry left because I was a disappointment to him. I wasn't good at sports, hadn't discovered running back then. He was always telling me to man up, stop being so sensitive, that kind of thing.'

'That couldn't have been easy,' Zoe said, reaching out with her foot under the table to nudge Win's ankle. He smiled at her, a smile that was a pure distillation of the man she'd married: quiet, knowing, warm.

'It wasn't. And so secretly I was pleased and relieved when he left and then I felt guilty for being pleased, especially as Ed did really genuinely miss him, but life was still much better for all of us once he'd gone.'

'Jackie said the same thing. She got quite emotional,' Zoe said, removing her foot as Florence started trying to lick her toes.

'She got very emotional in the middle of Pizza Express when I said Gav had been more of a father to me than Terry ever had. She even cried but then she swore it was because her doughballs were too garlicky,' Win said with a smile. 'Then when I thought we were over the worst, she started on at me about babies.'

Zoe widened her eyes. 'Oh? Did she?' She looked down at her half-finished mug. 'I might have mentioned babies in passing too.'

'Not fair, Zo,' Win admonished with the tiniest hint of a bite to his voice. 'You said you'd be patient.'

'I'm the definition of patient,' Zoe said with a bite to her own voice.

'You really aren't,' Win told her. 'And I had Mum going on and on about our superior combined genes and how she's counting on us to buck the trend and provide her with a granddaughter, which she's going to dress all in pink because she has no time for gender-neutral child-rearing. I've heard quite enough on the subject of babies for this week.'

There was plenty Zoe had to say about that but then Win rubbed the bridge of his nose and yawned and she decided, for once, to let it drop. He made it sound as if coming to terms with his father's disappearance and twenty-odd years of hurt and confusion had been a breeze, but Terry had been right, Win *was* sensitive (it was one of the reasons why Zoe loved him) and she knew it must have been emotionally exhausting for him, so now really wasn't the time to plead her case. Though it was starting to feel as if it would never be the right time.

Better to change the subject entirely. Zoe picked up Libby's diary. 'I read this to the end. I can't believe that Libby went all the way to Paris to bring Freddy home.'

'And then there was the showdown with Pamela,' Win said eagerly, as if he were happy to change the subject too. 'Who has to be Hugo's wife, right?'

They speculated about Pamela over dinner. Win said that he'd try and find a wedding certificate for Pamela and Hugo, scour newspaper archives to see if there were any records of their divorce.

'So, do you want to carry on, Zo? All the signs are pointing in a direction that's, well, not good,' Win asked, as Zoe washed the dishes and he dried.

The answer was a tentative 'yes', because Zoe had come this far and she had to see it through to its bitter conclusion. It was inevitable from the baby clothes in the suitcase to a diary that ended with a doctor's appointment for the eleventh of November then silence, that the conclusion of Libby's year, her story, would be bitter. Zoe also knew how diligent, how thorough Win would be when he had a target in his sights.

If anyone could find out what had happened to Libby, then Win could.

Libby dried her hands on a tea towel and picked up the diary again. All those blank pages for the rest of November, December . . . but there was something else.

The pages of the eleventh and twelfth of December were stuck together by the gum from an envelope that had been wedged between them. Inside the envelope was a piece of paper. A note.

11th December 1936

Dearest Libby
'Come live with me and be my love.'
I'll be waiting at the house for you.
Hugo

'Did you see this?' she asked Win, holding it up. 'Right at the end of the diary?'

He shook his head. 'I can't believe I missed it!'

The letter was like the clouds parting to allow the sun to beat feebly down on an otherwise dark day. 'This makes me feel better,' Zoe said, as she handed Win the letter. 'Maybe it did come good in the end.'

'Maybe,' Win said. 'Just don't get your hopes up is all I'm saying.'

'Whatever, Eeyore!'

But it was time to let Libby go for the moment. Win could carry on without her, while Zoe drew robins until robins were all that she could think about.

41

Libby

Every evening when she got home from school, Libby would go straight to bed and ask Hannah to bring her supper up. Then the girl would linger no matter how hard Libby would yawn and drop heavy hints about how exhausted she was.

'Are you sickening for something?' Hannah eventually asked, her eyes fixed on Libby's belly, no matter that it was obscured by blankets, bedspread and a couple of library books. 'You are looking quite peaky lately. Pale as anything.'

'I always look pale, don't I?' Libby murmured vaguely, then she shut her eyes and stretched out her arms. 'Gosh, I'm so sleepy. Be a love, Hannah, and switch out the main light for me.'

Libby still hadn't got used to Willoughby Square being on the electric – light pouring into places that had been in the dark for so long. Millicent was never happier than when she was touring the house and snapping off any light that she found merrily burning away while moaning about how the bills would send her poor Freddy into penury. Libby could

351

hear her mother-in-law's tread on the stairs as she lay there and thought about how she should be lying in another room, in another house a mile or so away.

Except the life that Libby had imagined with Hugo in Highgate seemed like a fever dream. Since the scene with Pamela, more draining, more deadly than any tragedy that Libby had performed on stage, she'd had no word from him.

She'd called his office several times from the phone box on Hampstead High Street, always furtively looking over her shoulder for fear that Virena Edmonds was about to appear and demand to know who Libby was speaking to. Not Hugo, in any case, but his secretary who always sounded as if he were humouring Libby when he said that Mr Watkins was unavailable.

So Libby didn't know if Hugo were in London, Manchester or Timbuk-bloody-tu. Didn't know if Pamela were acting under his orders, though how could she be? Hugo had told Libby how happy he was countless times. Had bought a house for the two of them to share because he loved her and she was carrying his child, which was more than Pamela had ever given him.

Yet his silence was deafening and Libby's thoughts, her fears, the creeping doubt chased around and around in her head like a series of bogeymen, each more terrifying than the last, and the most terrifying thing of all was the pain in her side, on both sides now, and her heart raced even when she was lying flat on her back and trying to take deep, calming breaths.

Her only recourse was to go back to the women's health centre where she'd been pronounced pregnant. They'd written to her once requesting she attend an expectant mother's clinic but Libby had decided it was best to leave well alone. All that poking and prodding couldn't be good for the baby.

Except now something was terribly wrong. Libby was sure of it, dreaded the confirmation, but still made an appointment for later that week.

On the Wednesday after school she caught the Tube to Goodge Street. On her own this time – no Beryl for moral support. Libby took her seat in the waiting room and, out of habit, rearranged her coat to hide her tummy.

There were two girls sitting opposite her, not much older than Hannah. The one with the belly as big as Libby's caught her eye, and refused to look away, a challenging tilt to her babyish face, while her friend gazed at the floor, red staining her cheeks, lip caught between her bottom teeth.

It could be worse, Libby thought to herself. I could have got caught when I wasn't very much more than a child myself. Now she was a grown woman and actually it didn't help matters much. She might have a husband but the baby wasn't his, her lover was gone and the whole affair was a bloody shambles, whichever way you looked at it.

She put one hand to her chest as her heart began to thump, the other to her left side as that niggling ache sawed into her. When her name was called she could barely stagger to her feet, much to the fascinated horror of the two girls on the other side of the room.

It was the doctor she'd seen the first time. She was as kindly but as young as Libby remembered, taking her arm to gently guide Libby to the consulting room.

'We had hoped to see you at one of our clinics,' the doctor chided her. 'I'd say you were what, five months along now?'

'Six months,' Libby gasped and then she found that she couldn't say much more than that because it had become so terribly hard to speak.

The doctor called in a nurse and between the two of them they helped Libby out of her coat and her dress and hoisted her on to the examination table. The doctor palpated her stomach then the pretty dark-haired nurse held what looked like an ear trumpet to the bulge. 'Baby's fine,' she said with a smile and Libby managed to breathe out again. 'Got a real live wire. Doubt he gives you a moment's peace.'

'Just growing pains,' the doctor said, explaining how Libby's body was stretching, expanding, to accommodate the new life inside it, but her expression became grave as the nurse took Libby's blood pressure then measured her pulse. 'Do you tend to suffer from your nerves, Mrs Morton?'

'I have been anxious,' Libby confessed as she struggled to sit up, though anxiety hardly described the long sleepless nights she'd suffered. 'Worrying about the baby and things.'

'Thirty-two is really quite old to be starting a family,' the doctor said with a frown. 'Now I could write out a prescription for something to calm you down but the best medicine I could prescribe is strict bed rest for the duration of your pregnancy.'

'But I can't. I'm a teacher. I agreed I'd finish the term.' On top of everything else, now Libby would have to have another unpleasant conversation with Beryl, who'd barely said two words to her these last few weeks.

The doctor shook her head. 'Bed rest,' she reiterated, scribbling notes on a sheet of paper. 'Straight home and under the covers. You're only to get up when nature calls. That's an order.'

The nurse helped Libby get dressed again and the doctor talked about asking a colleague who had a surgery in Belsize Park to visit Libby weekly; that if her blood pressure and pulse still remained high she'd have to deliver the baby in hospital. The doctor's words floated around the room. Libby pressed her hands against the constant fluttering above her breastbone.

'But the baby's really all right?'

'Yes, but baby will only continue to thrive if you take my advice, and if I find out from my colleague you've been disobeying my instructions, I'll be having words with your husband, Mrs Morton.'

Freddy would find that an absolute scream, Libby thought, but she promised that she'd take a taxi back to Hampstead and go straight to bed and stay there for the next three months.

She found a cab soon enough and after she settled herself on the seat, the cabbie turned around and asked, 'Where to, my ducks?'

There was one thing that she simply had to do before she took to her bed.

'Park Lane. Near the Dorchester. It's a car showroom.'

It was close to six now. People leaving offices and shops, pouring into Tube stations, queuing for buses.

They had a slow run down Oxford Street and around Hyde Park Corner. Libby peered out of the window as white mansion blocks and hotels, the Marriott, the Park Lane Hotel and finally the Dorchester, loomed up like art deco monoliths in the dusk.

'Just here, please,' she said hurriedly as she spotted the illuminated sign, Watkins Motors, before she saw the sleek, gleaming cars raised up on plinths and displayed under spotlights in the windows.

Libby hesitated at the door. She saw a flurry of movement at the back of the showroom, a group of men gathered round one of the cars. It was easy enough to step inside then. Heels clicking on the marble floor, her course set, her path clear.

Hugo in shirtsleeves, his jacket discarded, was leaning over the open bonnet of a long black car next to two men in overalls, a younger man hovering on the sidelines. He caught Libby's eye as she tottered towards them.

'I'm afraid we're closed, madam,' he said, moving away

from the group. He had a bandbox, wet-behind-the-ears look to him as if his mother dressed him every morning and warned him in no uncertain terms not to let his clothes get spoiled. 'Would it be possible to come back tomorrow?'

But Libby only had eyes for Hugo as he peered into the car's innards and murmured something she couldn't catch.

'Hugo! I don't bloody call this Manchester!' Her voice was perilously high, the men all looking at her now, curious but wary because Libby realised that she must look an utter fright in the baggy crumpled clothes she'd been wearing all day, her hair flat and frizzy. As she'd got out of the taxi, the driver had even felt moved to say: 'If I were you, love, I'd have a tot of something as soon as you get home. You look like you're about to keel over.'

'Where have you been, you bastard?' Libby demanded in the same shrill tone. 'Have you any idea what you've put me through?'

Hugo was at her side in an instant, eyes flashing a warning, his face a hard, rigid thing. 'Elizabeth,' but his voice was as soft as feathers, 'I was expecting you ages ago. Did I give you the wrong directions? Did you get turned around?'

'What? What on earth . . . ?'

'This is Elizabeth, a friend of Pammie's,' Hugo threw at the men, who were staring at Libby as if they'd never seen anyone heartsick and half dead with it before. They didn't stare for long as Hugo was already tugging Libby past them and through the door at the back of the showroom, his fingers a vice around her wrist. 'Said I'd give you a lift home, didn't I?'

Libby's reply, her renunciation of the glib excuses that had fallen so smoothly from his lips, was drowned out by the door slamming shut behind them. 'You've got better at telling lies,' she said furiously, her thoughts turning as they so often did to that first weekend in Brighton. 'Oh, I don't even know who you are any more! You go to Manchester and I don't hear a word from you and then Pamela, precious, *bloody* Pamela, comes visiting. Did you put her up to it? Did you hatch the plan together to steal my baby? Did you? Did you? Answer me!'

Hugo was silent and still pulling Libby along, down a corridor, the smell of petrol and grease growing stronger. Then he shouldered open another door and they were outside in a courtyard, which must have originally been part of a stable but now there were cars waiting patiently on the cobbles instead of horses.

'You're hysterical,' Hugo said evenly and Libby supposed she was because she was crying without even knowing how long she'd been crying. 'Get in.'

He held open a car door. Libby climbed in, still sobbing. She scrabbled in her bag for her handkerchief as Hugo walked round the car, got in the other side. Libby glanced at his clean, pure profile as if her tears, her words, her despair had simply bounced off him like stones skimming the surface of a still lake. Then she saw that throbbing tic at his temple, which even Hugo couldn't control, and the stones she'd made from her sorrow sank below the surface.

He turned the key in the ignition and the car roared into life. Hugo manoeuvred out of the yard and nudged into Park Lane and the evening traffic. They drove in silence for a while punctuated only by Libby's shuddering, hiccupping sobs. Every time that she thought she must be done with crying, more tears burst forth. It was exhausting.

'You said . . . you promised we'd be together,' Libby finally managed to say. 'When did you stop loving me, Hugo?'

'Of course I still love you,' he said, so perfunctorily that even the most inept director would have shouted, 'Once more with feeling.' Hugo glanced over at Libby, she was limp and quiet now, and his face lost a little of its rigidity. 'Though I wish I didn't love you because it's all shot to hell. I can't get a divorce, Pamela won't agree to it.'

It had been hard to hate Pamela when she'd been sitting across from Libby with her tears for all the babies that weren't to be, so that Libby couldn't help but feel a kinship with her. Now she could hate Pamela without impunity for being fickle and faithless. For taking a lover then running to Hugo when the affair soured, knowing he'd have no choice but to take her back.

'Freddy says that they'll change the law soon,' Libby remembered. 'There's some MP, a Mr Herbert, with a bee in his bonnet who's going to propose a bill or whatever it is one does to change the law.'

'Fat lot of good it will do. The baby will still be illegitimate. Even if I give him my name, in the eyes of the world, he'll be a bastard.'

It was such an ugly word to describe the little being that they'd made from their love. 'Leave her. "Come live with me and be my love,"' Libby quoted and she was calm now, so deadly calm. 'Let's live in sin in Highgate. Not even Highgate. There's a whole world out there that doesn't care one jot about our business.' She warmed to the idea. 'We could find a little island and live on coconuts and pineapples. You have the legs for a grass skirt.'

'Now you're being silly,' Hugo said, but he seemed relieved Libby wasn't crying or shrieking any more. He rested his hand on her knee and she relished the warmth of his touch. Then remembered that Pamela had ruined that too.

'You told her about us,' Libby said quietly. 'About the things we've done. She said—'

'It doesn't matter what she said,' Hugo insisted. 'There was one night when we were in Suffolk . . . she was upset,

358

contrite ... I said I wouldn't have her back, but she's been my wife for so long. She noticed that I was changed ... the things I did ... were not the things we, Pamela and I, used to do. She accused me of going with ... well, never mind about that. I told her about you. That I'd fallen in love.' He was stammering and stuttering, and drove straight down the Finchley Road instead of turning right when they reached Swiss Cottage.

Despite his stuttering and stammering, it was perfectly clear what Hugo was saying: he'd made love to Pamela. If he'd done even half the things to Pamela that Libby had taught him then no wonder Pamela was so desperate to have him back. Hugo was quite the demon lover these days.

When Libby thought about it, Hugo had been withdrawing, distancing himself by degrees, ever since he'd returned from Aldeburgh. She'd hardly noticed – there had been all that business with Freddy and having to go to Paris – but now she felt the loss of him even as she sat next to him. Libby knew she could live without Hugo if she had to. She'd got used to losing men before, had managed to survive the heartache, the grinding pain of a lover departed, but why should the baby be deprived of its father?

'We must go away,' Libby said. 'We can start again. Be new people. Have a new life. You, me and the pickle.'

'I'd like that,' Hugo said wistfully then he tensed again, swore under his breath as he missed another opportunity to turn right. 'It's impossible. Robin and Susan ...'

'They're not yours.' It was a mistake; Libby knew that as soon as she said those three words. 'The baby is your flesh and blood. Our child, Hugo.'

She took his hand that was still on her knee and lifted it to her belly. The baby had been restless all day, shifting inside her, but now it was still. Hugo snatched his hand back.

'I can't go away. It's impossible,' he said again. He sucked in a breath. 'Would you even consider letting us, Pamela and I, raise the baby?'

'*Oh!* You really are a bastard! How could you even ask me that?'

'Just think about it. If you love the baby, love me, then you'll want what's best . . . '

'What's best? How could you possibly think that I'd agree to that?' She was crying again and Hugo tried to reach for her but Libby batted him away, flailing her arms and she thought she might have scratched him for he cursed, then had to wrench the steering wheel to keep the car straight. 'I would die before I'd let you take my baby.'

'You're hysterical again. Nobody's taking the baby,' Hugo said quickly as if he hated the words. 'But it's something to consider when you're feeling . . . calmer. I know it sounds cruel, unreasonable, but please, if you'd just think about it, you'd see that it makes sense if—'

'Stop the car!' Libby gasped. There was no air and she was choking from it. Tried to open the door but Hugo reached across and yanked her hand back.

'Are you trying to kill us?' he roared and for the most fleeting of all moments, Libby thought it might be the answer.

'I wish I were dead. No! I wish *you* were dead. That I'd never met you!' But even that was a lie because the baby was moving again. She couldn't even hate Hugo because without him, she wouldn't have this miracle.

Then it all stopped. Hugo pulled the car into the kerb on the corner of Willoughby Square. 'We can't leave things like this, Libby,' he said, this time stilling her shaking hand so he could open the door for her. 'Think about what's best for the baby.'

'I'm best for the baby.' Libby got out on wobbly legs as

Hugo leaned across the seat to say something. Some other ludicrous reason why Libby should let him and his precious Pamela steal her child, but she slammed the car door so she wouldn't have to hear it.

'Clear off! I never want to see you again!' Libby doubted he could hear her so she banged on the roof of the car so he'd get the message.

'Libby! Why are you standing in the middle of the road shouting at stationary motorists? What will the neighbours think?'

Libby turned round as Hugo drove off to see Freddy on the corner by the postbox. She stood there, tears streaming down her face though she would have thought that they'd have stopped by now. Surely it wasn't possible for one person to have so many tears?

Freddy took a couple of steps towards her and his amused expression changed to one of concern. 'What's the matter, old girl?' He looked down the road, but Hugo was long gone. 'Come and tell Freddy all about it.'

He held out his arms and Libby stumbled into them. 'It's as if all I am to him is an unwanted parcel,' she sobbed and Freddy stroked her hair until she calmed down enough to let him lead her across the road to number 17.

'Bed,' Freddy said firmly but quietly so that the ladies chattering away at the dinner table wouldn't hear them as he helped Libby up the stairs. 'You're to go to bed and stay there. I was a dab hand at knots when I was in the Scouts, I'll cuff you to the bedpost if need be with some of Father's old ties.'

Even once Libby was in her nightgown and in bed, Freddy stayed to listen to her incoherent, tear-soaked woes and stroke her hair.

Finally, when Libby settled down, covers tucked up to her chin, Hannah sent up with toast and sweet tea, then sharply dismissed, Freddy sat on the edge of the bed and took Libby's ice-cold hand in his. 'Libby, why do you always fall in love with the most awful people? And yes, I count myself among that number.'

'Why do I always end up making such a hash of it?' Libby asked but she could feel sleep licking at the edges, pulling her down and she drifted off before Freddy could reply.

42

Zoe

For much of the year, the days had stretched before her without purpose, now her days had more purpose than she knew what to do with. One hundred and twelve illustrations to draw and colour before the twentieth of December and contrary to what many people thought, including Win, who really should have known better, she couldn't just 'bang out' ten drawings in a day.

Zoe was up at seven as Win and Florence set off for their morning run and was still working when Win came home nearly twelve hours later. In the meantime, she would have sketched and coloured her family of robins sledging and building snowmen, wrapping presents, opening presents and other assorted festive, family-friendly activities. Zoe's only respite was to take Florence across to Highgate Woods for an afternoon walk and while Florence stalked squirrels, Zoe was on high alert for any robins who happened to be cavorting about in the vicinity.

It was where Zoe was one Friday afternoon in late October,

sitting on what she thought of as their bench down a path they'd nicknamed Squirrel Alley. The light was fading as Zoe sketched the clearing in front of her. The trees were sparse but still green, even though the leaves that carpeted the ground were on the turn; a glorious melange of acid yellow to the palest gold. The clocks would go back that weekend and at nearly six the light was fading fast – Zoe was already listening out for the warning bell that signalled fifteen minutes before the gates were locked. One time, she'd had to tuck Florence under her arm to outrun the wood-keepers in their little buggy.

'Hello, stranger,' Win said, startling Zoe as he sat down next to her. 'You look a lot like my wife who disappeared about two weeks ago.'

'You look a lot like my husband, except he doesn't usually finish work this early.' It was warm enough that Win wasn't wearing a coat over his suit but the tips of his ears and his nose were pink. In the woods the air was thicker now, the smell of leaf mould pervading the atmosphere, the benches slightly damp when you first sat on them. 'Time off for good behaviour?'

'Something like that,' Win agreed and he settled back to watch Zoe work; her pencil making lightning quick strokes across her pad, scribbling notes to herself about the colours she'd use later to create a winter woodland scene.

Zoe finished her sketch and turned to Win as he pulled out a bottle of champagne and two plastic cups from his work bag.

'Happy anniversary,' he said a little smugly because he thought she'd forgotten.

'Happy anniversary,' Zoe replied, leaning over to kiss his cheek. 'I wouldn't open that just yet. The bell's about to go. We can have it after we get home tonight.'

Florence had been deep in the undergrowth but now she emerged, ears cocked. She caught sight of Win and stilled apart from her tail, which wagged with a force that looked painful. 'Hey, pretty lady,' he called to the dog as she bounded over. 'Who's my bestest girl?' There was no competition. 'Where are we going tonight?'

'I booked a table for eight thirty at Andrew Edmunds but maybe you'd prefer to take Florence, your bestest girl,' Zoe said drily. 'Although I'm not sure she'll want to come when she could be having a sleepover with Darcy and Bingley.'

Darcy and Bingley were two sandy-coloured puggles besotted with Florence, who loved them both equally and loved the squeaky tennis balls that their owner Jack bought even more.

'I thought you wouldn't notice the date, what with the robins and everything.' Win pushed Florence away as she tried to jump up with muddy paws.

'It's our anniversary. Thirteen years and we've managed not to kill each other,' Zoe said, because they always celebrated the anniversary of their first meeting. 'I think that deserves a night off.'

'It does, but Andrew Edmunds? Can we afford it?' Win cringed. 'Sorry. I didn't mean to ruin the mood before the mood even had a fighting chance.'

'You haven't ruined anything and I had an unexpected Brazilian royalty payment.' Zoe raised her eyes to the heavens. Her attention suddenly focused on a group of trees; their branches drooping gracefully if forlornly. 'Thank God for the children's-book-buying public of Brazil. Hang on! Just need to take some pictures.'

She pulled out her phone as Win asked Florence how her squirrel stalking was going. 'What was that?' He looked behind the bench. 'Is that a pesky squirrel?'

'One day she'll catch one and we'll have to deal with the bloody aftermath. Not to mention the fact that Florence will become a stone-cold killer.'

'I don't think we have to worry. She's the very opposite of stealthy,' Win observed as Florence thundered through a gap in the bushes. 'Oh, you're doing another sketch? Won't they be ringing the bell soon?'

'Yeah, but see the way those branches are starting to droop? If they were heavy with snow, you could imagine two mischievous little robins skiing down them, couldn't you?'

Win made a noncommittal noise but said nothing until Zoe was done. 'You're so observant, Zo. You always see the little details that other people miss. I suppose that's why you're an artist.'

Zoe felt herself swell with pride – just a little bit, not enough to bloat her. 'Well, I like to think that I've honed my visual senses over the years.'

'Yeah, exactly, so how come you've never noticed *this* before?' Win gestured at the worn brass-coloured inscription on the bench that Zoe was certain she'd read a hundred times before. On her first forays into the woods, she'd made a point of reading all the bench inscriptions. There was even a bench that she always avoided because its plaque was in memory of a child who hadn't even made it to its first birthday. So, of course, she'd noticed this one before.

She huffed a little at Win who pressed his lips together like he was trying hard not to laugh, then she leaned across to peer at the faded engraving.

IN MEMORY OF MY DEAREST LIBBY
'*The woods are lovely, dark and deep,*
But I have promises to keep,
And miles to go before I sleep,
And miles to go before I sleep.'
All my love, HW

366

It was the same jolt as seeing the face of a loved one suddenly materialise in a crowd. Zoe traced each word with the tip of her finger.

'It's Libby and Hugo,' she said, looking imploringly at Win. 'It can't be anyone else, can it?'

'It absolutely can't. It has to be them. Wow. I can't quite get my head around the idea that they walked along this path eighty years ago.' Win rubbed his eyes as if the ghosts of Libby and Hugo had suddenly emerged through the trees. 'That they might have sat here and looked out onto this view, like we've done countless times. I'm a little spooked, like someone just walked over my grave.'

It was Zoe's turn to shiver. 'I often see Libby so clearly walking through the woods or around Soho. Like there's a film of her playing in my head.'

'You're an artist, you can imagine things like that, I need a bit more to go on.' Win smiled ruefully.

Zoe traced the first line of the inscription again. '"In memory of my darling Libby". So she did die then.'

'It was eighty years ago,' Win pointed out. 'She had to have died at some point.'

'Yes, but . . .'

The bell rang then. Of course it did.

'We'll come back tomorrow,' Win said firmly as if he knew that Zoe wanted to run to the little office by the café and badger the staff to start looking through their records. 'If you still need answers, we'll come back tomorrow.'

It felt odd to get all gussied up.

Zoe wore the APC dress she'd splurged on a couple of years ago when they'd had money to splurge; a long-sleeved charcoal-grey crêpe with a graphic floral pattern in two different shades of pink. She put heels on for a wobbly walk from front door to Highgate Tube then hobbled from Leicester Square station through Soho. She'd even done something with her hair that was more than scraping it up into a ponytail and her lashes were weighted down with mascara, lips sticky with a soft matte pink. It felt a little like playing dress-up when she'd spent the best part of the year in a motley and ragged assortment of jeans, yoga pants and jumpers that all had holes in the cuffs from where she had worked her thumbs through.

She was back in her own skin, skin that had been denuded of extraneous hair, exfoliated and moisturised. So different from the long months when she had left her legs, eyebrows and underarms to become Hobbit-like and had done nothing more with her face than splash it with cold water; this from the woman who used to have a five-step skincare regime. Some of it was due to their primitive bathroom facilities and some of it was that Zoe had stopped caring. She didn't know when it was that she'd started caring again but she was glad that she had.

'I tell you what, Zo, you scrub up all right,' Win said as they sat in Andrew Edmunds, the small Soho restaurant where they celebrated all their significant moments, from anniversaries and birthdays to promotions and publishing deals. It was cosy and intimate, a wood-panelled room with windows misted up so Zoe couldn't see the world outside. All she could see was Win, his face soft and glowing in the light of the candle placed in a wax-encrusted wine bottle, their knees bumping underneath the table.

'You don't look so bad yourself,' she said, raising her glass in a toast. 'It's been thirteen years and I still like you lots and lots.'

'I like you even more than I did then.' Win cocked his head. 'You've improved with age.'

Zoe didn't think the last thirteen years had been that kind.

'I miss my nineteen-year-old body. It was much bendier, less achey. Though I don't miss my nineteen-year-old sense of fashion. I'm so grateful selfies weren't a thing then.'

'I did used to wonder why your foundation was four shades too pale for your complexion,' Win dared to say and was rewarded by Zoe kicking him under the table. 'Ow! It was a bit Kabuki, is all I'm saying.'

'Not four shades,' Zoe said, with her hands covering her inevitably rosy red cheeks. 'Two at the most. And you can hardly talk when you used to put so much product in your hair that it was crunchy to the touch.'

They reminisced fondly over past fashion disasters: Zoe's big mohair green jumper that had left a trail of fuzz like lichen everywhere she went. And Win's shoes with square toes so long and narrow that they'd eventually curled up at the end.

'Just as well we found each other,' Zoe said, as she wiped away a stray happy tear before it wrecked her mascara. 'Nobody else would have had us.'

By now they'd made serious inroads into a bottle of the cheapest sparkling wine on the menu, dinner plates were waiting to be cleared away and they were holding hands across the table.

It was perfect, for tonight at least.

Win raised Zoe's left hand to his mouth and kissed her ring finger just above her wedding band and Zoe was all ready to melt when he fixed her with his cool blue stare.

'I hate to kill the mood, Zo, but do you really think that if something bad happened to Libby, to her baby, that it means the same thing will happen to you?'

It did rather kill the soft-focus good cheer but if Win had asked her the same thing when she wasn't a little tipsy, a little nostalgic for good times past, then Zoe knew she'd bristle and get defensive. She was still learning how to think about the possibility of having a baby without bursting into tears. Now she considered the question carefully. And when Win put it like that ... 'I know we're not the same. You didn't get shot during the Spanish Civil War, for one thing.'

'And you haven't had an affair with a car salesman, as far as I know,' Win offered and Zoe smiled before her expression grew serious.

'Eighty years ago, they didn't have a fraction of the technology or medical knowledge that we have,' she said. 'They didn't have ultrasound. God, they didn't even have penicillin. It's amazing the infant mortality rate wasn't higher ...' She had to swallow hard, blink back that warning prickle of tears and she wondered if there would ever be a time that she could think about that failed pregnancy and be at peace with it. Win kissed her hand again, but he didn't interrupt, just nodded his head as if he understood and that need, the hunger, rose up again. 'You have to tell me once and for all – do you want children, Win?'

He closed his eyes. 'Why does that feel like a trick question?'

'It's not and I know you need time but please, you have to put me out of my misery. Are you still ambivalent or have you made up your mind?' It was hard to breathe because this need felt as if it would eventually override everything. If Win didn't want a family, then their love might not be enough to compensate for the loss of what they could have had, of what they could have been.

'I don't want a child,' Win said baldly and his face grew blurry and indistinct as Zoe willed back the tears that had already begun to marshal. 'But we're talking about *our* child. *Our* children. Having a family with you.'

'I want to have a family with you.' Zoe felt as if she might dissolve where she sat.

'Would you, Zoe?' Win looked doubtful. 'Would you really? I know that you think about the baby we lost all the time, I do know that, but I don't because still all I can think about is how you nearly died. Not an exaggeration, Zo. If I hadn't come in when I did, if the ambulance had been delayed, if the doctor on call hadn't known exactly what was wrong ... '

'If ... *when* I get pregnant again, I will be the most annoying, most paranoid, most Type A pregnant woman the NHS has ever dealt with. I'll be insisting on scans and blood tests every time I so much as sneeze.' Zoe took a shaky breath. 'So, you've reached a definitive conclusion about any babies that we might have together?'

They stared at each other. Zoe wondered which one of them would blink first then Win smiled. 'Yes, I do want to have a baby with you. And yes, sooner rather than later. No more five-year plans, I promise.'

Zoe let out a very slow, very shaky breath. Her first reaction was, unexpectedly, panic so she had to clutch hold of the edge of the table to keep herself seated, anchored, and not blurt out, 'Oh God, but I'm not ready yet.'

She took another deep breath. And then, it was as if the devil that she'd carried on her back had finally been banished. She wriggled her shoulders, felt instantly lighter without the burden. 'Between you and me, I've never been a big fan of the five-year plan,' she said with a watery smile. 'But I'm a big fan, huge fan, of sooner rather than later.'

Win smiled back. 'It's been strongly intimated that I'll make partner next year, which means we'll have a bit more money coming in. I think our new year resolution should be to make a baby. Much more fun than the year when my resolution was to run a sub-four-hour marathon,' he added, which wasn't exactly the ringing endorsement.

And it didn't do any harm to ask for clarification. Maybe even written confirmation. 'You definitely want to have a baby? Babies. Plural. Because one baby would be great to start with but I don't want to stop at one.' Zoe glanced down at her stomach almost as if she expected to see her belly distended and round, a life growing inside her; a little person with its own distinct personality and likes and dislikes.

'Babies. Plural. Why not? Just think, you might even be pregnant for our fourteenth anniversary,' Win said and in that moment Zoe swore that she felt something in her body, something atavistic and embedded deep within her, clench as if to say 'gimme gimme gimme'.

'If we get the bill now, throw caution to the wind and order an Uber, we could be home in thirty minutes,' she told Win and she wanted him to look at her like he had when she'd come down the stairs earlier as he waited in the hall and had seen her all dressed up for the first time in ages. He'd licked his lips and given her a slow once-over, not even realising that he was doing it and it was, always had been, sexy as hell. A few more of those lingering looks, maybe a little fondling under the table because there was a spot just below her knee that was extraordinarily sensitive, would have Zoe raring to go on their new project.

She wasn't even averse to snogging like horny teenagers in the back of the car on the way home. On the contrary, she was completely up for that.

Then Win pulled out his phone. 'No, I think it's best to wait until January. There's a lot of prep work to do first. Although I've already downloaded an app. It combines an ovulation calendar with a fertility tracker so we'll have some baseline readings before we get down to it. I'll put it on your phone too.' He smiled kindly at her. 'I haven't just been researching our Mrs Morton these long nights while I've come poor second to a family of robins. It gave me time to seriously think about this and explore what our various options were. I didn't want to get your hopes up and greenlight starting a family if it was only going to lead to more disappointment. Anyway, it turns out there are lots of things we can do to optimise our chances of conceiving naturally. They have these kits; the best one combines a touch screen monitor with urine tests, so we know which days every month you're at your most fertile. Of course, there are other ways to gauge it. Changes in your cervical mucus, for instance, right?'

'Urine tests? Cervical mucus? My God, I have never wanted you more,' Zoe said flatly and Win's face closed off.

They weren't holding hands any more.

'Too much?' he asked.

'Much too much.' Zoe tried to smile. 'You are literally trying to micromanage my vagina.'

He pulled a face. 'There have been times when you've enjoyed me micromanaging your vagina,' he pointed out, which was true but they were so long ago, Zoe could hardly remember them.

She rested her elbows on the table so she could gaze at Win. She still loved him. Even at their worst, their most estranged, that love had still been there, holding them together when nothing else could. But they were different people to who they'd been thirteen years ago. Different people to how they were a year ago even. They loved each other, but they still hadn't fallen in love with the new people they'd become.

They didn't even look the same. Zoe had her scar, her badge of courage, and a faint furrow between her eyes that was there to stay. Win had the shuttered, closed for business set to his face far too often for Zoe's liking, streaks of grey running through his hair.

It had been one hell of a year and they'd both tried to deal with it, make sense of it in their own way. Zoe had found solace in her imagination, in telling stories. It was probably why she'd become so obsessed with Libby. The pages of her diary were another story to get lost in, why she was so desperate for Libby to have a happy ever after.

But while Zoe made stories out of what she didn't understand, Win had his spreadsheets and schedules and apps so he could corral the present and try to contain the future. Break them down into a series of small tasks that he could action, then put a line through them.

Both of them were just muddling through as best as they could because they were never that great on their own. When they were a team, working together, complementing each other, they were golden. Solid.

They needed to learn how to be a couple again, before they could become three.

'I don't think we should start trying for a baby,' Zoe said, her head speaking and not her heart, which felt as if it were slowly collapsing. 'Not if you're going to plan it like a military operation. Leaving nothing to chance. That's not how I want our child to be conceived.'

'So, now you're saying that you don't want to try for a baby?' Win looked up the heavens. 'What do you want then? Do you still want me?'

'Of course I want you but the consultant said that trying for a baby should be fun, that we should be at it like bloody rabbits. Do you know how many times we've made love this year?' Zoe hated to end on a cliffhanger but their waiter had arrived to moot the possibility of pudding.

Win waved him away with a vague promise of coffee in ten minutes. 'Once,' he sighed after he'd done the maths. 'Well, technically not even once! How can that be possible?'

'Most couples who buy a house make it their mission to have sex in every room,' Zoe said. 'Just like we did when we moved into our old flat. We even did it in the shared cellar.'

'And the little lean-to by the back door.' Win smiled, his nose wrinkling, as if, like Zoe, he was remembering how they'd had to be very quiet as he bent her over the rainwater butt because two of the girls who lived next door were standing outside to have a cigarette and a bitch. Zoe had bit her lip for all she was worth until Win suddenly let out a startled cry and thrust deep when a spider landed in his hair. Then the girls next door had screamed, 'Who's there?' and Zoe had got the giggles, which finished Win off far too soon.

It hadn't been the best sex they'd ever had, but at least they'd been having sex.

'You. Me. Sex. In every room,' Zoe decided. 'Even the pantry. You can make a schedule.'

'I don't have to schedule everything. You make it sound like I'm the worst kind of control freak. That I alphabetise and colour code everything we own. I'm not *that* bad,' Win said a little huffily, though there had been a time earlier this year when he had so many different coloured stickers on his renovation wall planner, even he'd forgotten what the colours represented. 'I thought the idea of having more sex was to loosen me up, get us back to our happy place.'

'It is, it was.' It had never used to be like this between them – being so quick to take offence, to nurse grievances. 'I just thought a schedule would be ... '

'Let it go, Zoe.'

' ... fun. With rewards every time we unlocked a new level,' she said.

Win raised his eyebrows. 'Wouldn't the sex be reward enough?' he asked archly. Even more arousing than the spot just below the crease of her knee was when Win raised his eyebrows and said things in an arch way. 'I suppose we could have stickers though. Maybe even gold stars.'

'And whoever gets the most gold stars wins a prize,' Zoe decided.

'Are we going to call in an independent adjudicator to award these gold stars?'

'I was thinking a simple points-based system.' Zoe had been thinking no such thing, until that very moment. 'Contingent on, I don't know, position, difficulty of position . . . '

'Frequency and duration of orgasm?' Win suggested and under the table his fingers found that spot just below the crease of her knee that made Zoe wriggle and forget her own name. 'Do you think we should skip the pudding, get that Uber you were talking about earlier and go straight home so we can discuss this further? Agree the small print, any additional clauses?'

'I think that can be arranged.' Zoe raised her hand so she could wave frantically to get their waiter's attention. 'I'll get the bill, if you order the car.'

Win reached for his phone then paused. 'Just to be clear, we are going home to have lots of sex, aren't we?'

'We are,' Zoe stated firmly then it was her turn to pause. 'Are you in?'

Win's smile was equal parts anticipation and promise. 'Oh, Zo, I'm *all* in.'

43

Libby

Who would have thought that Freddy – *Freddy!* – would turn out to be such an absolute trooper. Certainly not Libby, but it was Freddy who had held Millicent back when she stood outside the bedroom door to demand entrance. 'I've never known anyone enjoy ill health as much as Elizabeth,' she'd proclaimed, which was rich coming from her.

He'd also hand-delivered Libby's resignation letter to Beryl. 'Burst into tears,' Freddy reported cheerfully. 'It's just as well I've grown accustomed to women weeping all over me. Says she's sorry for being so quarrelsome and wants to come and see you but I told her that you weren't to be upset, so we agreed she'd leave it a week. Odd little creature, isn't she?'

Nothing was too much trouble. Freddy even sent Hannah out to the Flask for a bottle of stout and a steak pie every evening and stayed with Libby while she ate. They'd play cards or he'd read one of the aunts' lurid romances, putting on all sorts of silly voices to make Libby laugh.

Libby suspected that this was Freddy's way of making

amends for how he'd been when it was his child that she was carrying. So diffident, so dismissive, even before she'd got pregnant, even when making love to her. Libby had never felt as if she truly had Freddy's attention, certainly not his love.

This time she'd been sure that she had Hugo's love, otherwise she wouldn't have given him her own poor, abused heart to do with what he wanted. So, despite everything, she mourned the loss of him. Wished that she could hide and nurse her wounds until the end of time even as she knew that this present state of affairs couldn't last.

'I can't stay here,' she announced to Freddy, some time into her confinement after a doctor had been sneaked upstairs to pronounce Libby quite well though her blood pressure was still cause for concern. 'Your mother won't be fobbed off with stories of contagious stomach ailments for much longer.'

'You can't be on your own,' Freddy said. He was lounging in the armchair by the window. The weak winter sun lit up his hair, his features, so he looked impossibly young.

'I've been on my own most of my life,' Libby said, without heat because Freddy was right. What if she were to be taken ill again in a rented room with no one to hear or care if she cried out? She thought longingly of the white house in Highgate, of the life she'd been planning for the three of them.

Her future had been mapped out and now, in the space of a few short weeks, it was as uncertain as it had ever been.

'We could get a place together. A small flat in town,' Freddy suggested because guilt really had made a man of him. 'I'm still quite flush and my publisher was talking of another book about the scourge of Fascism. I'd have to travel to Germany and Italy but that would be next year. You'd have had the baby by then.'

'I couldn't expect you to take on another man's child,

Freddy.' Libby had been playing patience; she looked up from the cards arranged haphazardly on the eiderdown. 'What a pity you weren't this kind to me when we were together.'

Freddy dipped his dark head. 'When we were together I did a lot of things I'm not proud of, Libs. And then that night in Paris . . . ' He turned to stare out of the window. 'It was as if I'd broken you with my own carelessness.'

'What happened, it wasn't your fault,' Libby said, though she had always blamed him a little. It was far easier to have someone to blame than admit that terrible things often occurred for no good reason.

'What happened after was my fault though,' Freddy said and he made sure that he was looking at Libby now, so she wouldn't be in any doubt that he meant every word. 'It's just . . . I'm a coward, Libs, always have been and I thought that if I didn't have to see you, face you, then I wouldn't have to face up to my own shame.' He sprang up from the chair to kneel by the side of the bed. 'I'd like to make it up to you now, if you'll let me.'

'Oh, Freddy . . . ' It was too late for them now, but Libby could feel her anger, the coruscating anger towards Freddy that was always in the background, lifting away. 'It's ancient history. Let it be done now.'

He lifted up her limp hand from where it rested on the quilt and kissed the place where he'd put his ring. 'I'm happy to do it; to take care of you and the kid. You know that all that nonsense, propriety and such, doesn't mean a thing to me.'

'I'll think about it,' Libby promised because there was nothing to do all day but think. At times she was restless, quite desperate to get up and go outside, and other days, she was so tired that if she could find a comfortable position, propped up with pillows, she'd try to sleep.

When she did sleep, she had such terrible dreams. The baby slithering out of her in a river of thick, black blood, its body still and blue and lifeless.

The baby alive and pink and her heart's song, only to be snatched out of Libby's arms by Pamela, her fur coat suddenly transformed into a snapping, snarling wolf that held Libby back.

Hugo walking away down that secret path of theirs in Highgate Woods, then turning to give Libby one final, cold look. 'You're a whore. One doesn't fall in love with whores.'

Then Libby would struggle to wakefulness, panting, her heart racing, the pickle turning somersaults and somehow Freddy was there. Maybe she'd cried out. Maybe he'd fallen asleep in the chair by the window, but he'd get on to the bed, careful not to jar her, one arm around her, the other hand smoothing down the sweaty strands of her hair. It awoke a half-buried memory of being a child, hot and sticky with fever, and her mother performing the same action, murmuring soft words of love.

Then one December evening Hannah brought up a letter along with Libby's supper of a cup of Bovril and a couple of malted milk biscuits. Said that a young boy had come by on a bike to deliver it.

'Be a dear, Hannah, and shut the door quietly, I've got one of my heads,' Libby said so Hannah wasn't tempted to linger, then when she was gone, grumbling under her breath, Libby was able to open the envelope.

Dearest Libby
'Come live with me and be my love.'
I'll be waiting at the house for you.
Hugo

44

Zoe

Win's infamous wall planner had been repurposed and pinned up in the kitchen. On it Zoe had drawn symbols for each room they'd had sex in. A sofa for the living room, appropriately enough as that was where the deed had been done – among other places – Win still had the rug burns. A stove for the kitchen. An artist's palette for her studio. They'd also amassed a number of gold stars between them, though Win had the lion's share. He was far more competitive than Zoe and had his eyes on the prize, which was a weekend when the victor had their every sexual desire catered for.

Not that Zoe was worried. She'd been sleeping with Win for the last twelve years so she was pretty sure that he wasn't going to blindside her with a request that she don a gimp suit or whip him with an egg beater. Besides, he was really going all-out in the pursuit of those gold stars, which worked in Zoe's favour.

The sex was good, some of the best sex they'd ever had, but much as Zoe relished the length and frequency of her recent orgasms, what she relished even more was the closeness she and Win shared afterwards.

'I never stopped loving you, Zo,' Win had said the night before. They'd made love in their own bed for once then showered together and eaten dinner in the front room. With their empty plates still on the coffee table, they were lying top and tail on the sofa to accommodate Florence who needed a wide turning circle so she could snuggle against either of them at will. 'But I feel like I'm falling in love with you all over again.'

'Me too,' Zoe had said, though that wasn't an adequate way to describe how Win could make her experience all the best emotions: lust, tenderness, joy and a warm cosy glow all in the space of an hour.

To the casual observer, Zoe knew that their lives would seem unremarkable, even boring, but she cherished where they were right now. In a state of very domestic bliss and soon enough, it would be shattered by ovulation thermometers, pregnancy tests and dreading the thought of her period arriving.

But for now the world outside 23 Elysian Place receded and even Libby was the last thing on Zoe's mind, so when an email arrived from Parminder, their solicitor, it was an unwelcome intrusion.

She opened the email with some trepidation.

To: zoe@zoetropedesign.com, wrowell@smpac.co.uk
From: BarmyParmy81@gmail.com

The vendors' solicitor finally got back to me. He's been in contact with one of the vendors, a Mrs Leigh, who says that she's not sure that she would be any help. They found the deeds to the house among her father's papers when he died – that was the first they knew of its existence.

Apparently this Mrs Leigh spends most of the year abroad but is in London next week to do her Christmas shopping (nice for some!) and could meet then. Her solicitor is a dry old git but was moved enough to reveal that she was intrigued about the suitcase. She's happy to come to Highgate. Why don't you suggest somewhere and I'll get back to them?

This is turning into quite the saga. Must have full debrief after. Maybe over pizza and wine?

Parmy xxxx

As she and Win walked to Highgate Woods with Florence in tow, Zoe's mouth was dry and her stomach juddered with every step she took.

'What's the worst that can happen?' Win wondered, when Zoe told him how she felt. 'Best case scenario is that this Mrs Leigh is Libby and Hugo's daughter or granddaughter. Or else she's horrified that her father or grandfather had a mistress and it all becomes incredibly awkward. Still no reason to throw up. You won't, will you?' he added with a wary glance at Zoe. 'You do look a bit green.'

'I'm not,' Zoe confirmed. 'I just don't want Libby's story to end badly. It will break my heart and also tragedy can leave a sort of indelible psychic stain on places. If something awful happened to Libby in our house, then it will have left a dark atmosphere, a bad energy, and we're stuck living there.'

'The house does not have a dark atmosphere and if it did, which it doesn't, aren't you meant to burn sage or something? Though if it were my choice, I'd rather have a dark atmosphere than the house reeking of sage.' Win pulled a face. 'It's my least favourite herb.'

'No, it's not.' Zoe rolled her eyes at Win who smiled in a maddening way. 'Let's not forget that you're the man who wrote a letter of complaint to Pret a Manger about them putting coriander in all their sandwiches.'

'The devil's herb,' Win agreed cheerfully. 'Still, sage runs a close second.'

They'd reached the open air café in the centre of the woods. Though it was a colourless, cold November day, there were quite a few people sitting at the tables, bundled up in hats and scarves, hands curled round steaming mugs.

Zoe peered at them all in turn, not sure who she was looking for. Then she caught the eye of an older woman, sitting with a man of similar age. The woman gave Zoe a searching look then raised her hand imperiously in greeting.

'Is it just me or does that feel a lot like a royal summons?' Win muttered.

It did and Zoe thought she might really throw up as she unlatched the gate and tried to smile, though it was more of a frozen grimace.

'Ah, the couple from that *charming* home-made book,' the woman said as Zoe reached their table but before introductions could be made, someone sitting nearby told Win crossly that dogs weren't allowed in that part of the café and they all had to retreat to the cordoned-off dog-friendly area.

Eventually, all parties were settled with a hot drink and cake for those who wanted it, Florence had been fussed over, Win and Zoe had thanked the couple for agreeing to meet and Zoe could turn to the woman who'd greeted them when they'd first arrived.

She was tall and elegant, with tanned skin and what must have once been fair hair, now turned white. She had a dancer's grace and the look of an ageing fashion model. There was something quite Avedon-esque about the jut of her impressive cheekbones. 'So, are you Hugo's daughter?' The woman frowned and Zoe realised her mistake. She couldn't be Hugo's daughter when she looked as if she was only in her sixties. Not unless Hugo had had her late in life. 'His granddaughter?'

'Who on earth is Hugo?' the woman asked. 'My father was Frederick Morton.'

Win and Zoe looked at each other. 'Freddy?'

'You knew Freddy? But how? This is all very confusing. Let's start again.' The woman threw up an elegant pair of hands, her long tapered fingers covered in rings and finished with long red nails. 'We haven't even introduced ourselves. My name's Marisa Leigh. I'm Freddy's youngest daughter and this distinguished gentleman is my older brother, Arthur.'

Arthur had the same long limbs and snowy-white hair as his sister and, despite the November chill, was wearing a cream suit and a panama hat accessorised with a thick, stripy scarf. 'We had an older sister, Luciana, but she died in a car crash a couple of years ago.'

'So sorry for your loss,' Zoe murmured while Win made similar noises. Zoe was in an agony of not understanding the connection. Why was she sitting across a plastic table from Freddy's (*Freddy's!*) two children? How did Freddy fit into all this?

Zoe realised that they were all sitting there in a stilted silence. 'This suitcase we found, that we wrote to your solicitor about, it belonged to a woman called Elizabeth, known as Libby, who was married to Freddy.'

'No, that's not right. Daddy wasn't married before, was he?' Marisa said to Arthur, who shook his head. 'We'd have known if he was. Though the name Elizabeth Edwards does ring a vague bell.'

'It does rather,' Arthur agreed.

'She was an actress,' Win explained.

'Oh! Was she a very famous actress?' Marisa asked. 'Would we have seen her in anything?'

385

'I doubt it,' Zoe said. 'But I do have a picture of her.'

She opened her bag to take out the file where she'd placed a few of the more important documents.

'This is Libby,' she said, putting one of Libby's publicity photographs on the table where Arthur and Marisa could see it. 'She married Freddy in September of nineteen thirty-five at St Pancras Town Hall. Libby was pregnant when they got married. They went to Paris for their honeymoon and she lost the baby . . . '

'Oh, how sad. Daddy would have been devastated. He absolutely adored children,' Marisa said and Zoe and Win shared another look.

Win nodded once as if to say, I've got this. 'I'm afraid it wasn't quite the case,' he said, swallowing hard. 'Libby was still in hospital in Paris when Freddy left her. We have letters. He went to Spain to cover the start of the Spanish Civil War for the newspapers and Libby came back to London where she lived in Hampstead with Freddy's mother, Millicent—'

'Millicent! Granny Morton! The house in Willoughby Square! Good God,' Arthur exclaimed. 'Terrifying woman. She lived to well in her nineties, you know. Daddy lived to one hundred and three, can you believe? We seem to do longevity rather well in our family, apart from poor old Luciana.'

'I wonder why Daddy never mentioned that he'd been married before?' Marisa fished out a pair of glasses from her handbag and put them on so she could scrutinise the photo of Libby. 'Tell us more about this Libby.'

Zoe, with Win chiming in, told them what they knew. About Hugo. The affair. Libby pregnant again. Freddy getting shot and Libby going to Paris to bring him home. Libby still planning to leave Freddy and move to Highgate with Hugo and then nothing . . .

'The diary just peters out and we couldn't find a birth certificate for the baby or any details of Hugo or Libby's divorces.' Zoe sighed because it never got less frustrating. 'None of it makes sense. I'm at even more of a loss now. How did Freddy's children come to own a house that we thought was bought by Freddy's wife's lover?'

'We knew nothing about the house until Daddy died,' Marisa said. 'His affairs were in a terrible mess. It was years before we reached probate.'

'Shall we tell you a little about Freddy?' Arthur suggested and Zoe and Win both nodded because Freddy might be the key to solving the puzzle of Libby. 'Well, he was a journalist, but you already know that. He had a book published in nineteen thirty-seven warning about the rise of Fascism, which had him pilloried for scaremongering, though events proved him right and subsequently he went on to have a very good war, as they say.'

During the war Freddy had worked for an undercover outfit in Whitehall, devising all sorts of ingenious schemes to gather intelligence and turn German agents; techniques which would later form the basis of modern spycraft. After the war he'd returned to his beloved Spain where he'd married the younger daughter of a minor Swedish aristocrat and wrote the first of the Jack Faraday novels, about an RAF flying ace turned private detective, which had become part of the same cultural pantheon as James Bond.

'He worked with Ian Fleming during the war,' Arthur said. 'Fleming couldn't stand him, told everyone that he was a terrible hack, which Dad thought hilarious. He'd always send Fleming a bottle of champagne and a clipping of *The Sunday Times* book charts each time a Faraday novel hit the number one spot.'

'Frederick Morton. I never made the connection. I was

obsessed with those books when I was a kid.' Win turned to Zoe. 'Jack Faraday was always getting into these tight spots, surrounded by thugs, certain death five minutes away, and he'd wriggle out of it by doing something cunning with a bunch of keys and a box of matches. Me and Ed would see the films with my granddad the weekend that they came out. Did you never read them?'

She shook her head. 'No, but I'm sure my dad has a few of his books.'

Every man and boy in Britain owned at least one Jack Faraday novel so no wonder Freddy was able to provide his family with an idyllic life; dividing their time between Hampstead and a huge villa in Ibiza surrounded by olive groves and orchards, long before Ibiza became fashionable.

'He was simply the loveliest, kindest man,' Marisa said a touch defensively as if she were still bristling at the suggestion that Freddy would have abandoned his mysterious first wife while she lay in a hospital bed. 'He was always such great fun and we were so lucky to have him with us for as long as we did.'

When Freddy died in 2007, his estate was in disarray and before order could be restored, his eldest daughter Luciana had contested the will and sued her brother and sister.

'I hate to speak ill of the dead, but Lucky didn't have a lick of common sense,' Arthur said.

'She was the proverbial cuckoo in the nest,' Marisa said crushingly. 'Married for the fifth time to a horrible little man half her age. They produced a letter, supposedly signed by Daddy, which left everything to Luciana. Arthur and I were almost bankrupted by legal costs. Then Lucky caught her husband cheating, began divorce proceedings and admitted the letter was a fake. Written by a friend of her husband who dabbled in art forgery. She was killed in the midst of all this.'

'We had to sell the house in Hampstead to pay off the lawyers,' Arthur said. 'It went to a property developer who carved it up into flats that mostly sold to foreign investors, so when we found the deeds to the house in Highgate we wanted to find a buyer who'd turn it into a proper home.'

'We haven't even told you how grateful we are. We'd never have been able to afford a house in London if—' Zoe got no further than that when Marisa clicked her fingers at Arthur.

'The deeds,' she said. 'What *were* the names on the deeds? I'm sure one of them was a woman's. And the other chap, Hugo? His name sounds familiar too. Where are the deeds now?'

'The building society has them and I think man will land on Mars before they ever get round to answering our request for a copy,' Win said.

'Curious and curiouser.' Arthur rubbed his hands together. 'No other clues?'

'We've reached a bit of a cul de sac,' Zoe said. Win covered her hand with his.

'I'd love to have a look at the diary,' Arthur said baldly, then gestured at his sister. 'And this one loves snooping round other people's houses. She's the type who goes to a party and rifles through the host's bathroom cabinet when she's meant to be powdering her nose.'

'You can tell everything about a person from their bathroom cabinet.' Marisa looked quite unrepentant. 'Do you mind?'

45

Libby

Thirty-two years she'd been on this earth and yet Libby could bundle her whole life up into two suitcases and a carpet bag.

The days spent in bed had made Libby bigger, rounder. She had to leave the side buttons of her loosest dress undone, bending down to buckle her shoes took a lifetime, but soon she was inching down the stairs on unsteady legs.

'Where do you think you're going?'

'Freddy! This habit of creeping up on me, I don't like it at all,' Libby hissed as he surprised her by slipping out of the drawing room, usually the domain of the ladies. 'Hugo's sent me a letter. He's waiting for me. He wants us to be together.'

'How nice of him and how very forgiving of you,' Freddy noted. 'You're meant to be in bed.'

'It's not going to take any time to get to Highgate and then I'll go straight to bed.' Freddy let out a long exasperated sigh but Libby persevered. 'I can't stay here much longer and I love him and if he loves me then perhaps the situation isn't as impossible as I thought it was. He may well have left Pamela. If I were him, I'd have left her months ago!'

They couldn't very well argue about it in the hall, not with Millicent (who they could hear berating Hannah in the kitchen) so close by. Freddy grabbed his coat from the portmanteau and took both cases from Libby.

'I'm coming with you just in case there's something rotten in the state of Denmark,' he muttered and insisted on hailing a taxi though the cabbie said that he'd only take them as far as Highgate Village and even that 'was in the back of beyond'.

Libby had no choice but to waddle the rest of the way. She felt huge, like a beast of burden, as she lumbered down Southwood Lane.

'This is the road,' she said to Freddy, as they turned into the street of new houses. So new that at the furthest end there was still scaffolding up on the very last plot, but number twenty-three was done, finished, waiting for Libby and Hugo. 'This is it.'

'All these identical houses for identical people with their identical little lives,' Freddy groused as he followed Libby up the path.

'They're not identical. Some of them are mock Tudor or neo-Georgian,' Libby said loftily, quoting the builder's advertisement. 'We went for the Moderne style and I don't know why you're being so stuck up. All the houses in Willoughby Square look the same.'

'That's different,' Freddy said, but he didn't explain why. In fact, he was quite silent as Libby unlocked the door, felt a moment's hesitation, fear curling its way down her spine, then stepped inside.

There was nothing to worry about. The house was still a lovely place to come home to. 'I'll be much more comfortable here,' Libby said. 'No queuing for the bathroom, for one thing.'

She showed Freddy around, expecting him to marvel at the electric lights, the boiler in the kitchen, the built-in cupboards, but he was silent.

'You can't stay here, Libs,' Freddy said eventually when Libby came to the last room, the back bedroom where she and Hugo would sleep and she could open the curtains of a morning to see beyond the huge back garden to the treetops and green expanse of Highgate Woods and their life would be bucolic and wonderful. 'Don't be ridiculous.'

'Why shouldn't I?' Libby bristled.

'Because, you silly woman, there's not a single stick of furniture in the place. No carpets, no curtains. Not so much as a tea kettle.'

Hugo had told her to come and Libby expected that when he got here, he'd have furniture with him. She'd never gone back to Heal's; Pamela's visit had put paid to that, but they'd talked about what they needed, colour schemes and so on, and Hugo was very good at being practical, at organising and delegating.

'It will all be fine,' Libby said. She gestured at the larger case, full of things she didn't need but couldn't bear to parted from. Her old theatre keepsakes, the dress she'd been married in, the clothes she'd knitted for the other baby. 'Could you put that on the top shelf of the cupboard, please?'

Freddy did as she asked but grumbled about that too, so Libby left him to it. She was tired. Ankles and feet throbbing, an ache in her lower back, but as she came down the stairs she saw a dark shape through the glass panel of the front door. Her heart quickened. It had been so horrible, the last time they'd seen each other, they'd both said such unkind things, but it was far better to begin the rest of their lives together with a smile and a promise not to let the past cast a long shadow over the future.

'Hello, darling,' she said, as Hugo came through the door. 'You don't know . . . you can't even imagine how glad I was to get your note.'

Hugo paused, one hand raised to take off his hat. His eyes swept over her, lingering on the ripeness of her belly. Libby placed her hand on the underside, on the particular spot that the pickle liked to press against.

'You look well,' he said.

'I think you mean I look like a whale.'

He smiled and when Libby reached the bottom of the stairs, he was ready to help her down the last step and kiss her on the cheek.

'There's nowhere to sit,' he said, shrugging helplessly. 'Let's perch here.'

He gently pulled her down on the stairs then sat down next to her. It was a tight fit but it was so glorious to have Hugo next to her, cleaved together. He smelt as he always did of the woody, peppery scent of his aftershave layered with tobacco and underneath that, the metallic tang of engine oil. It was such a masculine, comforting array of aromas.

Libby took his hand. 'So we needn't run off together after all, then?'

Hugo shook his head. 'I've signed the house over to you. Had my lawyer put the deeds in your name.'

'You didn't have to do that!' Libby was aghast. Mr Shaw, the builder, had advertised the house for nine hundred pounds, but that was before Hugo had insisted on central heating and a shower and so many other extras that Libby dreaded what the final cost might be. 'Is it because of Pamela? Having to hide your assets? Was she very angry? Of course she was.' Why was it that she always babbled when she was with him? Whereas Hugo was always so quiet, so considered, as if there were no point in speaking unless the words had real meaning. 'You have to know, Hugo, I don't hate Pamela. I can understand a little of how she feels, why she's done the things she has. It can be very hard to be a woman. When so little is expected of you, only that you'll be a good wife and mother, then to not even be able to achieve that, it's very hard to know what your purpose is. Do you see?'

Libby glanced across at Hugo hopefully. Waited for him to squeeze her hand, lift it to his mouth for a kiss, but he turned away to look at the wall. 'Oh God,' he said faintly then he stood up so he could look down at Libby. 'I do see. You won't be a good mother, Libby. How could you be? It's not your fault, of course, I'm not saying it is, you lost your mother when you were still a child yourself and since then, well, the way you've been living.'

'What's wrong with the way I've been living?' Libby felt her nails digging into the wooden steps but it was impossible to get purchase. They skated over the smooth surface.

'On the stage, on your wits.' Hugo at least had the guts to look her in the eye for what he had to say next. 'You've had lovers. You told me so yourself. You were pregnant when you married Morton.'

There was nothing of the lover left in Hugo, of that man with his sleep-soft face next to hers on the pillow as they'd shared kisses and promises. Now he was like the Hugo in her dream, who thought her little more than a whore. Condemned her for simply wanting to be loved, when it had been he who'd pursued her, dismissed all her protests and fears about loving him back. She'd been right to be afraid because Hugo was just like all the others. Worse than them, in fact, because they'd never pretended to love her.

'You were one of my lovers, what does that say about you?'

It felt as if something was pressing down on her chest so Libby could hardly raise her voice above a croak.

'It's different for men. We're weak, prone to temptation,' Hugo said as if he were trying to convince himself. 'But you're carrying my child. I have certain rights. If I had to sue for custody, and I don't want to do that, the courts will clearly find in my favour so let's save ourselves that unpleasantness, shall we?'

'Yes, let's. Because you can't prove paternity,' Freddy calmly said from behind Libby. 'If needs must, I'll say the child is mine. Didn't you learn about Occam's razor in school? Let me take a moment to remember.' Libby swivelled round as best she could to see Freddy strike a pensive pose. 'Ah yes, "The principle states that among competing hypotheses that predict equally well, the one with the fewest assumptions should be selected." A married woman is pregnant, both she and her husband insist that he's the father and then there's this other chap, married to another woman, claims that it's his. Who does the judge believe? Occam's razor, old pal.'

Libby didn't know what razors had to do with any of it but Freddy seemed to be making enough sense that Hugo faltered. For a few moments he lost the high colour he'd had and went quite pale. Then he shook his head. 'You were in Spain. Filing stories for your paper, all very conveniently dated, whereas Libby and I were being followed by a detective to gather evidence for my divorce.' He smiled without any warmth, with no humour. 'He was very comprehensive with his note-taking. There are even photographs of us engaged in quite, um, intimate displays of affection around the dates that conception must have occurred. And yet, all that time you were abroad.'

It was ghastly to have the faintest of hopes raised then dashed in the next breath. 'You can't have the baby. I'll run away, I will!'

'Libs.' Freddy's voice was a warning. 'Nobody's going to take the baby away. For God's sake, man, she's already lost a child, what kind of people would try to take this one?'

'Libby. I'm not a monster.' Hugo dropped to his knees, placed his hands on either side of the stair that Libby sat on so she was trapped, boxed in. 'The baby, he'd want for nothing. I know that giving him up would make you unhappy, but I have to weigh your unhappiness against my unhappiness and Pamela's, the children too, because you'd be depriving Robin and Susan of a younger sibling to dote on. And what about what's best for the baby? You can't give him the life that he deserves, that he's worth. You'd be making so many people unhappy just to get what you want. Isn't that rather selfish?'

Hugo stared at her with blue eyes so beguiling that Libby could easily picture a little boy with the same eyes playing in a garden much bigger than the one at the back of this house. There'd be an elder brother who'd teach him all sorts of useful things and an older sister to spoil him with kisses. Hugo would take him for rides in his fastest cars as a special treat, call him 'little man'. Pamela would tuck him up every night and though he wasn't hers, she'd fall in love with him because he would be so easy to love. He'd go to a good school, learn Latin, play cricket, then Oxford or Cambridge, the world would be his.

Hugo could give the baby all that and all Libby could give him was love. It didn't seem like a fair trade. Then she thought of giving birth to the baby. Of how it would feel to have him snatched away by nurses, given to Pamela in her fur coat and diamonds, how Libby would never hold the baby in her arms. Run a gentle finger along a cheek as soft as rose petals. Would never feel him suckle at her breast. Would never have the chance to wipe away tears and savour every smile, memorise each peal of laughter, soothe skinned knees and wasp stings. Love him with everything she was.

'How can you even ask her that? What kind of monster are you?'

Libby had never heard Freddy sound so angry. She'd never thought he was capable of anything even approaching fury.

Hugo gave Libby a long, disappointed look then rose to his feet. He sighed. 'All I care about are the best interests of my child and they lie with me. There isn't a court in the land who would disagree.'

Freddy thundered down the stairs, squeezing past Libby so he could square up to Hugo. There wasn't much between them. They were a similar build and height. Libby had once thought they looked similar too but standing chin to chin, Freddy was all whip-cracking energy and fizz, eyes gleaming with a combative glee.

Hugo was as still and cold as a grave.

'Best interests! Ha!' Freddy was spoiling for a fight. He cocked his head at Libby sitting splay-legged and ashen-faced on the stairs. 'The best interests of the child are to stay with its mother. No one would ever love it more than Libby.'

'All your cant about doing the decent thing when really you don't have the first clue what the decent thing is,' Libby said dully. 'This is my child, Hugo. *Mine.* Already I love him more than you ever could.'

It was the only truth Libby knew for certain and she clung to it even as she rested her huge weight on her hands and attempted to get to her feet.

'I will take you to court,' Hugo said, stepping past Freddy to put a hand under Libby's arm and haul her upright. 'Love doesn't make you a fit mother.'

'Take your filthy hands off her!' Freddy dragged Hugo's

hand away, then patted down Libby's sleeve as if he could obliterate Hugo's touch. 'You won't go to court. Your sort hate the whiff of scandal. Couldn't bear that people, your friends, business associates, would know you had a bastard.'

'No, Freddy! Don't say that word,' Libby begged and somehow the three of them were moving towards the door that Hugo hadn't bothered to close, Freddy pulling Libby after him, Hugo equally determined that she stay and face his wrath, his condemnation. He took hold of her hand again, fingers crushing hers so hard that Libby wanted to cry out. 'Don't call the baby that horrible word.' Little wonder she was crying again.

'You're too highly strung to deal with a baby,' Hugo pointed out. 'I could have you declared mentally unsound. I don't want to, Libby, don't want to do any of this, if only you'd just stop being so . . . bloody minded.'

'You really are a cold-hearted bastard. She's not meant to get upset. It's bad for her, bad for the baby that you claim to care so much about . . . I told you to take your hands off her!'

They spilled out into the little front garden, Hugo and Freddy squaring up to each other again, Libby in the middle. They each had one of her hands and she wondered if the simplest solution was to let both of them tug and tug at her until she split in two. No more Libby. No more baby. Problem solved.

Hugo pulled her around in a parody of a lover's embrace. 'You can have the house. You and he can start again. You could have another baby. Stop acting as if this is the end of the world for you. It isn't.'

Libby was so tired of it all. Exhausted to the point where her legs no longer wanted to hold her up, but somehow she had to find the strength to fight. 'You don't care for me at all! You never did.'

Then Freddy was there, pushing his way between Libby

and Hugo. An odd kind of knight, his shining armour a threadbare tweed coat, a shirt with frayed collar and cuffs. 'Get away from my wife, you son of a bitch.' His voice was murderous and low. 'Do you want to make her ill? Do you want her to lose this baby as well? You'd have that on your conscience every day for the rest of your life. Are you man enough for that? Not fucking likely!'

Hugo took a step back. Held out a hand towards Libby who cowered away. 'You'd know about that, wouldn't you, Morton? About causing her pain.'

'You really are a callous bastard. Not a day goes by when I don't hate myself for how I treated Libby. I wish that I'd cherished her like I promised. Perhaps then things might have turned out differently. You do know that, don't you, Libs?' Freddy turned to Libby, but she was gone, unlatching the gate and walking up the road, ignoring the clump of people who'd come out of their neat little houses to see what all the commotion was about.

46

Zoe

'We've only been here the once,' Arthur explained, as they walked along Elysian Place. 'To see what state it was in before we put it on the market. We decided to leave it as it was, apart from clearing the garden. There were rumours of Japanese knotweed, which turned out to be unfounded.'

'My mother-in-law thanks you for that, by the way,' Win said as they reached their gate so they could see what Nancy had done in the front garden. Then, because the days were so short and the light was almost gone, they showed Marisa and Arthur straight through to the back garden.

Zoe would never grow bored with showing people around the house but Arthur and Marisa were mostly silent, though Marisa made an approving noise when she saw that of all the rooms, the bathroom was the one that had had the least amount of work done to it; the original tiles and sanitaryware still intact. 'I'll be back to poke through your bathroom cabinet later.'

At last they came to Zoe's studio. Arthur and Marisa looked at her draughtsman table and the old archive desk with its narrow but deep drawers, which Clive had given her as a housewarming gift, her prized collection of battered Ladybird books stacked on the shelves along with editions of Zoe's own books. The old jam jars and scented-candle glasses filled with pencils and pens in every colour, the festive-themed sketches pinned to one wall.

'Someone likes robins,' Arthur said jovially as Zoe opened the cupboard door and reached in to take down the suitcase.

They went back downstairs for tea and the apple cake Win had baked the day before. To have Arthur and Marisa walk through the house had been daunting enough, but to see them touching Libby's things was harder still.

Or perhaps it was just seeing those items again. The sad things that made up a life: a dress to get married in, a layette for a baby that had never been worn, faded photos of an actress whose work now languished in obscurity. 'This is the diary,' Libby said, taking it out of the sideboard and peeling away the bubble wrap.

When Marisa picked it up, Zoe wanted to snatch it back. 'I've kept everything, all the letters and clippings and things, exactly how it was left,' she said quickly, in case Marisa decided to start pulling pieces of paper out at random. There had been a time when Zoe had debated the ethics of reading someone's diary and made her peace with it, but now, as she saw Libby's spider-web scrawl marching faintly across the pages and Marisa put her glasses on to squint at the words, it felt like the worst kind of trespass.

'This copy of *The Times*, what's the significance of it?' Arthur asked, picking up the yellowed newspaper, which was in the suitcase along with everything else, though Zoe had never given it much thought.

'I have no idea,' Zoe said. 'I suppose it belonged to whoever left the suitcase behind. Shall I make some more tea?'

There was no reply. Marisa had removed one of Freddy's

letters and was reading it, her brow knitted together, and Win and Arthur were looking through the newspaper.

'It's dated seventeenth of December, nineteen thirty-six,' Win reported, as he traced a finger along the masthead.

Zoe cleared away the tea things. Libby was more elusive than ever. As if she'd never really existed. A trick of the light.

'Morton! Oh, well spotted, Win,' she heard Arthur say. It was his turn to take out a pair of half-moon spectacles from the breast pocket of his shirt. 'Now, let me see. "Morton, eleventh December, nineteen thirty-six in London, Elizabeth (née Edwards) late of Hampstead, actress and teacher. Deeply regretted by her husband Frederick, family and friends. Private funeral. Family request no flowers." Oh dear, I did hope this story might have a happy ending.'

'What? Let me see that!' Zoe all but ripped the paper away from Arthur. How could the answer have been there all the time? It wasn't possible. This was not what Libby's ending was meant to be.

'Zoe!' Win got up from the table so he could stand behind her, his arm a solid comforting weight around her middle as he pointed out the right column. 'I'm sorry, Zo. There must have been complications with her pregnancy again.'

Zoe shook her head. 'There was no death certificate,' she insisted. 'If she'd died there would have been a record of her death. The eleventh of December is the same date as the note Hugo wrote asking her to meet him here. No! I refuse to accept this!'

'But it's *The Times*!' Marisa looked up from her letter. '*The Times* would never get a death announcement wrong. My dear girl, why are you crying?'

Zoe shook her head, tried to mop up the tears that were streaming down her face. It was irrational, because whether it had happened eighty or eighteen years ago, Zoe knew that

Libby was dead. Despite what Win said, there had always been a symmetry between the two of them, Libby and Zoe, so that the promise of Zoe having a baby seemed impossible now if Libby's second pregnancy had ended so badly. Fatally. More than that, she was grieving for a woman she'd never met but whom she'd known so well, had loved in a strange kind of way.

She tried to explain it to Marisa when the older woman took her upstairs so she could wash her face.

'I lost a baby too. Hardly a baby. I was only eight or so weeks along.' It still hurt to say the words out loud but, at the same time, it was easier to say them too after so much time had passed. 'We're trying for another baby and when I found out that Libby was pregnant again, I thought . . . oh, I hoped . . . ' Zoe stopped to let a fresh wave of tears crash against the breakers.

Marisa perched next to Zoe on the side of the bath. 'I'm sorry you lost the baby,' she said. 'But you mustn't think that this house is a conduit to events that happened a long time ago. I happen to think houses take on the personality of their current owners, like people resembling their pets.'

'What about houses where people have been murdered or tortured, so they have mysterious cold spots or stains appearing on the walls?' Zoe asked. It was a ridiculous question; she knew that as soon as the words popped out of her mouth, and not just because Marisa snorted. 'Or poltergeists,' she couldn't help adding.

'Does this house have all sorts of other-worldly things going on in it?' Marisa asked and Zoe was forced to admit that it didn't, although their blighted radiators rattled when the central heating first came on.

'The house in Hampstead, when my grandmother lived there, was the gloomiest place imaginable. As far as I can gather, a couple of aged aunts died *in situ* and Daddy used to talk of this man called Potty . . . '

'Potts,' Zoe corrected. 'His name was Potts. He was always borrowing money off Libby and never paying it back. She kept a running tally in her diary.'

'That sounds very much like the fellow Daddy described. Raging alcoholic. Got shellshock in the First World War apparently and fancied himself as a medium. Claimed to regularly commune with the spirits, then one day he saw my late grandfather, Arthur, sitting in his chair in the drawing room, though he'd been dead several years, and this Potts fellow dropped down dead himself of a heart attack. It's hardly surprising the atmosphere in that house was funereal. I used to hate staying there when I was a child but when Granny Morton eventually died, I moved in there with my husband Philip as newly-weds.' Marisa smiled fondly. 'We got rid of all the dark, Victorian furniture, painted everything bright colours. I've never been as happy anywhere as I was in that house.'

'It's been a long, hard expensive slog, but I think Win and I are beginning to be happy living here,' Zoe said. 'We're not *quite* there yet.'

She and Win weren't completely there yet either; back to normal. Or their new version of normal, but instead of being stressed and leaden-bellied about it, Zoe knew it wouldn't be long before the last few pieces of them slotted back into place.

'This is precisely why we chose you and Win,' Marisa said. 'You showed us how happy this house could be with a little love and lots of imagination. That it could be a home for a family, though we were grateful that you didn't mention school catchment areas once.'

'We did think about it,' Zoe said but it would be a long, long time, if ever, that they needed to worry about being in the catchment area for a good school. Before she could feel that piercing ache of loss again, though, she heard Win calling.

47

Libby

Walking towards the main road was like wading through suet. Libby was weighted down by her engorged body. There was a painful pull deep, deep inside her, the straps of her shoes cutting into her swollen feet. She wasn't sure her legs could hold her up for much longer.

'Libby! Libby! Wait!'

Freddy easily caught up with her, his anger disappearing as he took in the tear tracks, the pain evident on Libby's face.

'He's gone and he's feeling pretty ashamed of himself too,' Freddy said. He put down Libby's smaller suitcase and carpet bag, which Libby had completely forgotten about, and fished a piece of paper out of his coat pocket. 'Left me with the deeds. Come back to the house.'

'I won't ever go there again,' Libby said. She had to cling on to someone's garden fence to stay upright. 'I just want to go home, Freddy.' Then she remembered. 'I don't even have a home to go back to.'

'Come on, old girl. Things aren't so bad,' Freddy said

though all evidence pointed to the contrary. 'Stop crying, Libs. You never used to be this much of a crier. Can't be good for the baby, you weeping every five minutes.'

'It's not even born and already I'm a terrible mother,' Libby all but wailed.

'Enough of this,' Freddy said sharply. He took the case and her carpet bag in one hand and put his other arm round her. 'You look like you need a drink and Lord knows, I could do with one. Let's stop here for a while.'

There was a large pub on the corner of the Archway Road. Freddy hustled Libby through the door. She was almost knocked sideways again by the comforting fug of tobacco smoke and warm beer, the lively hum of people talking and laughing. Freddy guided her through the public bar to the saloon where there was a fire burning and a table free in the corner, where he deposited Libby as if she were a package marked fragile.

'You're a shocking colour,' he noted with a frown and watched as Libby unbuttoned her coat and tugged off her gloves. Despite the warmth of the cosy room, she shivered and Freddy took her hand. 'You're cold too. I'll get you a brandy.'

'A whisky mac would warm me up just as well,' Libby insisted and as Freddy walked to the bar, she tried to light a cigarette with shaking hands.

The wireless was playing something light and orchestral and on the other side of the room, a young girl sat with her sweetheart who gazed besotted as she sipped a pink gin and twirled a strand of corn-yellow hair around her finger.

By the time Freddy returned with their drinks, Libby was quietly sobbing again. With a sigh he pulled out a slightly grubby handkerchief and passed it to her. 'It will all come good in the end, you'll see.'

Libby shook her head. 'No, Freddy, it won't. Hugo's got money and he's respectable so if he insists on going to court, they'll find in his favour. I know they will. They'll take the pickle right out of my arms. I'm the mother. I should have some say, shouldn't I?'

The pull in her gut now felt like a belt tightening sharply round her middle, so Libby longed to loosen it a couple of notches. She shifted in her chair, unable to get comfortable, and she was so very cold yet sweat was breaking out on her forehead, her upper lip. She rubbed her arms while Freddy nibbled the tip of his thumbnail.

'I'll think of something,' he said hoarsely then he looked at Libby as if she were naked in front of him. Not just unclothed but as if he could see past her skin and bones, right down to her heart and past even that, to all her secret hopes and desires. Then he nodded as if he'd reached a decision. 'There's nothing else for it, Libs. We'll have to leave London. Go away.' Freddy pinned her with another penetrating look. 'I really don't mind taking the kid on. I owe you that much. Owe you a damn sight more than that, if I'm honest about it.'

Libby lowered the handkerchief from where she'd been trying to stem the never-ending flow of tears. Freddy was offering her everything that she'd wanted so desperately when they'd said their wedding vows.

One year later. The world had turned full circle. 'You don't love me,' Libby stated calmly because it was the simplest of truths. 'You never did. No, it's all right,' she added when Freddy drew himself up, opened his mouth to protest. 'I rather forced your hand, didn't I? It wouldn't work, Freddy. You really don't want to be saddled with a wife and a child, especially a child that isn't yours. I'd rather be on my own than with a man who didn't really love me.'

'I do love you, Libs. In my way,' Freddy amended when she raised her eyebrows at him.

'Love is for fools.' Libby could hardly get her words past the pain, which sharpened then blunted to a dull, dull ache, so it was a perfect match for the agony in her heart. 'I thought he loved me. But then I always do, don't I? None of you have ever loved me enough.'

'Don't say things like that.' Freddy took her hand and rubbed it. 'You're so cold. One day, I promise you, you'll find someone who loves you like you deserve to be loved and I wish it were me. Look, I'll stay—'

'Keep it down over there!' someone shouted and Libby and Freddy looked up to see that everyone had gathered round the wireless on the other side of the room. 'Eddie's about to give his crown the big heave-ho, isn't he?'

The papers had been full of speculation for days that Edward would abdicate if parliament refused to allow him to marry Wallis Simpson, but Libby had barely glanced at them. It seemed so long ago that the old King had died and she'd travelled across the city to a hotel in Victoria to meet a man, her fate, her future.

Only the pain was the same and she screwed her eyes tight shut as she listened to the plummy tones that sounded as if they were coming from a distant room.

'But you must believe me when I tell you that I have found it impossible to carry the heavy burden of responsibility and to discharge my duties as King as I would wish to do, without the help and support of the woman I love.'

'It's so romantic,' the girl with the corn-gold hair sighed. 'Giving up his throne for her.'

What use was a love like that? So selfish and destructive that it scorched anything that got in its way.

' ... one matchless blessing, enjoyed by so many of you and not bestowed on me – a happy home with his wife and children.'

'It has to stop,' Libby whispered to Freddy who was listening transfixed. 'No good can come of this.'

'What's that?' Freddy turned to her and his mouth hung open, eyes wide. 'Libby! What's wrong?'

' . . . *I lay down my burden. It may be some time before I return to my native land.*'

Oh! The pain had Libby on her feet, then falling back down to land hard on the chair, which was damp under her skirt and she didn't need to bring her fingers down and have them come away stained red or hear Freddy's shocked gasp to know that she was bleeding.

'Not again! Dear God, not again.'

Libby slumped forward and Freddy fell to his knees to break her fall. He said something. People were crowding around them all talking at once. Then they faded to silence so all Libby could hear was the old Sunday school catechism echoing in her head.

Betwixt the stirrup and the ground, mercy I asked, mercy I found.

Not much of a life to look back on and beg repentance for her sins. A life full of loss. Of goodbyes.

Libby slips through time and space, away from the pain, to a place where she's with her dear departed.

Her father, in his shirtsleeves by the fire, his kind eyes and smile, the soft tickle of his droopy moustache as he holds her close and kisses her cheek, runs his fingers through her hair still damp from the Sunday evening bath.

Her mother hums a tune, claps her hands, skirts twisting and twirling, her long hair free and flowing in the summer breeze as they dance in the long grass together, their picnic things forgotten. 'There's few things in life so bad that they can't be made better with a dance and a song, my darling.'

Charlotte. Sweet little Charlotte. The steady sound of her breathing as she sleeps and her smile when she wakes is like the sun coming up.

Her grandparents. Her uncles, Clarence and Albert, dying

409

in the same foreign fields as her father. The brother that had only lived a few hours. Libby sees them all.

The years speed by in a procession of dressing rooms and cheap digs. Blinded by the footlights. The smell of greasepaint, cheap perfume and rough tobacco. Girls she's known, men she's loved.

The married theatre owner who seduced her. The ageing matinée idol who was the first man to break her heart. The director who Libby had followed all the way to America for all the good it did her. Then Freddy. Foolish, fickle Freddy, and Hugo who, when all was said and now was done, was simply the last man in a long line of men who'd promised her everything and given her nothing but ashes.

Two last faces float into view. The little boy she'd lost. Nameless, faceless, but now she sees him so clearly; dark hair, dark eyes, delicate limbs and a smile that melts her soul.

And the child that would never be born. Pickle. Funny little pickle whom Libby would have loved best of all if she'd been given the chance.

Then they're gone. All the ghosts. Libby is on her own because she's been on her own since she was fourteen. She's had friends, she's had lovers, but she'd always been so lonely.

'Libby? Libby? Hold on, Libs. Please hold on.'

It's not been much of a life but she's lived it as best as she could.

48

Zoe

Downstairs, Arthur already had his coat on and was waiting by the front door like a small child who'd been promised a trip to the park.

'We're giving Arthur and Marisa a lift back to their hotel in Bloomsbury,' Win said, which was the polite thing to do when it was getting on for six and dark outside.

'I said that there was no need, but Win wouldn't take no for an answer. I hope he doesn't boss you around this much,' Arthur said to Zoe.

'He likes to try,' Zoe said, shooting Win an amused look.

'And I hope you don't mind me taking Libby's diary.' Arthur patted his bag because apparently it was very much a *fait accompli* and now the look she gave Win was more wounded, more *how could you*?

Marisa and Arthur, as if they sensed an atmosphere, chattered non-stop on the drive into town about their plans while they were in London. Then, as soon as they'd dropped them off outside their hotel in Bloomsbury, Zoe turned to Win.

'That diary holds every clue we have to finding out what happened to Libby,' she burst out. 'I can't believe that you let them take it!'

'But how could I say no when Arthur asked for it?' Win protested as they drove back to Highgate. 'I think, legally, it's theirs anyway.'

'It's not the point,' Zoe said. 'Without it, we've got nothing. It's like Libby was never there.'

'But we *do* know what happened to Libby now,' Win pointed out softly. 'And anyway, we extrapolated all the relevant information. It's on a spreadsheet.'

'Of course it is,' Zoe muttered. She decided that she didn't have the energy for an argument and now that she knew the truth about Libby, what good did it do to pore over the woman's diary? All those words, giddy with love for Hugo, for the baby – never imagining she'd be dead before the year was out. Zoe remembered an artist friend of hers who'd put together an exhibition of the last photos taken of people before they died. A man on Death Row faced with an inevitable demise. A 1940s' Hollywood starlet papped on Santa Monica Boulevard who'd be shot by her gangster lover that evening. Selfies taken by partygoers minutes before the building was engulfed in flames. Death sneaked up on you when you were least expecting it.

'Maybe it is best to have it out of the house,' Zoe said. 'We should have given them the suitcase too. Just to be free of it.'

They were both silent after that until they reached Elysian Place and Win carried on straight up Southwood Lane, instead of swinging right.

'Hey! You missed the turning,' Zoe said. 'We'll have to see if we can work our way round.'

'Backseat driver.' Win caught her eye in the windscreen mirror. 'I want to ... there's somewhere I think we should go, OK?'

'OK.'

Win sounded so grave, his mood infecting Zoe so that they drove on in silence.

They passed through Highgate Village then along Hampstead Lane. Zoe knew this route very well. Had walked it with Cath and Florence so many times, except they always turned down a little path that led straight to the grassy outer fields of Hampstead Heath.

Still, they drove. Waiting to let the oncoming traffic through when the road narrowed down to one lane outside the famous Spaniards Inn, onetime haunt of highwaymen.

They took a left and travelled along the little twisting roads between the heath and Hampstead High Street until they came to a stop in a pretty square of stucco-fronted houses. In the middle of the square was a little green with a bench at the centre, where on sunnier days people could sit and watch the world go by.

The evening air was cold and biting but once Zoe and Win got out of the car, they walked over to the bench and sat down. They could see number 17. Or rather, they could see that someone was home in one of the top-floor flats because the lights on a Christmas tree twinkled through the murky gloom of the November evening.

'Oh God, what kind of people put up their Christmas tree in mid November?' Win asked with genuine alarm. 'It will be shedding needles by the beginning of December. Come Christmas Day, it's going to be as bald as Bruce Willis.'

'Win!' Zoe looked up at the house again and her expression grew serious. 'What are we doing here?'

Win took Zoe's hand. 'We're here because it seems fitting for what I want to tell you. That the difference between you and Libby is that you have me. You will always have me.' Win threaded his fingers through Zoe's. 'I know I drive you bonkers.

That I'm a control freak who's obsessed with making lists, never leaving anything to chance, panicking if our bank account dips below a certain amount, but it's my own peculiar way of taking care of you.' He tightened his grip on her hands as if he'd never let her go. 'In a way that my dad never took care of us.'

Zoe tugged her hands free so she could put her arms around Win and kiss his cheek. 'I really wouldn't have you any other way.'

'So, you understand why I am like I am?'

Zoe realised that she'd still been harbouring her resentment at Win for his transgressions of the last year and that in order for them to really move forward, she had to let her resentments drift off in the night breeze. 'You wouldn't be you without your lists, and colour-coded wall planners and your one-year and five-year and ten-year plans and I love you.' Win was funny, kind and he had two smiles in particular that made Zoe's pulse race and he was also uptight and unyielding and drove her bloody mad on a daily basis. That was love. You loved someone because of all their best qualities and in spite of their worst ones. 'Besides, I don't follow your plans unless they fit in with my plans.'

'I had noticed that.'

'But you don't have to take care of me all the time, Win,' Zoe said gently. 'We can take it in turns. And I'm sorry if I shut you out but I was so sad about the baby, so bloody sad, that all I could focus on was how I was feeling. I never stopped to wonder how you might feel.'

'Truthfully, it's only these last couple of months that I've been able to grieve for the baby. Before that, all I could focus on was how I'd nearly lost you because without you ... I wouldn't even be me any more. Sometimes, I still can't quite get my head around the fact that you love me even a fraction as much as I love you.' Win stroked Zoe's cheek with the back

414

of his hand, then looked over at the house. 'So, for the record, unlike Freddy or Hugo, I'm not going anywhere.'

'Glad to hear it,' Zoe said, because she was. 'I might let you go away for the odd stag weekend or work trip, but that's about it.'

Win put his arm round Zoe and hugged her tight against him. 'And we will raise a happy family,' he promised. 'When I really thought about babies and the having thereof, the one thing I knew with any certainty was that you'll be an amazing mother.'

'And you will be the best dad, I have no doubts about that. Kind, caring, excellent at helping with maths homework, king of the birthday cakes.' Zoe could have continued for several minutes listing all the ways that Win would make an exemplary father but the man himself pulled a face as if he was yet to be convinced.

'Who knows? Not like I had a great paternal role model growing up.' Win sighed as if he were about to slide into despondency all over again. 'We should get back. You know Florence doesn't like being left on her own after dark.'

Zoe nudged him. 'See! Nothing wrong with your dad gene. Nothing at all.'

'I thought we agreed that Florence wasn't a child substitute,' Win said sternly but he was smiling as he got to his feet and held out a hand to Zoe to haul her up too.

'Hate to break it to you, but she is our dog daughter,' Zoe said and Win moaned in protest, any dark thoughts banished now.

Before they went back to the car, they both stood and looked at number 17 for a moment. Funereal, Marisa had called it, but Zoe prayed that amid all the tragedy, behind that gate, between those four walls, Libby had laughed and loved and at the very end she'd gone gently into the good night.

49

Freddy

Watkins was waiting for Freddy at the entrance to Highgate Woods.

It had only been a week since they'd almost come to blows in the street, but in those seven days, the other man had aged a decade. His face, hair, clothes, all of him, grey. There was a heaviness to his movements, even in the way he clasped Freddy's hand and said, 'Morton. My condolences.'

Watkins gestured at the copy of *The Times* tucked under Freddy's arm. 'I saw the notice. Has the funeral already taken place, then? That was very quick.'

'Not yet and when it does, it will just be family, close friends,' Freddy said firmly because Watkins didn't fit either description.

Instead of walking through the woods, they'd crossed over the road and seemed to be heading in the direction of the house.

'I hope it was . . . that she didn't suffer.' Libby had suffered at Watkins's hands, for his whims, long before she'd started to bleed and bleed until Freddy had thought she'd die right there in his arms on the floor of the pub. 'I can't help but feel that I'm responsible.'

'Maybe that's because you are responsible,' Freddy said coldly. He wasn't one to kick a man when he was down but if Watkins wanted absolution then he was looking in the wrong place. Though it wasn't as if Freddy was entirely free from blame. 'Partly responsible maybe. For God's sake, you knew she'd already lost a baby. Why on earth would you put Libby through the mill like that?'

They were now walking down the street that Libby had rhapsodised over. All those houses swallowing up every available patch of green space. Not that Freddy had ever been one for the glories of nature but these fancy little boxes with their laughable pretensions to history were an abomination. Still, he supposed people had to live somewhere.

'Because I'm a fool,' Watkins said dully. 'A relic. She was right when she said that I was so preoccupied with doing the decent thing that I don't even know what the decent thing was.' He motioned again at *The Times* Freddy was holding. 'Seems that nobody cares for decency any more. That man, Edward . . . no sense of honour or duty.' He made a hopeless, despairing sound in the back of his throat. 'Whole world's going to hell at great speed.'

They'd reached the gate and Watkins slumped against the post, his face even greyer now.

'Why are we here, Watkins?' Freddy asked, then he remembered what he had between the pages of the newspaper. He took it out. 'I have the deeds. I tried to give them to Libby that night but—'

'No, don't,' Watkins said faintly as if even the sound of her name was a torment. 'Keep them. I'd signed the house over to her, so they're part of her estate and you're her spouse so QED and all that. Here!'

He thrust a set of keys at Freddy. Freddy thrust them back. 'I don't want the house. Sell it. Give it to someone else.'

'In the end, it was the only thing I ever gave her, and in the beginning, you have to believe me, Morton, my intentions were true. I really did love her. I never stopped loving her but it was absolutely impossible for us be together.'

'If you'd really loved her you'd have found way to be together,' Freddy told him, as Watkins pressed the keys into his hand. Freddy was a fine one to talk – as if he were any expert on love.

He'd never loved Libby enough. Hadn't even tried, which was why he was here now. Doing penance. Making amends. Clearing up the mess that he and Watkins had made of her.

'I know that now and it's something I suppose I'll just have to live with,' Watkins said. 'When you bury her, my heart will be in the coffin too.'

Then he shuddered as if he could hear the earth from the gravedigger's shovel hit the wooden casket. This was so much harder than Freddy had thought it would be.

Watkins was offering his hand again. Freddy shook it. How civilised they were when they hated each other's guts. But above all else, they were Englishmen so they shook hands.

'Goodbye, Morton. I doubt our paths will meet again,' Watkins said and Freddy knew that if they did, one of them would cross over the road to avoid the other. Thank God.

'Goodbye then,' Freddy said and he watched the man walk away, up the road, out of their lives.

50

Zoe

The parcel arrived the second week of December and was left with all the other unopened post, stacked deep on the sideboard in the hall.

Zoe was cloistered in her studio working on her robins and Win was living a life of sheer hedonism. Not that Zoe was bitter or resentful that she was surviving on cereal while Win was taken out to lunch by grateful clients and had a party every night. He'd return home anywhere on the drunk scale from mildly merry to absolutely steaming. One night he'd collapsed into bed reeking of tequila (apparently someone had dropped a tray of shots over him) and the kebab he'd eaten on the way home and Zoe had made him sleep in the spare room.

Then it was December the twenty-first. The robins had been signed off and Win's office closed at lunchtime, not to open again until the new year.

'Who are you and what have you done with my wife?' Win asked when he came home to find Zoe dressed in something that wasn't sagging yoga pants and a baggy jumper, vacuuming while Florence cowered unhappily halfway up the stairs. 'You need to use a different setting for rugs and also, this isn't a criticism just an observation, moving the sofa rather than trying to get the vacuum head as far under it as you can would be a lot more effective.'

'Or you could just do it yourself,' Zoe suggested. Win muttered but he put down his briefcase and took over the Miele, which Zoe relinquished with a serene smile. 'I'll go and make lunch.'

The big Christmas supermarket delivery had come that morning so they could have something fancier than cereal and Zoe was just taking the cheese and Parma ham sandwiches out from under the grill when Win came into the kitchen with one of the piles of post.

'Some of this is from three weeks ago, Zo,' he said in a tone of the mildest censure. 'And all of it is addressed to you.'

'This is just like the old days,' Zoe said breezily. 'Not opening my post until you perform an intervention. Will you fish out anything that looks like a Christmas card so I can make a list and write mine out tonight?'

'I've already written out and sent off our Christmas cards because the last posting date was Tuesday gone.' Win sighed. 'I'm like the god of husbands.'

'You absolutely are.' Zoe wasn't going to argue about that.

They started on the post as they ate lunch. Minus the Christmas cards that Win had already dealt with, the rest was a motley collection of catalogues, special offers and financial statements and it wasn't until they tackled the third and final pile that Zoe got to the bulging jiffy bag.

Inside there was something swathed in an ocean of bubble wrap, a document folder and an envelope addressed to Zoe.

'Maybe the contract for *The Highgate Woods Mysteries* and

a lovely box of chocolates from my new publisher,' she said hopefully as she took out a handwritten letter.

Dear Zoe and Win

It was wonderful to meet you the other week and to see the miracles you've performed on an unloved old house. Arthur and I are very happy that we chose you as the new owners.

Now, onto more pressing matters. Having scanned and copied the contents, we're returning Libby's diary and papers, as we feel that they belong with you and the house.

As we told you, Daddy left behind a staggering amount of paper spread between three different houses in three different countries. Someone from Daddy's literary agents has been pulling it all together along with another chap who'll be writing his biography.

Neither of them had heard of Libby but then they hadn't had a chance to look at any of Daddy's correspondence that pre-dated his Faraday novels.

Well, when they did, they uncovered something quite extraordinary! Daddy's first piece of spycraft, as Arthur calls it. I won't reveal any more but direct your attention to the collection of letters we've had copied for you.

Do get in touch once you've read and digested everything. Can't wait to hear your thoughts.

Fondest regards
Marisa

Zoe handed the letter to Win who read it quickly, then turned to Zoe with a resolute expression.

'We have to start on the Christmas shopping this afternoon,' he said with grim determination. 'We've left it to the last moment and you know how I feel about that.'

Zoe was already reaching for the document folder. 'If we make a list, a very targeted list, and we get up ridiculously early tomorrow so we're at Brent Cross as it opens, we can get most of it done in a few hours.'

'No! We said we'd do it this afternoon.' Win's eyes drifted to the folder that Zoe was waving in front of him. 'OK, look, we can read a couple of letters to find out what happened to Freddy after Libby died. What's the matter? You look like you've just seen a ghost.'

Zoe felt like she'd just seen a ghost too. She'd taken out the first letter and well, she'd recognise that handwriting anywhere, but the date . . . the date was wrong.

The Gables
Primrose Lane,
Chertsey, Surrey

21st December, 1936

Dear Freddy

 Such a shock to see one's own death announcement but as you said, no one would dare question the veracity of anything that appeared in The Times. *(I do hope that your friend who works there won't get into any trouble.)*

 It's quite a sobering thought to think that practically everyone I know, from your mother and the aunts to Potts (though if Potts is really in touch with the other side I'm sure he already knows that I've been unavoidably detained) and all my old theatre pals believe that I'm dead and because they do, I can never go back to my old life.

 It's also quite ghoulish but I rather wish there was a funeral so I could sit unobtrusively at the back and find out what people really thought of me. Though Beryl, who came to visit on Saturday, said it wouldn't be much fun if it turned out that people thought quite horrible things about one.

Anyway, though I am alive, I'm not in the rudest health. I'm so awfully tired but finding it hard to sleep with the pickle kicking like they're in the chorus line at the Gaiety. I'm not allowed out of bed at all, a nurse bustles in with a bedpan every hour whether I need one or not.

But I am so grateful to be alive. We've told a wicked lie, tempted fate, but I believe with all my heart it was the right thing to do. That the pickle and I belong together and nothing else matters.

And so I thank you and Beryl (as you know, I was wary of involving Beryl at all but I never imagined that she had it in her to be so devious) from the bottom of that same heart.

Keep everything crossed for us.

Libby xxx

'Next one,' Win said hoarsely.

Zoe was already reaching for a letter written in an unknown hand.

January 19th, 1937

Freddy

Just a quick note as am almost out of the door to catch the train to Liverpool and then the boat to New York!

Matron called to say that Libby was taken to the local hospital and delivered of a baby girl this morning. A little earlier than hoped for, but baby is doing well, though on the small side. Five pounds, three ounces. Healthy set of lungs — Matron said that she screamed blue murder as soon as she was born.

Libby is quite weak but they don't expect any complications from the surgery. Still, one does worry about infections and the like so she and baby will stay in hospital for the time being.

Such happy news when a few weeks ago we thought we'd lost both of them.

Please do go and see Libby when she's back at the nursing home and take pictures. Will write en route with New York address etc.

Best wishes

Beryl Marjoribanks

The Gables
Primrose Lane
Chertsey, Surrey

February 14th, 1937

Oh, Freddy!

You should see her. My pickle. She's so perfect that my heart breaks, then mends again, every time I look at her, hold her in my arms, take her to my breast. My whole world is new now that this precious, gorgeous girl is here.

I'm back at the nursing home and though I'm happier than I've ever been, there are times that I feel quite, quite sad.

I suppose I wish that things had been different. I know that if he could see her, hold her, then Hugo would love the baby too and it feels rotten to have played such a cruel trick on him, but what else could I have done? I can't help but cry when I think that the sweet pickle won't know her father but I'll just have to love her enough that she'll never feel his absence.

Please come and see me, Freddy. Now that Beryl's gone, you're the only person who knows I still exist and I'm lonesome and blue.

Kisses from me and the pickle.

Libby xxx

March 7th, 1937

Dear Freddy

I've been moved from the main building to a little cottage in the grounds that I share with another girl and her baby, whose people are in Kenya.

I'm being readied to return to the real world and the prospect seems terrifying, but then, also rather exciting.

It was lovely to see you the other day and though your offer was so sweet and generous (oh, why couldn't you have been so sweet and generous first time around?) we both know that we would never make each other happy.

Besides, you're about to go off to Germany and Italy to write your book about the Fascist menace and I've decided that it's for the best if I go overseas too.

Beryl has offered me a job teaching dance, music and movement again. Her new school isn't in New York but somewhere in the suburbs called Scarsdale and accommodation would come with the position. It seems a good solution to this rather large problem.

What I will accept is your offer to buy the house. Not for what it must have cost Hugo — you don't have that kind of money. Shall we say four hundred pounds, which is untold riches to me? If you could send me one hundred pounds initially to cover my medical expenses and get me to New York then you can wire me the rest, as and when you're able. Does that sound fair?

One last thing, Freddy. I'm so much better than I was and the pickle (I will have to start calling her by her name soon, otherwise she'll be going off to school and I'll still be calling

her the pickle) is such a good baby, hardly fusses at all, but I'm
dreading the journey to New York on my own.

Do you think Hannah could be persuaded to leave Willoughby
Square and come with me? It means that you'll have to break it
to her (gently, please, Freddy) that I'm not dead after all – you
said she'd been so upset and I do hope she'll forgive me. Knowing
Hannah though, I'm sure she'll adore all the intrigue. I'll pay her
twice what your mother does and if she's unhappy in America,
I'll pay her passage back to England.

If she agrees, would you bring her down to me, Freddy? I
would so love to see you one last time before I leave although it
won't really be goodbye. I wouldn't be surprised if five years or
fifty years from now we bump into each other in a bar or at a
hotel and it will be as if the time had just melted away.

What you did to keep me safe means that you will always have
a piece of my heart that I won't give to anyone else, just as a piece
of my heart will forever belong to Hugo because he gave me my
beautiful girl. And yet, I still have plenty of heart left, that's the
wonderful thing.

Love
Libby xxx

Zoe stretched her arms above her head. It was just after
three. Already the shadows were lengthening, the sky
glimpsed through the kitchen windows darkening.

Libby. Lovely Libby had cheated death. Or rather Freddy
had cheated death on her behalf and now she had a brand
new baby, was on the verge of a new life. Zoe felt ripe with
possibility herself. Except she hadn't had to move half a world
away for her second chance, it was here in the city she loved,
in this house that she was growing to love, with the man
who'd once been the boy she'd fallen in love with.

Like Libby, she still had enough heart, still plenty of love to go spare, to lavish on new people, even the ones that weren't here yet.

'Don't cry,' Win said and he brushed a tear from Zoe's cheek with the pad of his thumb. 'Look, we could leave the Christmas shopping for tomorrow, if you wanted.'

Zoe followed his gaze to the folder, which was still thick with paper.

'I'll put the kettle on, shall I?' she asked, making no move to get up but instead pulling out the next letter.

The White Cottage
Santa Monica
California

12th October, 1937

Dear Freddy

Well, we never made it to New York! I met a charming man on the boat (he was travelling with his equally charming wife) who'd been talent scouting in England for MGM.

To cut a long story short, I'm now employed at MGM as their 'Charm Director'. I spend my days schooling young starlets in how to deport themselves. To enunciate clearly – they do so love to drawl and slur their words. To hold a knife and fork correctly. How to do their hair and make-up. Even how to walk in some cases – they are lovely girls but most of them have all the grace of savages.

For my skills (which I'm making up as I go along) I'm paid $50 a week and we're renting a charming cottage right by the ocean. Life is so easy here, Freddy, far away from all the bad news from home. The pickle is growing bigger by the day, still completely bald but she has big blue eyes and a sunny smile, which delights everyone who meets her.

Hannah is well too. She's always angling to come to the studio

427

with me so she might be discovered and cast in a film, preferably
opposite Clark Gable, but until that happens, she's so good with the
pickle and she's lost that pasty look she had back in London.

I did see in the papers that the divorce laws in England will
change: instant divorce for cases of adultery or after three years for
desertion. Not that I think it would have done Hugo and me much
good if it had happened last year. Do you hear anything of him?

And how are you? Are you back from Germany now? I hope
you managed not to get shot again, Freddy. You are so awfully
good at getting yourself into trouble.

Much love
Libby xxx

751 Kingman Avenue
Santa Monica
California

27th March, 1939

Dear Freddy

Sorry I haven't written in ages, but your letter arrived this
morning along with a copy of your book and the money order, for all
of which I thank you!

One hears such terrible news from Europe and I can't help but
worry. I pray there won't be a war. Not after last time. Though I
suppose you would know better than me.

But England, and across the sea to France, Germany and
beyond, seems a world away. Here, the sun always shines. I'm sure
there have been days when it was raining but I never seem to notice
them.

The pickle is walking and talking. Mostly talking. Lord, she
never stops! We hoped she might turn blonde, but she's a redhead
like her mama. Hannah brought her into work one day and one

*of the producers asked if I'd thought about putting her in pictures.
That she could be the next Shirley Temple. I politely declined.
Well, not so politely!*

*Besides, I won't be at the studio for much longer. I'm opening
my own little academy offering dance and modelling lessons,
deportment, elocution. All the things I do for MGM, but I won't
have to answer to anyone but myself.*

*I was sorting through some things the other day to get ready for
the move and I realised that I don't have any of Hugo's letters.
They were all in my diary for that year. Goodness, 1936 seems a
lifetime ago. I have the vaguest recollection that perhaps I stuffed
the diary into my suitcase that awful night that Edward abdicated
and we both thought I was done for. The last time I saw Hugo.
No wonder that I'd all but forgotten about them. Could they still
be at the house in Highgate? I was going to ask you to ship the case
and its contents, but I've decided that there's no point. I'm not that
person any more – the one who wore that dress to get married in,
posed for those pictures, wrote that diary. I was broken. But here
in this magical place with my magical child, I feel as if I've been
made anew. Better, kinder, more complete than I was before.*

*One thing though, Freddy. Would you to go to the house in
Highgate, when you have the chance, to see if the suitcase is there,
though I can't imagine where else it could be? I'd like you to send
me the layette that was in that case. It's the only thing I can't bear
to be without. The only thing left of that baby snatched from me
without any warning, with no chance to say goodbye. It's as if he
were never real, though I carried him for six months and I grieve for
him every single day.*

*Yes, I'm sure he was a he. Wilfred (for my father) Arthur (for
your father) Morton.*

Do you ever think of him, Freddy?
Love
Libby xxx

Zoe was crying so hard she could hardly read Libby's still appalling handwriting and Win was wiping the tears streaming from his own eyes.

At some point it had got dark and they'd turned on the light. Later, they'd order pizza and eat it straight from the box while they carried on reading.

The war years. A worried Libby sending Freddy frantic entreaties to *stay safe. So thankful that you did get shot in Spain as surely you must be unfit for active duty? Selfishly, I'm pleased that the pickle, Beryl (she was here last month, has plans to start one of her schools on the West Coast) Hannah and I are safe but oh, how we all worry about you, Freddy!*

Then in 1943. *I hope you're sitting down because I have some shocking news. I'm getting married! His name's Lenny and he's frightfully rich, made his money in real estate, but I wouldn't care if he were a pauper. I really wouldn't. He's so funny, all I do when I'm with him is laugh until I ache from it, and he loves me as much as I love him. I never knew love could be such a joy when it's returned tenfold.*

The only sticking point, Freddy, is that I'm still married to you. There's no earthly reason for either of us to want to stay married but I'm worried that if we're granted a divorce – you'd have to sue me for desertion – not only would it take three years, but worse, the story might make the papers. If it did, then it's quite likely that Hugo would read about it and realise the truth.

It doesn't bear thinking about. Finding out the woman you've mourned is no longer dead would simply be too cruel. And what if he made good on this threats and tried to take the pickle from me? So, could we just pretend that we're not married? Who's to ever know? What harm would it do? You always insisted that you weren't one for propriety so are you game, Freddy?

It seemed that Freddy must have been game because Libby married her Lenny and after the war, Freddy married his minor Swedish aristocrat and Libby sent him a crate of champagne and fervent congratulations. She also sent him a crate of champagne each time he had a book published, which she could well afford as she now had three charm schools, two in LA and one in New York, and *the girls call me Mrs Elizabeth (everyone else calls me Lizzy) and behave as if I'm the most terrifying creature they've ever met. As if anyone could ever be terrified of me.*

There was more champagne for the birth of each of Freddy's children and news of the pickle, *though she gets so cross if I call her that. She's the most delightful thing, has such a wicked sense of humour, but she's stubborn as anything. I don't really mind that. I'd hate to have raised a girl who let people walk all over her.*

In the fifties, Libby sold her business in LA and she, Lenny and the pickle moved to New York, where the pickle had riding lessons, ballet classes and *Beryl is quite cross about it but I decided not to send her to a Steiner Waldorf school. We've enrolled her at Spence. She's so bright that I don't doubt she'll be the first woman president.*

Soon the pickle was at Smith, and Libby owned one of the most successful modelling agencies in New York. In 1958 she wrote, *How lovely it was to see you last month. Such a pity I have to be kept secret from Lola and the children – I would so love to meet them. But to think that one of your novels is going to be made into a film! Oh Freddy, I'm so proud of everything you've accomplished and so glad that despite all the past heartbreak and the ocean between us, that we've become such good friends.*

By now, Zoe and Win were halfway down a bottle of Merlot and there was only one piece of paper left unread.

'I know what's coming because it's inevitable but I'm not ready for it,' Win said.

'But she had a good life in the end, so it's sad but it's not unbearably sad,' Zoe insisted, though taking up the next piece of paper was one of the hardest things she'd ever had to do.

She didn't recognise the neat, tidy handwriting as if all the letters had been lined up with a ruler.

28th November, 1961

Dear Freddy

I'm writing with bad news, I'm afraid. Mom passed away a couple of days ago. She went to bed early complaining of a headache and never woke up. The doctors said it was an aneurysm and that she wouldn't have suffered in any way. I'm trying to take comfort from that, but how hard it is that I never got to say goodbye.

You knew Mom for longer and better than anyone else, so you know how special she was. How her smile lit up a room – just the sight of it always made me feel like I'd come home. I can't imagine the world without her and that smile in it.

The funeral's next week. Do call if you can come. That's as far ahead as I can think. Other decisions will have to be made, but not now. Not when the shock of her gone is a body blow.

So much we never talked about. So much I wanted to ask her. We planned to come to London next summer, when I finished my Masters, to revisit some of her old haunts and I wondered if then, she might tell me about my father. Beryl and Hannah both say that he was married and that it was a very complicated situation. Those two things always go hand in hand, don't they?

I've often wondered about him. If I should like to meet him and if he would want to meet me but then I imagine that Mom took me away from him for a good reason. I don't even know why I'm telling you this now when all I can really think about is the loss of her, but I suppose you'd be the person to ask, as you've always been the keeper of Mom's secrets.

I have to go now. I'm having this sent overnight to reach you in time.

I'm so sad, Freddy. I've never known a sadness like it.

Love

Charlotte (the pickle)

A couple of days later, after they got back from their morning walk in Highgate Woods, before they'd had a chance to take off their muddy wellingtons, Zoe and Win unlocked the back door and hurried down the garden.

There was a strip of earth next to the shed where they were planning to plant a vegetable patch early in the spring. Now they took two spades and began to dig. There'd been a thick frost overnight and the ground was hard. They had to work at the earth again and again.

It took ages and Zoe's back twanged in protest until Win deemed the hole deep enough.

Zoe retrieved the Maison Bertaux box from the shed where she'd put it before their walk. It was nestling in several sheets of bubble wrap, then placed in a thick plastic bag and taped up.

The other night, after they'd finished reading Libby's letter, she and Win had talked about why Freddy had never honoured Libby's wishes when she'd asked him to send her the layette. It was impossible to know his reasons. Libby's letter had been written at the end of March 1939. Perhaps, by the time Freddy received it, war had been declared and got in the way of his good intentions.

Or else thinking about the baby was too painful, so he simply hadn't.

Either way, it was up to them, Zoe and Win, to honour their unborn – also in the box, tucked under the tiny, yellowed baby clothes, was Zoe's hospital tag. And in the house, on her dressing table, in the small, carved wooden box where she kept all her most prized treasures was the cherry button that had fallen off that impossibly small cardigan their first night in the house. Zoe had carried it with her so long, had held onto it through the worst of her grief, that it had come to symbolise not just Libby's loss but her own too.

'Have you thought about what you want to say?' Win asked.

'I'm waiting for inspiration to strike,' Zoe said but inspiration remained unstruck. She stood there for long moments until at last she squatted down and placed the package in the earth.

Win took her hand as she straightened up, their gloved fingers curled around each other and still she was silent. Zoe heard Win's sigh and then: 'We bury this box in honour of Wilfred Arthur Morton and our own ... our ...' He stumbled to a halt.

'I think we would have had a boy too,' Zoe said. 'Boys tend to run in your family. What about Norman after your granddad?'

'Bit old-fashioned, isn't it?' Win mumbled and if he started to cry, then Zoe would too, though she'd been sure she was all cried out after reading Libby's letters. 'Did you have any names picked out?'

Zoe could picture the baby's face so clearly but he'd never had a name and she hadn't dared to start making lists of what they might call any future children.

'What about Paul for *your* granddad, Zo? Paul Norman Rowell. How does that sound?'

Zoe nodded. 'We bury this box in honour of Wilfred Arthur Morton and our own Paul Norman Rowell ...' She choked on the name and Win's grip on her hand tightened as she swallowed down a sob.

'You can do this, Zo. You have to do this,' he murmured.

'Two baby boys who never lived but were loved all the same.' Zoe turned away and Win caught her, cradled her against him as the wind picked up, lifted her hair, dried her tears, and it felt as if she and Win weren't alone at the bottom of the garden; that there was someone else standing, grieving, alongside them.

51

Zoe

It was after Christmas dinner and everyone was still seated at the table in a pleasant post-turkey tryptophan haze.

Previous Christmases they'd crammed around the table in Jackie's kitchen diner, the nephews annexed around a pull-out picnic table in the lounge, under pain of death not to drop anything on the carpet. Or Zoe and Win would go up to Yorkshire to stay with her parents, which was always lovely until her father's unmarried sister, the godfearing Aunt Margaret, descended on them and she was hard work. But this year Zoe and Win were hosting and hopefully starting a new Christmas tradition. Ken and Nancy, Jackie and Gavin, Ed and Amanda, the four nephews and Win were all seated, more or less comfortably, around their huge kitchen table.

Zoe looked past the cracker debris, plates smeared with streaks of gravy and cranberry sauce, the serving dishes empty apart from a couple of forlorn roast potatoes and a few stuffing balls, to where Win was playing jumping jacks from a cracker with Medium and Small. He looked up and smiled at Zoe. She smiled back and blew him a kiss, which he pretended to catch while Large made gagging noises until Amanda threatened to take away his new iPad.

Zoe still had that warm, mellow feeling like a Ready Brek glow around her soul later when Win's side of the family had gone home. Her parents were in the front room. Ken curled up on the sofa with Florence sprawled across his chest, their stereophonic snoring rattling the window frames, while Nancy Skyped with her sister in Walton-on-the-Naze. She and Win were in the kitchen putting away the last of the glasses, which Win had insisted on hand-washing. Once they were done, he pulled Zoe into his arms and gently spun her round while Frank Sinatra crooned in the background.

'Happy Christmas, wifey,' he murmured in her ear, even though Zoe had told him never, ever to call her that. Ever.

'Happy Christmas, hubs,' Zoe replied then pulled free. The tension was thrumming through her. 'Actually I've got one last present for you.'

'Really?' Win tried not to look eager, but failed miserably. 'Because you've had all your presents.' He pulled out the pockets of his jeans. 'I've got nothing left to give you.'

'This is a present we can both share,' Zoe said and she took the small, narrow gift box out of the drawer where she'd hidden it. 'Here you are. Hope you like it.'

Win gave Zoe a curious look because her voice was so high and squeaky it was a wonder Florence hadn't come bustling in to see if they had mice. 'I'm sure I will,' he said, taking the box from her and tugging the ribbon bow loose.

'It's a bit unhygienic, but I gave it a wipe down with the antibacterial hand gel,' Zoe assured Win as he opened the box. 'And I know it's a bit naff, wrapping it up. Even clichéd, but the occasion warranted a cliché, right? Sometimes you have to embrace the cliché.'

'Oh,' Win said, his voice breaking. 'Oh.'

'Is that a good oh or a bad oh?' Zoe asked, and now she knew what was meant when people said their heart was in their mouth because it felt as if her heart had risen up her chest and was making it hard to get her words out.

'Are you sure?'

Zoe nodded. 'About ninety-five per cent certain.' Immediately, she was back in Win's arms as he kissed her hair, her forehead, her eyelids, the tip of her nose, her mouth and stayed right there, peppering kisses against her lips so she couldn't speak. Didn't want to.

Finally he let her go and held up the strip of plastic that could change a person's life. Two persons' lives, because soon two would become three.

Win sat down abruptly as if his legs wouldn't hold him up and pulled Zoe onto his lap.

'How do you feel?'

She smiled damply. 'This time I feel pregnant. My boobs are sore, which is why I elbowed you in the head the other night when you were too enthusiastic, I cry whenever the John Lewis Christmas ad comes on. I even cried when the Superdrug Christmas ad came on, and bad smells make me want to retch.'

'Is that why you'd declared Christmas a Brussels-sprout-free zone?' Win asked.

'Not so much the sprouts as the thought of Gavin's farts after he'd eaten the sprouts,' Zoe said and then she wished she hadn't because she retched while Win looked at her as if she was truly enchanting to behold. 'I wanted to tell you before but I was scared that I wasn't. And now I'm scared because I'm pretty sure I am but I'm excited too. You know what? I don't even know how to explain how I feel.'

Despite Win's Christmas schedule, inevitably Zoe had

found herself in Boots in Wood Green at three in the afternoon the day before doing battle with all the other last-minute, panicked Christmas Eve shoppers. Heading for the tills after snatching the very last Soap & Glory gift set off the display, she'd seen a shelf full of pregnancy tests and had grabbed one almost as an afterthought. She'd vowed to herself that she'd wait until after Christmas. That her period was late because she was stressed about the robins, stressed about hosting Christmas for the very first time and her body was probably still adjusting after years and years of having a contraceptive implant releasing progesterone into her system. Anyway, it was too soon. They'd only just started trying.

She'd felt like a kid too excited to sleep the night before Christmas and had sneaked out of bed at five that morning to put herself out of her misery. But it turned out that misery had nothing to do with it.

'I think it's all right to be scared,' Win decided. 'I'm scared too. It's all I can do not to get up right this very minute and throw out all the raw tuna and soft cheese that's in the fridge.'

Zoe wound her arms round his neck. 'We don't have any raw tuna in the fridge.'

'I know, but I still want to make absolutely certain.' Win rested his forehead against hers. 'I'm going to be a very attentive and a very, very annoying expectant dad. You've unleashed a monster and the spreadsheet potential . . . Oh . . . I'm going to be a dad. We're going to have a baby. Our baby. That's huge.'

'The hugest,' Zoe said and it was early days. They'd been down this road once before and it had ended in disaster, but all she could do was hope for the best. There was always hope.

She shifted on his lap so she was snuggled against Win's chest. He wrapped his arms around her, and rested a hand on her belly.

They were home.

Acknowledgements

I feel like I've been cloistered forever while I wrote this book shunning all human contact, but surely that can't be the case. So thank you to Eileen Coulter and Mr Eric for company on restorative dog walks.

Sarah Bailey, Natasha Lunn, Hannah Dunn and all at *Red* Magazine for keeping me gainfully employed and funded during the times I wasn't novelling.

As ever I'm indebted to my agent, Rebecca Ritchie, and Melissa Pimental, Alice Dill, Martha Cooke and all at Curtis Brown and to the team at Sphere in particular Manpreet Grewal, Thalia Proctor, Stephie Melrose and Emma Williams.

Thanks also to Rob Baker, author of the wonderful *Beautiful Idiots And Brilliant Lunatics*, for the wonderful pictures of vintage London life that he posts on Twitter (@robnitm) especially as he has an uncanny knack for finding pictures that are so relevant to my writing interests. It would also be terribly remiss not to thank the original dog named Beyoncé and her owner, Victoria Jones.

I also owe a huge debt to the late Sir Alan Patrick Herbert whose very funny novel, *Holy Deadlock*, was an invaluable help in understanding the punitive divorce laws of 1936. As an interesting aside, Sir Alan, was an independent member of Parliament from 1935 to 1950 and introduced the Matrimonial Causes Act, which came into law in 1937 and meant that people could finally obtain a divorce without evidence of adultery.